Chapter One

"Winona, are you sure you want to do this?"

"Yes, Danny, I've never been so sure of anything in my life." Winona looks up at me with those big, brown eyes. My heart melts.

"But, we just met. Aren't you married to Scott, or is it Keanu?"

"They mean nothing to me, now, Danny."

She seems quite insistent, and I am, after all, but a human male.

"Well, if you're sure…"

Winona lies back on the bed and spreads open her legs, inviting me down with a 'come hither' motion. "Danny, come get me."

What can I do? I bury my head in her bosom and navigate in my heat-seeking missile. Slipping easily into the moist, warm, happy cave.

"Oh, Danny, Danny, Danny."

"Oh, Winona. Oh, yes."

"Danny, Danny, Danny." Her tone changes as I thrust,

deeper, harder, faster. Her hands on my shoulders, shaking me. "Danny, Daddy! DADDY!"

"Ugh. What?"

My eyes creak slowly open, the harsh light blinding me. Wetness at my groin.

"Daddy, I need a pee."

"Ethan... Ugh. What time is it?" Winona has left the building, replaced with my eight-year-old son, standing next to my bed in his Spiderman pyjamas.

"Six-thirty-eight."

"Jesus Christ."

"I need a pee!"

"Well, go to the toilet?"

"There's a big poo in there. I'm scared."

"Flush it?"

"It's scary."

"Ethan, it's poo. It isn't scary. Just flush it away."

"No! Can you do it for me?"

I can barely speak, let alone get up, and there's the mess in my underpants to take care of.

"You know there's another toilet downstairs, don't you?"

"Oh, yeah. Thanks, Daddy." His face lights up and he runs off down the stairs.

I check my watch on the nightstand. He's right. It's the wrong side of seven in the morning on a Saturday. I was hoping for a lie-in. Some chance of that. Maybe if I just stay here, Winona will come back?

Now, where was I?

Winona, lying in my bed, the glisten of sweat on her lips from our heated passions, her hair flowing over my pillows, "Do you want another go, Danny?"

Do I ever? I roll over onto my side, my hand caressing her milk-white breast.

WHO NEEDS LOVE, ANYWAY?

ADAM ECCLES

For Robin & Willow

"AGHHH."

A scream comes from downstairs.

I roll back over. "NOW WHAT?"

"I stepped in cat puke."

Wonderful. Game over, I suppose. Save it for later, Danny, you never know, tonight could be your lucky night.

I pull on a threadbare dressing gown. Must have shrunk in the wash, because it used to fit me fine.

The toilet, as mentioned by Ethan, is indeed harbouring a floater that would put a sizeable dent in the Titanic. One flush alone is not enough. I throw my pants in the bin, wipe away the excess love juice and aim, bleary-eyed. Perhaps the force of my piss-stream will break the shit-berg in two?

"ROSIE! Please flush the damn toilet after you go."

From her room, a distant, matter-of-fact, "I did."

"Well, you didn't get rid of it. You know Ethan is scared of poo."

I move to the sink and wash away the eye crust and sleep sweat. Gradually, feeling and sensation come dribbling back to me. I didn't drink last night, but it was around one in the morning before I lay down. I check my sleep tracker app, which confirms; Five hours and fifteen minutes. A sleep debt of thirty percent. Try to get to bed earlier tonight, the cheery message pops up.

Bugger off.

I turn to exit the bathroom and jump, startled. Rosie is standing in the doorway, arms folded.

"Sorry, Daddy. I did flush."

"Okay, sweetheart. Just make sure it does the trick next time, eh?"

"Yes, Daddy. Would you like a cup of coffee?"

"Fu… I mean. Yes, please, Rosie. That would be wonderful."

Almost a teenager, she will be the death of me someday.

3

Cute as a button, smart, dangerously innocent and spoiled rotten. I'm dreading when the boyfriends start to appear.

"Can you see what Ethan stepped in, please?"

"It's not cat puke. I dropped a tea bag earlier."

Well, that's something, I suppose.

"Why are we up this early on a Saturday?" My little family and I are assembled around the dining table, enjoying a healthy breakfast of oatmeal, sprinkled with fresh fruit and seeds. Okay, that's not strictly accurate. I am sat at the table with sweet black coffee, Rosie is on the couch, Ethan on a beanbag. They both have iPads and toast. The TV is blaring some inane shit into the void. Ethan opted for jam on his toast, Rosie for brown-sauce.

"We're going to the park today." Ethan pipes up.

"But that's in about four hours?"

"Got to get ready." Rosie looks up. "We need clean clothes, or Mum will call the police again."

Oh, yes. Meeting Mummy at the park, won't that be a riot?

"Right. Is the laundry done?"

"Nope."

"Can you do it?"

"Nope."

"Thanks."

"We've got homework, Daddy." They both flash me a saccharine-sweet grin and return their attention to YouTube.

Shit.

always, leaving the house is as close to impossible as it gets. three failed starts, we manage to leave the driveway, only traight back because Ethan forgot his iPod headphones. r failed starts, we trundle along through Saturday traffic tion of the park.

Their mother, Elise, my second wife no more, is a vindictive bitch. Only, there's nothing for her to get revenge for. She shagged some guy called Brian. She decided to leave us. She got a load of my money. She took the decent car. What more could she want? Blood, apparently.

We meet on neutral ground, not according to any schedule, but whenever she decides she wants to see the kids. She butters them up with toys and sweets, then flits off back to her love cave with Brian, and we don't hear from her until the next guilt trip.

Not that I'm bitter or anything.

We arrive three minutes late, my beautiful prior BMW already waiting for us. Elise taps her wrist at me through the window as we bundle out into the car park. I ignore it. I bet she only just got here herself.

Through clenched teeth, I smile back at her, and under my breath mutter 'go fuck yourself, Elise.'

"Hi! How are you guys?"

"Have you got any presents for us, Mummy?" Ethan is straight to the point at least.

"Wait and see, darling." She looks up at me with a look that translates as 'Why do you teach them to ask for gifts? You selfish bastard.'

I look away.

"I'll come back in two hours, then?"

"If you can trouble yourself to be on time, Danny, that would be great."

I kiss and hug the little ones and offer a wave towards Elise, but she's already turned away and walking off into the park. Her black hair blowing in the wind. It was her thirty-ninth birthday last week. I suppose I should have got the kids to make her a card or something. Oh well. She looks younger, like she did when we got married. Bright and made-up like a dog's dinner. An aura of patchouli perfume surrounds her perpetually.

Things were simpler back then. We loved each other,

genuinely. We cared, made plans, and we had amazing sex. Did things that would make Winona in my dreams blush. But now, I feel the gaping black void of hate when I look at her. Funny how things change so drastically.

Love? Don't make me laugh. Love is an ideal sold by the media to keep people in check. I don't believe in love anymore. The spark of romance in me died when Elise told me the same lies and bullshit that my first wife did. That one lasted eighteen months, before Steve, or was it Simon? I can't remember now, came along and stuck his dick in my first love.

I shudder away the dark thoughts. I've got a date tonight. Can't all be bad, can it?

Back at home, I have time for a shower and some breakfast before I go back and get the kids again. Don't want to be late for Her Majesty. Then I need to get some shopping done, before the babysitter arrives.

The steamy hot water massages my back, finally breathing some life into my tired old bones.

In retrospect, I probably shouldn't have stayed up as late texting with Maria; whom I'm meeting for the first time tonight. A blind date, because she doesn't have a photo on her dating profile. I'm usually wary of those, but she assures me she's real, and a 'genuine, kind, bubbly girl at heart' and more poignantly, she says I'm a handsome catch.

I'm a forty-two-year-old single Dad, who works to pay the bills, dreams about a movie-star no one even knows these days, and hasn't had 'the sex' for many a cold year. I take what I can get. Maria may be a cave-troll, hiding behind a claim she doesn't want to be stalked by weirdos, hence no photos. But at least she's a female cave-troll, who wants to spend time with me.

I shrug and let the shower rain run down my back. Turning around and washing any remnants of dried cum from my crotch with a scrubby pad and some minty shower-gel. Ooh, that smarts. But in a good way.

Freshly clean, eggs on toast scarfed down, twenty minutes of PornHub surfing to find something worthy to edge to, and I'm back in the car again to the park.

Thinking about it, I probably should have given the kids some lunch before they went to see Mummy. They must be starving by now. Never mind, we'll stop at McDs on the way home. It's a treat day, after all.

I swore, in my youth, that my children would never see fast food as a treat. Instead, I joked it should be a punishment to eat the clown-food. But here we are. Convenience outweighs ideals every time. At least they eat it and I don't have to wash plates.

"Hi, guys. Did you have a nice time?" Elise and the kids are waiting in the car park as I pull up.

"They are starving, Danny. Did you feed them, at all?"

"We're going for a special treat, aren't we?"

"Fast food, again?"

"No, not 'again'. Just fast food. It's a rare treat."

"Well, thankfully I had a couple of protein bars in the car, or they'd have passed out."

I look at the kids. Ethan plugged into a game on his iPod, Rosie listening to music. They seem fine to me.

"Come on then, let's get you home…" Via McDs and Tesco's. Oh, what a joyous Saturday afternoon.

Elise makes a show of hugging the kids and then ignoring me as she gets into MY car. Winding down the window as she turns around. "Ethan trod in dog-poo, and Rosie has a big hole in her leggings. Please try to take care of my children, Danny."

Bugger off.

. . .

The dog-poo proved too ingrained to be scraped off with a patch of grass.

I'm now forty quid down on the day, and Ethan has new shoes. Rosie new leggings, courtesy of Tesco finest. He rode in the trolley until he got the shoes, much to the disgust of various old biddies who stuck their noses into our business. "He's too old to be in the trolley."

I ignored them, but these stabs in my back all add up. There's only so much bullshit a man can take before he explodes and 'accidentally' slams the trolley into someone's fat arse as he goes by.

Back at home, I pack away the shopping into the cupboards and fridge. Tumbleweeds roll by in the empty silence. Weird, because only a few seconds ago there was a multitude of children, strong and able to help put the food away. I trust they are busy somewhere, doing their much-celebrated homework.

The sitter should arrive around six, which gives me time to relax for a while and then make some dinner for the kids. Fish-fingers and beans, they asked for, which means they'll eat hot dogs and popcorn, or similar. Always have a backup plan for dinner. I learned that the long, expensive, hard way.

Jessica, the babysitter, is a young lass from a few streets away. She's been a godsend the last year or two. She wanted to make a few quid, and I wanted to have the odd evening off. I know the kids love her, and she's trustworthy. Wins all around. Quiet girl, studying for med-school or something. I usually leave her some food in the fridge and she gets the kids to bed, then watches some tripe on Netflix until I get back.

I pop a text to Maria. A nervous, paranoid, final check that she wants to meet me this evening. Because another stand-up is not what I need right now.

The last time I tried to lure a woman out for the evening, I ended up sitting for an hour on my own in the Chinese, then finally getting a text that she had an "unexpected family situation" and couldn't make it. I never heard from her again. I have my suspicions that the 'unexpected situation' was more to do with a younger and less off-sprung man that had suddenly contacted her. The arrangement had been sketchy in the first place. She told me, "Yeah, sure, I don't know what I'm doing yet." when I asked if we could get dinner, maybe?

Maria replies that of course we are still on for later and she's very excited to meet me.

I wish I could drum up the same level of enthusiasm, but my expectations are set very low, after so many failed attempts. There's no point in getting my hopes up, only to have them dashed against the rocks again, breaking every optimistic bone in my body, once more. They say a broken bone grows back stronger, but I feel as fragile as a teenager asking a crush to go to a school dance. I'm rapidly exiting the first half of my life and screeching to a dreadful halt in my midlife crisis.

Dating sites, miserable cans of beer with Netflix, alone. Oven pizza that tastes like cardboard, and the churn of work, school-runs, and masturbation. This is the life I have carefully carved out for myself. My parents must be deeply proud.

I don't know what Maria expects. I've been honest, told her my situation, my loneliness.

My dating profile says, 'Just see what happens.' as my goal. I don't think I know what I want either. I mean, a casual shag would be nice, but ultimately, do I think anyone will wake up next to me, year in, year out, until one of us, probably me, dies in the arms of a loving spouse? Those dreams of 'happy ever after' seem like an unreachable utopia. Does anyone actually have a happy relationship? I struggle to believe it. At least if they are sentient and intelligent. I don't think men and women are designed to live together, long term.

Maria has told me barely anything about herself. All I know is: She's female, aged thirty-two, never married, no kids, speaks English.

Ah well, I suppose I'll 'Just see what happens.'

The doorbell rings bang on time, and I open the door to Jessica. But it's been a few months, maybe six, since I saw her last. She's grown a bit, upfront. Her homely look is replaced with downright sexy. Made-up, hair styled, and dyed black and blue, a nose piercing and an outfit that would make a prostitute blush. She smiles, and waltzes in like nothing has changed.

"Hi, Jessica."

"Hey, Danny."

"You look… Good…" I'm hesitant to say pretty, in case she takes it the wrong way and I'm arrested for sexual harassment or something. I think she's nineteen now, but until five seconds ago, I saw her as an older child. Now she's definitely a woman. A bloody hot one, too.

"Thanks. You aren't so bad yourself." She smiles and goes through to the kitchen. "Normal plan, is it?"

"Yeah. Food in the fridge. Kids on their iPads. Help yourself to Netflix, and whatever drinks you want." I know it's safe to say that as she won't touch my "nasty beer." She told me before.

"Where are you going?"

"Got a date. Going to the Kings Head, then the Italian."

"Nice." She gives me a 'look' that I can't interpret and then dives into the fridge, pulling out a beer.

"Jessie!" Ethan and Rosie appear in the kitchen like a couple of Tasmanian devils, laughing and roaring. Jessica gives them both a hug and spins them around, giggling. The kids haven't noticed her recent puberty changes.

"I'll leave you to it, then?"

Jessica nods and they vanish off into the living room with bags of crisps.

I elected to walk into town rather than drive or get a taxi. It's a nice evening, I rarely get to take a few minutes to myself, and I could certainly use the exercise.

The Kings Head is where I used to go with Elise when we were young and excited about our marriage, but as that excitement turned to hatred, and she found other outlets for her entertainment, I haven't been in a long while. It could be a mistake to meet a date in the same place, but Maria suggested it, and I know where it is, so I agreed.

Doesn't matter, I suppose. I don't have the energy to be sentimental about a pub I don't go to anymore.

I look around as I go in, but as I don't have a clue what Maria looks like, the task seems pointless. There aren't any obviously single women floating around.

I drop down at the same barstool I sat in all those years ago, when we first found out Elise was pregnant with Rosie. She asked for a Guinness. Said it was good for the baby. Iron and all that.

I flag down the barman and get myself a pint with a whisky chaser. I need something to calm my nerves as I'm suddenly freaked out. Maybe a blind date was a bad idea. What if she's totally not my type, will it be awkward? What is my type, anyway?

Female, with a pulse, at this stage.

. . .

I'm spared from too much self-indulgent pondering by a tap on my shoulder. I spin around to a small woman, shoulder-length brown hair, a simple blouse and skirt, suede jacket and matching boots. She's... Okay looking. Her nose is a bit bigger than I'd normally be happy with, but who am I to judge? No, she's nice.

"Maria?"

"Yes. Hi, Danny."

Chapter Two

Two drinks in and so far, so good. Maria has listened to me rant and moan about kids, life, work, and shopping. Especially shopping. Something I violently hate, yet have to do three times a week. Sometimes more. Maria listened patiently, laughing in all the right places. We moved on to the Italian.

I snap off a breadstick and hold it like a cigar. "Got a light?" I joke. I've never smoked in my life. As I do it, I realise the epic fail Dad joke level I've sunk to. She sniggers, but I feel like it was strained.

"Tell me about yourself?"

I often do this. I forget that there's someone else in the conversation, and I rant on about my life and problems, and never stop to consider I'm hogging the floor. Something Elise told me drove her to shag Brian, who listened intently. Twat.

"Oh, there's not much to tell."

"Well, what do you do? Do you have a job?"

"I'd rather not say."

"Oh, okay." Unexpected. Is she a spy or something? "Well, where are you from?"

"Does it matter?"

"I mean, not really. Just making conversation."

"I'd rather not say."

"Right." Well, this leaves me a bit lost. What else is there? "Err, do you have any hobbies?"

"Honestly, I'm not comfortable talking about myself. At all."

"Right, okay. Any reason?"

"Stalkers."

"Stalkers? Like, men who spy on you in secret?"

"Yes, I've had some stalkers before."

"From the dating site?"

"I'd rather…"

"Rather not say. Yes, okay." This is rough. I'm sorry she's had a bad experience, but I'm obviously not a stalker. She contacted me; I would never have messaged someone without a profile photo. "Well, I'm hungry. Better take a look at the menu."

I look up at her across the table. Candle-lit, she doesn't look as bad as I thought at first, maybe the alcohol has given her a soft-focus effect.

"Why are you looking at my face?"

"Sorry?"

"You were looking at my face."

"Well, yeah. Where else would I look?"

"Why were you looking?"

"Err. I don't know?"

"I'd rather you didn't look at me."

This has gone south, all of a sudden. I can't ask her anything or look at her face? This relationship probably won't blossom. All the humour has gone, and we're left with the naked psycho core. Something bad has happened to this woman, and I'm sorry for that, but I'm not the man to fix this.

"Look, Maria."

"That's not my real name. Don't try to look me up."

"Jesus. I'm not a stalker, and I'm sorry you've had to go

through that, but I've been totally honest with you. You know my name, my kids' names, for fuck's sake." Suddenly, I'm not hungry anymore and going home to microwave chips, PornHub and an early night seem like a great plan. I stand up to leave.

"What are you doing?"

"I'm exhausted, Maria, or whatever your name is. I'm going home. Sorry."

"Oh, but I enjoy talking to you."

"Really? But you haven't said anything."

She looks blank.

"Frankly, I've told you all about my life, and now I'm worried that you are the stalker. I know nothing about you."

"I'd rather not say."

"Yes. So I've heard. Well, I wish I could say it was nice to meet you, but I don't think I have met you, so…"

I leave a ten-pound note on the table and exit, stage right.

The slow walk home in the cool evening air gives me time to think, and perhaps I was a little harsh. I open up my phone to text her an apology, but find a message from her already waiting. It's a long, ranting moan about how rude I was, how she was being perfectly reasonable in her eyes and something something something. I didn't read the rest of it. Deleted and blocked on the dating site. I'm the opposite of a stalker, 'Maria'.

Rather than nasty microwave chips, I stop at the chip shop near my house and get a nice large portion of curry chips and three battered sausages. An extra couple for Jessica, because, as I recall, she likes a good sausage. That sounds very wrong, now.

I'm home early, but the peace and quiet as I open the door signify the kiddos are nicely asleep. I'll offer Jessica her sausages while she waits for a taxi home, and I'll sink into a deep, troublesome sleep. With any luck, visited by movie stars of the 90s, ready and willing to relieve me of my spunk.

I creep into the kitchen, dump my food, keys, and phone, then go back into the living room to find Jessica. She's typically half-asleep in front of a Netflix show when I get home. This time is a little different. The TV is muted, playing a children's show. Jessica is on the couch, but instead of being half asleep, she's crying her eyes out. Make-up running down her face.

"Oh, my god! What's going on? Are you okay? Are the kids okay?"

"Danny!" She jumps up and flings her arms around me, burying her face into my chest. A rush of adrenaline floods my veins. I gently push her back.

"Are the kids okay?"

"Yes, they are fine. Sleeping. It's not that."

"Oh, thank god. What's wrong then?"

"My boyfriend. He… I just broke up with him." She motions to the phone in her hand and replaces her head on my chest. Tear streaked and raw. Bloody hell. More emotional women.

"Err. I'm sorry, Jessica. Would you like to tell me what happened?" I look, longingly towards the kitchen, and my deliciously hot, stodgy and disgusting curry chips, that will now cool, turning into a gelatinous mess of starch, and whatever the hell is in that curry sauce, while I listen to the woes of a teenager, as she discovers that relationships are all poisoned, tainted, evil concoctions of society.

Poor girl.

Poor chips.

Poor me.

"I was looking on Facebook." Here we go. "And I saw he was 'liking' a lot of pics from this girl."

"Do you mind if we move to the kitchen? I need a drink." And my dinner.

I pour her a glass of water, and myself a beer, but she picked up the beer and sucked it down before I could correct her. Okay, then.

She continues with her story. I'm only half-listening, sneaking bites of my dinner when she's deeply engaged in the sordid details. I'd summarise the evening's events with a simple one-liner if it were me. The little twat wants to dip his wick into any pussy he can get his meaty paws onto. Because that's what teenagers do. Nothing new here. Don't expect to be in a lifelong, deep, and meaningful relationship with a kid. That's all I'm saying. She's still elaborating on the details. There is history, and this girl, Megan, 'always liked' Brett since school.

I really don't care. But Jessica is still talking and the streaks of makeup on her face, coupled with her heaving bosom as she vibrates with anger and emotion, not to mention the alcohol in my system and I can't help but wonder, what if…?

She moves closer, occasionally hugging me again for moral support. Then she looks up at me, puts her hand behind my head, and pulls me down, planting a soft, deep kiss on my lips. Hot, wet, and so much passion. Fuck me. It's been years since a woman kissed me. I feel my pants grow taught as my knob springs into action. My face flushed red.

"What was that for? I mean, not that I'm complaining."

"Thank you, Danny, for listening to my bullshit and not judging me."

"I… Well, of course. The least I can do." And I got to eat some of my chips, after all.

She takes my hand, stands up and leads the way to the living room couch. Pushing me down onto the cushions.

We engage in some 'heavy petting' for what seems like hours. For someone this young, she's skilled in the art of oral pleasure. I found my hands straying to her arse and tits several times and had to pull back. I can't do this. Can I? The moral implications. The inevitable loss of a babysitter. What if Rosie comes down for a drink of water? The last thing I need is the kids to see my naked arse bobbing up and down on their beloved Jessie.

"Jessica, sorry. I need to pause for a moment."

"What's wrong?"

"Nothing… I just need to pee. Sorry, I didn't get a chance since the pub and…"

"Of course. Come right back. Okay?"

"Yes. Okay."

In the downstairs bathroom, for fear of waking the sleeping babies, I switch on the light, look at myself in the mirror. I see a sad, pathetic loser of a man staring back. Trying to bang the babysitter. How clichéd can you get? Midlife crisis going swimmingly here.

I can't do this. I'll regret it. She'll regret it. The kids will hate me. No, I can't. But… She started it, I mean, all I wanted to do was eat my chips and wank over Winona. I didn't ask for this. Maybe I'd be helping her out. Get the remaining Brett out of her system, show her what a real man can do?

Who am I kidding?

I'll take any chance I can get. Desperation fills my veins. Jessica will forget all about this in a week, but I'll relive it in my dreams, over and over, helping me through the remaining decades of celibacy that inevitably follow.

A pathetic realisation comes to me. I don't own any condoms. My previous stash long since passed the use-by date and discarded in a wallet clean of 2017. I seriously can't get the babysitter pregnant. That would be the ultimate in shameful behaviour. I can see the look of scorn on the face of Elise, after the kids tell her at the park one day that they now have another little sister.

"The babysitter, Danny? You pathetic prick. She's a little girl!"

Screw you, Elise. Brian is fifty-five. Yes, I do know that; I stalked his stupid Facebook page. Ha. Take that Maria, Elise,

Brett, and Megan, you can all collectively suck my hairy nuts. I will show Jessica how a real man behaves, and I will pull out well and truly early.

My fate sealed, I piss and wash my hands, face, and dick in the sink. I don't look back at the mirror though. I don't need to see that judgemental look again.

Back at the couch, Jessica is looking much better. "Now, where were we?"

"Oh, my god. I can't believe it. I'm so happy!"

"Ha, just wait till I…"

"We made up."

"What?"

"Brett and me, it was just a misunderstanding. He doesn't like Megan. He asked me to get engaged!" She squeals and dances around, then once again, throws her arms around me. This time, my dick remains flaccid.

Shit.

"Oh, that's… Wonderful, for you." I manage a smile and step back from her embrace.

"He's coming to get me. Can I go clean up?" She motions to her face, still streaked in mascara.

"Right, yes. Of course."

My chips are nearly cold now, but guess what? I have a microwave and I'm not afraid to use it. In they go, with all three sausages. I have a feeling Jessica will get plenty of her own battered sausage tonight.

She emerges from the bathroom, makeup fixed and still bubbling with glee. Casually stealing one of my sacred chips. You know, maybe it is time to look for a new babysitter, anyway? Kids enjoy meeting new people sometimes.

A car pulls up outside and several loud beeps follow, with flashing lights to boot. This is a residential area, Brett, you little twat. I don't need the cops coming over on top of this wonderful day.

"That's him. I'll be off then."

"Right, well, thanks for watching the kids, Jessica."

"My pleasure. I love them. Hey, you got my money?"

I hand over forty quid, and she stuffs the twenties into her bra.

"Call anytime you need a sitter. Bye, Danny." She doubles back. "Oh, I nearly forgot. How was your date?"

"Terrible." I flash her a fake smile, and she's gone. Leaving behind a sad, broken old man. Taking with her the last remnants of my dignity.

"Goodbye, Jessica. You little tease."

Right, where's my laptop?

Chapter Three

M onday morning is the typical chaos. Five alarms
snoozed, and I finally drag my arse out of bed to find
the kids oblivious to the impending rush. Buried in blankets on
the couch. iPads and game controllers in their hands instead of
clothes, school bags, and most importantly, homework that
wasn't done. I spend fifteen minutes helping Ethan with Maths,
English, Science, and Geography.

Well, helping him Google the right words, anyway. We've
had all weekend to get this done, but Monday morning is when
the urgency suddenly hits. I can't complain, since this is exactly
how I spent every single weekend when I was a kid. Nothing
changes. Life goes on.

I didn't see how homework enriched my education back
then, and I still don't see it helping Ethan and Rosie. Life is shit,
why make it worse? Kids need a break, same as I do. But it has
to get done, regardless. We all begrudgingly serve the system.

What happened to Sunday? I can't really remember, but there
was a lot of sitting around on our various electronic devices, and
somehow, inexplicably, we had to go back to the supermarket for

more provisions. My Tesco Clubcard has seen more life than I have.

I drop Rosie off first at her school. She pecks me on the cheek and then merges off into a group of girls, heading in the school's direction. Then a nip across town to Ethan's school.

I dread this part.

There's nowhere to park the car, of course, because the school yummy mummies have taken up all the good spots with their vast SUVs. I'm convinced they get up at five in the morning, just to get their makeup, perfume, outfit and hair all perfect and get the best parking. Sad, really, when you think about it. Why do they care so much? It sure as hell isn't for my benefit.

I open the door for Ethan and he bolts out like a greyhound to join his friend, Jack.

"WATCH THE ROAD, ETHAN!" Luckily no cars were coming, but Ethan didn't know that. He'll give me a heart attack one day.

"Bye, Daddy."

I walk behind him, not in a rush, because I can see Jack's mother, Maggie, in a gaggle of mummies near the gate. For some unknown reason, I seem to be her 'pet project'. Last month she gave me a big pot of stew for our dinner, claiming it was leftovers. But it was a huge pot, seemingly uneaten from. This may have been triggered by Ethan showing his class a large collection of 'Happy Meal' toys at their show and tell. Anyway, once I'd dumped a whole bottle of Tabasco in it, it didn't taste too bad. Then I had a full week of her asking for the pot back because every day I forgot to grab it as we left for school.

Ethan and Jack are meandering in the wrong direction to the school door. I do my sheepdog impression and herd them back. If I don't see Ethan go into the door, I can't rest all day, wondering if he made it in. I'm sure they'd contact me if he wasn't there, but still.

It's a razor edge dance, because I don't want the teacher to see me.

"Mr Watts?" Ms Sanders calls from the doorway.

Shit.

"Hi, sorry. I'm in a rush, actually. Got a meeting." I hold my hand up, pinky and thumb outstretched in the universal signal for 'piss off, I'm busy.'

"If you can pop in later, please. I'd like to have a word."

No surprise there. She's had more words than Rachel bloody Riley. I nod and turn around, back to the car.

"Morning, Danny." Maggie tries to catch my eye as I go past. She's standing with three other mummies, all directly from the salon, amidst a cloud of noxious vapour, also known as perfume. How any of them can breathe, I don't know.

"Morning, Maggie. Ladies." I nod but keep my head down. I really do have a meeting to get to.

"Did you have a good weekend?"

"Yes, thanks." I lie as I quickly walk back to the car.

Got away fairly lightly there.

Back home, where I also work from, my first port of call is the coffee machine. I'm not fit to address the minions without caffeine.

While it brews, I fire up the laptop and connect to the network, typing five different passwords, swearing, re-typing passwords, then finally logging into the chat and email.

I note that Alex is online. I ping her a smiley, then a coffee cup emoji. She sends me back a thumbs-up.

Alex is my second in command. I'm the regional manager. No idea how I managed that, but I'm not complaining. Well, not too much, anyway. We collectively manage a huddle of roughly fifty tech support agents, who, in turn, aid and assist the masses of the tech-ignorant across most of Europe.

She's a nightmare, and my best friend, if I'm honest. If there was a God, she'd be much more, and permanently naked. She's gorgeous, but I'm so deep into Friendzonia with her that I don't have a hope of ever emerging. She's almost married, too, which doesn't help.

Still, I enjoy her company virtually. She's based in the Netherlands. We talk every workday, on the phone and in chat windows, but it's a rare occasion that I get to see her in person. Probably best. I'd be driven mad with the frustration. I know she likes me, as a friend, although I can't imagine why. But again, not complaining.

Fetching my coffee, I stop at the doormat and pick up the wad of junk and bills. Dumping most of it straight into the recycling bin. Bills, letters about new bills that will come soon, notifications that my car will need tax, test, insurance, and probably a blood transfusion next month. Nothing good ever comes through the letterbox. If it's an Amazon parcel, they leave it outside the door.

Reluctantly, I stumble back upstairs to my little box-room office. Next to my bedroom, conveniently located near the bathroom.

"Good morning, team." I wait for the wave of coughs and grunts to subside and open up my email, then share my screen. "Let's have a look at the daily download, shall we?"

Alex takes control and reads out the bullet points of new problems and reported issues we should all take note of. Doesn't matter what she's reading. I could listen to her voice for hours. She's got that sultry, husky tone. Her accent isn't quite Dutch, but a mix of that and Romanian, I think. She speaks eight languages, which is how she comes to be the team lead of the European tech support department at only age twenty-seven. I speak exactly one language if you don't count bullshit.

I mute my microphone, and slurp at my coffee, fiddling with the executive toys on my desk that have been there since Elise bought them for me, as novelty Christmas presents when I first got the job. Thirteen years with this company now, and although I've climbed the ranks, the pay is nothing to sing about. Still, I don't have a commute. I don't have to take many support calls, these days, and, I get to chat with Alex. It's not the worst job.

After the team call, our tradition on a Monday is to have a direct one-to-one. Just Alex and I. Ostensibly to talk through all the figures and issues from last week, but usually just a good old gossip and natter about all and sundry. Alex was having a barbecue over the weekend. I will no doubt hear all about it.

"Hiya."

"Hey, Mister Danny. How was the date?"

Christ. I'd forgotten about it. Now I get to recount the dreadful event all over again. "Disaster. Can we skip that?"

"Oh, no, mister. You will tell me all the disgusting details."

"Thought you'd say that. But I want to hear about your barby."

"Is nothing to tell, we cooked meat and drank beer. What happened at your date?"

"Ah, where to start?"

"At the beginning, like every good story. I have my pastry and coffee here, you talk."

I step her through the gory details. She wants to know the colour of Maria's blouse, what did she drink, was her nose really that big? "Pinocchio, when he's been caught by his wife with stripper-glitter on the end of his wooden stalk." I put on my falsetto. "Lie to me, Pinocchio!" She laughs, squeals and generally agrees that the whole situation was a nightmare. Why did she come on the date if she didn't want to talk about anything? And didn't she prefer I looked at her face than her tits?

This is why I like Alex. I'd give my left nut to have been on a date with her, instead of Ave-bloody-Maria. Who am I kidding? I'd give both nuts and a leg into the bargain.

Lunch is a depressing Pot-Noodle at my desk, while I compile the reports from last week. I know I could automate this stuff, but doing that would leave me with almost nothing to do. I pretend it's just easier to keep doing things manually.

As long as the big-wigs get the data, and we keep looking productive, they leave me alone. For the most part.

Alex sends me a selfie from her barbecue. She's wearing a skimpy bikini and holding a can of beer. Jesus Christ. I send back a panting face emoji. I have to close my messages or I'll end up shooting a load in my pants again. Another message comes in. 'You thirsty for the beer or something else? ;)'

Such a tease.

I was a little cagey about telling Alex what happened with Jessica, but we tell each other everything, so I divulged all when she probed for more juicy details about my weekend. "You snooze, you lose, Danny." She told me. True. If I could make a decision in the heat of the moment, without stopping to ponder the nitty-gritty ins and outs, I'd be a shag up on the deal. I'm sure I'd be regretting it now, anyway, but in a different way, and I'd have got to swap body fluids with a beautiful teenager. It's probably for the best we didn't go all the way. But, a man can dream, can't he?

Before I know it, I'm back in the car again, doing the school runs.

I suppose I'm lucky to have a flexible job that I can do this. I sacrifice my lunch hour for my unpaid taxi job.

This time, the order is reversed, Ethan first, then Rosie. She has an after-school music lesson, which means I have a few spare minutes to drag across town.

I doubt if I can avoid the lecture from Ms Sanders forever. So, I brave the school halls and wait outside the classroom.

Schools always smell the same. Kids, disinfectant, crayons and blackboards. Even if they don't use those things anymore, the stench of previous decades persists.

I hated school when I was a kid, and adulthood has changed nothing. I feel sorry for the poor sods in there, bored to tears, counting the seconds until they can explode out into freedom.

The bell rings, and promptly, thirty-something sprogs burst from the door. Ethan is one of the last, with his buddy, Jack, in tow.

"Daddy!" He rushes up to me and clasps around my legs. I usually meet him outside. He probably knows something is up.

"Hey, dude. You okay?"

"Yeah. Can Jack come over to play?"

"Err, not today, Ethan. But maybe soon." I offer a smile that I hope doesn't seem too empty. My kids are bad enough, add another one into the mix, and it's my personal version of hell.

Jack isn't too bad, but I constantly worry I'll be sued if he falls over, or swells up like a balloon from a peanut or something ridiculous. Back in my day, peanuts were not weapons of mass destruction. What has happened to the world?

"Mr Watts, thank you for coming in." The 'nails on chalkboard' voice comes from the open door. She does like to keep things formal. I'd prefer if she just called me Danny as everyone else does, but that would infer a level of humanity that I don't think she's capable of.

Stephanie Sanders is a dried-up raisin stuffed into a blouse and skirt. She's seen it all, taught since the Black Plague ravaged the land.

I nod to Ethan. "Hey, dude, go play for five minutes, okay?"

"Okay, Daddy."

I'm ushered into the now empty classroom. The whiteboard is covered in indecipherable scrawls and lines. I assume some kind of equation solving problem, but I'd be hard-pressed to figure out the answer myself.

"Mr Watts."

"Danny will do."

She ignores my attempt to lighten the mood. "I don't know how to bring this up, other than to simply say it." She pauses for effect.

"Okay." She does like the dramatic buildup. Spit it out, woman. I haven't got all day.

"Ethan has been saying very inappropriate things to some of the girls."

"Oh, yeah? Like what?" I feel the heat of embarrassment flood my face. What has he been up to now?

Ms Sanders fumbles on her desk for a scribble on a sheet of paper. "He told Emily her mother was a M.I.L.F." She spells out the letters. I stifle a laugh with a fake cough. He's right. Emily's mum is a MILF.

"Did he?"

"Yes, and to be perfectly honest, I had to ask one of my colleagues what that meant." She pauses again, dragging out the punchline. "I was quite disgusted, Mr Watts, that an eight-year-old boy would say such a thing!"

"Yes, I can understand that. I'll have a word with him this evening."

I can't imagine where he got that from…

"There's more."

"Go on." I attempt my most 'concerned parent' frown. I feel like I've been caught peeking into the girls' locker room when I was a lad. Boys will be boys.

She looks at her paper again, before screwing up her face, even more wrinkled than before. Something I hadn't thought possible until I saw it with my own eyes. "He asked Ruby if her mother liked 'anal'."

"Ah. Are you sure you heard right?"

"Quite sure, Mr Watts."

I suppose there's no point in asking what Ruby said? Enquiring minds and all that.

"Okay, I'll talk to him immediately when we get home. I have to pick Rosie up now. Thanks for the tip."

"See that you do."

She's about to start ranting about something else, but I turn and exit, post haste.

Out in the yard, Ethan is sitting on the wall alone. There's a gaggle of older kids lingering nearby, but Jack and his other buddies have all gone.

"Dude, we need to have a chat. In the car, now."

I buckle him up and give him a little bottle of water, then slowly walk around the car and get in my seat. I find these lectures easier to dish out when he can't see my eyes. I'm torn between laughing it off and yelling. But he's calm and quiet, the last thing I need is crying all the way home.

"Ethan, sometimes Daddy says things that are only for adults to hear. Sometimes I say bad things because I forget that you and Rosie are listening." That came out awkwardly, but Ethan just looks blankly as I watch in the mirror.

"You can't say words like MILF and anal in school."

"Why not?"

"Those are things only adults can say."

"Well, that's stupid."

"It may be stupid, but that's just the way it is."

"It is stupid. Why can't everyone say everything?"

"Ethan! Just don't say things like that at school, or I'll have to take your iPad away."

"DAD! No."

"Are you going to say bad words at school anymore?"

29

"No." He sulks.

"No problem then." I look in the mirror. "We cool?"

"Yeah, sorry Daddy."

"All right, dude. Hey, you want a game of two-player Mario later?"

"Yeah!"

Parenting level-up achieved.

Picking up Rosie is a breeze, compared. She's waiting at the school gate as I arrive, and she hops in without any comment. At least I've got one sensible child.

"Did you have a good day, sweetheart?"

"Yes, Daddy."

"Learn anything interesting today?"

"Not really."

Fair enough. I throw another little water bottle back and head home. Kids need to be hydrated.

The darlings settle in with their iPads, and I go back to my desk. They might be done with the institution for the day, but I still have two hours before I can clock off.

I log back in with my dozen passwords, perform my banal tasks, check who will and won't be working tomorrow, and refresh the report page once again. With all that bullshit completed, I'm free to chat with Alex again before she logs off for the day.

I ping her on chat and recount the lecture I just got at school. She sends a page full of LOLs, followed by a 'Sorry' and a smiley emoji. I'm glad she thinks my life is funny. If I couldn't laugh, I'd have to cry.

. . .

I'm making my infamous Spag-Bol for dinner, my recipe passed down through the ages; if you can count a Christmas present recipe book from Granny, as ages. Adapted over time, enhanced with my secret ingredient, which is 'not giving a shit'. I find a good-sized dollop of that makes any meal a pleasure.

Rosie shows up in the kitchen without any electronic devices in her hands, which is a rare event.

"Can you teach me to cook, Daddy?"

Oh, wow. That was unexpected. I smile and look her in the eye in case she's messing with me, but there's no sign of a joke.

"Sure, sweetheart. I'd love to."

I get all the ingredients out. Onions, minced beef, tomatoes and an extra pot of sun-dried tomato paste, which really brings out the flavour. A mix of herbs, a pot of fresh pasta, and we're good to go. I hand her a small knife and a chopping board.

"Knives are dangerous, Rosie."

"I know, Dad." She rolls her eyes.

"Peel and chop up those onions, don't touch your face once you've cut them. After, rinse your hands with COLD water."

"Okay, why cold?"

"Hot water opens up the pores of your skin and the onion juice goes in. It makes you cry like a baby." I make a boo-hoo face. "But cold water doesn't do that, and the onion stuff just washes off."

"That's neat."

"You did learn something today, in the end."

She flashes a smile, and I see her mother in her eyes. Her mother from when we were young and happy, not cold, bitter and full of loathing, as she is now.

Dinner is delicious, of course, and Rosie helped, watched and learned. Maybe she can make it herself soon. I make a mental list of all the dishes I can teach her. Curry, stir-fry, quesadillas, lasagne. If I can delegate evening dinner duties to Rosie sometimes, that will help ease my tired bones, a little.

"Do you like your dinner, Ethan?"

"Yup." He's gulping it down in spades.

"Rosie made it."

"AGH!" He spits out a mouthful and makes a face.

"Don't be silly, she did a good job."

"Just kidding. It's really nice." He makes the thumbs-up sign and Rosie smiles back.

Monday didn't turn out too bad, after all.

Chapter Four

B ollock naked, sat on the shitter, swiping through dating apps, seems to be my morning ritual lately. One of the few times during the day that I get any peace before the daily churn begins. The crop of ladies this morning is particularly depressing. Anyone in my age bracket that hasn't already been snapped up seems to be real bottom-of-the-barrel material. I suppose that's me as well. I've sent a couple of 'winks' but I don't expect to get any replies.

The door bursts open with Ethan behind it.

"Hey, what the…"

Before I can flinch, he cries out and opens up the floodgates to a torrent of hot puke, which lands squarely on my crotch, phone, and splats over most of the bathroom.

Wonderful.

He grabs a towel and runs away, sobbing, leaving me with shit on my arse, puke all over my knob, and a sick child on the loose.

"ROSIE! HELP."

First things first, I wipe the chunks from my phone with a

wad of toilet paper. I can easily wash my body, but getting a new phone is an expense and pain I don't need.

"He's okay, Dad. He's gone back to bed."

"Get him a bowl, please. I'll be out in a second."

I stand up, trying not to drip vomit all over the place, and turn the shower on.

"Hey, you okay, little dude?" I feel Ethan's forehead and he's a bit warm. He shrugs and slumps down into his bed. He seems pale and quiet. Crap. This means a three-hour sit in the doctor's waiting room, catching even more bugs.

"I don't feel good, Daddy."

"You caught a bug, that's all. You'll be okay soon."

"Can I stay home today?"

"Yup, you have to. No school for you today, mate." He seems to cheer up with that news.

"But Rosie has to go. Are you okay to get in the car?"

He looks up, a ghastly shade of green. Okay, nope. That's not going to work. The last thing I need is a car full of barf.

My choices are limited. I can't leave him alone, and Rosie can't get to school alone. Taxi?

I pull out my phone and check the various apps, but there's nothing available until well after nine-thirty. School run cabs are probably booked up months in advance. We're just outside the bus routes where we live, and anyway, I'm not comfortable letting Rosie catch a bus on her own. I'm out of ideas. I guess she's staying home with us, too.

I call both their schools and leave messages that neither child will be in today, due to sickness. Then send a text to Alex that I might be late for the meeting today, can she run it? She pings back a simple 'NP'. I don't know what I'd do without her. She's a stalwart.

. . .

The coincidence hasn't escaped my attention, that the day after Rosie makes her first dinner, Ethan gets violently ill. But I'm fine, so far, and Rosie seems to be. I put it down to a school bug, rather than a food bug. But I'll be keeping an eye on all of us, just in case. Ethan is sedated with Calpol, water and iPad in bed. Rosie makes toast for herself and I gulp down my coffee. My work routine is broken now, I'm not sure what to do. If I'm on a call, I may not hear if Ethan needs help, and I can't let Rosie look after him all day. She's quietly dealing with the changes from our normal routine, but it wouldn't be fair to make her look after a sick kid.

With my office door open, I relay the morning's events to Alex, who tells me to log off, look after the kids and she'll do the reports for the day. I really couldn't want for a better colleague, but I can't just dump all my work on her either. I can do the simple tasks and keep an ear open for Ethan.

A sudden rush by my door, and the roar of another puke explosion, seven-point-five on the Richter scale this time. Poor fella.

"You okay?"

I grab another towel and wipe his face. He bursts into tears and puts his arms around my waist.

"No. My head hurts." His words are a bit slurred but I can't tell if that's the tears or if he's genuinely sick. I guess we're going to the doctors.

"Rosie, get dressed. We're going out."

Ethan in his pyjamas and dressing gown, like a miniature Arthur Dent. Rosie somewhat annoyed but trying her best. We sit, in limbo for all eternity, in the waiting room of doom. Ethan on my lap, I can't even browse around on my phone. He keeps changing colour from green to red like a set of manic traffic lights. We've been to the toilet on three false alarms already.

Seriously, why do they have appointments at all if they are that far behind? I know there are other sick people, but why tell us to come in if they know we won't be seen for ages?

We sit. Patiently. Resorting to reading the magazines on the table, celebrating the Royal wedding of Charles and Diana, in 1981.

Time stands still in the waiting room of doom. Hashtag: Album title.

"Mr Watts?"

Finally, we are called. The receptionist waves us over. There is a God.

"Sorry, but Doctor Evans has had to leave on an urgent house call. She'll be out for the rest of the day. If you'd like to come back in the morning?"

I look the receptionist in the eye, Ethan almost asleep on my shoulder as I stand at the little window. Rosie within an inch of gnawing off her leg to relieve the boredom. No words come. I am beyond words now. God has left the building.

We turn, calmly walk down the brightly painted corridor, and exit, stage right.

"It's probably just a twenty-four-hour bug, he'll be right as rain in the morning." My mother reassures me over a FaceTime video call. At least it cheered Ethan up a little, as Granny read him a bedtime story over the Internet.

"Hope so. Thanks."

"Got plenty of Calpol?"

I turn the phone around and show her three bottles of the pink stuff, along with wipes, towels and a bowl.

"Give him a dose now, before he sleeps. Check his

temperature and, most importantly, don't worry. Kids bounce back very quickly."

"Right. Thanks, Mum."

"Call in the morning. Night, Danny."

Mum hangs up the call, and I stick the thermometer in Ethan's ear once more. It's just over thirty-eight degrees. Not too bad, but I squirt the medicine down his throat, and sit down by his bed.

I know there are much worse things than a tummy bug, but when my babies are sick with anything at all, I panic. I don't know what to do, and I can't stand to see them uncomfortable.

I slept for twenty minutes at a time, one eye open, keeping a check on his little Lordship. He got up once in the night and I jumped up from the chair, ready with a bowl and towel, but he just went for a pee. I sat back down. Eventually, I must have passed out.

I woke this morning around ten, no sign of Ethan in his bed. A panic ensued, and I found him downstairs on the couch, playing a game. Toast in one hand, game controller in the other. Absolutely fine, totally oblivious of why I was worried.

Rosie was still in bed, watching YouTube and reading a book at the same time.

Since they aren't at school again, and I'm not at work, I should probably take the opportunity to do something worthwhile with the kids. It's a rare occasion that we all have spare time like this. I try to think of something to do, maybe go to the zoo? The park? Nope. Don't want to go too far. Maybe the swimming pool or skating rink? I ask the kids which they prefer, and they shrug their shoulders. They just want to stay home, they say. Suits me. Costs less than going out.

I feel a bit guilty about Rosie missing school though, so I come up with a plan. They can use their iPads if they do some spelling and maths first. Each question they get right buys them five minutes of iPad use.

I'm totally winning this parenting crap lately.

They agree to the plan, but only because I turned the WiFi router off to get their attention.

"Okay, the rules are simple. Correct answers get five minutes of Internet. Twenty questions up for grabs."

They groan but seem to be listening.

"Spell 'Antidisestablishmentarianism'. Go."

"Dad!" They both yell out at the same time.

"What?"

"That's too hard." Ethan protests.

"Not really. Break it down into chunks. Anti-dis-establish…"

"Can you just do an easier one?" Rosie is chief negotiator for the children's association of fair use Internet access.

"Ugh. Fine. Spell 'Caramel'."

They laugh and start scribbling down letters. I count down ten seconds, then sing the countdown music. "De-da, de-da, diddly-da, boing." They both laugh.

"All right, what have you got?"

They hold up their papers and show me. Not perfect, but they were under pressure.

"Excellent! Five minutes each."

We carry on with some more spelling challenges and they get all of them right. I fear they may be too simple. Instead, we switch to a maths problem. For this, I give them a few minutes to figure it out while I stick the kettle on for a cuppa.

"Aghhh!"

There's a scream from the living room, followed by a whoop and a laugh. I rush in and find the children holding my phone.

"WHAT IS THAT?" Ethan looks at me in horror.

"Dad, why have you got a big naked lady on your phone?" Rosie enquires, stifling a giggle.

"Err, what? Give me that."

I snatch the phone away and look at the screen, my mouth falls open and my cheeks flush red. There is indeed a big naked lady on my phone, but I don't know why. I quickly lock the screen and put the phone in my pocket.

"Okay, break time. You've done really well, you can have your iPads back now." I switch the WiFi back on and retire to my office for some investigation.

Cindy Jiggles, and, I have to wonder if that is her full legal name, is apparently a big, beautiful woman or 'BBW', who's up for anything, and somehow, one of the ladies I 'winked' at yesterday morning when perusing the dating apps. I don't recall the name, but her profile photo looks absolutely nothing like the nude selfie she subsequently sent. Must be the angle...

There's a message; asking me what I'd like to do to her body. I don't think she's looking for 'run from it, screaming in terror,' as the answer, but that's my gut reaction. Speaking of guts, hers is a canvas to a heart shape, drawn in red lipstick, with an arrow pointing down to a muff in serious need of some topiary. Cindy Jiggles could have a steady one-woman sideline supplying mattress stuffing.

Another photo arrives, this time from the rear, bent over doggy style. An acre of flesh with a crack torn open like the entrance to a mine. Deep, dark and full of scary surprises.

I delete the photos and close the app with a sigh. Am I this low? For a nanosecond, I consider replying to meet her, but I'm not that desperate, just yet. Am I?

. . .

"Daddy's phone was the victim of a malware attack. I've fixed it now. It's all safe again." Best I could come up with at short notice. I don't know if they'll swallow that bullshit though.

"Is that what happens when you get attacked? They send you naked ladies?" Ethan isn't buying it. Change the focus.

"What were you doing on my phone, anyway?"

They act like they've been caught with their hands in the cookie jar, fidgeting awkwardly.

"Looking up the answer to the maths question." Rosie admits.

"Right, well that's called cheating. I should take away your iPads for that, but I won't this time. Just leave my phone alone in the future, unless there's an emergency. Okay?"

"Yes, Daddy. Sorry." They retort in unison.

"What do you want for dinner?"

"McDonald's!" They both yell out excitedly.

"Nope. Not today. Real food. You don't want your mother moaning at you for eating junk, do you?"

"Fish Fingers?" Rosie suggests.

I sigh. "Fine." That's not real food, fish don't have fingers, but still, it has to be better than fast-food, doesn't it?

Chapter Five

E than's school has a forty-eight-hour policy when it comes
to barf. Don't come back until it's all gone. I suspect
many other parents don't adhere to this precautionary process,
which is how Ethan came to be spraying Jackson Pollock's in the
first place.

However, I do believe in keeping germs in the home, which
unfortunately means I'm working and babysitting at the same
time today. Rosie is at school. Ethan is on the couch. I'm in my
office, popping down every few minutes to make sure he's okay.
He says he's fine, watching crap on YouTube, but without any
kind of supervision, he's bound to get up to no good, sooner or
later.

I should probably investigate some kind of child-care place,
but I'm sure they also operate the same sickness policies, and of
course, they would want to be paid.

I manage during school holidays by planning activities and
getting Rosie to be my eyes and ears. That works, up to a point,
when I know it's coming, but for ad hoc situations like this, I'm
just increasing my stress level exponentially.

It doesn't help that one of my minions is also out sick today, and I've had to take some support calls. I'm a little rusty and reading the verbose terms and conditions out repeatedly is driving me insane. People absolutely do not listen, care, or give a single shit. The world is run by clueless lawyers and insurance firms. We all do these pointless tasks, hiding behind the rules and processes. To what end?

Alex said she'd help me as much as possible, but she's already doing her calls and some of my reports. In the end, the work has to get done somehow, so, here I am.

Today is also a sad day.

Not for me, but for another of my team who will be getting fired, once I can drum up the energy to do the firing.

He told a customer to, and I quote: 'Shove their fucking phone up their fucking arse.'

I had to listen to the recording. He had a point. The customer was angry to begin with, absolutely technically inept, and apparently couldn't follow simple instructions. Why they even had a phone at all makes no sense. Some people should stay in the dark ages and go find red telephone booths. The phone in question was one of the larger screen models. There's no way it would have gone in without a fight.

I sympathise with the lad, Ryan. I've felt like saying something like that, many times, but unfortunately, policies and lawyers run the show, and I have no choice but to 'let him explore other opportunities elsewhere.'

We aren't even allowed to say the word fired, in case of litigation against wrongful dismissal.

I pop down and check on Ethan, who is still glued to his iPad, then ping Alex to join me on a call to dismiss Ryan Ashton. It's a shame because he's one of our best chaps usually. Never had a day off sick, turns over a good number of calls, never caused trouble before. But as the customer complained publicly on Facebook, and head office saw the post, I have been instructed to deal with it quickly and cleanly. There's no point in trying to fight the cause because the bastards would kick me out, too, which wouldn't help with my stress level or bank balance.

Alex joins me on a conference call. We wait until we can see Ryan has hung up on his last ever customer and then drag him into the conference.

"Hey, Ryan. How are you doing?"

"All right, Danny, Alex. What's up?"

"Is everything okay, at home and stuff?"

"Yeah, why d'you ask?"

I borrow a line from Ethan's teacher. "There's no easy way to say this, mate, so I'll just say it." I can hear him sigh and then his line goes silent as he hits his mute button, probably to swear in the background. "You told a customer to insert their smartphone into their anal cavity." I have the audio from the call, ready to playback again, in case he contests the accusation. Calls are recorded for training purposes, after all.

"Right, yeah. Sorry, I did, but I was meant to be muted. The stupid headset is playing up, in't it. Works most of the time, but that one slipped through."

"I listened to the call. I can understand your frustration, but you deal with people all day. What happened?"

"Just had enough, Danny. You know how it is."

"Yeah, I do. But you know what this means?"

"Shit."

"I'm afraid the company policy is very clear in these matters, and we must terminate your employment immediately. You'll be paid to date, and your remaining holiday days added to the final payment. If you wish to protest this decision, you are free to seek legal representation and lodge your complaint with head-office within thirty days of this notification." I read out the script from my screen, verbatim.

A volley of angry curses then rattles our headsets for a full minute, accompanied by what could be the sound of a keyboard being pounded and smashed on a desk. Some knocks and bangs indicate that his headset was removed and flung down, then a muffled but still audible argument ensues with a female voice in the distance.

"They're fucking firing me! Bunch of stuck up bastards. One fucking mistake and the miserable twats are firing me!"

"Ryan, you know you aren't muted? We can still hear you…"

There's another series of curses and bangs, then his line goes dead.

"Alex, you still there?"

"Yes, I'm still here."

"That went well, don't you think?" She bursts out laughing.

Now we're two people down, and I have to pick Rosie up from school. Today is not a good day to have a problem with your personal electronic devices. Just saying.

… [please hold while we try to connect you. Your call is important to us, please stay on the line, and we'll be with you shortly] …

I prise the iPad away from Ethan and drag him back to the car. As it's Friday, I'll let them choose dinner. Which typically means eating with the clown, again.

My weekend outlook is as dismal as the British weather, cloudy, dull, and no chance of any extra-curricular activity.

Aside from Cindy Jiggles, I haven't had a single bite from any of the plethora of dating apps I subscribe to. Perhaps I should update my profile photo again. Make my 'selfie' into a 'sexy'. Who am I kidding? I'm unlikely to turn any heads, no matter what filter I use on my mug.

No, I'm looking at a lifetime of weekends with Netflix, shopping, tidying after the kids, and the occasional grind through PornHub for relief. Such is the fate of the single dad, until the kids leave me, and I'm left to rot, alone, spiralling into dementia and shouting at people in the post-office. Although I'm quite looking forward to that part.

A depressing stop at McDs on the way home from school, where the staff don't seem to be much older than Rosie, we get back home and eat our food, not around the table in some semblance of family unity, but dispersed throughout the house. Rosie in her room, Ethan on the couch, and I had to go back to my office and finish off some work.

Once I'm done with the reports and paperwork for Ryan's elegant and swift exit into job-seeker land, I ping Alex for our evening chat.

I'll have to write Ryan a good reference, because we're all humans, in the end, and humans make mistakes. You shouldn't have to pay for a single screw up for the rest of your life.

"Hey, Alex."

"Hi, Danny. Do you have any dates lined up for this weekend?"

"Don't make me laugh. My only definite date is with the crematorium."

"Ah, don't be negative. You are in your prime. You should be out there, having fun."

"I think you dialled the wrong number, this is Danny Watts. To whom am I speaking?" She laughs that tinkly laugh that makes things stir in my loins.

"Shut up, Mr Danny. You are funny, handsome, smart, kind. Any woman would be lucky to be with you."

"Well, thank you, Alex, but if you are looking for a pay rise, I'm afraid I'm not authorised to approve that."

"Shush. I mean it. If things were different…" She tails off.

"Ah, don't tell me things like that." My loins stir again. She's going to be the death of me. I need to change the subject because this could get awkward. "How about you, what wonderful weekend plans do you have with Niels?"

"There's a beer festival in Amsterdam, we're going to pop along."

"Oh, wow. That sounds great. Not that I'm jealous or anything."

"You should come."

"Yeah, I'll be there in twenty minutes." She laughs again. But there's a hint of sadness in it.

"It's a shame you are so far away."

Rosie appears in my doorway. "Hey, Daddy, I'm going to jump in the shower."

"That sounds dangerous, Rosie. You should probably just wash in there."

A groan simultaneously comes from Rosie and my headset. "Thank you, thank you. Danny Watts - international Dad Joker. I'll be here all week, folks."

Rosie rolls her eyes and walks away in mock disgust.

"I better go, Danny. We are going out for dinner soon. I have to make myself look beautiful."

"Ha. You don't need to do anything to be beautiful, Alex."

"Aww, thank you." She types in a kiss emoji on the chat window and disconnects.

My mobile rings. A rare event in itself. Usually, just a spam call when that happens. Who rings a phone these days?

Elise. That's who. The caller ID shows her photo from years ago. I took that photo myself, on the beach in Lisbon. Better times. That evening we shagged like wild bunnies after too many Ginjinha's. Come to think of it, that's when Rosie was conceived… What does she want now?

"Hello?" I don't know why I pretend I don't know who's calling and act surprised when she speaks, but it seems like the done thing. From a time before we could glimpse a few seconds into our future, with predictive texts and caller ID.

"Danny, I got a call today from Ethan's school."

Shit.

"Oh?"

The school should know that Ethan's mother is mostly out of the picture. They have been informed of the parent/guardian situation. But these government agencies all still insist on contacting the mother, primarily. The trouble I had getting the child benefit moved into my name and bank account was ridiculous. Daddy isn't considered important when children's welfare is in question.

"Has he not been in?"

"Tummy bug, been out for a day or two. I did tell them."

"You didn't tell me, did you? Don't you think his mother should know if he's sick?"

"It's nothing to worry about. I'm sure you are busy with whatever it is you do…"

"I'd still like to know, from you, rather than his teacher."

"Yeah, sorry. Didn't cross my mind. I've been rather busy, looking after him, waiting in the doctors, working, and looking after Rosie, all at the same time." No sympathy comes from the thin slab of glass and metal in my hand. Not that I was expecting any.

"Can you put him on the phone? I'd like to talk to him."

"Yeah, hold on." I plod down the stairs to Ethan, still stuck to his iPad.

"Your mother wants to talk to you, Ethan." He looks up,

shocked and a bit nervous. "It's okay. She just wants to know if you are better now."

I hand him the phone and leave him to it, heading into the kitchen to stick the kettle on. What a fun Friday evening. I don't even have any beer left. I guess that means yet another Saturday at the supermarket.

Ethan appears in the kitchen and gives me back the phone without a word.

"All right, little dude?"

"Yeah. She said I could get a treat, next time she sees me."

"Did she say when that would be?"

"Nope."

"Oh, well, fancy a game of Mario?"

"Yeah. You be Princess Peach, I'll be Mario."

"No. I'll be Luigi. Rosie can be Peach." I do have some dignity left, somewhere.

Chapter Six

Head office, in their infinite wisdom, have decided to hire a replacement for Ryan. That's a good thing since the typical policy would be to leave us a man down.

This means two things.

1. I have to interview people, which I find a horrific task anytime I've done it in the past.

2. I get to spend time with Alex!

We're planning a trip to Paris, which is where head office wants the new person to be located. French-speaking support is more in need right now than English speaking. I'm nervously excited. Three nights and most of four days in Paris with Alex, a mere hotel room away. Temptation and frustration will probably kill me. Add some booze into the mix... A dangerous combination. She'll help me with the interviews and translate if they can't speak English. She'll also tease me incessantly, no doubt.

Also, it means taking the kids to my parents' house, which is a ninety-minute drive on the motorway. Another few days off school. But they'll have a blast with Granny and Grandpa, who are already excited, preparing spare beds and activities. It'll be a little holiday for the kids, as they'll get to do all kinds of stuff they never usually do.

The team call this morning lasted all of ten minutes because I was desperate to get on our one-to-one with Alex to sort out all the details. Trying to act cool isn't my strong point. I probably came across like a kid in a sweetshop.

Suddenly, I have a load of things to organise. Kids laundry, hotel bookings for myself, Alex, and a conference room for our interviews. Flights, transport, schools. Probably many other things I'm forgetting.

We get a per diem allowance for travel. I like to keep well under it, which means I can actually make a few quid into the bargain.

However, as it turns out, staying in Paris is not cheap. So much so, that our per diem will barely cover the room, never mind food and drink. We'll be staying in something barely a step up from a hostel dormitory. That was fine for me in my teens, backpacking around Europe. But now, no thanks. I need a private en suite bathroom and a comfortable bed.

"What about this place?" I send Alex a link over the chat.

"Yeah, it's okay. But I have a better idea."

"What's that?"

"If we share, we could get a much better place and still have some money left over."

A jolt of adrenaline thuds through me as I realise what she's just said. Share a room with Alex? My mind flits back to that brief snog on the couch with Jessica, the danger of temptation. Frustration lingering just around the corner. "How you call it, two thin beds in one room."

"Err, I mean, yeah, that could work." Despite every rational bone in my body telling me this is a bad idea, my other bone is in charge of decision making. The choice is out of my hands, instead, in my pants.

"Do you snore?"

"Elise said I did, but she would find fault in a diamond."

"Niels says I snore like a mountain goat. Will be fine." I laugh, I wonder how he knows what a mountain goat snores like?

"He won't mind? The room sharing thing?"

"He knows you are harmless." She chuckles. I don't know how I feel about that statement. I probably am harmless, but that doesn't do my ego any good. He should be jealous and worried that his fiancé will be sharing a hotel room in Paris with a stud like me. Ha. The Dutch are probably just laid back about these things. Either way, I'm rather excited. Even the thought of interviewing candidates doesn't dull the mood. Speaking of which, I need to organise a job posting with a local agency.

"I've got a big surprise for you guys."

After school, in the car home is how I planned to break the news to the kids. I hope they will be excited and happy, but you never know. They could freak out and panic about it. Rosie can be shy sometimes, and it's been a long while since I was away from them for a night.

I need not have worried; They squeal in excitement, and within thirty seconds they are arguing over who would sleep in the spare room and who would get the couch bed. The fight is over who wants the couch, not the spare comfy bed. There's no TV in the spare room.

Kids sorted, I just need to drop a letter into each school, notifying them of the missed days and reason. If they don't like it, tough. The only other plan would be that my parents come to stay at my house and take the kids to school, but the logistical nightmare of that is not worth considering. They would need at least a month's notice and have to pack and repack their bags ten times. Not to mention the inconvenience of missing Bingo on a Tuesday night.

The other option, Elise, is not an option. The words I used were, "Over my dead body will you take the kids." And I stand by them now.

We haven't been to visit Mum and Dad since Christmas, and that was just one afternoon. I know I should take the kids to visit more often, but life gets in the way of living. Plans are all very well made, but carrying them out when I barely have the energy to get up off the couch is another.

Still, this impromptu event will be a little break from reality for everyone. Especially me.

Last time I was in the same place as Alex was about three years ago, as I recall. It was at one of our rare company get-togethers where everyone is invited. Costs a fortune to get all our spread out colleagues together for a massive piss up. Those gigs are as rare as rocking-horse shit. I didn't know her as well back then, but that didn't stop me from getting far too drunk and asking her to dance in the club after dinner. Spoiler alert: I can't dance. I've never danced in my life. Something about her just brings out the idiot in me.

With less than a week until we fly, our paths coordinated to meet up at Charles de Gaulle Airport on Monday next, I book one room for our accommodations. It feels weird to do that, knowing what I'm getting into. But the room is a twin, in a reasonable three-star hotel just outside of the city. Reviews look good; all the photos look elegant and bright. It's near a park too, in case we feel the need for a romantic stroll. Ha.

It will be fine.

. . .

Rosie and I are making lasagne for dinner tonight. She's going to stir the sauce, do the layers, and spread the cheese. I'm going to show her how to make the beef and the cheese sauce from scratch. We don't do jars of crap in my kitchen. The crap is reserved for takeaway.

I'd love to show Ethan how to cook, too, but he doesn't seem interested. Which is okay. I don't want to push it. He's certainly interested in eating the food we make, that will do for now.

After dinner, we organise a video chat with Granny and Grandpa to finalise all the details. The kiddos want to specify their sleeping arrangements, and I want to know what equipment, food, drink, chargers, blankets, and kitchen sinks we should bring. I'm sure we could show up with nothing and be fine. Mum and Dad know how to look after children, I know firsthand, but still, if we don't pack the boot of the car to bursting, I'll feel like something is missing.

Dad recently retired from thirty-something years working at the same company. He was a structural hardware designer for a large military supplier. This has given him an intensity and attention to detail like no one else I've ever met. When he bought a car, he virtually took it apart piece by piece and put it back together again, tutting at the choices the carmaker had made. His rework was better and stronger than before. He once made me a train-set using the metal from old soup cans, then painted it and made a landscaped environment which was an accurate scale model of the Ffestiniog Railway in Snowdonia, Wales. It had a real, tiny working steam engine powering the train. I was fascinated, enthralled, and utterly unable to learn from his teaching. When I tried to bend metal, I ended up nearly taking a finger off, and Mum forbade me from touching it again. I bet that train set is still in the attic, and would probably still work fine, given a fresh fuel tablet and a tank of water. Perhaps

Ethan will get the engineering bug, passed through my blood, into his. I'd be equally happy if Rosie was interested in steam engines and metalwork, but she's never shown any curiosity into that sort of thing. Still, she never cared about cooking until recently. Anything is possible.

Mum never worked for money, but kept the house in good order all these decades. She's the chairperson of her local bridge club, church choir, housing association, and probably a few other things I don't know about. She is one of the few people in the world who still uses a landline phone and has a paper Rolodex next to it, with all her contacts and numbers. She only got an iPhone to see the kids on video chat. Other than that, she never uses anything that was invented after 1986, which in her mind is seemingly a cutoff date for when things became too complicated and weird.

A normal, everyday family situation then. Apart from Roland. My brother.

We rarely talk about Roland and he doesn't come to family events. Not since he came out, anyway. Mum and Dad just can't deal with it. It's one of those things they don't understand and say they will never accept. Personally, I couldn't care less who he wanted to be with. He's the younger, more attractive brother. When we were teenagers, the fact that girls gravitated towards him somehow, and yet he had no desire to shag them, only benefitted me. Not that I managed to bed any of them, of course.

He's a great laugh and a decent chap. Smart, elegant, and makes way more money in one month at his graphic design job than I do in three. I rarely see him, but I put that down to him being busy, rather than any resentment. I keep hoping Mum and Dad will come around someday, and we can get back to being a homogenous, loving family, but thus far, that hasn't happened. Roland is taboo.

I don't blame Mum and Dad, and honestly, I don't think Roland does, deep down. They just come from a different era when sexuality was stifled and hidden away. They aren't bad people, just set in their ways. Secretly, I think they are equally disappointed with me and my divorce. But I often hear - "Thank God you gave us those grand-kiddies before she ran off." Which is my saving grace. I knew they'd be useful for something, one day.

Arrangements made, kids suitably designated sleeping quarters, there is one small spanner in the works. My parents don't have WiFi. The only Internet connection is through Mum's phone on 4G. This means that the darlings can't watch YouTube all day.

I've made the executive decision not to tell them this nugget of information; They'll just have to deal with it. Last time they stayed over they didn't have the iPads or the YouTube addiction.

I'm hoping that Granny and Grandpa have enough tricks up their sleeves that they won't even notice. It will do them good to be cut off for a while.

Chapter Seven

I t's good, sometimes, just to let your mind wander. Process the information you already store, cancel all further input for a little while. That's why driving opens up thoughts and memories that would otherwise be smothered by normal day-to-day banality.

As we get closer to what used to be home, memories flood back in tsunami waves. I pass by my old school, then the first place I worked, the pub where I got my first real snog. Going home is always a melancholy trip to nostalgia land. Those days always seem simpler, but I'm sure, at the time, they didn't feel that way.

The kids, however, desire constant stimulation. On a long journey like this, they inevitably fall asleep.

Suits me. Some peace is just what I need to sort my head out for this trip.

I'm staying at my parents' house tonight and Dad is driving me to the airport in the morning. He insisted, and it makes more sense than going all the way back home first or finding a hotel at the airport, which would eat into my budget.

As we pull into the driveway, the little things are what I

notice first. Mum has new hanging baskets with dangling ivy coming from them. There's a new doormat, and I'm pretty sure the letterbox is different, but it might just be painted.

The kids wake as the engine stops and excited yelps and screams replace the peace.

"We're here."

They scramble to unbuckle and exit, but the child locks keep them in place for a second while I creak my bones and stretch out. Just standing up is becoming a chore these days.

"HURRY UP!" Rosie roars, repeatedly plucking at the door handle to no effect. I pause because it's funny to watch them squirm for a second.

"Okay, okay. Keep your hair on." I open the door and Rosie bolts out like the hare at a greyhound race. At the front door within a microsecond. Ethan follows, he doesn't wait for me to go around and open his door. I wonder if they are happy to be here?

Amid the chaos of the dining table, there's a calm sense of safety and warmth. Mum has gone all out, making a big Sunday roast with all the trimmings. Something we haven't had for many a moon. The kids pick at their broccoli, but there's a sweet carrot dish that Ethan is gobbling down.

Dad is telling the kids all the activities he's got planned. This is why I'm not worried about them missing a few days of school; they'll learn more here in three days than a year of school. No doubt about it. Dad is a wealth of information on every topic, from machine screw thread diameters to space shuttle orbit paths. He'll happily explain either in great detail, given the chance. Mum teaches by osmosis. She suggests things to stimulate the mind and you come away wondering, eager to go and find out more on your own. Honestly, I should just leave the kids here for the whole school term. Sadly, life isn't that simple.

After dinner, Dad drags me out to his shed to show me all the things he's tinkering with.

"See that can of beer in your hand, Son?" I nod.

He holds up a nugget of shiny metal, "That's a future project."

"Hey?"

"My latest distraction, I've built a little aluminium smelter behind the shed. Makes no sense wasting all that good metal. I melt it down in batches and make these little nuggets."

"Incredible. What for though?"

"Ah, you never know, Danny. Might come in useful, one day." He taps his nose and winks.

"Please, don't let Ethan touch it. What temperature does it get to?"

"Oh, not too hot. About six or seven hundred Celsius. Give or take." He chuckles.

"Yeah, please don't light that up while the kids are here."

"Don't worry, no plans to fire her up just yet. Don't throw that can away, though."

He's never happier than when tinkering.

Someone suggested a game of Trivial Pursuit, and although it sounds uncool and cheesy, it's quite fun, even if Dad is slaughtering all of us. Rosie and Ethan are cheating and getting pie slices when they shouldn't be, but who's counting?

In the car, Dad regales me of his last trip to France, sometime in the early 1700s.

"'Course, things have probably changed a bit since I was there. You should try to see some sights, Danny, not often you get a chance like this."

"It's a work trip, Dad, probably won't do anything except work."

"You'll have a couple of evenings, though?"

"True. I'll see what I can do." I know what I'd like to do in the evenings, but the chances of that are between slim and none.

"Did you tell Elise that the kids are with us?"

"Oh, bugger. No, totally forgot."

"She is their mother, Danny."

"Yeah... I'll sort it." I didn't completely forget, I knew I had to do it in the back of my head, I just put it on a to-do list that was a mile long, at the bottom. I'll send her a text when I get to Paris. If I remember.

"Here we are, the majestic monolith of Gatwick Airport. Safe flight, Danny."

"Cheers, Dad. See you in a few days. Hope the kids behave."

"They'll be fine. Don't worry about a thing."

I grab my suitcase and wave him off, stepping into the unknown. A break from normal life, released of responsibility for a brief reprieve. It feels like I'm young and free again, off on a trip to try to get laid. Try being the optimum word. While my mates always seemed to score on holidays in Spain, I'd be the spare knob at the bar, alone and wasted at three in the morning. That was a long time ago, though. Have I learned anything useful yet? Probably not.

After an uneventful flight, I land, on time, in Paris. I call Mum quickly to say I've arrived and to check on the kids.

Now I have a short wait for Alex to get here. I find somewhere to sit and fire up my laptop. Work still has to be done, and I need to keep up with emails and reports. With Alex here too, we don't have anyone else who can do the admin tasks. The truth of my evenings is likely to be catching up on all the boring crap we have to churn through. Seeing the Eiffel Tower or browsing the Louvre is unlikely to be high on the list of priorities. Work travel sounds glamorous. But in reality, it's tiring, tedious and quite stressful.

Despite telling the team there would be no call this morning, my Inbox is littered with people wondering why there was no call. I send another reminder to everyone that there won't be one tomorrow, or the next day either, and to carry on with their normal tasks as usual. You just can't get the staff these days. Well, I hope we can get at least one; otherwise this trip will be rather embarrassing. The agency has lined up a dozen or so candidates, and we have the arduous task of narrowing that down to a few potentials. It sounds like a simple job that almost anyone can do, but we pride ourselves on going the extra mile with our support. Any old Jean, Pierre, or Jacques isn't who we're looking for.

I find it hard to focus when there's noise all around me and people constantly walking by. I try to block out the background ambience. But when my name is called on the PA, I prick my ears up. The message repeats "Could Monsieur Danielle Watts please bring his sexy butt to the information desk, s'il vous plaît." I must be still asleep on the plane. Did they really say that? I'm dreaming this, surely? But no, I'm definitely awake. I stand up and look for signs to information.

When I get there, I'm expecting it to be a prank, played by my wonderful colleague, Alex. But she's nowhere to be seen.

"Bonjour, err, Je suis Danny Watts." My French classes utterly fail me, but I remember a few basics.

The lady at the desk looks up and smiles. "Oui, bien sûr." She nods and motions behind me, and as I turn around, I'm physically assaulted by Alex, running and leaping towards me, arms flung around my neck, legs wrapped around my waist. Knocking me backwards into the desk.

"Agh!" She squeezes even tighter and then kisses me on the forehead, dropping down onto the floor.

"Hello!"

"You couldn't just have met me at the bar?"

"Where would the fun be in that?" She slaps me on the arse. "And you do have a sexy butt, the world should know about it."

I smile, "If you say so, Alex." I desperately want to return the compliment, but it doesn't seem right. We are on a work trip and she is my subordinate, after all. "You look amazing, by the way."

She's grown her hair longer than when I last saw her, and it may be a different colour. But she's also somehow tripled in gorgeousness. When you don't see someone for a while, your mind's eye picture of them fades. I see her Skype avatar every day, but it's a tiny thumbnail of an old photo. Now she's here, in full stereoscopic real life and there's a radiance from her that lights me up.

She stands back and eyes me up and down. "Thanks, you too."

"Let's get out of here."

By way of various forms of public transport, none of which I understand, but Alex seems perfectly comfortable with, we arrive close to our hotel. We pass by a café on the way, which looks ideal for lunch. I'm starving, but dumping the bags and checking-in first seems like a good idea. Aside from platitudes and directions, we haven't talked much yet.

Alex is energetic, bubbly, enthusiastic. She's the antithesis to my demeanour. We're yin and yang.

"Daniel Watts, I have a room for three nights." No point in even attempting to speak French, I've already used up the few words I can safely say. Everyone speaks English, don't they? Apparently not, and the lady at reception looks blankly at me.

Alex jumps in with her perfect French. All smiles, she's immediately having a long conversation as if they are old friends. They both look at me and then laugh, then carry on talking. Not that I'm paranoid or anything. Alex turns to me.

"We can't check in yet, too early. But we can leave our bags and come back in an hour."

"Oh, well, that's fine."

"Yes, but there's one other thing." She looks me in the eye. "The hotel is fully booked and the only room they can give us is a double bed."

"What? But I booked a twin."

"Yes, she apologised and offered to find us another hotel, but I already told her it's fine."

"You... What?"

"Do you mind?"

Do I mind having to sleep in the same bed next to this gorgeous young woman? My team lead, my best friend? If things were different, I'd climb mountains to sleep next to her, but...

"I... No, it's fine."

"Yes. Will be fun." She pokes me in the ribs. "No funny business."

"No, god. No."

"Kidding! of course there will be funny business. I snore like a mountain goat, remember?"

I offer a nervous laugh. I have no idea what I'm letting myself in for here, but honestly, at this moment, I don't care.

We dump our bags in a little room behind reception and head back out towards the café across the road.

I feel like I'm in the film, Amelie. The little café is the perfect example of all things French. I suspect some of it is for the tourist ambience, but, nevertheless, it's a change from the normal Starbucks.

"Did you have a look through all the CVs? I think there are some good ones."

"You want to work, already, mister boss?"

No, I don't really, but I'm at least trying to be professional. "Well, I suppose we can relax, a little."

"That's better. You want some wine?"

"You trying to get me drunk, Alex?" I smile, and she flutters her eyelashes.

"You need to loosen up."

She's right. This isn't a holiday, but away from home, away from the kids, it's probably as close as I've had to a break in a long time.

"Right, let's just see what happens, then."

Alex waves over the waitress. "la carte des vins, s'il vous plait."

"We do need to review those CVs though, later."

"Interviews are tomorrow, aren't they?"

"Yup, all day, then we call one or two back on Wednesday for a second round, then choose someone, and make an offer before the trip home on Thursday."

"We have time…" Alex smiles at me, melting my heart.

I have all the time in the world for her.

Chapter Eight

I'm woken by the constant drilling of a jackhammer into the back of my skull, and a tonne of dry, arid desert sand that's been deposited into my mouth by the night elves. Not to mention the bursting deluge of hot piss residing in my bladder. But also, the gentle snore of Alex, facing me, drooling all over my hand. I try to move but the thud of the jackhammer stabs deeper.

If there's a deity, I'm in great need of a miracle cure right now.

She's still deliciously pretty, bed-head hair, drool and snores aside. None of that is important. She's wearing my t-shirt, and I seem to be naked and we're together in the same bed. Something very sticky all over my genitalia.

Rewind.

After the café de beaucoup de vin, we stumbled back to the hotel; I remember that clearly. Alex showered while I tried to catch up with some email. That lasted all of five minutes until she exited the bathroom, wrapped only in a small towel. How was I meant to concentrate? I tried my best to avert my eyes, but she stood right next to me, talking about what we'd do in the evening. I'm only human. In the end, I let my eyes wander. She didn't notice, or if she did, she didn't mind. Holy crap, has she got some amazing body?

Our evening plans were scant, at best, but we'd already discovered that eating and drinking out was expensive. Once Alex dressed, in front of me with nary a care, we took a walk to a supermarché and stocked up on wine, beer, and questionable fruity coloured booze-pops, along with a selection of food that can be eaten from packets. When we got back to the hotel, I felt like a teenager again, laughing at the array of junk and booze laid out before us.

At some point, reason and responsibility came to me, and I called Mum and spoke to the kids. All fine, they barely realised I wasn't there. Then Alex found a music channel on the TV, lay down on the bed, and demanded that I bring her wine.

I didn't take much convincing, and it wasn't long until I was also sitting on the bed, guzzling down the silly water.

Wine run dry, we switched to beer, and somehow I found myself massaging her feet as she lay on her front. Feet turned to calves, calves to thighs, and then I stopped, embarrassed, nervous, and trying desperately to fight the voice in my head that knew this was a bad idea. Before I could react, she jumped up and grabbed some olives and cheese. Laughing as she spat the pips at me from across the room.

It was when we moved to the fruity stuff that things got really silly. I can't remember if it was me or Alex that said those fateful words 'truth or dare', but as we ran a circuit around the hotel corridors together, hand in hand, stark naked, giggling, that I realised how much I absolutely loved the crap out of this woman.

Thankfully, Alex had grabbed the room key, and we made it

back with no one seeing us, I hope. She grabbed my shirt off the floor and I managed a pair of underpants. She went to the bathroom. I lay down on the bed, the room spinning slowly around me. Next thing I knew was the elastic of my pants being pulled up, my hopes raised, only to be squirted down by a whole can of shaving foam, and the cackling howl of laughter as Alex fell on the floor, leaving me and my creamed underpants to wallow in our drunken stupor.

She stayed on the floor for some time, until I picked her up, snoring, and dumped her in the bed, took off my foam pants and crept in next to her.

She's still gorgeous, and even through the throbbing headache, I desperately want her to be my girlfriend and soul-mate. As valuable and wonderful as it is to have her as my best friend, it leaves a gap in my brain where the relationship should be.

I manage to move my arm enough to see my watch, it's eight-thirty and our first interview candidate is at nine.

"OH, SHIT! ALEX."

I jump out of bed, the pain in my head now pounding and beating, then I realise I'm still bollock naked, my dick covered in dry foam and, no longer drunk; I am not comfortable in this predicament. I leap into the bathroom and turn on the shower.

"Ugh." There's a groan from the bedroom. Then the door opens and Alex, bleary-eyed, walks in, sits down on the toilet and pees, rubbing her eyes.

I think it's safe to say she's very comfortable around me.

.   .   .

The only saving grace; Our commute consists only of going down in the lift to reception, where we have a small conference room booked for our interviews.

"Ask them to bring ten litres of coffee. Promptly."

Alex is somewhat more alive than I, being many years younger and able to soak up the booze quicker. She laughs, but groans a little, too. Surprising how quickly she has polished up. She looks professional, in a long skirt and blouse. I, of course, remain unshaven.

"What are those pastry things, the curly ones."

"Croissant?"

"Yeah, get a load of those, too."

A nervous chap rolls up at the open door, knocks, and waits patiently while I slowly turn my head, and somehow prick up a smile and nod for him to come in. Standing up is too much effort, but Alex gets up and shakes his hand.

"Monsieur Watts? Mademoiselle Vasiliu?"

"Yes, err, Oui. Come in, asseyez-vous."

I offer him coffee and a Croissant, but he only takes coffee. Good, more for me. I squint at my laptop screen and the open CV.

"Victor Jacquard? Tell us about yourself."

The lad is twenty-three, studied language, philosophy and computer science at the Sorbonne, has a hipster beard and a brand new suit, dark blue and two sizes too big for him, with a flourish of a white buttonhole flower. He's extremely polite, well-groomed. Honestly, we could skip the rest of the interviews and hire him now. He's perfect. Alex runs through the questions and slides, then she conducts a fake support call to him in French, switching occasionally to English and Dutch. The lad keeps up, and he's found his confidence. He's way over-qualified, which is the only thing that worries me. He's not going to stick around in a tech support job for long. Staff turnover is always a concern; training and investment in someone takes time and money.

Our forty-five minutes are up quickly, and as the coffee soaks into my system, I'm feeling more alive.

I stand up and shake Victor's hand.

Although I couldn't understand half of the interview, I see talent and knowledge in him. I feel like this has flipped around. At this stage, we are courting him to come and work for us.

The money isn't wonderful, but also not terrible. The hours can be flexible and there's no office to commute to. However, you have to deal with angry technophobes yelling at you all day, every day.

Yin and Yang.

With fifteen minutes before the next candidate, I run to the bathroom to freshen up.

In the mirror, I see a tired old man, designer stubble, the dregs of a hangover lingering. Why does that beautiful woman like me?

"What did you think?"

"He was very good, no?"

"Yeah, too good, almost." I explain my theory that he'd leave us in a heartbeat when he undoubtedly finds a better job soon.

"Then we come back and do it all again." A smile creeps onto Alex's face.

"I'm too old, Alex. I can't drink like that anymore."

"I think you had fun, last night."

"Oh yes. No doubt. But I'm paying for it now."

"You will pay for the rest of your life if I am pregnant."

"What?" A slam of adrenaline floods my veins, all the blood drains from my body and a stab of electric shock hits me in the guts. Alex is deadly serious, hands-on-hips. My mind races, I don't remember any sex? I would remember, wouldn't I?

She pauses for a moment before a grin erupts onto her face, then she bursts out laughing.

"Just kidding! Your face, ah-haha."

"My God, Alex, you are going to give me a heart attack."

"Was that true, what you said last night?"

"Jesus, what did I say?"

"You don't remember?"

"Give me a clue."

"The question was how many sexual partners have you had."

Shit.

"Ah, you know, truth or dare should remain in the realm of the drunken night, never to be spoken of again."

"But, just three? In your whole life?"

"Alex!"

That is an accurate figure, sadly, but I was married to Elise for ten years. Before that, I had one real girlfriend, who turned briefly to a wife, before deciding she needed much more penis in her life, and then there was a drunken one-night-stand with someone called Kayleigh in Royal Tunbridge Wells. And, unlike the song, I don't remember thinking it was confetti in her hair. More like fag butts from the bus stop.

It's been a while.

I'm spared further embarrassment by our next candidate arriving, Mademoiselle Georgette Baume.

"Salut, bonjour."

Georgette is clearly pregnant. I jump up and pull out a seat for her. She's thirty-two, well educated, but nothing as elaborate as Victor.

The beauty of the home-based tech-support role is that pregnancy and babies aren't too much of a problem. If she wants to continue to work once her baby is born, she can shuffle her hours and calls to fit the baby's schedule. I let Alex take over with the questions in French and the fake call. She does equally well as Victor, with the added bonus of her authoritative tone when she reads the verbatim text we must force every customer to listen to. Rather than rush through it, she enunciates eloquently. I understood about half of the French.

"She was good, too, right?"

"Yes, very good. I like her."

"This is going to get tricky to pick if they are all as good. Let's get lunch before the next one?"

"Same place as yesterday?"

"Yeah, but please, Alex. No wine today."

She laughs. "Okay, Mister Danny."

We wander over the road to the café; I slump down into the leather seat. "Water, please, lots of sparkling water." Alex laughs at me again. "Wait until you are in your forties, Alex. Then I'll laugh at you."

"You will be in an old people's home then."

"Shut up!"

After a light lunch, we went back to the hotel and interviewed another six candidates in the afternoon shift. A variety of quality, ranging between utterly terrible, barely audible, and generally okay. None as good as the two morning people though; The choice is certainly between them. Alex calls the agency and asks for Victor and Georgette to come back tomorrow for a second round. This time, we schedule them for a reasonable hour.

I'm forced to face the reality of the workload and compile our reports for the day, then check in with head office that our trip is going well. By the time I'm finished, we're both starving again.

Paris, being known for fine dining, we decide to head out despite the cost and celebrate a good day's work.

There's plenty to choose from, but we settle on a place close to the hotel. Convenience outweighs adventure. Dad's idea of doing some sightseeing while here is so far removed from reality that it sounds utterly insane now. I suppose if we hadn't got wasted last night, we could have spent that time exploring, but honestly, I think I had a much better time than I would have had walking around a museum filled with musty old paintings. Art has its place; I'm just too tired to appreciate it at the moment.

The bistro is elegant but unassuming. It isn't too busy, but there are quite a few locals dotted around. The waiter lights the candle on our table and I remember to say "Merci". Getting the hang of this now.

Candlelight, wonderful food, beautiful company, just the one glass of wine, and Alex is looking more and more desirable with every second. I have to keep telling myself, she's engaged, to a nice chap. She's my best friend. I can't fuck this up. But the millions of years of DNA evolution in my body say screw all that, this girl is amazing, you have to be with her.

It's going to be tough when I have to say goodbye on Thursday. This is a work trip, but I never want this moment to end. I miss the kids if I'm honest. Despite them being utter and complete pains in the derrière, I love them to bits and it feels weird now, them not being around.

"What are you thinking?"

"Oh, nothing. Just missing my kids a bit."

"Aww. You will be home soon."

"Yeah. But then I'll miss you."

"Danny! You'll make me cry."

"Told you not to get the onion salad."

She kicks me under the table, but gently.

. . .

She takes my arm on the walk back, snuggling in close. Every step flips on my perspective. I need to tell her how I feel, maybe she'll somehow be with me instead of Niels. Then no, I can't do that to a couple. I can't ruin someone's life just because I have a crush on a girl. She's more than a crush though, she's a part of me. We get along wonderfully. In the years I've known her, we've never fought. Maybe that's because she lives in a different country and we work together?

I'm so torn, I can't think straight.

As we get to the hotel, my phone rings in my pocket. I flinch because there are only two reasons someone would call me now; Elise, wondering where the kids are because I forgot to tell her. Or Mum and Dad, if there's a problem. I pull my phone out and it's Mum. Adrenaline slams through me again.

"Hello? Mum, is everything okay?"

"Hi, Danny, yes, it's fine. But the kids miss you. They didn't want to go to bed without seeing Daddy."

"Oh, that's a relief. I thought something was up."

"They've had a wonderful day. I'm sure they'll tell you."

"Give me five minutes and I'll call you back on FaceTime."

We go to our room and I'm conflicted about showing them Alex. On the one hand, I'd love for them to meet her, but on the other, it may raise too many questions now. Why is there a girl in your bedroom, Daddy? No. Best to leave introductions to another day.

"Hey Alex, I need to call the kids, but, sorry to ask, could you hide for a minute while I do it?"

"Ha, I embarrass you?"

"God, not at all. But it's just complicated now. They want to see me and I don't want them making up stories before I can explain properly."

"Just teasing, of course, I understand. Shall I go out?"

"No, it's fine. Sit on the bed or something. I'll just face the room and they won't see."

"Okay. Don't worry. I'll be quiet."

"Thanks, Alex."

I pick up the phone to dial Mum, and Alex sits on the bed. "Danny, come back to bed. I need you."

She makes a mock sexy panting noise. I ignore her, but I can't help but smile.

"Hey, guys."

"Hi, Daddy!"

"Are you having a nice time?"

"Yes, but we miss you. When are you coming home?" Rosie is holding the phone. Ethan is in his couch bed.

"I'll be there on Thursday."

"Can you read us a story?" Ethan begs.

"Err, well I don't have a book with me. What story do you want?"

"Pooh."

"Right, tell you what, I'll have to do it from memory. I might need to improvise a bit."

"What's that?"

"He's going to make it up." Rosie says, matter-of-factly.

I tell the story of how Pooh and Piglet have to get jobs at the bakery, but Pooh eats all the bread with his honey, and the baker tried to catch Piglet and eat him for his breakfast. In the end, Christopher Robin saves them, with the help of Owl and Tigger, who cause a diversion by crashing a London bus into the building. An unorthodox twist on the usual tales, but not too wildly off canon.

The children seem to love it, and there's laughing and yelping throughout. When I see Ethan yawning, I wrap it up.

"Night guys. Sleep well, see you very soon."

"Night Daddy."

"Love you both very much."

"Love you, too." they both screech out. I hang up the phone.

I stand up to get a drink. Alex gets up off the bed. I'd almost forgotten she was there, silent as a mouse.

She intercepts me before I get to the table, grabs me by the arms and kisses me, firmly, long, hot and passionate on the lips.

Before I can speak, she puts her hand over my mouth.

"You are a good man, Danny. A wonderful Father."

"They are my babies." I shrug. "I can't imagine life without them. They are everything I have. The only people I can trust won't leave me one day."

Alex wipes her eyes, choking back tears.

"You deserve to be with someone very special."

I can't argue with that.

Chapter Nine

No, we didn't have a wild night of epic sex that would make a porn star blush. No, she didn't leave Niels and ask me to marry her on the spot. No, it isn't happy ever after, at least, not yet.

Nothing has changed. I still adore her. She's still my best friend. But we cuddled, a lot. In bed, on top of the bed, standing next to the bed. I'm more frustrated than ever, but I appreciate the sentiment. It's nice to have some human contact, other than my kids jumping on me to wake me up on a Saturday morning.

Alex fell asleep in my spoon-cuddle, her hair tickling my nose, my iron-hard boner causing me to twist my back in case I impaled her.

I lay awake for a long time, pondering the decisions I have made in my life that led me to be here, in a hotel room in Paris, cuddling the only woman I feel any connection with. So close I could feel the heat of her breath on my arms clasped around her. Yet so distant, that she'll leave me soon, and our relationship will default back to daily online chats and team calls.

How did I get here?

If I try to pinpoint exactly when I knew my marriage with

Elise was over, I find I don't really know. When my parents asked me what happened, I honestly couldn't answer. We just drifted apart. Then she drifted onto someone else's cock and set sail to new lands. But how did we come unfurled? Who knows? Maybe that's just what happens to people?

Lying next to Alex, I can't imagine a time where I would find her unbearable, but rewind to Elise and me, just before Rosie was born, and I'm sure I felt the same way.

Life, it seems, is always complicated, no matter what you do.

Alex is still sleeping, still entwined in my embrace, while the morning light creeps in through the crack in the thick hotel curtains. I have to piss like Niagara Falls, but as soon as I get up, this moment becomes a memory, and I flow on the torrent of crashing river back to reality and work. I hold it just a little longer.

Our second round of interviews starts at noon today, still a few hours away.

Alex begins to stir, a gentle awakening. Nothing like the explosion of yesterday morning. I shuffle away and head to the bathroom to let loose the torrent.

"Good morning."

Alex sits up in bed. "Jesus, I need a smoke."

"Oh, I didn't know you smoked?"

"I don't, not anymore. But sometimes you get a craving, you know?"

"Never smoked in my life." I shrug.

"Lucky." Her face changes to a beaming smile. "Okay, that's over. Good morning."

A slow wake-up procedure involving two showers - I suggested we share one to speed things up, she said that wouldn't speed it up at all, probably true… And we find ourselves at breakfast in the hotel restaurant.

"Last day of this adventure. We have to make a choice today."

"Georgette or Victor?"

"That, yes." I suppose the other choice is already made. Do I tell Alex I want to be with her? No, obviously not. If she wanted to be my girlfriend, she already would be. I'm banished to Friendzonia for life.

"You think the second interview will sway the decision one way or another?"

"Probably won't make any difference. First impressions are what count."

"What was your first impression of me?"

"Ha. That's easy. I thought 'holy crap, she's gorgeous.' Everything after that just made it better."

"Is that why we are friends? Because you have the hots for me?"

"No, Alex. You know that isn't true. We have something special, don't we?"

"Just kidding. But yes, we do."

"And your first impression of me?"

She tilts her head. "He's a nice man. Trustworthy, funny, handsome, and just a bit complicated."

"Really?" She nods. "I'm flattered."

I think that's enough mushy crap for now. I stand up to get more coffee.

In reverse order today, we meet Georgette first. She's bang on time, wearing a dress that accentuates her baby bump. She's got the beautiful glow of pregnancy about her. Something I found incredibly attractive in Elise. I suppose it makes sense when creating a new life that the host body would be a little magical. Okay, Danny, we agreed no more mushy crap.

"Thank you so much for coming back, Georgette."

"Ah, Oui, thank you for inviting me."

We run through our second set of questions, which are around how she would deal with a tricky, angry customer. This time I pretend to call her, using lines I picked directly from the call that got Ryan fired. I was obstinate, belligerent, technically challenged and downright annoying. It was quite fun. She put me in my place, politely and accurately. She has the patience of a saint. That will come in handy for her when the baby is born.

"Is this your first?" I nod to her bump. I find it useful to get close to someone I'll be working with. She's passed all the usual interview-type questions; Now I need to know if we click.

"Oui, first and last!"

"It will be a wonderful adventure. Scary sometimes, absolutely terrifying others. Another human who utterly depends on you. And a noisy, smelly, annoying one at that."

She chuckles. "Ah, yes. My sister has three. I am well prepared."

"That's good. The more help you can get the better."

"Especially as the Father is gone, yes. I will be alone."

I nod. I know that feeling well. Alex looks up at me and offers a smile.

"Err, Merci beaucoup, Georgette, for coming back to us today. We'll let you know very soon."

We've got an hour for lunch now before Victor comes back. We stroll over to the café across the road once more. This place will become the lore of the trip. In the movie of my life, it will be the focal point where my character realises something deep and meaningful. He'll sit opposite the most beautiful woman in the world and bet everything on the toss of a coin. Will he ask her to marry him, disrupting his and her life, not to mention the background characters we never meet. Or will he leave things alone, as they are, staying in his unfulfilling life of routine?

Simplicity in the repetition. Change is complicated, stressful. It takes courage and stupidity. But deep down, don't we all crave a little complication?

In the movie, my character would propose. Theatrically, on one knee, using a napkin ring instead of an engagement ring. Alex would put her hand to her mouth, tears filling her eyes, then she'd look me directly in the eyes as she said: "Yes! Yes!".

In the real world, I pull the napkin ring off and hold it between thumb and finger. Rolling it up and down. I look up at Alex, the most beautiful woman in my world, and take a deep breath.

Alex leans forward, smiling. "I'm going to piss. Order some beer?"

I fucking love this woman!

Victor is already waiting as we get back. He's in a different suit today, dark grey, still a size too big. A new buttonhole flower, cornflower blue. We shake hands, vigorously, and go into our little room. Coffee awaits us and I pour all of us a cup.

We run through the same questions, and I do my angry customer routine again. Victor politely helps me figure out why I'm utterly wrong, so smoothly that I didn't even notice. He's good, and he goes off-script to suggest some tips and tricks to aid my life in the world of complex smartphones.

"Where do you see yourself in five years, Victor?"

He looks up. This is a trick question. Because if he tells me he sees himself in the same job, or even in my manager job, I'll know he's full of shit. This isn't a career for someone as talented and smart as him. It's a temporary stepping stone to get him through his early life. He'll meet someone, settle down, get on his real career path, and slump into a routine of school runs, work, TV dinners, and sleep, while his marriage breaks down, silently without him noticing. Then he will wake one day, crying, unable to face the world he has made for himself. Yet he has no choice. He'll put on a brave face, clinging to the threads of hope that one day, somehow, everything will finally come together as he planned and hoped. Spoiler alert: It won't.

"I hope to start my own business. I have some friends who write code." He taps his fingers at an invisible keyboard in front of him. "We have an idea for an app." He smiles. The confidence and optimism of youth. Good for him. Correct answer.

"All the best of luck with that, mate. You'll need it."

Once Victor is gone, Alex and I move to the bar to make our choice. This is a tough one. Definitely requires a beer. "What do you think?"

"You know, I have many feelings about both of them. I can't think."

"Same. In an ideal world, we'd hire both, but that's not going to happen now."

"How do we decide?"

How, indeed? Either of them would be a great fit in the job. Georgette needs the job to support her baby. Victor needs it to start on his great life journey.

"Toss a coin?"

"What, seriously?"

"Yes, if we can't decide, let fate take its course. The universe will make the choice for us."

She laughs but nods in agreement. I find a Euro coin in my wallet.

"Heads for Georgette, tails for Victor. Okay?" And in my mind, heads for keeping my mouth shut, tails for telling her my feelings. Betting my future on the toss of a coin. Because fate knows best.

"Okay."

With some nerves and trepidation, because I'm genuinely

concerned for these people, not to mention my secret fifty/fifty, I flip the coin and catch it. My hand over the top.

"You look." I shut my eyes and take my hand away.

"Heads."

"Heads it is. Fair enough. Will you call the agency and let them know?" And I'll leave our relationship as it is. Friends, happy, fun and no pressure. I feel some relief and sadness. But, honestly, this is the right choice.

"Well, this is our last evening in Paris."

I do my terrible impression of Humphrey Bogart. "We'll always have Paris, Alex. Here's looking at you, kid."

"Will you shut up?" She giggles and hits me on the arm, softly, with love.

"What do you want to do?"

"Something weird? Different?"

"My Dad told me I should see some sights while I'm here."

"That's a good idea. But not the normal stuff like Eiffel Tower or Louvre. Probably busy."

"How about going underground and looking at the skeletal remains of millions of dead people?"

"Ah, the Catacombs. Yes."

"I saw a leaflet in reception. Something about skipping the queues. Shall we?"

"Yes, why not?"

After I call the kids and make sure all is well, we head into the city and descend into the dark depths of Paris, amid thousands of tourists. But encased in walls of bones, it feels quite alone. The amber light gives it a sickening feeling. I assume the plague virus is long gone, by now?

"Do you think anyone will want to pay money to see my dried-up bones, in a few hundred years?"

"Yes. You have beautiful bones, Alex. I would pay now."

"I'll get an X-Ray for you."

"Show me some tibia, baby." She giggles and lifts a leg. "I know no one will want to see my bones. No one wants to see my boner now as it is."

"Ha! I felt it."

"Oops. Sorry."

"It's okay. It was reassuring."

Well, that's a first. No one ever called my dick reassuring before. "Say what?"

"Women like to be appreciated, Danny."

"No doubt about that. I appreciate you very much."

We walk through the grave corridors in silence for a while. Hand in hand, romantic, deep in a massive coffin.

"Well, these bones are all very interesting and stuff, but how does a litre of wine, a movie and a massive pizza in the hotel room sound?"

She laughs. "That sounds wonderful."

Chapter Ten

It doesn't take long for the memories of the Paris trip to fade, and the harsh reality of the normal schedule of work, school-runs, eat and sleep to slap me full-on in the face.

Paris was a crazy adventure with a wonderful friend. A diversion from normal day-to-day life. I needed it. Especially all the cuddles. But back home, where my bed is still empty, my thoughts default back to the constant loneliness. And, despite my acceptance that I'm likely to be single for the rest of my life, my DNA stubbornly refuses to believe it.

I need a girlfriend.

But the vast collective of women on every dating app available pass me by, no matter how many winks and flirts I send out into the ether. Women, women everywhere, nor any lips to kiss. Isn't that the line from the famous poem - The rime of the ancient single dad?

Well, apart from Cindy Jiggles, who still occasionally sends a 'naughtie'. I've since discovered these flesh pics aren't directed solely at me but go to a large group of people. Why she does this, I can't fathom, but I don't know how to get out of the group. I just delete the photos when I'm done with them.

. . .

Alex has been training our new recruit, Georgette. Things are going well. I have listened in on a few of her calls, but I can't understand much. Customers sounded happy, though, and Alex tells me she's great. The trip was a success; Head-office is happy. We didn't spend too much money, and things are getting back into the normal swing. I compile my reports, check the weekly schedules, drag my arse to take the kids to school and spend half my income on grocery shopping.

Life goes on.

Rosie and I are making our new signature dish for dinner tonight; chilli spaghetti. A mash-up of cuisine that should probably never exist, but we all like it.

I have to tone down the spice for the kiddies, then supplement mine with separate hot sauce. The only spice I get in my life.

"Where are we going for holidays, Dad?"

"Holidays?"

"Yeah, it's half-term next week."

Crap. I totally forgot.

Since Elise left, I've treated the kids to a little week-long break at half-term.

Before she left, we'd do things locally, occasionally venturing to a zoo or water-park, but since they don't have their mother around, I feel like they need to be spoiled sometimes. This year, I haven't given it a thought. Now I have to come up with something on the fly.

"Well, you guys are old enough now. You choose." This brings cheers of rejoice. Smooth move.

"Disneyland!" They cry out in unison.

Shit.

"Ah, well, I don't think my budget can stretch to that, guys. It's very expensive." This revelation brings sobs of woe.

"How about something even better?" Yelps of joy.

"Like what?"

"Hold on. I'll show you." Buying myself time to get my iPad and Google for last-minute deals, scroll through available options, and find something suitably child-pleasing and cheap.

"How about," I pause for a buildup, "Forest Parcs!" Tumbleweeds blow through the dining room. "It's really cool wooden cabins in the woods and loads of amazing activities. Look." I show them the website; They continue to be unimpressed.

"How is that better than Disneyland?" Rosie asks, matter-of-factly.

Well, it's about three grand cheaper, Rosie, that's how. "You'll see. You can err…" I look back at the website, "Make a pizza, go swimming, get a face painting done, see farm animals, braid your hair…" Their faces say it all, 'are you taking the piss, Dad?' "Here, I'll send you the link and you can look yourselves. You'll find something good, I'm sure."

"They have quads, COOL!" Ethan has found something to get him excited. One down, one to go. Quad bike riding sounds dangerous, but presumably, they have safety procedures and instructors?

"Oh, my god. Laser quest and paintball!" And that's Rosie signed up. Excellent. Before they can change their minds and the discount deal expires, I book us five nights in a little cabin with all the activities included, for slightly less than one ice-cream at Disneyland. Job done.

I send Alex a text message to let her know I'll be taking a week's holiday. She'll be my backup. Shame she isn't coming with me, but I have to leave that dream behind and move on. Hey, maybe I'll meet someone at the resort? It must be a magnet for single mums also looking for a cheap way to entertain the kids while they drink and shag their way to oblivion? This could turn out quite fun for all of us.

I should probably let Elise know we're going away. I didn't tell her about the Paris thing and she never asked, no harm done. The kids haven't seen her for a while now. I suspect that when she hears we'll be away for a week, she'll want to organise a visit, just to annoy me. She knows I'll be busy, getting things ready.

Yes, I'm sure she is that petty. She'd never admit it and I'd be persecuted for suggesting it. As usual, I'll bite my tongue and just smile through gritted teeth.

She replies promptly to my text message.

'Why didn't you tell me?'

I just did. Didn't I? How could I have told her before I even knew about it? A follow-up text arrives.

'I've been planning a whole day out with the kids on Sunday.'

Oh, really? Well, why didn't you tell me, Elise?

What does she mean by a whole day? I'm not sure I like that idea.

'I'll pick them up at nine. We're going to a wildlife park. Back at dinner time.'

I know last-minute plans when I see them. I'm sure she's been planning that for all of two minutes.

"Kids, your Mother is taking you out on Sunday, all day."

"Where to?" Rosie asks, sceptical.

"She wasn't specific, but a wildlife park. You know, where monkeys come and chew off your windscreen wipers and stuff."

"Oh."

"You'll get to see all the animals close up. Be fun."

And I get a whole day to myself. I could go back to bed, play games, watch movies. Generally sloth around all day until dinner time. Sounds great.

"Do we have to?" Ethan doesn't sound enthusiastic.

"You haven't seen her for a while. So, yes, you do. Sorry, dude."

———

Sunday morning should be a time for peace and quiet. Reflection on the week that has passed. Coffee, toast, and relaxing. Perhaps some classical music softly playing in the background. This is not my experience, especially today.

Why bother with an alarm, when I have two children capable of air-raid siren decibel levels?

I have plans for myself today, once the kids are off with their mother. I'm going to do a lot of bugger-all, some scratching my arse, a little staring out of the window, and probably a good chunk of porn watching. I may even lay in the bath and do all of those things at once. The house will ring with the sound of silence and bliss.

But first, the kids have to get ready, which involves a lot of exasperated searching. Socks, shoes, jackets, hats. Once those are found, inexplicably, socks have to be re-found, before we can all gather at the breakfast table.

When I say breakfast table, I mean couch, beanbag and armchair. With the TV blaring out inane crap and everyone buried in their respective iPads. At least they are eating. Can't have everything.

At around ten-to-nine, the kids start to get antsy. Looking out of the window for their mother's car, sorry, I mean, MY car she took. With every passing vehicle, squawks of excitement and then rapid groans when it passes by. By nine, they are bouncing around in the corridor, taking turns to look out of the letterbox at the driveway. Come five-past, the anticipation is palpable, and they are virtually foaming at the mouth. Every few seconds, I'm reminded that Mum is now late. I know. But if I mention it to her, all I'll get is bitch-mouth and excuses. At nine-fifteen Rosie suggests I should ring her and find out where she is, but I have no desire to do that, and if she's driving, then she can't answer the phone.

The reason for their fidgets is probably because of the one time when Mummy did forget and never came to get them. They waited two hours by the door, before dispersing back to their iPads. Upset, and no doubt scarred for life. I had tried to ring her that day but got no answer. It wasn't until hours later that Elise called, in a panic, apologising to the kids, then later appeared at the door with toys and chocolate. I never found out what happened. Don't care honestly. But the kids don't deserve to be treated like that. It was heartbreaking watching them and I couldn't do anything about it. 'Mummy forgot us' isn't something they should ever be thinking.

"I'm sure she'll be here in a minute, guys. Just relax."

"Here she is." Ethan yelps out. Within thirty seconds they are both outside, backpacks on, waiting on the doorstep for her to park the car. My car.

"Hi, guys." The kids run over to her as she gets out, bouncing up and down. Not surprising when they haven't seen her for a few weeks.

"What time will they be back?" I don't bother with pleasantries or small talk. Elise never does.

"Six or seven, probably. I'll text you."

"Right. See you later, guys." They run back to hug me before bolting into the car. I stand in the doorway until they've gone around the corner.

Inside, as I shut the door, I pause for a moment.

Silence. Not just silence, but daytime silence. Not the few minutes when I get back from the school run, before trudging up to my work office. This is the silence of freedom. The house is mine. I could walk around naked if I wanted. Eat a whole bag of crisps on the couch and fart. Sit on the toilet with the door open. Put on music and sing, unfettered. This is the stuff of dreams.

Speaking of dreams, I could watch a movie. Dracula, or Heathers, maybe? I can do what I want.

But first things first, I stick the kettle on for a cuppa.

As I take my first sip of tea, the doorbell ringing interrupts the peace. Jehovah's, or something similar. I saw them coming down the road earlier. I plan to ignore them, but they ring again and then knock. I sigh and reluctantly open the door.

"Hello, we'd like to read you a passage from the Bible, if that's okay?" Two Marks and Spencer pensioner range models stand on my doorstep, perfectly groomed. Him with a shirt and tie under a woolly jumper, her in a pleated long cream skirt.

"No, that is not okay." I move to slam the door, but a better idea springs to mind. "Actually, I'd like to read you a passage from my Bible, if that's okay?"

"Oh?" They look surprised.

"Yes, I don't have it to hand, but I'm familiar with the text."

"Well, yes. Please do." The man beams in saccharine humility.

I clear my throat. "From the book of Daniel. Psalm thirteen: And on the sabbath, when the Lord takes pause to survey his kingdom," They are lapping it up, both filled with the joy of the Lord. Filled with something, anyway. "Lo, the Lord is sated, peace and tranquillity fill'd his cupeth."

"Sorry, which edition is this from?" The female zealot begins to look puzzled.

"It's a rare version. If I may continue?" They nod. "And the Lord takes his five-minute break from the constant churn of the duties of creation." They both look confused now. "The Lord values his peace above all else. Especially on the morning of the sabbath. He shall vent forth his wrath on those that dare to disturb the peace." They look worried now as the message seeps into their thick skulls. "I deliver this message from the Lord himself." They look up as my volume increases and my theatrics become Oscar-winning. "Go forth and multiply!" They tilt their heads in question. "BUGGER OFF!" I slam the door with mild satisfaction.

I sit down and sip my rapidly cooling tea. But I notice a large pile of the kids' laundry looming next to the washing machine. School uniforms, underwear, blankets, towels and duvet covers. With our holiday coming up soon, I better get that done before I settle down. Not to mention that the place could do with a good vacuuming, the kitchen hasn't been mopped in a while and the bathroom resembles a motorway service station piss hole. The Lord's work is never done.

Suddenly I'm in the mood for some classic rock. Something from Ozzy's early career, I think.

Chapter Eleven

H ospital waiting rooms aren't known for their happy moments. No one includes them in their list of venues for things like wedding receptions or nights out with the boys, for example.

That said, I'm feeling particularly emotional in this one, after a night of barely any sleep. Sat with Rosie, after Ethan was in the emergency room having a bone set by the friendly surgeon.

Rosie has a black eye, too, but that didn't warrant emergency treatment. Just a mild painkiller and some time to heal.

They'll be fine, but I'll never hear the end of this from their mother.

I'd better get my story straight.

The holiday started well. We had a great old sing-song on the drive up to Forest Parcs. The kids were in good cheer and I was looking forward to the week off. Who knew what adventure lay ahead of us? The kids had a long list of activities they wanted to do, and the evenings promised entertainment for adults.

One night would be an 80s theme night. I was looking forward to ogling all the women dressed up in their bright neon outfits.

The cabin we had booked looked awesome in the photos. But, like our frequent cheeseburger happy meals, the actual product was nothing like it. It stank of damp, there were mouse traps dotted all around the rooms, and you had to insert many coins to get any hot, sorry, tepid water for the shower. The kitchen facilities were basic, at best. But as we planned on eating in the restaurant most of the time, it didn't matter too much. There was a big swimming pool, and we assumed there would be decent showers there.

We were on holiday, and we were going to make the best of it.

When I checked in, they informed me of all the 'extras' that weren't included in my discount deal. Things like meals, drinks, parking, electricity, air conditioning, oxygen and water, if they could get away with it. Fine. I handed over my credit card to be abused. We were there already, children excited. Not much I could do about it.

The setting was nice, at least. We looked out onto a thick green forest, hidden away from civilisation. It had potential, despite the minor niggles.

After we settled in, the kids went for a swim in the pool, while I checked out the talent sat around the edge. There were some possibilities, especially after alcohol.

We went to the restaurant afterwards and sampled the fare. It wasn't terrible, but it was far from wonderful. Rather more expensive than I imagined.

This cheap deal holiday was working out quite the opposite. We skipped dessert and restricted to only one drink each.

There was a band playing in the big ballroom next door, and once we'd eaten, we wandered over. I got a pint of something resembling beer, and the kids had some elaborately decorated non-alcoholic cocktails. When the barman took my twenty and came back with only a few pennies, that put a cap on the evening fun.

The live music was provided by a one-hit-wonder cover band. They played everything from 'Never gonna give you up' to 'Barbie Girl' with an interlude in between from Right Said Fred and 'I'm too sexy'. The lead singer was good looking, but after my single beer, I should be so lucky…

Tired from the long trip and all the excitement, we went back to our cabin around eleven to find the power was out. I had to run back to the little shop, conveniently open until midnight, and buy a pack of candles. It was fun, at first. Really driving home the disconnect from the rest of the world. There was no signal on my phone most of the time, and the kids couldn't be stuck to iPads and YouTube.

"It happens all the time." The chap in the shop told me, as he brought out another pack of suspiciously expensive candles.

Aside from being woken several times by drunken louts yelling and singing, as they walked back to their respective cabins, the night didn't go too bad. By the morning, the power had come back on and I could boil a kettle for coffee while the kids charged their devices in a panic. When you don't know where the next electron is coming from, you hoard what you can.

Breakfast was a bit of a mess, as we battled the zombie-like hung-over revellers from last night. Some of them still wore the chicken-song feathers and were clucking as they walked around.

Still, there were eggs and bacon, toast and tea. Everyone happy.

The kids wanted to go swimming again. I jumped in with them for a minute. Braving the cold waters and discovering just how out of shape I am. Ethan lapped me six times, and I eventually gave up, got out and wrapped up in towels. The other patrons ranged from the violently fit exercise freaks, who probably started swimming at five in the morning, to the overweight grandfathers, standing around smoking and flicking fag butts in the foot-washing pool. Not many hotties around at that time of day, "Come back in the afternoon." one of the butt-flickers told me, with a wink.

The kiddy activities that day were face-painting, cooking, crazy golf, and a tug-of-war match. I stood around, avoiding the other parents who were already drunk, for the most part. I had visited the cash machine already, but I was saving my pennies for the evening and the promised 80s night.

We at least got to eat the pizza the kids made for lunch, which saved me a few quid, but I'm not sure why Ethan thought lettuce and cucumber were good ideas for pizza topping. Perhaps I should encourage him to learn to cook with Rosie and me.

Back in the cabin, the kids hacked into someone's portable WiFi network. They spent the afternoon catching up on whatever crap they watch on YouTube, while I took some well deserved Dad-nap time, getting ready for my 80s boogie night.

I hadn't brought any suitable clothes. All I could do was buy some hair gel at the Double-Price shop and spike up. Rosie helped me, while Ethan laughed and pointed. There are some photos on their iPads that I must delete when we finally get home.

The same band rolled out virtually an identical repertoire as the night before, mixed in with some Madonna, Michael Jackson, Musical Youth, and Frankie Goes to Hollywood. It wasn't as bad as it sounds. I was quite enjoying it for a while.

A blonde wrapped in white and fluorescent pink tried to get

me up for a dance, but I couldn't leave the kids, and, more importantly, as previously established, I don't dance. She was persistent and sat down with us.

I didn't catch her name, but she was pretty, back in 1989. Now she was a shadow of her former glory, if that shadow had lived the last thirty years eating chips and cheeseburgers, and smoking sixty Benson and Hedges every day. I can't judge, though, and I was enjoying the light flirting. That was, until her husband, the butt-flicker from earlier, came and dragged her away. Hurling abuse in my direction about trying to take his woman.

We had a walk around the ballroom, kids in tow with their colourful mocktails, me scanning the room for any available talent, and there were some cuties, but I'm not good at making the first move, and with Ethan and Rosie beside me, I felt a little hampered. Who am I kidding? Even if I was alone, with a T-shirt on saying 'come get me' I'd still be walking back to my cabin, carrying a pack of candles, on my own.

Aside from the power-outage, the frequent yelping outside that woke us, and the extremely drunk couple, mistakenly trying to unlock our cabin door with their key, but not taking no for an answer until I eventually had to call security to redirect them, the night went without incident, and with no chance of even a quick snog, I might add.

The next day, which was yesterday, I think. Time doesn't exist in this place, was when the fun really started.

After breakfast, Rosie had her paintball session. I was worried about it, but they assured me that with the protective helmet and suit, the worst that could happen was the odd small bruise, and that was 'part of the fun'.

In fairness, the black eye didn't come from a paintball, thankfully, but in fact from the elbow of one of her victims, as she pelted him with paint. He fell out of the castle he was hiding in, knocking her helmet off. I watched from afar as the incident occurred, Ethan was laughing his arse off, but by the time I ran over to Rosie, avoiding being shot myself, and found her on the floor crying, things went from funny to tense.

She was mostly fine, just shocked. The lad who fell was okay too but looked like he'd been swimming at the Dulux factory. Eventually, we all saw the funny side, and they awarded Rosie winner of the tournament. She's been wanting to play paintball since she got a video game with a similar theme.

We had lunch after. I got Rosie extra ice-cream with her aspirin to cheer her up.

Then it was Ethan's turn on the quad bikes. This obviously didn't end well. But he started out good. The quads were tiny, 'junior' sized, something like a built-up go-kart, which he's done before with his friend Jack. He was super excited, and in the lead of the second race, but lost control as he spun out on a corner and went 'agricultural' over the tire fence, then rolled over onto his arm, fracturing his humerus in two places, as we learned later from the X-ray. Not very humorous at all. Poor kid was in agony and scared shitless as Rosie and I ran over to him after I watched the scene unfold in front of me again, unable to do anything about it. The camp medic was at his side within sixty seconds and an ambulance came and picked us up soon after.

And here we are. We had to wait for I don't know how many hours, until they took Ethan for the anaesthetic and surgery, then they plastered him up, and now he's in limbo until he's awake enough for us to go home.

Rosie slept on my lap for a few hours, on a hard plastic chair in a waiting room full of the dying.

I have to admit, this has not been the most successful holiday we've ever been on, and now I have to find a way to explain this mess to Elise, who will undoubtedly blame me for letting Ethan onto a quad bike in the first place. No matter what answer I give, it will come down to me being in the wrong.

I feel terrible, but the doctor told us this sort of thing happens all the time, and that Ethan was very lucky it wasn't worse. Sure. Hospitals are always full of very lucky people.

Out of cash, the only source of nutrients being a vending machine, Rosie and I have eaten nothing since lunch yesterday. Ethan is probably starving too, but he might get some hospital food.

A nurse passes by, which is a rare occurrence. I flag her down.

"Can we go see Ethan Watts now, please? Broken arm. I'm his dad."

"I'll just check for you, Mr Watts." She disappears off, possibly to never be seen again. That has already happened during the night. Nurses just vanish after I talk to them.

This time, she comes back quickly. "He's asleep, but you can go in now."

"Oh, thank you."

I drag Rosie up, and we walk the corridors to where Ethan is gowned up in a bed, an arm freshly plastered, a few cuts and bruises on his face. Poor fella. He's been in the wars. Thankfully, he was wearing the helmet and protective suit. I suppose it could have been much worse.

"Have you been here all night?" The nurse looks sympathetic, which makes a change.

"Yes, we're tired, hungry, and meant to be on holiday."

"Oh no, that's awful. The canteen is open now if you want to pop and get some breakfast? He'll be out for a while more."

"I don't want to leave him." I look down at Rosie, whose

face falls. "Okay, no, let's get some food and we'll come right back."

"I'll keep an eye on him, take your time."

At this stage of exhaustion and stress, hospital canteen food seems wonderful. I feel a bit more alive after three cups of coffee and a full breakfast. Rosie looks perkier. I bought more aspirin for her in the little shop, as her poor face was still sore.

When we get back to Ethan, he's awake and chomping down his breakfast. A little hindered by the cast on his right arm, but he's managing okay.

"Daddy!"

"Hey, dude. You feeling better?"

"I've got a plaster cast."

"Yeah, you can get all your mates at school to sign it for you."

"Yay, cool." His eyes light up.

"Yup, coolest kid in the class now."

When we are finally allowed to leave, I'm in the predicament that my car is back at the park and we are in some unknown hospital, in a town I have never visited. My phone battery on the brink of dying, I have to find a payphone and call for a taxi to take us back.

Forty quid later, we're back at our cabin, and I think we should just call it quits and go home. Ethan is still woozy, but he'll sleep it off.

Rosie is upset, as there's a kiddie disco on tonight she wanted to go to, but we're in no fit state for that.

I promise them clown-food and we pack up our stuff and load everyone into the car.

· · ·

In the park reception office, checking out early, the jobsworth at the desk insists my booking was non-refundable, and I'll still be charged for the two nights I'm not staying, plus the safety suit that had to be cut off Ethan's arm at an additional fifty pounds.

If they want to play that game…

"That's fine. I assume you have public liability insurance? My son was thrown off your dangerous equipment and has a fractured humerus. We'll be seeking compensation, and of course, documenting the entire incident on social media. I have a video if you'd like to see?"

"Ah, let me have a word with the manager."

Yeah, mate. You go have a word.

He returns, promptly, a changed man. A smile replaces the smug grin. "Mr Watts, in situations like this, we're authorised to make a full refund of your booking and extras. I do apologise for the misunderstanding, and we sincerely hope you will come back one day once your son is better."

I could be a twat and demand more, but I have two tired children waiting, and I just want to get out of here. "Fine." I hand him my credit card and he does some kind of refund magic. "I also fed your shower meter at least ten quid. Oh, and the taxi was forty, plus candles in your ridiculously priced shop, and drinks…" He gets two fifties out of the till and hands them to me with my card.

"Thank you for staying at Forest Parcs, come again soon."

Chapter Twelve

E very time I get back to work from a break, the amount of
crap piled up waiting for me makes me wonder why I
bothered taking the holiday in the first place. Even with Alex
helping me, I still have hundreds of emails to churn through,
dozens more to write and send, then all the staff annual
evaluations to do before the end of this month. It gets to a point
where I look at my laptop screen and just want to walk away.
Not before throwing it out of the window, ideally into a river.

But bills don't pay themselves. I have no other method of
income, so here I am, slowly churning through the work.

That, and tending to Ethan every five minutes, because he
finds out another thing he can't do with his arm in a cast and
sling. Brushing teeth, wiping his arse, getting a drink, taking a
piss. Basically everything. Thankfully, he's figured out swiping
his iPad screen with his left hand. If I had to change his YouTube
every fifteen seconds as well, I'd probably go stark raving mad.

Sleep is another of those things that causes a problem. He
wakes all the time in pain if he rolls over onto his arm. Poor
fella. The doctors said he could go back to school anytime, but I
don't have the heart to send him. He needs a little time to come

to terms with the situation. But this means my work-life balance is all thrown wildly off-kilter.

It's times like this that I could use some help with the kids. I've looked up Au Pair finding websites, but the average wage I'd need to pay would mean we'd all be eating grass from the garden three times a week. Not going to happen right now. We'll just have to make it work.

My phone buzzes on the desk.

A text message from Roland. Wow, I haven't spoken to him for ages.

'Hey, bruv. I'm in your pissy little shit-town tonight. Wanna get a drink?'

Flattered, I reply.

'Yeah, if you can stoop down to our pissy little Kings Head level? You muppet. Of course. What the fuck are you doing here?'

'Meeting a client. Here with a colleague. Don't cream your pants over her. She's gay as Eurovision.'

He sends me a photo of him with his colleague. Christ on a bike. She's dangerously sexy, pierced everything. Glad he gave me the warning. I don't need to spend mental energy figuring out how I'd get in her pants. If they are a dead end, I won't even attempt to go down that road.

'I have to see if I can get a babysitter…'

The only sitter I know is Jessica, but as she's engaged to some dweeb now, she may not be interested in spending her evening bored in my living room anymore. But I don't want an unknown element in my house near my kids.

I send her a text asking if she can help. She replies within a few minutes and she's happy to come over. Says she could use any money she can get at the moment.

I text back that's great, but there's the added fun of Ethan and his arm. I hate to drop something like that on her, but it's either that or tell Roland to come to my house, and I don't think suburbia with kids is his cup of tea.

Jessica responds that she is glad to help. She broke her arm when she was younger too. She knows what to do. Brilliant.

Well, not brilliant for her. But I'm glad Ethan will be in good hands.

There's the awkwardness of our little sofa-snog to overcome yet. I wonder if she even remembers? I sure do.

Jessica rings the bell precisely on time, as usual. She's as pretty as ever, but no makeup today, and her hair is back to a chestnut brown. I prefer her this way. She's more real, somehow.

"Hey, Jessica."

"Hi, Danny." She comes and goes straight through to the kitchen.

"Thanks for coming at short notice."

"No problem. I was glad to get out."

"Thought you might be busy with, what's his name?"

"Brett? God no. That's totally over."

"Oh? Sorry."

"Don't be. He was dicking anything with a pulse. Ironically, Megan was the only one he didn't stick it in."

"Young fellas today, huh?"

"Yeah. Still, never mind. I'm concentrating on my studies. I'm going to stay celibate until I've finished Uni. Too complicated otherwise."

Damn.

"Probably for the best. I've been celibate for a long time. Not my choice though."

She gives me that sultry look again that I can't figure out.

"You should get out there. There's nothing wrong with you."

"Yeah, well. Going out with my brother tonight."

"Oh, that sounds good. On the pull?"

"Ah, no. He pulls a different thread to me."

"What? Ohhh. Really?"

"Yup. Haven't seen him for a while. Should be a blast."

Rosie and Ethan appear in the doorway.

"Jessie!"

Much hugging and squealing ensues. She's amazing with the kids.

"Oh, my god. Ethan. You've been in the wars, haven't you?"

"Yeah. I fell off a quad."

"Oh wow, that's pretty cool though. Did you win?"

"I won the first race."

"Awesome. You'll be back in the saddle soon enough." He nods. No, he bloody won't.

"Rosie. What happened to you?" Her eye has faded now, but there's a slight shade of a bruise left.

"A boy fell on me."

"Ha. Wait till they fall for you, Rosie. That's when the trouble starts." Isn't it just?

"Tell you what, I'll show you how to cover up that bruise with makeup if you want?"

"Oh, YAY!" Rosie bounces up and down.

"Is that okay, Danny?" Jessica looks over at me.

I nod. "If that makes you both happy."

"You want some makeup too, Ethan?"

He scrunches up his face. "No."

"We could make that plaster cast a bit more colourful and interesting. You got some felt tips?"

"Cool!" Ethan runs off to fetch some pens.

"Mind your arm, Ethan." I look at Jessica. The kids adore her. I'm quite fond of her myself. It isn't just that she's young and pretty, but the mothering quality in her is extremely attractive. "Thank you, Jessica. You are great with the guys."

"They are fab! Now, off you go, have a nice evening, Danny."

The walk to the pub is short and brisk.

I've been trying to remember when I last saw Roland, and it must be five years ago, at least. I was in London for a work thing and met him in the Devonshire Arms in Camden. In fact, every time I've seen him in the last decade has been in a pub of some kind. That time in Camden, he was with some guy called Blake. I don't think Blake liked me very much. I was freshly divorced and may have got way too drunk and tried chatting up the barmaid. She was wearing ripped fishnets and heels, a tiny skirt, and barely more than a bra. Hardly my fault she turned out to be Blake's sister. How was I to know?

"Danny Boy." Roland accosts me the second I enter the pub.

"Rollie! Bloody hell, you are looking good." I think Roland has spent the last five years at the gym and health spa. He's only four years younger than me. But I feel like I'm looking through a time machine at him aged twenty-five.

"Cheers, mate. I've been keeping fit, you know." He's picked up a bit of a London accent, too.

"Drink?"

"Don't mind if I do. Here, this is Saffy." He introduces me to the Indian Goddess of Love, Rati. She's even more stunning in person. I'm quite taken aback.

"Charmed. I'm sure." I hold out a hand and she offers a limp shake.

"Oh, he's right posh, ain't he? Sure he's your brother?"

"Quite sure."

She doesn't sound much like a Goddess. Not that I know

what a Goddess sounds like; I just never imagined she'd be from Catford.

"What can I get you, Saffy?"

"Vodka and coke. Cheers. That's short for Saffron. Parents thought it was funny to make me a spice girl. Haha."

"Beautiful name." I smile.

"Oi, mate. I told you, Saffy is only interested in fanny, aren't you love?"

"Shut up, Rollie. Haha. Roly-Poly." She punches Roland on the arm. "But yeah. Only interested in fanny, as he says."

"Shame." She looks at me and licks her lips. I feel movement in my pants. This evening is going to be fun.

"What are you people doing in my pissy little town then?"

Saffy laughs again.

"Told you. We have a client. We're meeting some marketing dildos tomorrow to re-invent their image. All that bollocks. Saffy is a marketing guru."

"Nice. Maybe don't call them dildos to their face, though."

"Don't worry, Danny Boy. I'm a fucking pro."

Our drinks arrive and Roland raises his glass for a toast. "To a fun evening ahead in pissy town."

"Indeed."

"What you been up to then, bruv? Haven't seen you in donks."

"Where do I start?"

I tell them the story of the wonderful time we had at Forest Parcs, and how Ethan broke his arm, Rosie got elbowed in the eye, and I utterly failed to get off with anyone. Then I tell them about Paris and my few days with Alex. I may have made it a bit too clear that I wanted to shag her brains out, but instead shared a bed with her and got nothing but frustrated. Then I told them about the terrible date I was on and how Elise treats me like dirt, picking up the kids whenever it suits her. I probably came across as a bit of a loser which I didn't intend on doing, in front of this beautiful Goddess, but it just sort of flowed out once I started.

"Bloody hell, Roly-Poly. This man needs to get drunk and laid, urgently."

"You took the words out of my mouth, Saffy."

I shrug. Drunk I can do. Laid seems to be out of my jurisdiction.

"Any good clubs in this pissy town, Danny boy?"

"No clue, mate. Never been to any."

Roland pulls out his phone and starts tapping the screen. "Slim pickings, but there is one place. The Agenda. Ever heard of it?"

"Can't say I have. But that isn't surprising. I only go to the kids' schools and Tesco."

"Five minutes in a taxi. You up for it?"

"Hey? You aren't suggesting we go tonight, are you?"

"I believe that is precisely what I'm suggesting, Danny boy. You are in dire need of some alcohol and body fluids."

"Mate, this is pissy town, and it's a Monday night."

"What's your point?"

"Well, first off, I doubt the club is even open, and if it is, it will be practically empty. I'm not going to get laid in an empty nightclub. Am I?"

"Ah. Yeah. You could have a point there, bud. I keep forgetting I'm out in the boonies here. Well, what do the kids do in this shit hole for fun?"

"I think they tend to sniff glue in the alleyway behind the cinema. But I have no interest in that particular pastime."

Saffy laughs.

"Well, that's scuppered my plans, then. Have to make the most of the Kings Head, I suppose." Roland waves to the barman for another round.

"What you up to then, apart from being here in pissy town for a client meeting? You still with that Blake chap?"

He looks confused for a second. "Blake? Who the fuck is Blake?" Then it dawns on him. "Oh, shit. No, forgot all about him. I was never with him, just hanging out."

"Oh, okay. Well, he seemed annoyed when I tried to flirt with his sister."

"That barmaid in Camden? That wasn't his sister, Danny. That was his Mum!"

Shit. I must have been more drunk than I thought.

"Oh. Damn."

Saffy bursts out laughing, spraying Vodka and Coke all over the bar.

"I'm seeing someone." He taps his finger on his nose. I guess he doesn't want to talk about it. Fair enough.

"Where are you staying?"

"Some shitty Travelodge place just outside town."

"You should have said. You could have stayed at mine."

"Didn't like to ask, also, I didn't realise this was your town until I got here. Sorry, bruv. I totally forgot where you lived."

I chuckle. It's okay, I know he lives somewhere in London, but I couldn't narrow it down much further. It's a shame we've lost touch. Roland is probably someone I need more of in my life. He got all the charm, bravado and looks from the family DNA. I got boring genes. Nerves, responsibility and organisation. That's all very solid and stable, but I'm no fun, and that's probably why I've only ever had sex with three women.

"Anyway, Saffy snores. Don't you love?"

She punches him in the arm again. "Shut up you. Mister forty minutes in the bathroom getting ready."

"I wouldn't mind. Alex snored like a mountain goat in Paris." I tell them about our truth or dare game, how we both somehow ended up stark naked, running around the corridors in the middle of the night.

"Sounds like a good idea, eh Saffy?"

"Not bloody likely. It's freezing!"

"Danny, if I may give you some general life advice?"

"What's that?"

"Don't stop to think about the consequences. Just get up, grab life by the balls, and take what you want. Women like a strong man. Ain't that right, Saffy?"

"He's right, Danny." She nods. "Well, not me, 'course."

"I thought nice guys were in, these days?"

"Nah, mate. Just fucking do it. Next chance you get, take it. If I find out you fucked up another lay, I'll be back up here, dragging your arse to that shitty nightclub. Mark my words."

"Noted." We clink glasses again. "It's not through lack of trying, Rollie. I'm just not blessed with the charm you have."

"Bollocks, Danny. You are plenty charming." He looks at Saffy. "Isn't he?"

"He's a fucking delight, Roly-Poly." She giggles and puts her hand on my arm.

"You just be you, Danny."

"Pretty sure I can do that."

By the time I get home, it's around midnight and I'm in the extremely merry stage of drunkenness. It was good to see Roland, and even better to meet Saffy. Brilliant night, all told. I unlock the door as quietly as possible and go through to the kitchen, dump down my phone and keys, and then go through to the living room. This time, Jessica is fast asleep on the couch. I'm assuming the kids are in their beds, the same.

"Jessica," I whisper. Nothing.

"Jessica." A little louder. Nothing.

Well, now what? I'm drunk, it's late. I have to get up for school and work. I gently shake her shoulder. She stirs and makes a groaning noise.

"Jessie, are you awake?" She opens one eye, slowly.

"Danny?"

"Yup. I'm home, you can go now. Looks like you are a tired bunny."

"Ugh." She closes her eye again. "Can I just sleep here?"

"On the couch? Um. Well, sure. Okay. If you want."

"Mhm." She snuggles down into the cushions. I suppose I better get her a blanket.

Chapter Thirteen

"Jesus!" Fifty shades of shit are scared out of me as I open the bathroom door and find Jessica, sat on the toilet, knickers around her ankles. I completely forgot she was here. "Sorry, sorry!" I back out and close the door.

"It's okay. I'm done now. Come in."

"Err, no, I'll wait until you are out, Jessica."

Rosie springs out of nowhere. "Jessie is still here?"

"Yes, she was really tired last night. She slept on the couch instead of going home."

"YAY! Ethan, Ethan. Jessie is still here." Squealing comes from Ethan's bedroom.

"Thank you for letting me stay, Danny." Jessica comes out of the bathroom. I'd love to be polite and friendly, but my head is killing me, my bladder is bursting and there's a school run to sort, not to mention work.

"Get yourself a coffee or something, we'll be down soon."

.   .   .

When I get downstairs, Jessica has the kids dressed, eating breakfast, and school bags ready. Ethan with his arm slung up and beaming a smile.

"Jessie is going to take us to school, and everyone will sign my cast."

"Huh, what?"

"Sorry, Danny, I didn't say that. But they asked."

"Can you drive?"

"Yeah, got my license last year. Don't have a car though."

"Think you can drive mine?"

"Yeah, 'course."

I pause for a moment. Insurance, safety, responsibility. I can't just let her drive the kids. But it was a nice thought, for a moment.

"Don't you want to get home, anyway?"

"I'm in no rush."

"I don't think you'd be insured, Jessica. But thank you."

"Aww, can she come with us?"

"Err, well, I don't know Ethan. Jessie probably has things to do."

"No, I don't today. I'll come with you, if that's okay, Danny?"

"Sure. If you want."

At our first stop, Jessica gets out of the car and runs around to open Rosie's door. They hug, and Rosie merges off into a crowd of her friends. At Ethan's school, she repeats the process, and instead of bolting across the road to Jack, Ethan gets out slowly, minding his arm. Holding Jessica's hand as we all cross the road, carefully. Things are going smoother than the usual chaos today.

. . .

"Thanks for helping me this morning. I can drop you home now, before my morning meeting, if you'd like?"

"I've been thinking, Danny." She looks over at me. "You need help. I need somewhere to stay for a while. Sounds like a mutually beneficial situation, do you think?"

"What? You want to stay with us and help out?"

"Yeah, I can't afford to pay you rent, but I'll help around the house and with the kids."

I look over at her. This is quite sudden. But I was just looking for an au pair, and Jessie is better, as the kids already know and love her. It has some implications, but the words of my brother echo in my head, "Don't stop to think about consequences. Just get up, grab life by the balls and take what you want." All right, let's give this a go.

"Are you serious? Oh, my god. I could kiss you right now."

"Ha. I'm staying celibate, remember?"

"Metaphorically. But wow. Of course. I'll clear out the crap from the spare room for you."

"All I need is the Internet and some peace to get my studies done."

"Well, our house is rarely peaceful, unless the kids are at school. I'm home all day at work, but I usually keep to myself."

"Sounds great."

"Just so I'm sure I'm not dreaming this. You did just offer to stay with us and help look after the children, didn't you? I'm not still asleep in bed?"

She reaches over and pinches me on the leg. "Nope. You are wide awake. I'm super excited."

"Great start to the day. Thank you, Jessica. How long do you think you'll stay?"

"Until I go to Uni if that's okay. At the end of the summer."

"Of course. The kids will be around all day, in the summer, but I'm sure we can work something out."

"If you could drop me home, I'll pack up some stuff and come back later."

"Sounds like a plan."

I say nothing to the kids when I pick them up. Neither of them remembers that Jessica came with us to school this morning, at least they don't mention it. Ethan reads out all the messages and signatures on his cast, showing me all the different pens they used. Someone seems to have drawn a 'pee-pee'. We may need to edit a little.

When we get home, they disperse immediately. Bags are flung under the stairs, shoes kicked into a corner, jackets hung on the bannister. Within thirty seconds, they are in front of the TV.

"Hey, Rosie, can you go up to the spare room for me and get the blankets for the laundry?"

"Dad. I've got homework."

"Are you doing it now?"

"In a minute."

"Right, well until you start, you are free to go get the laundry for me. Thanks."

Rosie sloths off the couch, every step a leaden weight for her. You can tell she's nearing teenage years. Each stair is an epic mountain to climb. Finally, she reaches the spare room door and I hear it open. There's a pause while she assimilates the scenario she's witnessing, then a scream and yell, "JESSIE!"

At this point, Ethan's ears prick up and he jumps off the couch to run up the stairs.

"Mind your arm, Ethan."

There's much squealing and bouncing up and down, then all three of them come downstairs amid a cacophony of chaos.

Good chaos, though. Happy voices, hugs all around. I better

tell them this isn't a permanent thing, in case they get too attached. Probably too late, already.

"Guys, listen. Jessica has come to stay with us over the summer to study in peace. That means you can't hassle her constantly. But she will help me look after you both, especially you, Ethan, while your arm heals. But then she has to go away to University in September. Okay? Do you understand?"

"Yes, Daddy. That's ages away."

"As I remember summers, they fly away quickly. Don't forget, okay?"

"Okay."

I know they will still be upset when September comes, but at least they understand the deal. I like to be extra clear when children are involved.

I go back up to my office to finish off the reports for the day. I've already told Alex the news. She said it was a wonderful plan. I agree. I needed help. Help arrived. The universe has delivered. Now, if only I could get a girlfriend delivered, that would be great. Even a random shag?

A couple of things have occurred to me that complicate this situation a little.

Firstly, I don't know why Jessica was keen to leave her home and come live here. I'm sure she's just of the age where she needs some space and peace, as she mentioned. I hope there's nothing sinister behind it. But I can't get that niggle out of my head. I should probably ask her, but there hasn't been time yet. This is what comes of grabbing life by the balls, you'll probably get a few rogue pubic hairs with it into the bargain.

Secondly, I'm now sharing my house with a young girl that isn't my daughter. She'll be everywhere. In my laundry, in my bathroom, kitchen, living room. Probably everywhere except my bed, in fact. This makes things like the occasional need for privacy a luxury I may never have again.

There's always the shower, I suppose. She'll leave eventually, and I'll have had sex by then. Somehow, won't I?

The benefits of having her here to help massively outweigh the problems. It will be fine.

Since it's a special occasion, I ordered pizza for dinner to much excitement from all. We ate it together, at the table like a family. A weird family, but, nonetheless.

It was nice. No one was glued to their iPad. We sat and talked, ate and laughed. A lot of questions for poor Jessica from the kids, but she never seems to get exasperated by them.

After dinner, I get up to clean off the table and kitchen, but Jessica jumps up and told me to sit down, she'd do it. She got me a can of beer from the fridge and made me sit on the couch.

Have I died and gone to heaven? No, because in heaven, presumably, the kids wouldn't have jumped on me, stolen the remote, and put their inane crap on the TV.

Still, this is pretty close. A lovely young lady waltzed into my life and immediately made things better. What's the catch?

I didn't want to bring it up in front of the children; But to silence the niggle in my brain, once they go up to bed, I'll try to have a chat with Jessica. I hope there's nothing weird going on, because having her around makes all of us happy.

Bedtime comes around and I continue to sit my arse on the couch, grabbing control of the remote as the kids go up, with nary a squabble. I've always wondered how she got them to bed when she was babysitting. She has some kind of Pied Piper talent. She sings a bedtime song and they join in, knowing the words by heart. They follow, after doing a circle around the kitchen and living room, marching up to bed. It's hilarious and heart-warming all at once. I wish I had this skill. Bedtime for Daddy is a battle that I rarely win.

When Jessica comes back down, she gets herself a mug of hot chocolate and sits next to me on the couch. Her feet up on the seat, knees under her chin. Oh, to be young and flexible.

I look over at her. She looks innocent now, back to the young lass who babysits for me. She's still got that flirt with sexy womanhood, but it's toned down, in her fluffy pyjamas. Quite different from the last time I was on this couch with her, catching a snog and a grope.

"What you watching?" She motions at the TV.

"Ah, nothing. I don't even know what it is. I'm just happy to be relaxing for the first time in a decade."

She chuckles. "It must be hard, alone with them."

"Nah, piece of piss." I cough out a laugh. "Just kidding. It's unimaginably hard. Day in, day out. Never any peace. You can't possibly know how much I appreciate your help."

"I'm happy to help, and you've given me some peace. I am in your debt, Danny."

"Did your Mum or Dad mind you moving out, suddenly?" Her face falls from a smile to a wince and she bites on her lip. "Hey, don't worry. You don't have to tell me details."

"No. I do. It's only fair. You have been very kind, you deserve to know."

I raise an eyebrow.

"Jessica, you can tell me anything you need or want to. But don't feel obligated."

"I want to tell you." She puts her hand on my arm. Then puts her mug down on the table. "They kicked me out."

"What? Your parents?"

"Yeah. Said I had to find somewhere else to live. I've been basically locked in my room avoiding them for days."

"Why? I mean, what happened?"

116

She pauses for a moment, bites her lip again in a devastatingly cute way. She knots her hands together, hugging her knees.

"You don't have to tell me."

"No, it's okay. I'm just. Agh."

I smile, offer my arm for her to come into a cuddle if she wants. She smiles back and scoots over next to me.

"I haven't told anyone else yet. But. Fuck it. Danny, I'm pregnant."

She breathes out a big sigh of relief as she says it. I had my suspicions that's what she was going to say, I mean, what else could it be when a young girl is involved. But still, this is a shock.

"Oh, wow."

"You aren't going to yell, or preach, or lecture me?"

"What? No. Not at all. Why would I do that?"

"Oh, my god. I love you." She moves to straddle my lap and wraps both her arms around me, burying her head in my chest and squeezing tight.

I hug her back until she releases her grip and eases off.

"All I've had for a week has been yelling, screaming, crying, lectures and preaching."

"Really?"

"They wanted me to marry the dickhead!"

"Brett?"

"Yeah. As if? I haven't even told him. I'll never tell that fuckhead."

"Your parents religious?"

"Just a bit."

"Well, you won't get any of that here, Jessica. Things happen. It'll be okay."

"You are so nice. You don't mind?"

"Why would I mind? It's your body. No one can tell you what to do with it. People do stuff, stuff happens as a result. It may not be the best thing in the world for you right now, but you'll be okay. You are wonderful with the kids. I know you'll be a great Mum."

She looks down at her hands, her eyes moist, chin trembling. "Thank you, Danny." I pull her back down into my chest and let her cry out the tears that have built up.

"You are safe now." I pat her back and stroke her hair, same as I do when Rosie or Ethan need a cuddle. No amount of talking can take the place of a good hug.

She gets up eventually, wiping her eyes and getting a tissue from the kitchen. "Do you want another beer?"

"No, thank you. Work in the morning. You get one if you want though."

"I can't."

"Shit, yeah. Sorry, forgot."

"Never mind. I wasn't big into drinking, anyway." She comes back to the couch with a jar of olives and a glass of milk.

"Do you mind if I ask, how long?"

"Six weeks."

"Did you take a test?"

"I did three pee sticks, over two weeks. That's how Mum found out. I left one in the bin in the bathroom. Forgot to put it outside."

"Oops."

"Yeah. I wasn't going to say anything, yet."

"They'd find out, eventually. But yeah. I know."

"They might never have found out."

I look up at her. "Oh?"

"I want to go to uni. I didn't plan this." She scowls.

"Hey. It's okay. I'm not going to judge you. As I said. It's your body."

"Really? You still won't lecture me?"

"Jessica. I promise you now, I will never lecture you or tell you what to do with your life. I'll support you in any choice you make and help you whenever I can. Whatever you decide."

Her chin wobbles a little again. "I wish you were my dad."

"Ha, then I'd make you clean your room and do your laundry."

She chuckles. "No, Danny, you are a great Dad. Rosie and Ethan are very lucky."

"Thank you. I do my best."

"Would you ever have another baby?"

"Ha. No, that's just pizza in my belly." I pat my gut, which does look a bit pregnant, now I come to think about it. Jessica slaps my arm playfully.

"No, you dope. With a woman."

"No chance of that. It's as dry as a Nunnery around these parts lately. Anyway, I'm too old. Doing all that again?" I point up at the ceiling. "I think it would kill me."

"You've got life in you yet. You'll find someone." She throws me her 'look' again.

"Babies are a young man's game." I stand up, groaning as I do. "Look at me. I can barely get up off the couch, let alone chase after a baby."

"You need a fit young woman to help you."

I look down at her, a dangerous grin on her face. "Yup, well, it's lucky I have one then, isn't it? Anyway, I'm off to bed. You got everything you need?"

She pauses for a moment. "Yes, I think I do now. Thank you, Danny."

Chapter Fourteen

Today is a DIY day. I'll be fitting a lock on the bathroom door. Probably long overdue, but it has now become an urgent matter.

Jessica has invaded my house, my life, my dreams. I'm not complaining. It has been wonderful having her here. But when she invaded me in the shower this morning, while I was… busy… I thought it best to install some precautions.

She gasped, laughed, and then backed out.

Well, what am I meant to do? My bed remains empty, but blood continues to run through my veins. Hath not a dad eyes? Hath not a dad hands, organs, dimensions, senses, affections, passions?

Well, this one does. I woke up in a sweat. Jessica took the place of Winona. I needed a shower to clear the backup of tension.

At breakfast, she said nothing. But there an air of sniggers about her.

She's out now, doing the shopping. I got her added to my car insurance, made sure she was a safe driver, and now I have one less tedious task. She says she likes food shopping. What kind of psychopath have I let in my house?

I'm a bit lost. Feel like I'm at a loose end, guilty that I'm not doing something productive. The laundry is all done, the kids' rooms are clean, sort of. They are fed, clothed, and beyond all reasonable hope and possibility, barely Saturday afternoon and all their weekend homework is done.

This novelty can't last. The kids will grow used to her and start rebelling as they do to me. But I will enjoy it while I can.

Ethan is coping quite well with his arm now. It's not the best situation in the world, but with help, we're getting through it. There is the issue of telling Elise about it still to overcome, but I'm going to postpone that as long as possible. Who knows, maybe he'll have the cast off before she can be bothered to see them again?

I've already got a bolt for the bathroom door. Bought it years ago, never got around to fitting it. I go out to the shed and dig around through boxes of junk, forgotten memories from a life gone by. Some of Elise's crap that she never took, baby toys that should go in the recycling bin.

I should use this extra time I have to do all the things I've put off for many years.

Who am I kidding? It's enough work to dig through boxes and find the bolt, charge the power screwdriver, then chisel a little square out of the door frame and fit it. A ten-minute job put off for years, but will hopefully give me back a little personal space.

I hear the car pull into the driveway and voices through the open window. I pop my head out and see Jessica with another woman, dragging in the bags of shopping.

"Hello." I wave down.

"Hey, Danny." She looks up. "This is Lily, my cousin. I bumped into her in Tesco. You don't mind if she comes over for a bit?"

"No, not at all. Hello, Lily." She waves up at me. This is interesting.

I pop down the stairs and help them bring in the shopping.

Lily looks to be late twenties, maybe thirty. Pretty enough. She's got that 'child of the nineties' rock-chick vibe going for her, and those dark brown eyes that mesmerise me on a woman.

"Pleased to meet you, Lily."

"And you, Danny." She smiles and shakes my hand. Delightfully alluring.

As we unpack the shopping, I notice a significant increase in the usual beer ration. Plus, a bottle of whisky.

I don't remember putting that on the list. Jessica isn't drinking, the kids sure aren't, which leaves me and… Lily.

"Jessica, come up with me for a second. I want to show you something."

She follows me up the stairs. We go into the bathroom and I shut the door.

"I fitted a bolt."

"Good idea."

"Are you sure you 'bumped' into Lily in Tesco?"

"Yeah, course."

"It's just, her skirt seems a tad short for grocery shopping?"

"She's a uniquely stylish woman, what can I say?"

"Okay… And the booze? It's nothing to do with this bolt, is it?"

"What? How could a door bolt have anything to do with Lily and alcohol?"

"Hmm."

She shrugs. "I don't know what you mean, Danny."

"Right."

"Is it okay if Lily stays for dinner?"

I look her in the eye. She doesn't flinch. I know I'm being set up here. Part of me is opposed to the idea. Part of me is seriously fucking grateful. But the morality of the situation is what makes me feel uneasy. My brother's words echo in my head again. Grab life by the balls. What can I do? I'm only human.

"Yes, no problem. What are we having?"

"Rosie wants to make lasagne with me."

"Great. Love it."

"While we're doing that, you can chat with Lily. Get to know her. She doesn't have a boyfriend."

"Oh, you just casually mentioned that, did you?" I can't help but chuckle.

"Yes, very casually." She looks coy.

There's a knock on the door. "Dad? Why are you talking in the bathroom?"

"Just showing Jessie the new door lock, Rosie."

I roll my eyes at Jessica and open the door. She blinks in innocence.

"I just hope no one regrets anything tomorrow."

"Well, be careful, Danny."

I nod.

Lily gets on with the kids just as well as Jessica, it seems. Within a few minutes, they are all best buddies, laughing and messing around. Rosie points out that they both have flower names.

As promised, Jessica and Rosie are in charge of dinner, making a fuss and clearing us all out of the kitchen so they can work their magic in peace. Ethan is engrossed with his iPad. He's found a way to prop it up on his cast, while he slumps down, headphones in. Leaving Lily and me virtually alone.

"What do you do, Lily?"

"I'm a hairdresser."

"Oh? Cool. Reckon you could make me look presentable?"

She eyes me up and down. "You ain't too bad as it is." A sly smile creeps over her. Oh, boy.

"Drink?"

"Whisky and coke, please."

"Oh, starting as you mean to go on?"

"Go hard, or go home." She emphasises the word 'hard'. I'm feeling a little tingly.

"Quite so."

I pour Lily her drink, and myself a beer, because if I hit the whisky this early, there won't be anything hard at all in this home later.

I'm a bit out of practice with this flirting stuff. I can't think of anything to say to keep the conversation going. If we were both teenagers, and Ethan wasn't sitting on the chair next to us, I'd probably go straight in for the snog right now. I think she'd reciprocate.

But here, now, possibly a tad more mature, I feel conditioned by society to at least get to know her a little before I jump on her bones.

The aroma coming in from the kitchen is delicious, and I'm hungry now. For food, as well as passion.

"Rosie makes a decent Lasagne. Do you like Italian food?"

"I love it."

"Do you like to cook?"

"Sometimes. I like to get my hands dirty." She brushes her hair back from her face and flicks me a smile. I don't need to be Sherlock Holmes to read these clues. Lily wants some fun after dinner. Christ knows why she'd choose me over the plethora of bell-ends available to a pretty woman like her, but perhaps I've just answered the question. Maybe she's bored with bell-ends, revving their engines? Maybe she wants something a bit more classy? Ha. Come to the wrong place, then, hasn't she?

"Come eat." Jessica sticks her head into the living room. I

unplug Ethan from his iPad and help him up off the couch. He follows his nose into the kitchen. I motion for Lily to go before me, always the gentleman. She brushes up against me, much closer than was necessary for the exit.

You know what? I think I might have pulled.

Dinner is delicious. Jessica has gone all out, with the help of Rosie. The lasagne is wonderful, and somehow there's a bottle of red wine on the table. Since Lily and I are the only ones to partake, by the end of the meal, I'm feeling quite merry. There's ice cream with grated chocolate sprinkles all over it. The kids are lapping this up.

Our mealtimes are typically bleak, with only me bothering to sit at the table most nights, alone, kids dispersed amongst the couch cushions. Tonight there's laughter, banter, two pretty women and two happy kids. I could get used to this.

Someone suggests we find something on Netflix, family-friendly. Once we all pitch in to clean up, Ethan excused, we adjourn to the living room. Jessica flicks through the movies and finds something suitably computer-animated, ostensibly about cats and dogs that talk, with mild humour hidden for the adults watching. Ethan takes up his place on the beanbag, Rosie in the armchair. Jessica and Lily sit at opposite ends of the couch, leaving me to sit in the middle of them. Lily pats the seat and looks up at me with a grin.

I sit down and Jessica bounces up. "Forgot the popcorn." She dashes off into the kitchen and returns presently with three bowls. One each for the kids and she dumps a large bowl on my lap, for us to share, presumably. She turns the main light off, then sits back down with the remote.

"Ready?"

"Yes!" The kids squeal in unison.

I'm sure I heard an "oh, yes," from Lily, too.

. . .

Not that I've been concentrating much, but the movie itself is dire. The animation is smooth and rich, but the plot leaves much to be desired. Still, the kids seem to like it. Jessica is almost asleep, phasing in and out of consciousness, but Lily and I... Well, it isn't PG-rated, that's for sure. The popcorn is on my lap, but somehow she reaches in the dark, not for the bowl. I gasp, but she turns and puts a finger over her lips. I sit back as quiet as I can and enjoy the grope. Rarely has there been women-folk in these parts. She better watch out, she might startle the badgers.

The movie seems to go on forever, and by the end, my jeans probably reek like the refreshments counter at the cinema. Good job this is just butter popcorn and not something weird like cheese.

As the credits roll, I look up and notice that both kids are asleep. Jessica is more or less out for the count. I get up and scrape Ethan up off his beanbag and carry him up to bed. Once he's settled, I come back down to do the same with Rosie, but she's up, and almost crawling up the stairs half asleep. I kiss her goodnight, and she goes into her room. Jessica is in the kitchen when I get down.

"I'm going up to bed, Danny. You and Lily be okay?" She flashes a grin and a yawn.

"Oh, I think so."

"Be good. Night." She kisses me on the cheek and fist bumps my arm.

"Thanks, Jessica. Night."

I grab another beer from the fridge and wander into the living room, not knowing what to expect.

Lily is noticeable by her absence. For a second I assume she's done a runner, decided that she wants nothing to do with a loser like Danny Watts. Maybe I should have groped her back during the movie? I don't know what the protocols are in these situations. As I say, it's been a while.

I needn't have worried. The downstairs bathroom door opens and Lily returns triumphant.

"Just us left?"

"Looks that way. Another drink?"

"Please." With the light back on, I can see she's quite tipsy. On the scale, she's probably two notches up from merry. I'm teetering not far behind. Taking things easy, because these old bones aren't as fit as they used to be.

I hand her another drink and she sits back down on the couch, pulling me with her. She takes a sip of the whisky and coke, then puts her glass down on the table, taking the beer out of my hand and dropping it down next to hers. She doesn't hesitate, pulls me towards her and kisses me violently. I can taste the whisky on her lips, her tongue pushing its way into my mouth.

She smells delicious. Perfume rising on her body heat. Her delicate skin smooth and warm. Just stroking my hands over her arms and legs feels amazing. Emotional, primal. There's a buzz of electricity coursing through us.

After a few minutes like this, she undoes the buttons on my shirt, revealing my bursting gut, but she doesn't seem to mind, running her hands over my chest, then kissing and licking.

She stands up, abruptly, and performs some kind of Houdini magic act, an inside-out striptease. First, she reaches inside her top and snaps her fingers. Her bra somehow pops off and is thrown on the floor. Then she spins around, deftly plucking a pair of knickers from under her skirt. Again, they land on my carpet. I'm in awe, mouth agape, but she soon fixes that by straddling me and clasping her lips around mine. She grabs my hand and clutches it to her breast under the shirt. I follow her lead and run my hands over her ample bosom. The faintest hint of sweat, the scent of sex, passion and lust. All the time she

127

kisses, deep, wet and hard. My hands caress her body until she finally takes my right hand, and directs it between her legs into the hot, lush, and soaking wet pleasure garden.

Sweet dreams are made of this.

My fingers slip in easily, she moans and thrusts down, encouraging me to push harder and deeper. She moves from my lips to my neck, biting gently, licking and teasing me.

She pauses for a moment, looks me in the eye, point-blank range, and says, "You should fuck me now, Danny."

Who am I to disagree?

Chapter Fifteen

I've never been one of those people who give names to inanimate objects. My car isn't called Steve or JimBob, my computer is just an object, not a personality. I've also never understood people who refer to their body parts as 'junior' or for women, 'the twins'.

But I feel I need to make an exception now. From here forth, my penis shall be known as Judas the Betrayer.

The little bastard let me down. Big time.

I've never been so embarrassed in my forty-two years. When naked in my living room, a beautiful woman lying in front of me, legs akimbo, begging me to fuck the living shit out of her, and every fibre of my being desperate to do just that, except those fibres that occupy my traitorous knob.

He remained quite blasé to the situation. I could hear him in my head.

'Nah, mate, I'm not in the mood right now.'

'Not in the mood? Not in the fucking mood? We've been preparing for this for the last five years; This is the time. This is the place. Look.' I begged of him, 'Look at the beautiful naked woman in front of you, with your one, treacherous eye. Take in her shapes, the scent of her womanhood, the warmth of her body. Soak it up, you bastard, and bone up. Now is the time.'

But no. He was having none of it.

Lily was getting impatient by this time. Touching herself, "Danny, fuck me." She moaned.

I looked down at Judas, raised my eyebrow. 'You heard her. Do it!'

'Can't be arsed, mate.'

'Come on, I am literally begging you now. What the fuck is wrong with you?'

Judas didn't answer, but Lily had by now noticed the flaccid, pathetic excuse for my male libido, hanging limp.

"Something wrong?" There was a nervousness to her voice. Not surprising. She thought she was getting laid; Instead, she's getting a load of nothing.

"Err, I don't know."

"Come here. Maybe this will get you going." She pulls me up to her face, French-kisses me like she's hoovering up an octopus, reaches down and squeezes Judas. He jumped at that. Started to stand to attention.

'Thank you.' I told the little bastard. Maybe he's just a slow starter tonight. Before he could flop, I whipped him down, thrusting into Lily's thirsty, tight love hole. But the double-crossing son of a bitch cut me off at the pass.

'Ha. Gotcha.'

It was like trying to hammer a nail in with a marshmallow. Not happening.

I tried thinking disgusting thoughts, dragging up the most obscure porn I could think of. MILFs in heat, tied up pussy, lesbian licking. None of it helped. The frustration building up in my brain was driving me mad.

'Why? Why now? Of all times?'

'Told ya. Not in the mood.'

'But you've been in the mood every single other night.'

'Time for a break then, innit?'

'You little bastard! You total and utter shithead.'

'Yeah, maybe, but you still love me, don't you, you dirty twat?'

I looked up at Lily, she was looking a bit concerned by then. My thrusts weren't giving her the expected result.

"Do you not like me?"

The spell was broken. She pushed me away, embarrassed, getting up off the couch and grabbing her clothes from the floor. Before I could say anything, she was gone, into the bathroom. I'm sure I heard her crying.

When she finally came out, fully dressed, phone in her hand. I was still on the couch, naked, head in hands. Feeling extremely stupid.

"Jessica asked me to come over. But if you didn't like me, why did you lead me on?"

"No, that's not what happened. I do. I think you are beautiful."

"Don't look like it." She looked down at my mutinous cock.

I couldn't look her in the eye. How could I explain this? "I don't know what's wrong. This has never happened before."

"Well, that's lovely, isn't it? I'm that ugly I broke your dick."

"Lily, no. That's not it."

Her phone buzzes. "My taxi is here. Thanks for nothing, Danny."

And that was that. The only chance at a shag I've had in years, and I totally blew it. Judas the Betrayer blew it. He screwed me royally. In a bad way.

Bastard.

I picked up my clothes, locked the doors, turned off the lights, and went up to bed. I may also have shed a tear for the death of my sex life forevermore.

. . .

You'd think that would be the worst it could possibly be, but Judas then had the temerity to wake me up the next day with dreams of Winona, rock-solid, ready for action.

I hate him.

As I sit at my desk, Monday looming like a dark cloud of hatred over me. Two staff out sick today, Alex on a day off, I'm forced to take customer care calls all day.

At least the calls take my mind off the rest of the worst weekend that Danny Watts has ever experienced. Second place going now to when Elise told me she was fucking Brian. What a joyous time that was.

Speaking of Elise, she decided yesterday was when she'd pay us an unannounced visit, arriving during an awkward breakfast where I tried to explain what happened to Jessica, via text messages sent across the room, so the children wouldn't hear.

'I thought you would like her?'

'I did. It's not that. I've been googling.'

'She's really upset. What the fuck did you do?'

'Nothing. It just wouldn't work. I'm sorry. Please tell her I'm sorry.'

I had been googling, while in the safety of the locked bathroom. But five hundred adverts for fake brand Viagra later, I had no conclusive answer.

Then the doorbell rang, and Jessica, clothed in just a t-shirt, answered. Maybe that was a mistake, but she jumped up before I could do anything.

Elise burst into the kitchen, took one look at Ethan and his arm in a cast, and calmly asked me what happened, while Jessica made us all a nice soothing cup of tea. Yeah, right. She went arse-bastard-ballistic, screaming, yelling, pointing, accusing. I recall something along the lines of "And now you've got this little slut living here?"

That didn't go down too well, needless to say. Jessica then joined the tirade of general abuse. Thankfully, at some point, Rosie and Ethan scarpered upstairs.

Then came the threats. Custody, child abuse, responsibilities. "Maybe if you didn't spend all your mental effort thinking with your tiny fucking dick, you'd look after the children better."

That was probably when I flipped. Custody being the trigger word. I told her, over my dead body would that ever happen and I meant it.

"It was an accident, he was having a great time. Kids take falls. They bounce back. Jessica is helping me look after them, there's nothing more going on. Not that it's any of your damn business."

After some more cursing, abuse, accusations of paedophilia, talk of lawyers and police, she left. A slammed door punctuating her exit. Jessica ran to the bathroom, crying.

My cosy family broken like a priceless vase into smithereens. I picked up the pieces, one by one. Then slowly, calmly, stuck them all back together, with the only glue I had. Love.

I started with the kids, going up to their rooms, making sure they were okay. Taking a cookie each, and a promise of reassurance that, under no circumstances would they ever be going from my house to live with their mother. No force on earth could take them from me. Some hugs and tears and they were eventually sated. I bought Ethan a game he'd been talking about for weeks, and Rosie gets to order something from Amazon.

Jessica was harder to placate. She bit at her fingernails, sat on the floor in front of the washing machine. "I left my parents' home to get away from fighting. Maybe this was a mistake?"

"No, it wasn't. I'm sorry, again. Elise will not be coming

back to the house, don't worry." I made her a cup of tea, sat with her on the floor, waited for her to calm, and then offered my arms for a hug. She looked up at me with a trembling chin. "Yeah. Fuck that bitch. How could you have ever married her?"

I didn't know what to say to that. Times were different, life was simpler? Things were better back then. All those words are empty clichés. Instead, I held Jessica close, kissed her on the forehead and told her she would be safe here, with us. She nodded, said she'd stay. But she did go upstairs and get fully dressed after.

At least the rest of the day went smoother. We all went out for dinner to a chain restaurant. Ethan got lots of attention from the waitresses because of his arm, everyone seemed to be in better cheer. Not the best weekend I've ever had, but we're back to normal now, I suppose. Except for Judas in my pants, who continues taunting me.

Life, such as it is, continues to go on. We ride the waves of drama, and ebb and flow with the tide. I'm keeping afloat, just about. Doing my reports in between phone calls.

Jessica brings me a sandwich for lunch, then flits back to her room. She's deep into some studies, always got her nose in a medical textbook. We haven't heard any more about Lily and I'm scared to bring it up.

Jessica pops out to do the school runs, and I take a moment to flip back to my medical research; regarding why doesn't my stupid dick function anymore. Information is abundant, but nothing is straightforward. The causes of erectile dysfunction range from psychological problems, stress, diabetes, or any number of unpronounceable conditions I don't want to even think about. Every single article resorts to telling me to visit my GP for more information.

That thought does not relish me with enthusiasm. For now, I will chalk it down to alcohol. This is now a dry house. No more booze. Can't hurt to eat more vegetables, go for a walk occasionally.

The cacophony coming from downstairs signifies the children returning from school. Promptly, shoes thud, jackets flap and doors slam as they bolt from room to room, picking up iPads, dumping down bags and switching on the TV.

Jessica appears in my doorway.

"Ethan got this letter." She hands me an envelope.

Shit. The only things that come home from school are spam, requests for money or, in this case, moans.

It takes some time to decode the spider scrawl cursive, signed by Stephanie Sanders. Rather ironically, she's penned a verbose diatribe on how Ethan's handwriting has devolved into an illegible mess and how his plaster cast is causing disruption in the class.

Ethan is right-handed. His right hand is covered in plaster. How the bollocking hell does she expect him to write? If he's doing it with his left hand, I'm not surprised the quality has dropped. As for his arm causing disruption, what am I meant to do about that? Magically heal it overnight?

I hand the note to Jessica to read. "I can't remember the last time I used a pen to write with. Can you?"

"No, who does that anymore?"

"Ms Broomstick up the arse Sanders, apparently." She sniggers. "ETHAN." I call down. He shuffles up the stairs, probably expecting a lecture.

"What?"

"Do you know what this letter is about?"

He looks down at his shoes. "No."

"How are you managing to write with a pen, dude?"

"I can do it with my teeth, or if I grip it hard. Look." He runs to his room and comes back with a pencil in his mouth.

"Ethan. That's not a good idea."

"But I can do it really well. Look."

He sets about writing his name on a sheet of paper he pulled out of the printer. I have to say, he's doing better than I expected.

"That's pretty cool, but tell you what, don't do that at school anymore, because you are just too cool for everyone else to deal with."

"Okay, Dad."

"It's all good, mate. You aren't in trouble." His face lights up and he runs off back to the TV. I think we can safely file that letter in the recycling bin.

My computer flashes and beeps, signalling an incoming support call.

"Gotta take this. You making dinner?" I flash Jessica a grin. She nods and smiles back, then leaves me, shutting the door.

"Good afternoon. My name is Danny, thank you for calling Help-Tech. How can I fix you up?" I cringe every time I have to say those words.

There's a snigger at the other end of the line, but this is not rare. I sigh, inwardly.

"Ah, well, it's a little embarrassing." A female voice announces. I check the details that have popped up on my screen.

"No problem, we'll have you fixed up in no time. Can I just confirm some details before we get going?"

"Okay."

"For security purposes, can you please confirm your name, date of birth and address? Your technology contains sensitive and private data. We just like to make sure you are really you." Our spiel is painfully cheesy, but she rattles off the details, regardless.

"Faye Lovering, the tenth of March 1984, and I'm at four Cedar Terrace, Abingdon." I read the details back and verify she's really who she says she is, as far as our limited investigation goes. It matches, and what's surprising is she's from my town. She lives over near Rosie's school, in fact. The name rings a bell. Where have I seen that name before?

"That's great, Faye. How can I help you?"

"My son, the little darling, in his wonderful way, has locked my phone up with a passcode I don't know and he won't tell me."

I stifle a chuckle. This is quite common.

"Oh dear, well, don't panic. We can get you sorted, no problem. There are a few steps to follow. Do you have a cloud backup?"

"Err."

"If you haven't set it up or changed the settings, it's likely on by default."

"Umm."

"Do you have a laptop or desktop that you can plug into?"

"Yes. I have a MacBook."

"Brilliant. You'll need to connect the phone to the laptop, go into restore mode, and then wipe the phone. After that, you can set a new passcode, run a restore from the cloud, and you'll be back in business in no time."

"Err. Can you repeat that?"

"Sure," I explain the steps again, slower, but I know she isn't listening. Some people just have tech blindness. The words won't sink in.

"How long does it take?"

"Well, it can depend on how much data you have and the speed of the connection, but not very long."

"I really need the phone to work. That sounds complicated and I don't want to fuck it up. Oops, sorry. I mean, I don't want to make a mess of it." I chuckle.

"I understand, Faye. If you follow those steps, carefully, you should be fine."

"Right. Err. Maybe I'll just get a new phone."

I can tell she's getting exasperated. There isn't much more I can do from my desk. In cases like this, we're basically stuck. If I was sat in front of her phone, I could sort it in twenty minutes.

Which gives me a crazy idea. She sounds nice, stressed, and frustrated. I know that feeling only too well. Sometimes you just have to go above and beyond and help a stranger. I stop the call recording.

"Listen, Faye, this is totally off the record, and I've honestly never done this before, but you live just down the road from me. Do you know the little café near the school? Jitter Beans, I think it's called."

"Oh, really? Yes, I do."

"You can say no if you want, and I'll still help you over the phone like this, but if you prefer, bring your laptop and phone to the café and I'll meet you there and get you sorted."

"That would be amazing. Are you sure? Thank you so much."

"I can be there in about half an hour if that suits?"

"Wonderful. Yes. I'll be there. Thank you. Err, what was your name, again?"

"No problem. I'm Danny. Danny Watts."

As I hang up the call, it hits me like a bolt from the blue where I've seen her name before. Of course, the school Facebook group.

I grab my phone, scroll through the pages, and sure enough, there are many posts from Faye Lovering in the school group.

Her profile photo is a shot of planet Earth from the International Space Station. The caption reads: We've only got one planet. Don't fuck it up.

Most of her posts are about environmental issues and autism. There's a definite theme as I scroll through her public feed. Then, Facebook shows me a photo album, and naturally, I click it.

Fuck me sideways with a yard broom. She's absolutely gorgeous. Wow. She's got that Winona look going for her, dark eyes, long brown hair. She's petite, tidy, and feisty looking. There's a photo of her on a beach holiday, bikini-clad and coy. Judas the Betrayer stirs in my undergarments.

Keep it professional, Danny. Don't be a stalking perv.

I'm a little nervous, to tell the truth. I know this isn't a date, but my body thinks it is. I'm going to help someone, not get in her pants. But you try telling my guts that. I probably shouldn't have looked at her photos, but how else would I recognise her?

It will be fine. I'll fix her phone, have a coffee, and we'll be on our ways. She'll leave a nice survey result for me and everyone is happy. I have to get back for dinner soon, anyway. Jessica is making fajitas.

I get to the café a few minutes early and order a drink and a little pastry, then take a seat at a big table near the door, so we have space to put the phone and laptop down.

Faye bursts in suddenly, laptop bag around her neck. She looks around the room and then rests her eyes on me; I raise a hand and wave.

She's as beautiful in real life as her photos suggested. She's in leggings and a black top under a long coat. Hair tied back, makeup subtle.

"Danny?"

"Yes. Hello, Faye." I stand up to greet her. Holding my hand out to shake. But she gets tangled up in her laptop strap while trying to take her coat off. She mutters curses under her breath, twists around, but only makes it worse. The strap is extra long, and it's got caught in the coat buttons.

"May I help?"

"Please." I take the laptop bag, decouple it from her buttons, and slowly lift it over her head. I catch her eyes as I do it. She smiles, so pretty. "I'm such a klutz."

"Don't worry about it."

She takes off her coat and flings it on the chair opposite. "Can I get you a coffee or something?"

"Thank you, but I got one already." I motion to my cup.

"Oh, that looks good." Her eyes widen as she spots the pastry. "I'll be right back."

She comes back with a coffee and pastry, the same as mine. Plops them down on the table, then slumps down opposite me.

"Let's get you sorted then."

She looks up at me as if she's forgotten why we're here. "Oh, yes! Sorry, I was miles away."

"I'll need your laptop and phone." I already know she won't have remembered the cable. I brought my own. She sets about unpacking the laptop, then gets the phone out of her jacket pocket that she threw earlier. No regard for technology, some people.

"I'm very grateful, Danny. I have a video call later I can't miss. Of course, this is when Josh decided to lock up my phone."

"Is that your son?"

"Sorry, yeah. Joshua. My son and my life. He's with my neighbour now."

"U2 fan?"

"Haha, yes. Just a bit." She grins.

I open up her laptop. It goes straight to a desktop full of cluttered icons. There's plenty of battery left, and, aside from a huge crack in the screen which causes me to frown, we're good.

I pick up her phone, locked and requiring the passcode to be entered to enable the fingerprint sensor.

As predicted, there's no cable in the bag. I pull mine out of my pocket and plug the phone into the laptop.

"Oops, I forgot that."

I smile. "No problem."

I start the process of restoring the phone to factory settings, which will take a little while.

"They insisted on a video call, otherwise I could have just used the landline."

"You know the MacBook has a camera?"

She shakes her head. "It hasn't worked since I dropped it."

"Ah." That explains the screen damage. "People love a face-to-face chat these days."

"Job interview. I'm quite nervous."

"What do you do? Sorry, don't mean to intrude."

"No, it's fine. I'm an Environmental Compliance Co-Ordinator."

"Oh, that sounds fancy."

"Not as glamorous as you might think. I try to make sure we don't end up ruining the planet, but most days, I think I'm fighting a losing battle."

"A noble cause."

She picks up her pastry and takes a bite. "These are yummy."

I nod. "Okay, you can go through the phone setup now, and set yourself a new password."

"Wow. Is it done already?"

"It's reset now. Blank. But we'll have you back soon."

She picks up the phone, squints, then rummages in her bag, pulling out a pair of glasses.

"Can't see a thing on the screen without these."

She begins tapping and scrolling through all the questions and terms and conditions.

"Bloody hell, everything is ridiculously complicated, isn't it? Ah, it's asking for a password again."

"That's the iTunes account password. Do you know it?"

"Err."

"I might be able to get it from your laptop. But I don't want to see what it is."

"Pff." She waves a hand. "Do whatever you need to do."

I fiddle around in some utilities and pull up the key-chain access. Search for the right password, then turn the laptop around to face her.

"See it?"

"Oh, yes! I remember now. Wow, you are good."

"Just doing my job, Ma'am." She laughs, and my heart melts.

Once she's logged in, she hands the phone back to me.

I kick off the cloud restore and make sure it starts working, then lay it down.

"Have you back up and running soon. It says about twenty-five minutes."

"Thank you, so very much."

"My pleasure." There's an awkward moment as I meet her eyes again. Such a simple thing for me and she's visibly grateful. There's an aura of energy about her. She picks up her coffee and takes a sip.

"My son goes to school here."

"So does my daughter."

"Really? What's her name?"

"Rosie."

"Yes! I know her. I knew that surname sounded familiar."

"Seriously?"

"Yeah, she's in Josh's music class."

"Oh, yes. Small world."

"Music helps Josh focus, for a while anyway. He gets lost easily."

"Kids, eh?"

"Josh is on the autism spectrum. I love him to bits, but he can be hard work." Her hands move to a locket around her neck. She clasps it for a moment, then lets it fall.

"Oh, I'm sorry. That must be hard for you and his dad."

"Ha. It would be if his dad was around." She huffs.

"I'm sorry, again."

"Don't worry." She scarfs down the rest of her pastry.

While the phone slowly sucks down all her data and apps, we respectively moan and groan about the school policies, cost of uniforms, quality of lunch options, and general day-to-day reality. Faye's life, albeit wildly different, is similar in some ways to my own. Her daily routine of kids, work, shopping and sleep sounds eerily familiar. She tells me random snippets from her past, like when she first saw U2 play at Wembley Stadium and how she nearly died when skydiving once for a charity event. I listen, because I hate when I talk to someone and it feels like they are just waiting for me to stop, so they can talk about themselves. I want to know every detail I can find out about this woman.

A buzz on the table drags us back to reality. I look down and the phone has completed the restore.

"Ah, here we go." I pick it up, unplug it and hand it back to her.

She types in the passcode then swipes around through her apps. "Oh, my god. It's all back how it was."

"Yup. See, no problem."

"I know I've said it a million times now, but thank you SO MUCH!"

I smile. My job can be fulfilling sometimes when I get to help someone out of a bind. But I've never had the pleasure of seeing the reaction face-to-face in real-time before. It feels wonderful.

I don't want to leave now, but I expect the kids are

wondering when I'll be back and Jessica probably has dinner ready.

"Well, I better be off. Kids will be waiting to eat."

"Your wife cooking?"

"Ha. No. She's long gone, and she couldn't cook, anyway. No. We have a friend staying for a while. She's making dinner."

"What do I owe you?"

"Nothing. The support was included in your purchase."

Faye smiles, then stands up and throws her arms around me. "I'm really grateful for your help, Danny. I know we just met, but it felt like catching up with an old friend."

"It did, yeah." I want to ask if I can see her again, but her phone suddenly blasts out a succession of message pings and she's distracted.

"Good luck with your interview."

"Thank you."

I don't remember the journey home. But suddenly I'm parked in my driveway and the world abruptly spins back into view. What just happened?

The blur is sharply pulled back into focus as I go in the house, and find Rosie and Ethan fighting over the TV remote, then Jessica dishes up the dinner on the table and I round up the children, dragging them into the dining room.

"Hey, Rosie, do you know a boy called Josh Lovering?"

"Yeah. He's in my music class." She makes a face.

"Is he your friend?"

"Well, not really. He's a bit, err, weird."

"Weird isn't bad, Rosie. Anyway, I just met his Mum. Faye."

"I know her. She's really nice."

"Yes. Yes, she is…" Jessica raises an eyebrow.

My phone buzzes in my pocket. A friend request from Faye Lovering. How 'bout that?

Chapter Sixteen

Hindsight is wonderfully clear, isn't it? It's that clarity that tells me it was not a good plan to order Rosie's two-hundred piece art set, including watercolours, pastels, pencils and crayons, along in the same package as my experimental penis equipment, also known in the industry as adult sex toys. I was just trying to get free shipping by combining packages.

"What's this? Eww!" Is the cry I heard from her room as she unpacked the Amazon box. How was I to know she had picked it up outside the door?

"I don't know Rosie. I think they must have sent that as a mistake. Here, I'll get rid of it."

"It says pocket pussy."

"Yes. Well, as I said, it must be a mistake and I'll send it back."

"What is this?" She holds up a tube of KY Jelly.

"Oh, that's just oil for the squeaky door. Give it to me."

As I exit Rosie's room, arms full of sex toys, of course, that's the moment Jessica crosses the hallway into the bathroom. She sniggers. "Must be a mistake, huh?"

"Yes. It certainly was a mistake…"

I stuff everything in my wardrobe and go back to my office. There's justification in the purchase. I'm trying to gauge under what circumstances Judas the Betrayer fails to perform.

Anyway, I don't have time for that now. We are getting the house ready for an invasion of pre-teen girls.

It's Rosie's thirteenth birthday tomorrow, and she asked for a sleepover with her friends. Six of them. The logistics of this event are proving to be rather complicated. I'm leaving most of it to Jessica to organise. She seems to know what she's doing and I'm just getting in the way. I handed over my debit card and told her to sort it out.

Quite why we needed three hundred quid's worth of food, drink and party accessories I don't know, but as they reminded me, Rosie only turns thirteen and becomes a teenager once. Thank the deities in charge for that.

"Danny!" Jessica yells from the bathroom. "DANNY!" It sounds urgent. I jump up and run to the bathroom door.

"Jessica? What's wrong?"

"Come in, please."

"Err, what? Into the bathroom?"

"Yes. Please come in."

I hear her flick the bolt across, then cautiously open the door. She's sitting on the toilet as I enter. Head down. I turn around and shut the door behind me. Then turn back to her.

She looks up, her face in tears. "Danny! Look."

She holds up a wad of toilet paper, covered in blood.

"Jesus! What happened? Are you hurt? Do you need an ambulance?"

"No. It's my period."

It takes a moment to flicker into my brain what she means. One minute I'm hiding a pocket pussy, the next I'm looking at menstrual blood. Life is certainly colourful.

Then it hits me. She's having a miscarriage.

Oh, shit.

"Err. Are you okay? Do you need a doctor?" I try to remember what the nurses said in our antenatal classes thirteen years previous, but I have to admit, I wasn't listening back then, in a room full of ripe women, all of them ready to pop out a tit at a moment's notice.

"I don't know." She cries out.

"Are you in pain?" She pauses for a moment, breathing deeply.

"No. I don't think so."

"Okay. Maybe just a shock then."

"Can you please go to my room and get my pads from in my big bag? They'll be somewhere at the bottom. Just tip it out."

"Yes, okay. Be right back." She nods, wiping tears away with a new wad of toilet paper.

Rosie is standing in her doorway, staring at me as I come out of the bathroom.

"Jessie just had a little scare. She'll be fine, Rosie."

"Did she get her period?"

"Yes."

"I learned about it at school. It's normal."

"Well, yes, it is. She just wasn't expecting it right now."

Seemingly satisfied, Rosie goes back in her room. I go into the spare room and find Jessica's bag, tip it out as she suggested, and dig through the pile of knickers, bras, tops and pants that spreads all over the bed. I find a pack of panty liners eventually in a colourful packet. This must be it. Not the cotton wool balls or the other circular pad things that also fell onto the bed. I have learned something in my years of marriage.

"Here you go." I hand her the pads. "Do you need me to stay?"

"No, it's okay now. Thank you."

"I'll be a yell away. Don't hesitate." She forces a nervous smile.

I hear the bathroom door open, then Jessica's room door close quietly. Oh, boy. I haven't talked to her about the pregnancy situation since. I wanted to give her time to think about what to do. I guess this puts a literal full stop at the end of that chapter in her life. It happens, I know. I went directly to my desk and googled. Seemingly, it happens in one in four pregnancies, but much less frequently in a woman of such a young age. But cold, hard statistics offer little emotional support. I know she didn't want a baby now, especially since the father is out of the picture, but logic and reason play absolutely no part in this. She's flooded with hormones and probably has no idea what she feels or wants.

I go downstairs and make a cup of tea for us, because tea is the ultimate cure for everything and anything.

Knocking at her door, she bids me enter.

"Made you a cuppa." I put it down on the nightstand. She's lying on the bed, clutching her phone. "You feeling okay? Need anything?"

"Just normal cramps. Thanks for the tea, Danny. I'll be okay. I've looked it up." She motions with her phone.

"Yeah, me too."

"I'm sorry, Danny, for causing you all this drama."

"Jessie, please. Never think things like that. What are friends for? You have nothing to be sorry about." She smiles through wet eyes, reaches up and grabs my hand. I sit down on the edge of her bed. There's no point in words now. We sit like this in silence for a good five minutes.

Eventually, I break the peace. "I'll make us dinner tonight, anything you like."

"Can we have spaghetti the way Rosie makes it?"

I chuckle. "Yes, sure we can."

Once we're settled at the dinner table, Rosie's special spaghetti on our plates, iPads closed, TV off, I'm reminded again how nice it is to have a regular family meal together. What's that old saying? You can only truly be a family once you have eaten, slept, and cried together.

"Are you excited, Rosie?"

"Yes!" She squeals, "Kirsty said she's bringing a new movie."

"No boys or drink. Okay?"

"No, Daddy." She rolls her eyes. "Just Kirsty, Chloe, Mia, Caitlin, Madison and Amber." She rattles off the names, counting on her fingers. "And me. And Jessie."

Sharing the house with eight young women. Ethan and I should take precautions. This is definitely not the harem of my obscure dreams.

"Dad, can I go to Granny and Grandpa's house?" Ethan suddenly looks worried. I know the feeling, mate.

"Well, it's a bit far, Ethan. Don't worry. We'll be okay." I fist-bump him gently on his good arm.

Tired after a long, dramatic day, I head to bed early, having asked Jessica a dozen more times if she was okay and needed anything, or medical help, or ice cream, even. She said she was fine.

I'm about to turn off my light and lie down when there's a soft knock on the door.

The kids rarely bother me at night these days. There were times, when they were younger that they'd come and cuddle in Daddy's bed. But not for a long time.

"Hello?"

The door opens a crack to Jessica. Even in the dim light, I can see the distress on her face.

"What's wrong?"

She comes into my bedroom, stands next to the bed, wringing her hands together, hesitating for a moment.

"I lost my baby." She bursts into a flood of tears.

I stand up next to her, open my arms, and once more, hold her close and stroke her hair until the pain goes away.

"There, there, it will be okay, sweetheart. Daddy will look after you." The words just came out, I suppose she's one of the family now. She doesn't object.

"Can I sleep with you tonight?"

"Of course, if you want to. I snore though, I've been told." She laughs through the tears but then lays down next to me. Resting her head on my chest. I dare not move until she's fast asleep.

"Happy birthday, Rosie."

"Thank you, Daddy." Rosie is bouncing around like a bunny on speed. There's a stack of presents on the living room coffee table from me, Mum and Dad, Jessica and even Elise. Patience is not something children have an abundance of. "Can I open my presents now?"

"Yes, okay, sweetheart. Go ahead."

She woke up with the birds this morning, too excited to sleep. She came to wake me up and found Jessica still in bed with me. I think she was shocked. But she said nothing. Later she asked, "Is Jessie your girlfriend, now?"

I had to explain that no, Jessica was just a bit sad last night, and she didn't want to sleep on her own. Sometimes people need a cuddle. She nodded, but I think she was disappointed.

Rosie opens up the parcels, a load of different makeup sets, bought on the recommendation of Jessica.

The squeals and gasps confirm it was the right decision to make, even if I'm not okay with a thirteen-year-old girl getting obsessed with her looks and makeup. It makes her happy to experiment with it. I opt for a happy life. It's not like she'll be going out to pubs done up like a hooker.

I got a little gift for Ethan, too, because otherwise he'd feel left out. A little box of Lego always pleases. They both seem happy. That's all that ever matters when all is boiled down.

Jessica seems better today. I expect she'll never forget this experience, but for now, the trauma is contained.

It isn't the gaggle of tween girls in the house that's bad, they mostly keep to themselves, if you ignore the noise. It's their insufferable parents that make me want to throttle baby dolphins.

They stand around, far too long, probably mentally tallying up how much money I make, based on the age of my TV and furniture. The small talk is excruciating.

I'm not one of the clique; I don't attend the parent evenings or participate in the community events, and I sure as hell don't feel the need to impress any of them.

The way they say it, they somehow manage to make phrases like "it must be hard for you, on your own…" and "you're doing such a great job!" sound condescending and derogatory. I want to tell them where to shove their fake sympathy. But Rosie, innocent as she is, will undoubtedly want to go to each of these girls respective birthday parties when they come up. I can't risk her being shunned because they think her dad is a twat. Well, they probably already think that, but if they think I'm a rude twat, then that will seal the deal and Rosie will inherit my twat-status.

Society is complicated, therefore, I mostly avoid it.

They deliver each girl with a list of dietary requirements and sleeping arrangement preferences. I wish I had thought ahead and made up a pillow menu, and asked the chef to prepare a vegan, gluten-free, peanut-friendly, non-dairy birthday cake. Instead, the little darlings will have to make do with whatever this Tesco cardboard cake is made of and their rolled-up sleeping bag hoods as pillows.

I won't remember that Madison is not permitted to watch MTV at all, ever. Or that Chloe must not eat an apple near a birch tree. Or that Amber does not consent to having her photograph taken and posted to social media. Or that all of them must cease all iPad and iPhone use at nine o'clock.

I don't know what kind of concentration camp these parents run, but my house does not go by these strict rules. Presumably, the girls want to have a fun time. I'll let them do whatever they want, within some limits like getting drunk, experimenting with drugs, sending nude selfies, and anything else that seems to come within the remit of common sense.

My parenting policy has some simple bullet points. Treat them like humans. Remember what it was like to be that age. Encourage them to know what the right thing is, rather than restricting what I think all the wrong things are, which only prompts them to want to do them.

Still, I smile and nod, urging the parental units to exit, post haste. Come back tomorrow and collect your offspring. No, I don't have third-party liability insurance.

Once all the girls are all delivered and parents gone, Jessica arranges the cake and candle ceremony, which Ethan and I attend. Then they all give Rosie their gifts, which range from the pretentious perfume bottle to the simple Amazon coupon.

After that, Ethan and I sneak off upstairs, where I've set up his games console on the TV in my office. We'll have our own boys' party here, while the girls wreck the rest of the house.

Jessica, much happier this evening, has arranged games, music, food, and soft drinks. Then they'll watch a movie of their choosing.

We'll get through this. It will be okay.

Even considering Ethan's handicap, he's still managing to beat me at every game we play. Part of that is my absolute ineptitude with games. Part is my paranoia that my home is being destroyed by a pack of crazed girls, while I hide upstairs. Part is the frequent distraction by people trying to find the bathroom. Either way, we're having a grand old time. A boys' night in.

I admit defeat and let him play the computer for a while, sit back and flick around on my phone for a break.

Interesting. I've been tagged in a post by Faye Lovering.

'By far the most amazing tech-support I've ever had the pleasure of receiving. Highly recommend.' She's also tagged our company social media department.

It's nice to see that. But I had hoped she would reach out to me for more than just work-related things. Perhaps she wasn't as excited about our chance meeting as I was? I've been going back over that evening in the café, how she smiled and laughed, how we live close, yet strangely distant, but also have many similarities. Both single parents, both busy and disillusioned with life.

However, after my recent encounters with women, I'm a bit scared to even think there could be 'something'. But Faye was lovely, and beautiful into the bargain, plus, we did seem to get along.

Oh, well. Who needs love, anyway?

. . .

Around eleven o'clock I go downstairs and announce to the throng of 'hopped up on sugar and excitement' girls that they should think about going to bed.

They complain, but start the bathroom cycle. Isn't a sleep-over meant to involve sleep at some point?

At one-thirty, the giggling and loud whispers cause me to go back down and tell them to be quiet. But by two in the morning, I just give up and let them fizzle out of their own accord. I think they wanted me to come and yell at them, to make it all seem more real and scary.

They won't thank me tomorrow when they have to wake up, but one day, they'll remember me as the coolest dad. Ha!

Chapter Seventeen

C all it paranoia, or call it genuine medical concern. My research into the lack of underpants activity led me to use my extra time, in the mornings and afternoons, to take a long walk. A bit of exercise to stimulate the old blood flow.

I quite enjoy it. Gets me away from the house, work and pressure.

I've carved out a little path down by the river, along through the park, then back home. Takes about an hour each time.

That led me to more extreme choices, like joining a gym. Quite what I was thinking, I don't know.

I went twice. Once to pay and take a look around, once more to attempt some kind of activity.

But, since the only activity I've done in the last ten years has been pushing a shopping trolley around Tesco, my atrophied muscles in my arms and legs violently disagreed. I think I need to warm up a little before I attempt to organise a public sweating event.

What does a middle-aged man, having a mid-life dick crisis, do?

Buy a bike.

.   .   .

So committed am I to this new plan, that Jessica has dropped me off at the bike shop, and on my insistence, driven home without me. I now have a choice. To walk home and drag a bike with me, or confront the demons and ride that sucker home.

In my youth, I was never off my bike. I'd ride to school and home again, then all evening until dusk. Never thought about it. That's just what everyone did.

At some point, an engine took the place of my legs as I dallied briefly with a motorcycle, but the warmth and comfort of a car soon replaced that. The rest is history.

Now, I'm back on two wheels. A smart, neat thing. Bike tech has certainly come along a bit since I was last in the saddle. It even has a phone holder, for checking Facebook while careening down a hill into oncoming traffic, no doubt.

It fits. I pay the man, who looked sceptical I'd be able to ride all the way home, but seriously, how hard can it be?

I set off in style. Suspension, comfy saddle, gears that work. Aside from having two wheels, one in front of the other, this bike is so far from my previous rust heap, that it shouldn't be in the same category. This is easy.

I navigate out of the town centre along the smooth roads, quite enjoying myself. The breeze on my face, the pumps of energy propelling me along. It's quite exhilarating.

I love that ticking sound that stalled pedals make as I cruise easily down a slight hill. This is much better than walking. There's a cool breeze that keeps the sweat away. And much faster. I should have done this years ago. I barely twitch the handlebars and take a long corner, changing down a gear to climb back up another hill.

The bike shop chap insisted I buy and use a helmet, which does detract somewhat from the experience. I feel like a bell-end in this, but never mind, I suppose it's better than dying in a… CRASH.

A truck comes out of nowhere, cuts in front of me, and slows down. I slam on the brakes and almost go over the handlebars, instead, colliding into the side of the truck as it swerves out of the way. I wobble but manage to keep upright and not roll underneath the huge truck wheels.

The truck stops completely, a hiss of brakes scaring another blast of willies out of me. I also come to a dead stop. My underpants are now much browner than when I set off.

I hear the truck driver's door open and close, then boots on the metal steps. A burly chap comes around the front and approaches me. Shit.

"You all right?"

"Err, yes, thanks. Got a bit of a fright, but I'm fine."

"You want to be careful on that thing." He points at my beautiful shiny new bike, raising his voice a tad.

"Now, hang on, mate. You pulled right in front of me."

"I've been trying to pass you for a mile. All over the bloody road, you was."

"Was I?" I thought I was doing quite well. "I just got this new bike."

"Learn to fucking ride before you go on the roads, pal. Bloody liability, you are."

Before I can object, he's back in the truck, revving up the engine and pulling away. I look around for someone to offer some sympathy, but absolutely no one looks in my direction. Probably for fear of becoming involved in a police investigation.

I get back on the saddle and set off home, somewhat more carefully, this time.

By the time I get back, my legs are utterly made of jelly. When I get off the bike, I fall immediately over, legs unable to support me. I lie in an ungraceful heap, bike on top of me, trying to get my keys out of my pocket and prop myself up somehow.

The door opens, three faces peer out at me.

"Told you not to ride all the way home."

"Help!"

Rosie pulls the bike off me, Jessica helps me up off the ground. Ethan laughs. I'm dumped onto the couch, but Jessica brings me a cup of tea.

"You okay?"

"Mostly. I'll be fine. Just need to get in shape again."

"What shape, Daddy?" Rosie teases me.

"Spherical."

"Practice by just going up and down the road, a few times a day. You need to build your muscles up."

"Yeah, that's a good idea. Shouldn't be many trucks trying to kill me here, either."

I tell them about my little incident. It wasn't bad. Only my ego was bruised, but it made me think a bit. I could have been a road pancake under a truck wheel. That's no good. Who'd look after my babies?

Once my legs return to something like normal, I crawl up the stairs to my office. I need to do some googling.

First off, I make sure my life insurance is all up to date. It seems fine but could do with some boosting up. I have basic cover, just enough to pay off the mortgage. That won't see the kids very far if I kick the bucket. I'll have to arrange a better package.

Then I look for an online resource to make a last will and testament. There's no shortage of choice. I select a site that says I can make a legal will document free and print it off. I don't have much stuff to leave to the kids, but it's probably best to have things clear and simple.

Then there are the kids. Who will look after them?

The obvious answer would be their mother, but even though I said 'over my dead body' I'm thinking of extending that a tad. I've got a few choices, but only one of them makes any kind of sense.

Mum and Dad. But they are getting on in years. I can't lumber them with two kids.

Alex, who would be a wonderful mother, and I know I could trust her, but she's in a different country.

Which leaves Jessica. Who is possibly a tad young? She isn't really that much older than Rosie. But she is wonderful with them. I make an executive decision.

"Jessica?"

She plods up the stairs presently and stands in my doorway.

"What's up?"

"Come in, can we have a little talk." Her face falls as if I'm going to lecture her about something. "It isn't bad."

"Oh. Okay." She comes in, closes the door and sits down.

"I had a little brush with death earlier." She laughs but then frowns. "Yes, I know. I will be more careful. But just in case. I want to ask you something. It's a huge thing, really."

"Go on."

"If I die, somehow. Hopefully not under a truck, but, however the life energy decides to leave my body, be it violent or malevolent calm." I may be going over the top here, must be all the legal crap I've been reading. "Err, what I'm trying to say is. Would you like to be a guardian for the children, you know, if the worst happens."

She gasps, her hand clasps to her mouth, then she squints away tears.

"Oh, my god."

"Is that a yes?"

"Yes!"

"I mean, I hope I'll see them grow up, this is all just in case. But I trust you. You get on with them, you are part of the family now. I don't know who else to ask."

"What about Elise?"

"Ah, well. I think she's busy with her own life."

"Wait. Did you just say I'm part of the family?"

"Well, yes."

"Danny!" She jumps up and throws her arms around me. Please, no more waterworks. I can't handle any more crying women.

"I mean. If that makes you happy?"

She slaps me on the back. "Of course, it does. Thank you, Danny. I don't think I say it often enough, but I don't know where I would be if you hadn't taken me in."

"What else could I do. And anyway, you have helped me and the kids a lot, we owe you a huge debt."

"Let's call it even, then?"

"Okay. Deal."

"Good. But you better not die. Okay? I'm not kidding, if you die, I'll kill you."

"Shush. What's for dinner?"

"Ha. You, if you aren't careful." She smiles and slaps my arm, then leaves me to it.

Alex tells me I've made a good choice. I told her about the will, the insurance and the guardian stuff. Good to have things neat and tidy. Just in case. She also tells me not to die.

As everyone in Holland rides a bike since they were still in the womb, she finds it hilarious that I'm struggling this much. I still can't easily get up off my chair.

Alex asks me what happened to Faye? And that's a good

point. She added me as a friend, tagged me in a post, but that's all. I've heard nothing more.

'Why don't you contact her, you fool. She is probably waiting.'

'Err, I mean, she probably has things to do, a life to lead. I don't want to intrude.'

'You said she was nice, that it felt like old friends?'

'Yes.'

'Well, that means you have a connection. ASK HER OUT NOW.'

'Ah, I don't know, Alex. Besides, I have that problem.'

'Danny, you don't have to fuck her immediately. Just get to know her. Have dinner, go to a bar. Do normal things. Enjoy life while you can and don't talk about dying anymore.'

'You think I should?'

'If I was there now, I would push my foot up your ass. Do it.'

'If you were here now, I would let you.'

'Danny!'

'Okay, okay.'

Here goes nothing. I switch to Facebook, open up my friends list, which is dismally small, and find Faye. She's online. I open up the messages app. What do I say? Do I start with a lengthy introduction, do I try to be cool, comment on her photos? Come up with some contrived crap about the state of the planet?

'Hi.'

Or do I make an absolute idiot of myself and say nothing but 'Hi.'?

Faye is typing… 'Hey, Danny.'

Well, so far so good, I suppose.

'How was your interview?' Smooth. I remembered something from when we first met. I'm totally in here.

'It went well, thanks for asking. I'm waiting to hear now.'

'That's good.' Okay, well now I'm out of conversation topics.

'I was wondering when you'd get in touch :)'

She was wondering? And a smiley face?

'I've been wanting to. But you know, life and kids. Rosie had her birthday party.'

'Happy birthday Rosie. She must be thirteen now?'

'Yup. I'm dealing with teenagers now. It's all downhill from here.'

'LOL. You'll be okay.'

'Probably. Have you been up to anything fun?'

I'm dragging this out, I know, but if I schmooze my way in, it's harder for her to decline my dinner date.

'Same old, work, school, eat, sleep. How about you?'

'I bought a bike today. Nearly got squished under a truck. Can't feel my legs, still, but I'm trying.'

'Good for you. Well, not about the truck. What happened?'

'You know what, Faye, that's the kind of story best told over dinner.'

'Haha, is that your subtle way of asking me out on a date?'

'Damn, you foiled my plans. Okay, yes. I admit it.'

'Well, then, I accept. :)'

I switch back to my work computer.

'Alex. She said YES!'

Chapter Eighteen

In the car going to pick up Faye, I feel like a nervous teenager.

You think adults must have all their shit together when you're a kid. You see people doing important things, making important decisions.

But the reality is, no one ever knows what they are doing, and every day is just a bunch of people making it up as they go along.

Here I am, cleaned up, teeth brushed, a dab of aftershave, but not too much. Jessica and Rosie helped me pick out a shirt. I went for casual dark green, top button undone. I tried another couple of buttons, but that may have been a bit too 'casual'. Also treated myself to new underwear, just in case... I even cleaned the car inside and out.

I think I like this woman.

Not that I'm Casanova, but over the years I've been on a few dates, yet, I don't think I've given much of a damn about the other women.

Since Elise, my expectations have been minimal. If they show up, that's a plus.

This one is different.

I drive the familiar route, over to Rosie's school, but turn off one street early and park right outside number four Cedar Terrace. This feels momentous like there should be emotional music playing, a huge build-up ready for an epic event - me ringing the doorbell.

However, the doorbell doesn't seem to make any noise. I press it again. Nothing happens. Now I'm faced with a problem. What if it makes a whole load of noise in another part of the house and you just can't hear it outside the door? If I press it a third time, and she's already on the way, it will seem like I'm an impatient twat. Don't want to start a date with her already annoyed at me.

On the other hand, what if the doorbell just doesn't work, and I'm standing here all night, like a total knob? At some point, neighbour curtains will start to twitch, and someone will call the police.

I wait thirty long seconds, then knock on the door.

Some time passes, I loiter, but then the sound of steps and the rattle of keys in locks signifies she's alerted to my presence.

"Hi, Danny."

"Hello, Faye." As I say the words, it hits me that perhaps I should have come brandishing a bunch of flowers or something. Isn't that the done thing? I'm a bit out of practice. What if she's allergic? We can't go around thrusting pollen in people's faces. But now, I feel a little empty-handed. She doesn't seem to mind.

"One moment, and I'll be with you." She flits away, barely giving me a chance to study her squeezable arse in a tight-fitting pair of jeans. I did get a tantalising glimpse of a plunging white top.

I stand at the doorway, waiting. Her house is clean, neat. At least the hallway is. I notice she has an old landline phone on a little table. That must have been where she stood when I first talked to her.

She reappears with a black leather jacket and bag to match. "Are you a vampire?"

"What? No. Not that I know of?"

"You didn't come in. I thought maybe you were a vampire, you know how they can't come into a house unless invited."

"Yes. They are very polite, aren't they? You wouldn't get those kinds of manners with a Werewolf, or a Sasquatch. I heard they just bust down the door and crap on your kitchen table."

"That's a big problem in the suburbs. They smell the rubbish bins." She nods, authoritatively. "You nut job. Come on then, where are we going?"

Good question. One that I have toiled over for long hours with Google Maps. I've only ever been to a couple of restaurants in town if you don't count McDonald's. I don't think she'd appreciate a trip through the drive-through.

I checked the star rating of every restaurant, made a spreadsheet of the pros and cons, and then threw it all away. We're going to the only place I know has good food.

"Italian."

"Brilliant. Love it." Good choice. "Thanks for picking me up. I feel like a teenager again."

Teenagers have all the fun.

"You not drinking?" Faye asks me as I order sparkling water.

"Err, no. Having a break. A cleansing, or something."

"Good for you. I don't drink much, either."

"Feel free to get whatever you want."

"It's okay. I'll join you in sobriety."

"It's quite bleak there, but the views are majestic, on a clear day."

"I've been, a couple of times. Cold in the winter."

"You have to find someone to snuggle up with." I flash a grin, she chuckles.

The waiter brings a glass of breadsticks and puts them on the table for us, along with a lit candle in an old Chianti bottle. The wax of decades accumulated in drips down the sides. I'm reminded of the last time I was here. I picked up a breadstick and made a stupid dad joke. I refrain, this time.

"Did you hear about your job after the interview?"

"No, nothing yet. Fingers crossed though."

"Is it a big change, from what you do now?"

"Similar, in different circumstances. More money, better opportunities. You know the kind of thing."

I get the feeling she doesn't want to talk about it. I rack my brains for something interesting to say.

"Lovely weather, we're having." Seriously, Danny?

"It is, quite clement." She laughs. "Don't worry. Conversation isn't my strong point, either."

I feel a grin spread over my face. "Sorry, without the old booze to loosen me up, I'm just a bit pathetic."

"Last time I was out on a date, he got absolutely rat arsed, started a fight and then ended up puking in the pub toilet. So, you're all right. I think I prefer the awkward chat."

"Oh, wow. Nice chap. Well, last time I was here on a date, she told me a fake name, said I can't look at her face, or ask anything about her life, then I got up and left."

"Sounds like fun."

"I haven't had the best of luck, with women, over the decades."

"Sounds like me with men."

"Well, tell you what. I'll try not to get drunk on, umm, water." I pick up my glass. "If you don't assume I'm a weirdo stalker. Sound like a deal?"

"Deal."

I raise my glass for a toast. "To better dates." She clinks my glass.

.   .   .

Food arrives, and we both tuck in. Faye doesn't hold back. I like a woman who eats, rather than picking at the food. It's all delicious, why waste it?

I pat my growing tummy. "I was starving. Didn't eat much today."

"You look starving." She chortles. "Oh, my god. I'm sorry. I didn't mean that to sound the way it came out."

"No, it's okay. I know need to lose a few dozen kilograms."

"I'm the other way around, I need to put on some pounds, but no matter what I do, I can't seem to gain any. High metabolism, or something."

"I bet I could put some weight on you."

She looks up at me with a smirk, eyes wide.

"No, I didn't mean it like that." I feel my face redden. "I mean, Rosie, my daughter, she's learning to cook. We make this awesome spaghetti dish together."

"Sounds delightful…" I'm sure there was a flicker of flirtation in her eyes.

Since we've both made a comical faux pas, the atmosphere seems to lighten. We chat effortlessly, like how we did in the café as I fixed her phone. It feels comfortable, easy, like chatting with an old friend again.

I don't get the feeling I'm being evaluated and judged, and I don't need to pretend to be someone I'm not. I tell her about my home situation, Jessica helping me with Ethan and Rosie. She says she wishes she had a live-in helper. Josh needs attention every minute he's awake. Luckily, her neighbours are great with him, their son his best friend.

Faye asks about the kids' mother and what happened. I give my usual answer. "I don't know. I suppose we just drifted apart." She tells me the same thing happened with Josh's dad. Things were sort of fine until the stress of a child with special needs showed the cracks in their relationship, darker and deeper than before.

Somehow, she's managed to carve out a career and retain her sense of humour, despite all the hardships.

With every snippet of information we share, I'm feeling a little closer to her. This isn't a throwaway date, never leading to anything, or, at best, a once-off shag. This could be something real. Can I possibly allow myself to wonder, what if?

I keep my heart locked away, these days. After many breaks, I don't know how much more pain it can handle. I don't know what I expected when I got in the car this evening. I hoped for the best, of course, but you just never know. Things can go wrong in the blink of an eye. One wrong word and the evening is ruined. People get hurt, hopes and dreams are delicately fragile. Isn't it just easier all around to keep them back at home, safely locked in a cupboard with all the old Tupperware that no one uses anymore?

But as I look over at Faye, now, midst a long and passionate rant about cheap toilet paper, and how the human race is no longer under the influence of Darwin's survival of the fittest theory. I can't help but feel a glimmer of warmth and desire, that this little feisty woman, long dark hair waving in slow motion as she gesticulates. Eyes like pools of black tar, lips that I'd crawl over broken glass to kiss, and the shadow of a black bra, beneath her white blouse, giving me glimpses of eye candy as she fidgets around. That this specimen of nature's perfect harmony could be someone in my long-term future.

When the waiter brings the bill to the table, I'm plucked from a deep and meaningful world, where Faye and I connect on some higher level. I feel like I've known her for decades, but the reality is only a few hours.

I look around, and the restaurant is empty apart from our table.

"Holy crap, I didn't realise the time."

"I know, flown by, hasn't it?"

"I better get you home, young lady." She chuckles. She has to get back to pick up Josh from the neighbours.

Stepping out into the cool evening air is a fresh blast, compared to the heat of the restaurant. Faye shivers, even inside her leather jacket. She takes my arm and snuggles up close to me as we walk to the car. It feels nice. I don't want to say anything and break the moment, but as we approach the car, she splits away. Silly moments like these are what I'll remember when I ponder in the shower tomorrow morning.

As I drive the short distance to her house, I'm trying to think of a way to extend the evening, but the fact is she has to get her son and I have to go home to the kids.

In another universe, we'd have the rest of the night together, but as it is, we have about ninety seconds.

"Well, thank you for the lovely evening, Danny. I had a great time."

"Likewise. Can we do this again, sometime?"

She looks over at me. "No. I don't think so."

"What?"

"Kidding! Your face." She roars out laughing.

"Ah! Don't do that to a man."

"I better get Josh, but don't be a stranger, eh? Message me when you get home."

Faye leans over and kisses me on the cheek, then she reaches for the door handle, pauses, and turns back to me.

"Actually, I want to get an upgrade on that."

She pulls me towards her, gently and slowly, kisses me passionately on the lips for a good minute. A very good minute.

When she finally releases me, I'm stunned, speechless.

"See you soon, Danny."

I manage an incomprehensible, "Ung."

An uncomfortable stirring in my underwear brings me back to reality. Judas, you sneaky bastard. Don't tease me!

Chapter Nineteen

A celebratory McDonald's trip was called for yesterday. Ethan finally got his cast removed.

His young bones have healed nicely, according to the X-ray, and the doctor was happy that all was well. There's some aftercare to do, and the poor chap will have some more pain to deal with, and physio to help his atrophied muscles. But he is certainly on the mend and is in great cheer, having regained the use of his arm. He's been dying to scratch an itch for weeks.

A rather distressing and unforeseen side effect of this, however, is that we've been invited for dinner with Jack's parents tonight. They put me on the spot, as Maggie rang my phone and more or less insisted. What kind of lunatic does that?

She said something about not seeing me at the school lately and wanting to catch up. Catch up with what? I had no idea we had any history, aside from the occasional casserole.

Rosie, Ethan, and I will visit the Goddard household for dinner. I don't think they invited Jessica, and she's certainly the lucky one. I'm not interested in socialising, but this is another one of those sacrifices I make for the wellbeing of my babies.

Ethan is excited. Rosie is ambivalent. I am dreading it. I suppose that means Jessica is Goldilocks?

I park outside the house, knowing it from the few times Ethan has been to visit Jack before. They have elaborate, flowing curtains that belong in Buckingham Palace more than this semi-detached suburban domicile. I'm sure that Maggie spends a ridiculous amount of money at the soft furnishings store every month.

Ethan bolts into the garden and up to the door.

"Mind your arm, Ethan."

Rosie and I follow, slowly.

"Hello, hello. Rosie, my, haven't you grown up?" Maggie greets us at the door, an explosion of words and hugs, with a kiss on my cheek that I could have done without.

"Come in, come in. Doug is in the kitchen." Ethan has vanished up the stairs with Jack. Rosie looks awkward. I forbade her to bring her iPad, thus, she's in a teenage mood. Now she's going to be bored to tears with strangers. Poor girl.

We are directed through to the kitchen. Doug is chopping what looks like Parsley, no doubt that he's grown in his herb garden.

"Danny. Good to see you. Hi, Rosie." Rosie offers a vague smile.

"Hey, Doug."

Out of the corner of my eye, I notice someone else. A woman sitting at the dinner table.

"Danny, this is Eleanor. Eleanor, this is Danny." She stands up. I feel obliged to go over and shake her hand.

"Pleased to meet you, Danny." Eleanor is mid-thirties, short bob-cut strawberry blonde hair, mildly overpowering floral perfume, in a long dark-red dress. She's covered in jewellery, bracelets, necklaces and huge hoop earrings. She picks up a glass of white wine from the table and takes a sip.

"Indeed. Likewise."

"Eleanor was at a loose end. We thought we'd make up the numbers. Can I get you a drink, Danny?"

"Water, please. Sparkling, if you have it?"

"On the hard stuff, eh?"

"Taking a break from alcohol for a while. Anyway, I'm driving." I offer a disarming smile because people can take offence at the strangest things.

"Good for you, water it is then. Maggie, do the honours?"

"Of course. Rosie, love, what would you like?"

"Nothing, thank you." She's shy, sitting down in a corner chair. Probably best to leave her alone and not draw attention to her.

"You sure?" Maggie fusses over to Rosie.

"She'll be fine, thanks. She'll have a drink with dinner, I'm sure."

I'm handed a glass of water. "Well, dinner will be a few minutes, let's go through to the comfy chairs."

"The kitchen is where everyone wants to congregate, Maggie, don't fuss."

"Just trying to be a good hostess, Dougy, darling."

Eleanor turns to me. "What do you do, Danny?"

I open my mouth to answer, but Maggie steps in for me. "He's the regional manager for a big tech support place. Very important, aren't you?"

"Err, well. That's it, yes. Not sure how important I am, though…"

"Don't put yourself down, you help people figure out their gadgets and whatnot. That's very important."

"I suppose." I turn to Eleanor to be polite. I have to remember to ask people questions I have no desire in knowing the answer to. It makes them feel comfortable. Since we are stuck here for at least the next two hours, it may as well be friendly. "How about yourself, Eleanor?"

"I'm an aromatherapist."

"Oh, really?" That explains the overpowering scent from her.

"Yes, I have a little shop. You should come by for a massage. Very soothing."

"Ah, wonderful." Spoiler: I will not be going by for a massage. There's something odd about Eleanor I can't put my finger on.

"I'll give you my card. You can get the friends discount." She flashes a wide grin and then digs around in her purse for the card. "Here."

'Scents of Paradise - aromatherapy, massage oils, healing.'

"Thanks." I nod and pocket the card. Changing the subject to something mind-numbingly boring, but I know it will take the focus away from Eleanor and her stink potions.

"Doug, did you grow that Parsley in the garden?"

"I most certainly did, Danny. This is the Italian flat-leaf. I know you are partial to the Italian foods, aren't you? I'll show you my Red Basil pots later if you like?" I nod and smile.

Twenty minutes of excruciating conversation later, food is finally ready, and Ethan and Jack are called down to join us. There's a game of musical chairs as we shuffle around and get seated, but somehow, Eleanor sits down next to me. I was hoping to use Rosie as a buffer, but she's opposite. She hasn't said a word, but I can sense a build-up of tension.

"Beautiful children, Danny."

Ethan and Jack are in their own world at the other end of the table, talking about a game or something. Rosie scowls at me. "Thank you. They are a bit of a handful, but great kids, most of the time." Eleanor beams across the table at the kids.

"Do you have any children?"

"No, not yet."

She places her hand down on the table next to me, nails painted in a red to match her dress, but whilst the rest of her is adorned in bling, there is a noticeable gap on her ring finger.

Ah. I think I know what's happening here. This is a honey trap. Maybe more of a sperm trap. The weird feeling I get from Eleanor is her wanton, almost tangible desire to procreate. Well, this is awkward. I'm not really in the market for another baby, plus I am kindling a potential relationship with Faye. I may need to pull out a 'Get out of jail free' card here.

"Delicious chicken, Maggie. Thank you very much for inviting us."

"Our pleasure. I wondered what you were up to lately. Haven't seen you at school?"

"Jessica has been helping with the school runs."

"Jessica?" Eleanor flashes a frown at Maggie.

"Our house guest. She's a student, lovely girl."

"Ah. Well that's nice, isn't it? Good to get some help. Must be hard, on your own."

"Yes. It can be." And then other times it doesn't get hard at all. I haven't pinned down the reasons, yet.

Dinner is finished off with a homemade trifle, which was pretty good. And then we are furnished with cups of coffee and led into the living room. They call it the lounge, though, and it looks like Maggie has recently upgraded the curtains to an even more ostentatious purple silk, billowing out into the room. The carpet is vacuumed into lawn stripes, a fake fireplace dominates the room with a warm glow.

Rosie, bored almost to real tears, looks so depressed I have no choice but to give her my phone to play with. She immediately pulls headphones from a pocket and plugs in. Like an addict getting a hit of drugs, she's visibly happier instantly.

I realise this is perhaps a little unhealthy, but these are extenuating circumstances. Ethan and Jack flit back upstairs to play Minecraft, leaving the adults to discuss important matters, like when the best time to harvest Basil leaves is, and Doug's strong opinion on sports teams that I don't follow.

Rosie found another corner to hide in, Doug and Maggie occupy one large couch, leaving Eleanor and me to sit on a smaller one, I think it's called a love seat.

There's nothing visibly wrong with Eleanor, as far as I can tell, she's not ugly, not obese, not too loud or obnoxious, but she's just not my type. At all. I can't help it. I'm simply not attracted to her. But I get the feeling she's motivated by something more than just physical lust.

Dinner with Faye the other night felt relaxed and pleasant, but here with Eleanor, I'm uneasy and on edge.

Eleanor turns to me. "Danny, can I ask you something?" The mood in the room changes, Maggie and Eleanor exchange glances. I look over at Rosie, she's still glued to the phone.

"Shoot."

"I want to have a baby. Soon. Like, really soon."

A flush of sweat rolls over me like a tsunami. "Err."

"You seem like an ideal father. Good genes, strong, healthy children."

"Eleanor. I'm flattered, but we just met."

"No, you don't understand. I don't want you to be my partner, just a sperm donor. Danny, I want your baby juice."

I look around the room at the faces. Doug, beaming a smile, Maggie, a weary grin of hope, and Eleanor, I can't decide if she's taking the piss or serious.

"What?"

"I'm at that age, my hormones are aching for me to procreate, but I don't have time for a relationship. I just want the baby. You'd never hear from me again."

"It's just practicality, Danny." Maggie pipes up. They had this all planned from the start. I'm feeling a bit cornered here.

"Aren't there sperm banks for this sort of thing?"

Eleanor shakes her head. "Too clinical, I want to be sure the donor is a decent man. I don't want a surgeon to implant the seed with a syringe. I want it to be natural."

My face is heating up here, sweat beading on my neck and back. Does she think this is natural?

"I see. Well, this is all a tad sudden. Tell you what, I'll have a think and get back to you."

"No, Danny. I'm ovulating now." Her voice deepens.

"You can use the spare room, mate." Doug chimes in. A grin as wide as his couch. "We'll put the telly on loud. You'll be done in ten minutes."

Has he been talking to Elise? Ha.

"I've got some of my oils. I'll give you a massage, get in the mood. You need to get your chakras aligned for optimal sperm flow."

"My what?"

"Chakras. The energy centres in your body."

"Sorry, let me get this straight. You want me to go upstairs now, and have sex with you to get you pregnant, and then I'll never hear from you again?"

"That's it, yes." Eleanor smiles, moving to stand up. "Shall we go?"

"Are you stark raving mad, woman? We just met. I already have two children." I point to Rosie, still oblivious. "I don't think I want to spend the rest of my life wondering if I have another child somewhere that I don't even know."

"I wanted to find someone smart, handsome and intelligent to father my children."

"Didn't we all, Eleanor?" Maggie scoffs.

"Hey!" Doug protests as he realises what she said.

"Maggie told me all about you. All that was left was to meet you tonight. I think you'd be perfect."

"Well, I'm very flattered, but I think I must decline, thank you."

"That's not the answer I was hoping for, Danny."

"Err, Rosie. Come on." I wave to get her attention. "I think it's time for us to get going. Can you get Ethan, please?"

"Go on, mate. You'd be doing her a massive favour." Doug stands up. "Bit of how's your father and it's all over for you."

I get up and turn to Eleanor. "Look, I feel your pain. I sympathise, and I wish you all the best. But I'm not your man."

"But why not, Danny?"

Ethan and Rosie are now waiting just outside the door. I can get us out of here alive if I play my cards right.

I look around the room at them all, grinning like baboons, waiting for my answer.

"Because… Err. Because I'm impotent!"

An eerie silence descends on the room. We stand frozen for an awkward moment while they comprehend.

Doug breaks the silence. "Well, that's a shame. I'll give it a go, though, Eleanor, if you like?"

"Douglas Goddard!" Maggie slaps him on the arm.

"Only trying to help."

"Thanks for dinner, we'll be off now."

As we drive home, the scent of evening air comes through the vents, a light mist starts to bloom on the lawns as we pass by.

"Dad?" Rosie opens her mouth for the first time all evening.

"Yes, Rosie?"

"You should have said you got a vasectomy."

Smart kid.

178

Chapter Twenty

Today is a 'kids at the park with Elise' day. Jessica helped get them ready. I slept in until a reasonable hour, getting up to a peaceful house with quiet children. I don't know what I'll do without her when she leaves us for Uni. Better enjoy this peace while I can.

I'm not looking forward to the park handover procedure, because last time we met Elise, things did not go smoothly. I'm trying not to think about it as we slowly roll through the town.

When I told Alex about our dinner party with the Goddards, to guffaws of laughter, she said that I'm probably the only man in the world who could walk into a brothel at happy hour, and still not get laid. She's undoubtedly right. I seem to always be in the wrong place at the wrong time. Or in the right place, in the wrong time of my life. It's a miracle I have two children.

I told her about my date with Faye, and how that seemed to go a lot better.

The memory of that kiss in the car lingers with me. I'm trying to keep my hopes down and not let my imagination get the better of me, running wild with possible future situations.

Where it's Faye at the park, not Elise, and she comes back to my house with me. We have a wonderful family dinner together, then shag all night, waking up still entangled, to shag again before breakfast. A lot of my daydreams involve shagging Faye, lately. But they are just dreams. I can't get my hopes up. It will only end in tears.

As we arrive at the park, I can see my beautiful old car already waiting. I'm five minutes early today. We pile out of the car.

Elise sees us and waves.

"Hi, guys." She's friendly sounding, not the reaction I was expecting.

"Hi, Mum, have you got any presents for us?"

"Ethan, I told you not to ask that." I turn to Elise. "Sorry, he's been really bored lately."

"That's okay. Yes, guys, but you'll have to wait and see what I've got for you." Ethan cheers up. Rosie looks sceptical.

"Right, well, I'll see you in a few hours then."

"Wait, Danny. Will you walk with us for a bit?"

"Oh? Err, sure. Okay." What's this about? Is she luring me deep into the woods to dispose of my body easier?

The kids run off ahead, leaving me with Elise to meander slowly through the neat tarmacked path into the trees.

"I wanted to apologise, for what happened last time." I look up at Elise in shock, she's sincere, a sheepish smile on her face. My instinct is to say: "Don't worry about it." But I'm glad she has worried about it.

"Well, thank you for that."

"Will you please pass on my apology to Jessica?"

"Of course."

"I overreacted, and it was wrong. I hope we can forgive and forget?"

"Yes, we can." There's no need to hold a grudge. We need to move on with our lives. For the sake of the children and our sanity.

"Good."

Elise smiles her pretty smile. When she looks like this, I see why I married her, all those years ago. She's beautiful, still. The years have been kind to her. I could flip through our wedding album and look at her now and barely see any difference. The nostalgia creeps up on me sometimes, and I wonder how everything has gone so terribly wrong when it all started so well. "I hope we can be friends, again?"

I nod.

Somehow, we get onto the subject of dinner with Maggie and Doug, and I recount the story once again about Eleanor. Elise says she knows the shop, 'Scents of Paradise', and has bought oils in there before. She laughed at my reaction and said I should consider it more. We do have beautiful, healthy children. Why not spread my DNA further? When she puts it that way, I suppose she has a point. I feel the moment has passed though, and I'm unlikely to be invited back for dinner at the Goddards. Not that I am at all worried about that. As long as Ethan doesn't have to suffer because of it.

I'm not ready to bring up the subject of Faye, with Elise. Even with our newfound friendship, some things are better left unsaid.

We end up walking the entire park circuit together, children running around us in circles, back and forth. They probably clock up three times as many steps as I do.

By the time we get back to the carpark, they are thirsty and hungry. But they haven't forgotten the presents Mummy promised them.

Elise opens the boot of her car, taking out a cool-looking skateboard for Ethan and a pair of roller boots for Rosie. They squeal in excitement and start rolling around in the almost empty carpark. Rosie, a few inches taller than usual in the boots, is the mirror of her mother. Beautiful. She's going to be a heartbreaker.

"Keep on the path, guys." The last thing I need is someone rolling under a car.

"Well, that should keep them busy over the summer."

I nod. "Thanks, Elise. They look very happy, today."

After some more rolling and boarding around, the kids hug and kiss their mother, and get back in my car, looking exhausted. I might get some peace tonight if they go to bed early. I wave goodbye to Elise, but she comes over to me for a brief embrace and a kiss on the cheek.

"See you all soon, then?"

"Sure. Take it easy."

Rather than stop for nasty fast food today, Jessica has prepared lunch. A spread of sandwiches, nuggets, dips, little Indian themed side dishes, and a jug of home-made lemonade.

She's quite the domestic goddess when she wants to be.

I'm surrounded by women every day. Balancing my life between Alex, Jessica, Faye and Elise, with the occasional crazy random one entering the fray, but somehow, I just can't seem to get anywhere. At least, in the way I want to. Perhaps I'm too fussy, and I should just linger around a bar in town, waiting for a woman drunk enough to let me on top of her for five minutes. But I've always had this sense of standard. I know I could have been a man-whore and slept around with any old slapper, but I didn't want that. I wanted the sense of achievement that a relationship brings. The luxury of knowing I didn't have to chase strangers for meaningless sex, not that I've ever done much chasing.

I've had brief periods in relationships where that was true, and those were the only times in my life when I felt content and serene.

I need to get that back.

I open up my messages app.

'Hi, Faye.'

'Danny, just the man I need.'

'Oh. I hear that a lot lately.'

'Really?'

'Yes, but usually in the wrong context.'

'Well, I'm helping organise a sponsored walk for World Land Trust next weekend, would you all like to come along?'

She sends me a link to the event page.

'That sounds great. Absolutely, but, one condition.'

'What's that?'

'Can we have dinner, after? Just the two of us, I mean.'

'Yes! I thought you'd never ask :)'

Well, that went better than expected, and I will put all my walking and cycling practice to good use. I don't normally partake in charity events because of all the self-righteous humble-bragging that people do. No one does anything now without making a big fuss about it all over their social media. They hide it behind bullshit phrases like 'raising awareness', but the reality is clear as day. They only do it for attention, and it makes me sick. I couldn't say no to Faye, though, and I'm hoping she isn't one of the braggers. Better tell the kids.

"Hey guys, I have some cool news." They barely look up from their iPads for a moment before looking back down. "Put those things down for a minute, will you?"

Jessica comes to my rescue. "Rosie, Ethan, listen to your dad."

They comply. I shouldn't need Jessica to help me get my kids to listen to me, but such is life.

"We're going to take part in a fun walk next weekend. To raise money for a conservation charity."

Groans of apathy are not what I was hoping for. But I suppose I should have expected them.

"We'll get ice cream after."

"Yay!" At least Ethan seems excited now there's an incentive. Rosie remains impartial.

A photo of a skinny young lad appears on Rosie's iPad. "Who's that?"

She reaches to hide it from me. My Dad-instinct kicks in, and I grab it before she gets close. I open the app and see a conversation she's been having with this fellow. I recognise him.

"That's the lad from holiday, he fell on you out of the castle."

Rosie bites her lip. "Yeah."

"Kian Kershaw." I scroll back through the messages. There's mild flirtation, silly jokes, links to music. Nothing bad. Rosie has sent him a couple of selfies, but thankfully they aren't anything naughty. I don't want to intrude on her life. I hope she's sensible enough to know to be careful, but I also realise she's far too young to be getting into boyfriend territory. But 'Girls just wanna have fun'.

"Rosie, can we have a chat?"

"Ugh. Can I have my iPad back?"

"Yes, you can. But listen first. You know I'm pretty relaxed about things. Most other kids your age wouldn't get this much freedom with gadgets."

She nods. I know her friends' parents have much stricter policies.

"I'm easygoing like this because I want you to know your

own rules and limits. You need to be careful, out in the world with people. Especially with boys."

"I know, Dad."

"You are a good girl, but… How can I put this? You are very pretty. A lot of boys will message you soon enough."

She blushes a little. But says nothing.

"I just want you to stay safe, don't get pressured into anything, don't make any arrangements to meet anyone, at all."

"Okay, I know."

"Just making sure. And if you ever feel weird about something, come to me, or Jessie." Jessica nods in agreement. "We won't be angry at you. Okay?"

"Yes, Dad."

"Well, all right then. But one more thing, sweetheart." She looks up at me. "Treasure your youth and innocence. Don't be in a rush to grow up. Trust me, being an adult is total shit."

She laughs. I give her back her iPad.

"We all up for the walk next weekend? Faye will be there."

"Oh? Yeah, cool."

I walk to the kitchen. After a parenting session like that, I need a cuppa to calm me down. Jessica follows.

"You're a good dad, Danny."

"Thanks. I just do what I think is best, and always try to remember, I was a kid, once."

"I wish my parents thought like that."

"I'm always amazed by how people forget so quickly. Or they hide behind the old adage about 'discipline and rules never did me any harm'. It did do them harm. They are contradicting their own words even as they speak them."

"Yeah, I think they just want to pass on the pain they had as children."

"Got to break the cycle somehow."

"A charity walk with Faye next weekend?" A conspiratorial grin breaks out on Jessica's face.

"Yep. What of it?" I laugh.

"Oh, nothing. I might come along to that. Seems like a worthy cause."

"Yes, it does, doesn't it?"

Chapter Twenty-One

There are way too many people in colourful shirts, being extremely enthusiastic at this ungodly hour of nine, on a Saturday morning at the park. Extreme enthusiasm typically has the opposite of the intended effect on me, leading me to want to run away, as fast as I can, rather than take part in whatever stupid crap is being peddled. However, this time, I'm somewhat biased, due to the bulk of the ardour coming from a petite, feisty woman, whom I'm becoming rather fond of; despite my cynicism towards the concept of ever finding a meaningful relationship again.

This little kitten has got me quite smitten.

The kids are getting excited, and Jessica seems happy. I'm trying. Very trying.

Some people have dressed up as whatever ridiculous costume they could throw together; Six-foot tall chickens, dolphins, various other unrelated creatures. Someone is dressed entirely in plastic bags, apparently representing the plastic in the oceans. Must be itchy. Others are in tight spandex, taking things far too seriously; doing warm-up routines and looking at stopwatches. Can we not just walk and have a laugh, then go back to our boring lives? Does everything have to be a competitive event?

Personally, I don't give a shit if I finish first, last, or if I happen to get sidetracked by a bus home. It doesn't matter, and the money is already collected. Not that I have much sponsorship. The only person who stumped up ten quid was Alex. I put in the other thirty myself. The kids did better at school, but I may end up funding those promises. Oh well. It's for a good cause.

We were hoping to meet Josh this morning, but Faye explained he didn't feel like it, in the end. He's with the neighbours again. Faye blew it off, but I could tell she was a bit disappointed. I expect she's used to Josh having his complications. This would be wildly out of his normal routine and she mentioned that he doesn't do well in big crowds. Probably for his own good he stays away. Shame.

Still, Faye met Ethan and Jessica for the first time, and everyone seemed to get on wonderfully. I'm hoping that when she finds out I'm planning to stroll the whole thing at my normal sedentary pace, she won't dump me for being a wuss.

We are somewhere in the middle of the throng. But as the starting pistol fires, and the momentum picks us up, the kids, along with Jessica, rush forward. I, however, stay firmly behind. There's no panic. I prefer to pace myself, to avoid exhaustion. Rather surprisingly, Faye stays with me.

"I hope I'm not slowing you down, Faye?"

She laughs. "No, not at all. I don't want to get all out of breath and sweaty."

I look over at her, in a bright blue t-shirt and tight lycra leggings, her hair tied back, no makeup, a huge number eight on her shirt. I wouldn't mind seeing her out of breath and sweaty. Probably not vertical, though.

"I'm not going to say what I'm thinking."

She laughs and slaps me on the arm playfully. "Watch it, mate."

I hold my arms out in innocence, "Dunno what you mean?"

"Thanks for coming, today. All of you."

"Pleasure. Happy to support you, and the worthy cause. Plus, the kids are loving it."

"That means a lot." She smiles a smile that would melt a Titanic busting iceberg, and possibly even my cold, dead, blackened heart.

We amble along leisurely, many people ahead, few behind. A camera crew pass on a slow-moving car, Faye yells out some slogans for their sound-bites. We may get on to someone's YouTube channel, which, these days, is far more important than being on the TV.

Jessica sends me a photo of the kids at the finish line, while Faye and I are still only about halfway around. We laugh but pick up the pace a little. Faye says there are free ice-creams at the end. We better hurry and get there before they are all gone or melted.

Near the end, it's me feeling out of breath and sweaty. I'll need a shower before we go out for our dinner date later. I'm sure Faye will also want one. We could save time and shower together… Or, as Alex said to me before, that wouldn't save any time at all.

"Where do you want to go for dinner tonight?"

"I'm that hungry, I could eat out of the bins behind Tesco."

"Ah, well that sounds like a cheap date. Tesco bins, it is."

"Do you think that requires formal dress?"

"Absolutely. Black tie. We don't want to offend the other tramps."

She laughs. "Are you saying I'm a tramp?"

"One can only hope." I grin.

She giggles and slaps me again, but this time on the arse. My luck could be in here.

"Daddy!" The kids see us and wave, then run towards us.

"Hey, guys. Well done."

"You've been AGES!" Rosie complains.

"Well, when you are as old as me, you'll understand. You enjoy the journey, rather than the destination."

"What are you going on about?"

"Nothing. Where's the ice cream?"

"All gone."

"Oh, well that's a shame. Come on then, let's go home and clean up." I turn to Faye, "Would you like to stop at ours and grab some lunch?"

"Sounds like a plan, man."

Faye follows us in her car. She's got a cool little electric vehicle. Very nifty.

I've been trying to think of a way to get her back to my place. My home ground advantage should help win her favour. Maybe we don't even need to go out for dinner if I knock up our infamous spaghetti.

I give Faye the thirty-second tour of the house, then she slumps down on the couch with a tall glass of cold lemonade. She looks at home, and I could get used to seeing her there.

Ethan can't help himself, and with his arm back in working order, he switches on the TV and games console. I'm about to protest, but Faye comes to his rescue.

"Hey, we've got that game. Want to see if you can beat me, Ethan?"

"Yeah!"

Fair enough. I leave them to it and look through the fridge for some lunch ideas. Jessica comes to my aid, and between us, we knock up a lunch fit for Kings. Or at least, poor Kings who haven't been shopping for a few days. But our table is full and there's lemonade and tea. Who needs anything more?

"Food." I yell through the house and a cacophony of footsteps precede the arrival of hungry people.

"Wow, nice job." Faye looks wide-eyed at the fare on the table.

"Lunch, à la the 'reduced to clear' fridge. Hope you like coleslaw?"

"Who doesn't like coleslaw?"

"Exactly. But I have heard of factions of 'slawaphobes trying to gain power in Westminster. Down with the government!"

"Down with knickers!" Faye fist pumps into the air.

"Seconded."

"You two are as bad as each other." Rosie laughs, and I feel a warmth around the table. Happy kids, pretty women. I could get used to this.

"Do you mind if I get a quick shower? Then we can head off."

"Please do."

"Oh, no. Do I stink?"

Faye laughs, "Kidding! Of course not. Go ahead. I'll play Ethan again. This time I'll win, buster."

"No way."

I grin. She's got no chance. Ethan is basically at one with the games console. He's entered the Matrix, his thoughts become reality.

"Back soon."

I head upstairs and peel off my sweaty clothes, throwing them in a heap on the floor. I can't help but think that Faye's clothes would look good next to them... One step at a time, Danny. Things are going well. Just get through this evening without fucking something up, and it could be game on.

The warm spray of the shower feels good on my back. My feet are throbbing in pain, my legs are jelly. But it feels good to wash away the sweat. I linger for longer than usual. I want to be super clean in every nook and cranny, just in case there's any bedroom activity later.

I have to pause for a moment and consider what Judas the Betrayer is guiding me towards. He always wants the same thing; to bury his head where the sun don't shine. But is that really what I want? I mean, yes, ultimately, doesn't everyone? It feels good for a few minutes, at least.

All my DNA is pointing me to that end goal. But that isn't going to help with the long-term plan. I don't want a one-night stand with Faye, and then game over. I hope she wants more than that. Relationships are more than just sex, but sex comes with a good relationship. Nourish and feed the former, and the latter should come in droves. Judas may need to wait a little longer, but it should be worth it.

For a brief second, I thought about declining the chance of a shag, if Faye brought it up, but I'm not that stupid.

Let's just see how it goes. How about not overthinking every single point, for a change, eh, Danny?

With the help of Rosie and Jessica, I had already planned my evening wear last night. Something suitable for a second date. Jeans and a comfy shirt. Not the same shirt as last time, but possibly the same jeans. Who can keep track? I suit up, dab on some aftershave, and go downstairs.

"Well, how do I look?" I burst into the living room, to a lacklustre response. "Oh, where's Faye?"

"Gone." Ethan sulkily announces.

"Hey?" A thump in my chest tolls the bell of woe. "Where did she go?"

"Home, I think." Rosie pipes up.

"Where's Jessie?"

"In her room."

How long was I in the shower? I left a happy home with a beautiful woman waiting for me, now I just have two apathetic children with monosyllabic responses.

I climb back up the stairs and knock on Jessica's door.

"Hey, Danny."

"Where did Faye go?"

"She said she had to go sort Josh out."

"Right. Okay. Err, did she say what happened?"

Jessica looks awkward. "Danny, you left your phone downstairs."

"Thanks. I was looking for it."

She hands it to me, biting her lip. "I thought I'd better take it."

"What?" I tap the screen. Oh, shit.

"Did Faye see it?" Jessica nods. "And did she leave soon after?"

"Yes. Ethan was playing a game, and that photo popped up. He yelped, I tried to take it, but he dropped it down on the table, and Faye had already seen it by the time I could grab it. She said something about perhaps you are into different things. Sorry, Danny."

"I don't know that woman. I just couldn't get rid of the photos. They hadn't come for a while. I forgot all about Cindy fucking Jiggles."

"You don't have to explain to me, Danny. But Faye seemed a bit shocked."

"Okay, thanks, Jessie."

I hang my head in shame and cross the landing to my office, slump down in my chair, and resign myself to a lifetime of solitude, because my obsession with tits has, ironically, denied me the chance of actually touching some.

You absolute twat, Danny Watts. Buggered it all up, yet again.

After some moping, sulking, ruminating and pondering, I've decided to delete all of my dating apps and the associated accounts. Nothing good came of them anyway, what's the use in trying if, when I finally get somewhere with someone I like, I go and mess it all up?

I should have figured out how to unsubscribe from the naughties list a long time ago, now it has cost me dearly.

The deletion process takes much longer than it should. Some of these apps are harder to escape from than the Jehovah's Witness chapter inside of Alcatraz. They really don't want you to go.

For one app, I had to phone a number somewhere in the US, re-routed to people in India who barely understood me, but after some threats and yelling, my account is now deactivated. All of them are. All six pointless dating apps I scoured for potential lays every day, all gone. My phone suddenly feels lighter.

With that done, I can now focus on the other problem. Faye. How do I convince her it was a mistake, and no, I'm not a pervert who gets dirty photos from some random BBW, while I'm meant to be spending time with the woman I do want to see naked?

I have to pause again, what if I am that pervert? How can I convince Faye that there's more to me than that?

. . .

I write an apology, then an explanation, then a long tirade about how I've been single a long time, alone in my bed, that I strayed into unknown territories, not because that's what I was into, but that's what was thrust into my face. I know I should have cleaned up, but I forgot about it. Mesmerised as I was by her delicate beauty.

Don't worry. I deleted that text well before I could press send.

After several more goes, toning down the bullshit an increment each time, in the end, I leave the phone on my desk. Sometimes you have to sleep on things to get the full perspective.

The best thing I can do right now is nothing. Can I do that without making a balls-up of it?

Chapter Twenty-Two

When the kids were younger, when they didn't notice much, we used to be able to celebrate a single combined birthday for both of them, about halfway between the two, as they are only around a month apart.

We also acknowledged the actual days. But the big event, with family and friends, cake and gifts, was much easier to plan as a one-day thing.

I can't get away with that anymore.

Today we're going to a skate park, with an as yet unknown amount of eight-to-nine-year-olds, whose parents can be bothered to drive twenty minutes to the nearest park.

Needless to say, this was not my first choice. But that's what Ethan wanted, encouraged by the skateboard his mother gave him. My gift was all the matching safety equipment because another broken limb is not what we need right now.

Jack is coming, which sadly means Maggie or Doug accompanying him, which could be awkward. I've been wondering if there's any reasonable way to take back my earlier statement of impotency, and explain it away with a misunderstanding, but I can't think of anything that would fly. The damage is done, and I'm just going to have to live with it.

But another parent is coming for sure, that I am rather glad about.

I somehow convinced Faye that I wasn't a pervert, that the photo on my phone was spam from a dodgy website, and that she should come and meet me again.

She took it quite well. The day after. I let us both sleep on it, then I called her. A real phone call, not a text or a Facebook message. I profusely apologised, explained the reasons, told her I had deleted all the apps and accounts.

She laughed, said she probably overreacted. Then she apologised to me and said it was none of her business what was on my phone. But that's the thing. I'd like it to be more of her business.

It was a tad stilted, but I think we're all good, again. Taking things very slowly, this time.

We arrive at the skate-park a little early, and there's been some drizzle already. It looks a tad slippery, which doesn't bode well. But otherwise, it seems well maintained. A few other kids are rolling up and down.

Rosie, already in her roller-boots, speeds off into the smooth concrete park. Ethan follows on his board. He's kitted out in his safety gear. It will be fine.

"Hello."

I turn around to the pleasing sight of Faye, black leather jacket, blue jeans, hair loose and blowing in the light breeze.

"Hey." I fluster for a moment, wondering if I should kiss her, but she saves me from my awkwardness by moving in for a peck and a hug. "Thanks for coming."

"Our pleasure, thanks for inviting us."

"Where's Josh?"

She turns around, motions to a boy standing by the gate to come over. He walks towards us with a jaunty skip. I can tell he's Faye's child immediately. He's got her features and dark hair. He's carrying a brand new skateboard.

"Hello, Josh. I'm pleased to meet you."

"Josh, this is my friend, Danny."

I stick out my hand, and he gives me a hearty shake. "I've got a friend called Danny at school, his real name is Daniel, but everyone calls him Danny. I suppose that's what happened to you, too?"

"Yes. It is, indeed." I smile.

"I'm called Joshua, but everyone calls me Josh. It's only two letters less, but it's quicker to say…"

"Josh, do you want to go for a skate around?" Faye interrupts the lad.

"I'll call you Josh if that's okay with you?" He nods in approval. "Rosie, Ethan, come and say hello." I wave the kids over. They notice Faye and change direction towards us.

"You know Rosie, don't you? From music class?"

"Yes, she's very good at Piano, but not great at Flute."

I laugh. "Well, everyone has their strengths and weaknesses." Rosie shoots me a look of daggers. "This is Ethan, it's his birthday today."

"Happy birthday, Ethan."

"Thanks. Woah! Is that an Element board?"

"It is, but I don't know the brand."

"They are super cool. Come on, let's see it go?"

"I've never skated before."

"It's easy. Look." Ethan speeds off into the distance. Josh looks over at Faye. She nods, and he stands on the board with both feet. Not moving.

"Push off with one foot." Faye mimes the movement.

"Right." He rolls slowly into the concrete. At least he's keeping his balance. Sensible kid. A few more taps and he's gradually speeding up into the park. I'm glad it isn't very busy.

Rosie kicks off back into her circle of the course.

I turn to Faye. "He's a great lad."

"He's having a better day, today. He is a good boy, most of the time, but he can have terrible moments."

"I know that feeling, myself."

"Well, hopefully, you don't tantrum and get obsessed with some ridiculous petty thing?"

"It has been known."

She laughs. "Typical man."

I notice Jack run past us, jump on his skateboard, and zoom straight over to Ethan with yelps of excitement. I turn around and, sure enough, Maggie is walking over to me.

"Hi, Danny."

"Maggie. Thanks for coming."

"No problem." She waves to Ethan. "Happy birthday." He looks up and waves back.

Maggie glances at Faye and back at me expectantly. I suppose I'm meant to introduce her. Do I say friend or girlfriend? Which one of those titles is potentially most inflammatory? If I say one, and Faye thinks she's the other, I'm screwed. Best to play it safe.

"Faye, Maggie, fellow mothers of boys." I awkwardly motion between them.

"Pleased to meet you, Faye." Maggie beams a smile.

"And you." Faye smiles back.

I'm glad that's over.

"I haven't seen you around the school?"

"Josh goes to Rosie's school."

"Ah, that would explain it."

I nod. The conversation is getting quite tedious. How long do I need to keep talking to be polite?

I suspect that no one else from Ethan's class will show up. The weather isn't wonderful and anything involving effort is frowned upon. He doesn't seem to be bothered about it.

Maggie looks between Faye and me. I think she's just clicked that we are more than just acquaintances. Then her face scrunches up, flicking into empathy toward us.

"Well, I'll leave you to it, then."

She walks back to her car.

Faye turns to me. "What was that look for?"

"Ah, well, Maggie may be under the impression that I can't get it up."

Faye tilts her head and raises her eyebrows. I explain what happened at dinner with Eleanor and Faye keels over in laughter. Seems everyone finds it hilarious except me.

"Rosie told me after I should have said I got a vasectomy."

"She'll go places, that girl."

"Indeed."

The heavens decide this is a good time to open up, and it starts to bucket down. There's no shelter here at all, so I wave the kids over and we rush back to our cars. Soaked by the time we get in.

Jack has piled into my car, Faye and Josh are across the car park.

I send a text to Faye.

'Well, this sucks.'

'It may pass, soon.'

'Hope so.'

I check my weather app; it claims rain for the next hour at least. Not good. It's a shame, but at least he got to play for a while.

"What do you want to do, Ethan?"

"Get McDonald's."

Should have known. I suppose it's his choice today. The little chap doesn't seem to be disappointed his birthday plans are a washout. I'm just glad he isn't having a freakout about it. Big boy now, he's growing up fast.

I switch back to my phone.

'Ethan wants McDs. You up for it?'

'A date at the drive-through? LOL, sure.'

I text Maggie and tell her play is called off due to rain, and we'll go back to my house after grabbing some food. She can pick Jack up from there. She replies promptly with a thumbs-up emoji.

Back home, we are assembled at the dining table.

"We should sing Happy Birthday to Ethan." Jessica starts off singing and everyone joins in. I fetch the cake we had planned for later and light the candles. Ethan is excited and happy; He's still young enough that cynicism hasn't taken over his life. Oh, to be that innocent. On my birthday, all I want to do is hide in bed. An increment to my age is not a good thing.

Ethan blows out his candles and we all cheer and clap. It's nice that Faye and Josh are here. They complete the picture.

After we eat, the kids settle down in front of the TV with the games console and take turns to battle it out. I think Ethan could have met his match in Josh. They both play with an intensity and fluidity I'm in awe of.

For a while, we went out on the pavement and rolled up and down with our various wheels. It wasn't quite what Ethan hoped for, but at least we got out for a bit.

Maggie picks Jack up at the designated time, and Jessica and Rosie sneak away to their respective rooms. Ethan and Josh are back at the games console, furiously killing each other on Mario Kart. At least Ethan can only injure his fingers this way. Which leaves me with Faye, virtually alone in the kitchen.

"Would you like to stay for dinner, Faye?" She scrunches up her nose momentarily.

"Sure, why not?"

"No pressure. We'll just have whatever I can knock up from the fridge. No ceremony here."

"Sounds good to me. Sometimes the best things in life are the simplest." She flashes a grin to warm the coldest of cockles.

"Absolutely. Take a seat in the living room, if you like, I'll get to work."

"No, I'm fine here, thanks. I like watching a man cook."

I look up at her, leaning forward on the counter, a sly grin on her face, twirling a strand of hair between her fingers.

"Fair enough."

Chapter Twenty-Three

I have been summoned to an urgent team meeting in Amsterdam, with little notice. Usually, these things are planned months in advance, but headquarters dropped this on me just a few days ago. Mandatory attendance required for Alex and me. We don't know the agenda, and I don't know the chap who's coming over from the US head office to meet us. I suppose we'll find out soon.

Alex is meeting me off the plane at Schiphol, and we're going directly to the hotel to meet Dewey Brannon the Fourth, or 'D4' as he told us to call him. Born and raised in Dallas, Texas.

On the brief call I had with him he was curt, rude, but straight to the point. Meet him in Amsterdam and make damn well sure to be there on time.

Luckily, Jessica stepped up and agreed to be left entirely in charge. I'm sure I can trust her; She's a good lass. But I asked Faye to stop by once or twice, just in case.

And here I am, about to land in Amsterdam, a bit nervous, to be honest. Are we all being made redundant? Couldn't they just do that over the phone? In the years I've worked for the company, this type of thing has happened only twice before that I recall.

Once was a team-building event, with lots of stupid games to make us all interact, plus a disco. Another when the company was acquired in a merger. They wanted to make sure we all knew, firsthand, that absolutely nothing would change. However, in the subsequent months, everything changed, except for my salary.

Since this is most certainly not a team-building event, I'm leaning towards it being some kind of bad news. The only saving grace, I get to see Alex again, unexpectedly.

As she lives in Amsterdam, she doesn't need a hotel room. Thus no shenanigans this time, especially with the boss-man watching over us.

Alex is waiting for me after I rush through the airport. The plane landed half an hour late.

"Alex!" No prank at the arrival gate this time.

She's wearing long black boots, blue jeans, a light jacket and hair tied back. As gorgeous as ever, but something isn't right.

"Danny!"

We embrace, but there's no laughter in her eyes. "What's wrong?"

"Ugh. Will tell you later. Come on. Don't want to be late for Mr Dee-Four."

"Right."

She leads me through the miles of airport, until we eventually find an exit, then up to where she's parked.

Her car appears to be older than she is. A faded old light-blue Saab. She reaches over and pops the lock for me to get in. The seat is leather, but more creased and cracked than an Elephant's back. There are two large suitcases on the back seats and a tall pot plant. Not a 'pot' plant as you might expect in Amsterdam, but some kind of large succulent.

"Err, shall I put my bag in the boot?"

"No. It's full. Sorry, can you hold it?"

"Okay."

I clamber in and awkwardly heft my small travel case on my lap and lean out to shut the door.

Alex pulls off immediately before I can grasp for the seatbelt.

"Do you normally bring a plant with you in the car? I suppose it gets like a greenhouse in the summer."

Alex turns to me as we negotiate the narrow car park roads. "I broke up with Niels."

"Oh, shit."

"Yeah. Shit is definitely the word."

"When did this happen?"

"Last night."

"Alex, I'm sorry."

"Don't be. I'm still angry."

"Do you want to tell me what happened?"

"Yes, but we don't have time now before we get to the hotel."

"Right, okay."

"I have a favour to ask."

"Anything."

"Well, you can see all my stuff here in the car. I have nowhere to stay. Can I sneak into your room?"

"Oh boy. Did you leave your home? Yes, of course you can. But what will you do after?"

"Will go back to Mum and Dad's house in Eindhoven. I will be fine. But for these meetings, I need to stay in Amsterdam."

"Wow. Okay. Don't even worry about it."

"Thank you, Danny. I knew you would help." She smiles, and for the first time since I arrived, the smile reaches her eyes.

.   .   .

We arrive at the Myatt Hotel. One of the best in the city, towering over the Amstel river. A lavishly appointed, unreasonably expensive, palatial monolith. Our per diem was scrapped for this impromptu trip. D4 told me to book somewhere awesome. I did some research, and this place has dozens of five-star reviews on the StayAway.com site.

A porter opens the doors for us and then peeks in at all the suitcases with a grimace. Alex says something in Dutch and he brightens up, then goes to the boot and takes out one small bag. I'm also thankful he took my suitcase off my lap.

The reception area is bigger than the plot of land my house is on. We traverse the cavernous space over to the check-in desk.

"Danny Watts, I have a room for three nights."

The beautiful reception girl flashes a smile that can only mean she's sat on some kind of buzzing electronic device. "Of course, Mr Watts." She looks up from her computer screen. "There is a message for you, from a Mr Brannan. He will be late, but would like to meet in the lounge bar at four o'clock."

So much for making damn well sure to be here on time.

"Thank you."

The porter escorts us up to the room on the sixth floor. Beautiful views across the city. The room has a separate bedroom and lounge area with a small bar in one corner. The bathroom has a vast champagne-coloured hot tub and a crystal clear glass shower cubicle that's bigger than my home office. We're going super swanky here. I hope D4 approves of it.

I hand the porter a five Euro note, and he slopes off.

I turn to Alex, who is standing at the window. "We have a couple of hours to get settled before His Highness wants to meet in the bar. Do you want to tell me what happened now?"

"Is there any whisky in that minibar?"

I open the cupboard door. "There's a selection of highland single malts, and a Jack Daniels."

"Give me the Jack."

I pour her a glass, with ice, and myself a long glass of sparkling water. I'm trying to stick to my plans of no booze for a while longer.

Alex takes a gulp. "Where to start?"

I motion to the couch and we sit down. Alex puts her glass down on the coffee table, then clasps her face in her hands.

"I suppose I should have noticed something was strange earlier, but you know, life is busy, we don't always have time for sex." I nod. I know that situation only too well. "But I think it was maybe two whole months, and he had no interest. You know, always something if I tried to get attention. He was tired, or he had to get up early."

"Two months? Ha. Try five years."

"Oh, my god. I know." She flashes a sympathetic smile.

"Sorry. I understand, carry on."

"Niels would always sleep naked, winter and summer, but the last month maybe, he's been wearing a shirt to bed."

"Weird?"

"I didn't think much about it, but he showed me his back yesterday. It is covered in bruises and sores. How you call these, welts?" I raise an eyebrow. "Danny! He's been going to some weird BDSM dungeon and getting whipped by a dominatrix."

"Holy shit. Really?"

"If that was all it was, I could forgive him. Everyone has their fantasies."

"Indeed. I have dozens." Alex rolls her eyes.

"Four years we were together, never once did he ask to be whipped."

"Seems like he's exploring his sexual fetishes, for sure."

"I would have done it if he asked. I don't understand."

"I guess he wanted something different."

"Well, she came to the house yesterday."

"The dominatrix?"

"Yes, banging on the door like crazy. When I opened it, she demanded to see Niels, screaming and shouting."

"What the fuck?"

"Long story short. She's pregnant, and she says it's his child."

"Oh, wow. I'm so sorry, Alex."

I offer my arms for a hug as her eyes moisten. "Alex, you should have said something, you didn't need to come to this bullshit work meeting with all that going on. I'll tell Dewey D4, whatever his stupid name is, that you are out sick."

"Thank you, Danny, but it's okay. It takes my mind off things. I will come to the meetings."

"Well, if you are sure…"

"I'm just glad that I found out all this before we were married. Now, this is only his problem and I can simply walk away."

"Life is never that straightforward, but I understand."

Just before four, we head downstairs to the lounge bar, which is nothing short of an opulent statement, claiming stake to the utmost in luxury here in Amsterdam. We sit down at the bar. I get myself yet another water and Alex a small beer.

We didn't get a photo of Dewey Brannon. We'll just have to wait for a brash Texan to make himself known. Shouldn't be hard to spot in the quiet bar.

Sure enough, a chap in his fifties steps up to the bar, orders himself a Martini, and makes a fuss about the specific ingredients and mix. He's greying, in a light suit, not obese, but hardly what you'd call slim. His accent gives it away though. I can imagine him riding around in a ten-gallon Stetson, driving cattle. I think we have our man.

"D4?" I walk over and stick out a hand. "Danny Watts."

"Hey, hey. Danny, my man." He shakes my hand so hard, I fear he may rip it off.

"You need a drink, buddy?"

"No, thanks. I just got myself a glass." I motion to the bar.

"What's that, water?"

"Yes, taking a break from alcohol for a while."

"Oh, boy, you are going to want to rethink that." I smile but intend to stick to my guns. Speaking of guns, I bet this chap has dozens of them back at home. I change the subject.

"This is Alexandra Vasiliu."

Alex stands up and is treated to a kiss on the hand.

"Hoo boy. Alexandra, it's a pleasure to meet you, Ma'am." D4 turns to me. "Your wife is quite beautiful, Danny."

"No, no. Sorry. Alex is my team lead. We aren't married."

"You're the team lead?"

"She speaks eight languages."

"Wowzers, is one of those the language of love?"

"You mean Flemish? Or maybe German?" I notice the flicker of a smile on Alex.

"Right. I have to admit, when I saw your name was Alex, I assumed you were a dude."

"Not a dude."

"Okay, well, that kinda messes up my plans for the evening."

"Oh?" I tilt my head, inquisitively.

"I was planning an evening of male bonding, shall we say? You know, here in good old Amsterdam."

"Ah." This is one of those kinds of business meetings. "D4, we assumed there was a work-related agenda for this trip?"

"Oh, there is. Don't worry, we'll get to that tomorrow. You gotta have some downtime, too." He slaps me on the arm, unnecessarily violently.

I force a chuckle. This is not going how I imagined. Did I leave my kids to get wasted with a horny Texan? I've seen this sort of thing before. If I don't play along, I'll be labelled as a miserable trouble maker. I'm sure Alex has no desire to take a tour of the red-light district after her recent experiences, or anytime, in all honesty.

"Alex wasn't feeling well. Perhaps she can be excused?"

He makes a sympathetic face. "Sure, you go lie your pretty head down, honey. Feel better soon, and we'll see you tomorrow morning, zero-nine-hundred-hours in your local time-zone."

"Thank you, Danny. D4." Alex gulps down the rest of her beer and heads off. I realise this has signed me up for whatever debauchery Dewey Brannon the Fourth has got in mind, but at least I saved Alex from the nightmare.

"Wow, she sure is some sweetmeat. Tell you what." He shivers and slaps me on the back. "I can see why she's the team lead."

"She's very talented, aside from her looks."

"Of course she is." He winks. Good grief. "Hey, I wanna thank you for booking this place. Top-quality hotel they got here. I was delayed in the fine massage parlour they have up on the fifth floor. Those girls sure know how to press the right buttons, if you know what I mean?"

"Never tried it, myself."

"Say what? We gotta get you loosened up, buddy."

"Can I ask, what's this all about?"

"You'll find out, Danny. Back in Texas, it's customary to get to know a man before doing business with him. 'Least for me, anyhow. You can't just jump right in at the deep end. Gotta ease into it."

"Fair enough."

"You got a wife and kids?"

"Had a wife, got two kids. Rosie is thirteen and Ethan is just nine."

"You got your hands full. Good man."

"I sure have. They can be a lot of work, but they are great kids."

"You need to get yourself a good woman to help you out, buddy."

"I'm working on it." I smile.

"Hey, hey. That's what I like to hear."

Perhaps I should be open-minded about D4. He's loud and brash, but he seems like a decent chap, underneath it.

"How about you, D4?"

"On my third wife, and sixth child. Darleen used to pole dance, which, incidentally, is how I met her." He laughs. "Eldest is at college now, down in Austin. Youngest just started grade school."

"Wow."

"Yup. Ain't no time for slackin'." He slaps the bar, waving over the bartender. "You ever been to Texas?"

"No."

"Beautiful country. Now, Mr Watts, I don't want to hear no excuses. Order yourself a real drink."

Here we go.

Several beers later, I'm feeling quite merry. D4 has told me all about his home, which is a ranch on the edge of a forest. I was correct about the stash of firearms. He spends his vacations shooting things, then cooking and eating them. I was invited to come and partake of some mindless violence whenever I fancied it. I don't think that will be anytime soon.

"You hungry, Danny?"

"Starving, come to think of it."

"They got steak here?"

"I'm sure they have."

We head down to the reception desk and Dewey relentlessly flirts with the girl, asking for a recommendation for a good steak restaurant and a taxi to it. She's putty in his hands, at least it seems like it. We are directed to a place nearby, and a taxi is already waiting outside.

Steak is always a risk with unknown company. Personally, I just order medium rare and eat whatever they bring me. Life is too short to be precious about the exact specifications and temperature of the meat. I don't need to know the life history of the cow, including the full family tree, holiday photos, and school exam results. But that's the level-of-detail D4 is asking for. The waiters are undoubtedly spitting in his sauce as he sends the plate back for the third time, claiming his meat is incorrectly cooked. He'd better leave a large tip or we'll end up lynched outside.

"You gotta keep people on their toes. Am I right?"

I smile and nod, but no, he's not right. Never piss off the people who bring you food.

"You run a pretty tight ship, yourself, Danny?"

"I do what I can. Alex helps, a lot."

"Got any trouble makers?"

"No, not really. Everyone just does their job, day in day out. The usual stuff with sick leave and holidays, people have good and bad days."

I'm reminded of poor Ryan, who we had to fire. I should check up and see how he's doing.

"That's good to know."

D4 seems satisfied his food is adequate now as the waiter brings another plate, and he orders up his umpteenth beer. I've got an idea to keep me out of trouble. I'm switching to non-alcoholic beer. I doubt if he'll notice as it looks and smells the same. I don't feel the need to engage in the bravado ball swinging of binge drinking alcohol to prove something. All it proves is that you are a twat.

That said, I've lost count how many drinks D4 has had, and he's none the worse for wear.

Over dinner, we move to the topic of women and marriage. Dewey has a catalogue of ladies that number more than his drink intake. When he asks me my story, it feels a tad pathetic.

I avoid the fact that I have had no bedroom activity since well before the current presidential administration.

"Brother, we need to get you fixed up."

"As I said, I'm working on something, back home."

"Faye?"

"Yup. She's a work in progress."

"Women are like deer. You gotta strike before they know it, or they'll run off and you'll never catch them."

He has a point.

"Fair enough, but I'm still eyeing up the target."

"You need the confidence to shoot."

"I suppose."

"Come on, I'm gonna help you out."

I raise an eyebrow. D4 calls over the waiter and pays the bill.

As we walk the late evening streets of Amsterdam, I don't think there's anyone on this planet who couldn't guess in which direction Dewey Brannon the Fourth was heading. I'm conflicted. A shag is a shag, but a brothel? I've never done anything like this. He could be right, maybe I do need to lighten up and live a little. What if it did give me the confidence I need to make a move with Faye?

Only one way to find out.

Chapter Twenty-Four

Alex was right. I am the only man in the world who can walk into a brothel and still not get laid.

I didn't let D4 know that. He went off with his choice of two girls, and I was led upstairs to a small room by a sultry looking eastern European girl. She turned out to be a lovely lass. She lay me down on the bed, started feeling my dick through my jeans, and next thing I know, a bra pings off and into my face.

I tried to get into the moment, but I just couldn't do it. It took every ounce of courage just to go into the place. Doing anything with Anushka was not going to happen.

I sat up, stress balling up in my throat, the guilt, the embarrassment, the weirdness of the situation overwhelming me with doubt and panic. I remember apologising to the girl.

No idea why, but I recall telling her about Alex back in my hotel room, then Faye and Jessica, and I may have even mentioned Elise. Her English was good enough that she laughed and told me to take my shirt off and lie on my front. She gave me a wonderful massage and asked if I wanted a happy ending. I turned over, told her she was beautiful, and that was happy enough for me. I know, I'm pathetic.

Our time was up, but she waved me away with a blown kiss. I regretted it the second I walked out of the door, but that's my life to a tee. This is not a story I'll want to tell my grandkids one day.

D4 was in great cheer after his threesome. And I'd bet my bottom dollar he made sure to get his money's worth. We ended up back in the hotel bar around two in the morning. I was tired, half-drunk, and conscious of his intention to start our business day at nine. Somehow, I made my excuses and went to my room, leaving him in the bar. He could have stayed there all night for all I know.

I found Alex asleep on the couch, and I didn't have the heart to wake or move her. I slumped down into the sumptuous bed and watched the ceiling gently spin, while I totted up all the mistakes in my life that I've made.

This morning, as I recount the evening's events to Alex over a coffee, before we go down to hear, finally, what this whole trip is about. I conclude that not having awkward sex with a prostitute was the right choice.

Neither of us felt like eating breakfast. We head down and meet D4 in a small conference room on the second floor. He's still psyched up, and far more hyper than any man should be at this time in the morning, after a heavy night. So much so, that I wonder if he acquired any Dutch courage in powder form from the girls last night. It wouldn't surprise me one bit.

He's tinkering with his laptop and trying to get the screen to project up on the wall. I help him hit the right combination of keys and up pops his desktop wallpaper. An eight-foot-wide image of a sprawling ranch house. Presumably his.

· · ·

"Alrighty. Now we're in business." He claps his hands together, too loud for my smouldering hangover. "No point in skirting around it. I've just got one word for you fine folks." If yesterday evening wasn't skirting around, I don't know what is. He pauses for effect. "Chatbots."

"Chatbots?"

"That's what I said. Chatbots."

Tumbleweeds blow through the room in the deathly silence, as Alex and I soak up what he just said.

"Can you elaborate?"

"I can do better than that. Let me show you."

He taps on a link in his email, taking him to a website. A pop-up chat window appears with the name Eliza.

'Hi, how can I help you today?'

"Guys, give me a typical support question you get every day."

"Err, maybe something like; My phone says it has run out of room for photos."

"No problem." D4 types in what I said, verbatim.

The computer responds immediately. 'Have you tried moving some of your data to secure cloud storage?' It then pops up a link to a photo storage service and a YouTube video on the same topic. He types in a few similar day-to-day questions and the machine does equally well, even if the phrasing and spelling are wrong.

"Incredible."

"You are looking at the state-of-the-art in artificial intelligence chat technology. This is NASA down in Houston grade stuff. We're talking about being able to field thousands of common tech support questions in a way that every user feels comfortable with. Right there in their messages app, as though they are talking to their nerdy buddy. And, like Alex here, it understands plenty of languages." D4 is quite animated. He is clearly very excited about this new technology. "How many team members do you have, Danny?"

"About fifty."

"You can field a maximum of fifty calls at once?"

"I suppose."

"Guess how many users this machine can deal with at once?"

"Err, more than fifty?"

"Try five thousand. And that's just one server. We can boost that up as high as we need."

"Amazing."

"You know how many smartphones are out there?"

"Literally billions."

"You nailed it. Billions. We need to scale fast. Taking fifty calls at once is a tiny drop in the ocean. With this tech, we can take the company into the stars."

"As impressive as this is, some people prefer to talk to a human." I'm reminded of the first time I met Faye; She needed the human touch, for sure. Still does, come to think of it.

"They still can, if they want. However, studies show that the emerging young adult demographic does not make phone calls. They text."

He's got a point. Rarely do we get calls from teenagers, but I had put that down to them knowing how to use tech, having grown up with it in their blood.

There's a coffee flask on a corner table. I get up and grab a cup for myself and Alex, D4 already has one. Alex hasn't said a word, and I'm not sure if she's just stunned, confused, or upset about the breakup. I don't want to call attention to her. I take the lead.

"I presume you aren't asking for us to give our opinions on this? What's the plan?"

"Straight to the point. I like it. We'll be integrating this into our operation, starting next month. I need you guys to make it happen. We've already rolled out a similar version back stateside, down in Austin. But I know." He holds his hands up before I can speak. "The European version is more complicated, with all the languages and regulations and all that jazz."

"Have to admit, D4, I'm not an expert on AI tech, myself."

"Nor I." Alex speaks for the first time.

"Worry not, team. That's why you got two full days here to learn."

I raise an eyebrow.

"Drink up, buckaroos! We're going on a field trip."

A taxi takes us out of the city centre to a dull industrial estate. We are deposited outside a nondescript building, and D4 leads the way inside to a clean and bright reception area. We are given ID badges and cloth bags to put over our shoes, then led through into the main building by the reception girl. I notice she is not wearing blue shoe-bags on her feet. She leaves us at a side office and then goes back the way we came.

A small, balding chap in his late fifties arrives at the door and is heartily greeted by D4, who introduces the man as Janwillem Van Herpen, and he will be our guide and tutor for the rest of today and tomorrow.

"Well, team. I've seen the demo already. I'll leave you to it. I'm heading back to TX tonight. I'll catch you on the flip. Jan here will fill you in with everything you need."

And with that, he's gone. Leaving us a bit lost and unsure of what is happening. I turn to Janwillem, who smiles broadly.

"Err, well, pleased to meet you, Janwillem. What exactly do you do here?"

He laughs. "D4, he doesn't explain?"

"Not really."

"Come, come. I show you."

He struts like a chicken as he walks. An interesting gait that leads us to a vast hall full of aisles of servers, racked up with thousands of lights blinking on and off. The noise is deafening from fans and air conditioners. Winding snakes of cables lead from the back of each machine up to a thickening coil on the roof of each cabinet. From there, up into the ceiling of the building.

"This, my friends, is the Internet." He pauses for theatrical effect. "Well, a small part of it." He chuckles.

"A data centre?"

"Yes, exactly. You have done your homework." He taps the side of his head, smiling. "You have the use of these servers here." He motions to a stack of computers. Flat and stacked twenty high on a six-foot rack. "This is where your robots live."

"Great, I suppose."

Alex turns to me and quietly whispers in my ear. "Danny, do you know what is going on here?"

"Not a clue, Alex."

"Okay, just checking."

Janwillem laughs. "All will become clear. Come."

We go back to the office and he motions for us to sit down. He takes a seat near a screen and then flicks off the lights with a remote control, and fires up his laptop and the projector.

Death, by PowerPoint.

By noon, I'm seriously regretting skipping breakfast. The presentation that Janwillem has been showing us is tedious beyond comprehension, utterly dull, and furthermore, boring as hell. The poor chap is doing his best to lighten it up, but explaining the intricacies of the AI engine seems rather pointless. He keeps saying he'll get to the meat of it soon, but we need to understand the underpinning methods first. I hope Alex is listening because I tuned out a while back. Lost in daydreams of simpler times, due to his accent, and the way he says the word bots to sound like boats. Now every time he says it, I think of Chat-boats floating down the canals of Amsterdam, talking to each other. Yes, I'm a mature adult with the brain of an eight-year-old.

We are taken across the data centre to where they have a small canteen. Janwillem says he'll meet us back in the office in thirty minutes.

The food is basic but passable, and free. I stock up my plate, not knowing where the next meal is coming from. I notice Alex doesn't take much from the buffet.

"How are you doing?"

"Ugh. You know…"

"Sorry."

"Not your fault. But this bullshit is not helping."

"Agreed. Not sure what to do about it. Apparently, we have no choice but to sit it out."

"Yes, but I don't know about artificial intelligence or chat robots. I have no interest in this."

"Same. It seems our job has just drastically changed."

"My whole life, in two days is upside down."

"Shit. I'm sorry, Alex. Do you want to say you are sick or something? I'll stay and do this."

"No, I won't leave you. We'll help each other stay awake. Okay?"

"Sure."

After we eat, we walk back to the office, where Janwillem is waiting. He doesn't eat. I have to wonder if he's one of the AI robots.

"Good, we get back to work."

Alex and I exchange a glance, and while Janwillem is

looking down at his laptop, I reach over and squeeze her hand. She nods in camaraderie.

After four long, painful hours with only one brief coffee break, we are let out into the sunshine again. My mouth dry and head throbbing from the relentless air conditioning. A taxi is called by the receptionist, and it promptly takes us back to the hotel. The ride is mostly in silence, aside from the inane babbling of Dutch FM radio.

When we get up to the room, Alex grabs her bag and vanishes into the bathroom for a shower. I slump down on the bed; the ceiling spinning. This time, with the vast amount of data my brain was just deluged with. It will take some time to comprehend all that Janwillem told us.

I take the opportunity to call home and see how the kids and Jessica are doing. All fine on the western front. I text Faye a message and give her the very brief version of what has happened since I landed in Holland. Skipping the entire red-light district part. No need to stir the pot.

She sends 'LOLs', but then apologises and sends sympathy. I need it.

"I don't feel like going anywhere for dinner, can we get something in the room?" Alex comes out of the bathroom, wrapped in a towel, still wet.

"That suits me. My brain is fried after today."

I pick up the menu and choose the simplest thing I can find, which is a burger, but infinitely more expensive and elaborate than our normal clown-food. I don't care. The company is paying, and D4 made it clear he didn't worry about expenses. Alex chooses the same, and then I call to order it up.

"How are you feeling?"

"Okay. Not great, but okay."

"Fair enough. Better than I would be."

"I have friends." She smiles.

"You certainly do." We lock eyes and linger for a moment.

"What do you think about these fucking chatbots?"

"Well, I mean, the thought that's been lurking at the back of my head all day is, if they have chatbots, then do they need us?"

"Yeah, that's what I was wondering."

"He said that people can still talk to humans, if they need to."

"I guess."

"Makes you wonder, though, doesn't it?"

"Screw it. You know, if everything will turn upside-down in my life, then maybe it is time for a change. Maybe the universe has plans for me."

"Maybe. But I don't feel like going back to job seeking. The very thought makes me cringe."

"Embrace the chatbots, then, Danny." She jumps up from the couch and into the bedroom. Her wet towel comes flying out of the doorway. "Hey, Danny. Order some wine with the food."

Chapter Twenty-Five

They say that the key to comedy is all in the timing. Delivery, maybe, but timing mostly. That's what makes my life so terribly comical. Bad timing.

Those were the thoughts my brain swamped me with, as Alex and I lingered in the hot tub, after our delicious dinner and a second bottle of wine. I think she suggested the tub, but she claims it was my idea. Either way, the timing was all wrong.

Last time Alex and I were together, I made a choice not to tell her I loved her. To keep us as friends. Little did I know that her fiancé was cheating on her with a dominatrix. If things had only transpired differently, it could have been more than just a soak in the bubbles in that hot tub. But now, while I'm still trying to nurture a relationship with Faye, I am once again on the wrong side of time.

Instead of telling Alex how I felt about her, I ended up telling her how I felt about Faye. She dragged it out of me, somehow. With those eyes, she can get anything she wants from me.

We talked for a long time, under the influence of blood-red wine, and the heat of the water. She asked me if I loved Faye. Love is a strong word, a dangerous word, used in the wrong context. Wars have been fought over love, lives have been lost, and hearts have been broken. My heart plenty, and now Alex's. Don't use the word frivolously.

I said I didn't know. Only time would tell.

After another tedious day at the data centre with Janwillem, honestly, we came out still rabidly unaware of what the hell we are meant to be doing. He emailed us training material, links, test servers and his promise that he's on call and available whenever we need him, which is likely to be often. Alex drove back to her parents' house in Eindhoven, leaving me on my own in Amsterdam for my last evening. Instead of going out and exploring the nightlife, I stayed in my room, messaging Faye.

My next few weeks of work will focus on figuring all this stuff out. But as I sit here, back at my home desk, staring at the quick start manual user guide for most of the day, I can only think about one thing; do I love Faye?

I don't know her that well, but over the last few weeks, we've been texting a lot, just general chat, back and forth. I tell her about my day. She tells me about hers. We make silly jokes and laugh a lot. When my phone buzzes now in my pocket, I look forward to reading the messages.

I've been trying to organise another date night with her, but once again, timing is my enemy. She's got a lot going on with work and Josh at the moment. I don't push it. We'll get together soon enough, I'm sure.

All I want from life is simplicity, peace, enough money to live, enough time to do all the things I've put off over the decades, and companionship. That would be nice, wouldn't it? To wake up next to someone I care about every morning. To have someone to complain about work with or go for a morning bike ride together. To spontaneously have sex with someone I don't need to wine and dine and get completely drunk first, wouldn't that be something?

But a simple life can be boring. Occasionally, we need some complication to stir things up. Faye is both of those things. I can see her being the woman who lies next to me, gently snoring, putting her cold feet on me in the winter. But to get to that simple life, I think I need to climb a mountain of complication first.

Does this constitute love? I don't think so. Yet.

"Daddy!" Rosie yelps from the bathroom. "DADDY!"

Oh, hell. What now?

"What's the matter, Rosie?"

"Can you come here?"

"Into the bathroom?"

"YES. Hurry."

I hear the bolt slide over and I open the door. Rosie is on the toilet, a bloody wad of toilet paper in her hand.

She cries out, "I got my period!" She's shaking in fear.

"Oh, boy. Err, right. Do you have any pads?"

"No."

"Okay, don't worry, it's fine. Remember, it's normal?"

"I know, but… My tummy hurts."

"Hey, it's okay, sweetheart."

"I'm scared."

"No, don't be." I try to laugh it off. "It's okay, honestly. You'll be fine. Err, Jessie just went out, but there are probably some pads in her room. Hold on."

"Okay. I need new knickers, too."

I feel guilty going into Jessica's room, but needs must. I find a pack of pads in her nightstand and take a couple. No idea what you do with them, but one step at a time. I grab a pair of undies from the laundry pile on the way back.

"Here you go, sweetheart. I guess, clean up a bit, then put this in your knickers?"

"Right."

"Oh, look, it has a sticky strip. I imagine that sticks down to keep them in place, err, then wrap those flaps over. Job done."

"I'll be okay, now, thanks, Daddy."

"No problem, Rosie."

I exit and breathe a sigh of relief. But a scary thought strikes me. My baby girl is a little woman, now. I know she's thirteen and I should have expected this, but I've been sort of ignoring it, hoping that someone would be around to help when it finally happened. She seemed to know the basics from school. I didn't think much about it.

I should have been better prepared and made sure Rosie knew what would happen. Can't rely on school teachers to educate these things properly. The clinical cold blackboard diagrams are no substitute for family care.

The years flash by so fast, it wasn't long ago that I was cradling her in my arms at the hospital. Such a tiny little thing changed my entire life forevermore.

I suppose this is another one of those life changes to make a note of. Does the tooth fairy have a period fairy sister? Do I leave a pound coin in her knicker drawer? What's the protocol?

When Jessica gets back, I explain what happened. She sympathises, remembers her first period experience. She knew what to expect, but when it happened, it was still messy and shocking. She was more scared to tell her religious parents than about the actual event. She thought she'd be chastised for doing something wrong. Amazing how such a normal, healthy, natural thing can be so stigmatised that young girls are nervous and scared about their own bodies.

She goes up to comfort Rosie, and I tell Ethan that Rosie is just feeling sad and off colour. He should be extra nice to her. No arguing about games or TV show choices. In fact, I recommend he leaves her well alone. I try to live by the same policy when I'm around menstrual women.

I take the car and head to the grocery store. Not knowing what I'm doing, and overwhelmed with choices, sizes, types and colours. I throw two of every mysterious feminine hygiene product into my trolley, guessing that the smallest size is what she needs. Something has to work for her, or she can try them all out and find what works best. I grab a little teddy bear for her as I pass the toy aisle.

The lady on the checkout looks up at me, confused.

"For my daughter. She just got her first period."

She smiles. "Ah. Good dad. Take some chocolate."

I chuckle. "Good idea, thanks."

I discreetly stash all the pads and tampons in both bathrooms, then take Rosie her teddy and the box of chocolates up to her room. I also gave Ethan some chocolate on the way upstairs to keep the peace. Rosie is lying on her bed with her iPad, as usual.

"How are you feeling now, sweetheart?"

"Fine."

"What you doing?"

"Just talking to Kirsty. She got her period last month." She motions to her iPad.

"Oh, okay, good." She can probably help more than I can. "I got you this." I wave the Teddy.

"Aww, he's cute. Thanks, Daddy. But I'm too old for teddies now."

"Never too old for teddies. I'll take him if you don't want him?"

She laughs. "Didn't say I didn't want him." I throw it over to her.

"Bet you won't say no to a Milk Tray box either?"

"Yay!"

"There're supplies in the bathrooms. I think you'll have everything you need. But, shout if you need anything else, okay?"

"Thanks, Dad. Oh. One thing…"

"Yeah?"

She blushes a little. "I might need a bra soon."

"Oh. Right. Do you want to go shopping?"

"Maybe." She looks bashful.

"Tell you what. I'll give you some money and Jessie can take you?"

"Yeah. That would be better." She smiles.

"I think that makes more sense."

Rosie needs a mother. Especially as Jessica is due to leave us for university shortly. I've been avoiding thinking about that, as it will be a traumatic event for all of us. She's become part of the furniture here now. I'll be utterly at a loss without her. But she has her own life to lead. I don't want her to feel bad about going. We'll get by, somehow.

My phone buzzes in my pocket. I'm glad. That means I can ask Faye for some advice. I suppose I should tell Elise the news.

I pull my phone out, but the message isn't from Faye. It's from Roland.

'All right bruv. I've got some news for you.'

'Hey! How are you doing? What news?'

'You'll have to come find out, won't you?'

'What do you mean?'

'I know you won't be doing anything at the weekend, being a sad bastard. Get your arse down here on Saturday at noon. You won't regret it.'

He sends me a map location of a hotel on the outskirts of London.

'What's going on?'

'Saffy will be there. Don't ask questions. Just come. Okay?'

'Right. Okay, then.'

'Seriously, don't cancel. This is important. And bring your overnight bag.'

'This is very mysterious, Rollie. I hope you aren't trying to set me up or something.'

'No, nothing like that. Told you, don't ask questions. Just be there.'

'Okay, okay.'

"Hey, Jessica," I call from my office.

"What's up?"

"Sorry to ask again, but my brother just told me to come down to London on Saturday and stay in a hotel overnight. He was very coy about the whole thing. I don't know what it's about, but I said I'd be there."

"That sounds like fun."

"You never know with Roland. I'm a bit scared, to be honest."

"Ha, you'll be fine. I'm sure it will be interesting, whatever it is. Of course, I'll watch the kids. But you know, I'm going on Monday?"

"I know. Don't worry. I'll be back on Sunday."

"I'll miss you guys."

"We'll miss you. No doubt about it."

"Stop. I'll get teary again."

"No. It's a good thing. You need to go into the world, show everyone your talent, become somebody wonderful and save a little corner of the world. Put a dent in the universe. Make your mark."

She smiles, blinking back tears.

"Sorry, Danny. You are so nice to me."

"Why wouldn't I be nice?"

"I'm just overwhelmed."

I stand up and open my arms. She moves in for the cuddle. I spend half my life holding women, but never anything more. It confuses old Judas in my underwear. He doesn't know what to think these days.

"You can come and visit us anytime you like, you know?"

"Really?"

"Of course. Bristol isn't that far away. But I suspect you'll soon have plenty of friends and things to do. Don't forget us."

"I'll never forget you."

"That's settled then. You'll be fine, sweetheart. Now then. Rosie's choice for dinner tonight. Let's get cooking."

Chapter Twenty-Six

The drive down to the hotel that Roland summoned me to is about an hour. I set off mid-morning. I should arrive in plenty of time.

Despite my repeated attempts to get more information out of him on what this is all about, I've got a load of nothing. I've researched the hotel and location, but that's all. It's another Myatt, coincidentally. Same chain as I stayed with in Amsterdam. The reviews are all good, and this one is the very first, opened just over one-hundred years ago by Charles Myatt, just outside of London in a sleepy little town, according to the spiel on the website.

But the details of what I'm to expect when I get there, why he's chosen this particular place, or why Saffy, the Indian Goddess of Love will be in attendance, remains a mystery.

I'll find out in about ten minutes, according to the Sat-Nav.

Roland has always had his secret side. I suppose brought on in part by our parents' problem with his sexuality, but definitely a big part of it is his love for theatrics. He's all about the build-up and big reveal. When he first told me he was gay, he did it with an elaborate stop-motion video he'd made, using peg dolls as the characters. He'd narrated a story over it about how Mr and Mr Peg decided they wanted different things than other people. He waited until our parents had gone out, then made me watch his animation. He's always been very creative. But I never figured out why one Mr Peg needed to die in a horrific helicopter crash, right after he professed his love for the other Mr Peg.

The hotel has that old world charm, set within beautifully tended gardens. The car park is awash with vehicles that cost more than my annual salary. I step with trepidation into the reception area and then walk through to the bar where I'm to meet Roland.

I sit down, check the time, and put my phone away. I'm five minutes early. I glance up at the mirror behind the bottles, smooth down my hair. I'm the only one here.

A chap around Roland's age comes in with a heavily pregnant woman, he helps her sit down on an old leather couch. The bartender nods at them then comes over to me.

"What can I get you, Sir?"

"Err, well I'm meeting my brother here in a minute. I'll just have water for now, please."

"Certainly."

I look around at the opulence surrounding me. Quite different from the grotty Kings Head I normally frequent.

I hear a woman cackle in the distance. The unmistakable squawk of Saffy. Sure enough, she bursts into the bar with Roland two steps behind, then another man.

Saffy doesn't notice me, but she goes straight over to the couple on the leather couch, and squeals in delight.

"Hey, Keith." She turns to the pregnant lady. "Oh, my god. You are so big, Lotty."

"Thanks, Saffy. That makes me feel wonderful." They laugh. The man gets up and kisses Saffy on both cheeks.

Roland and the other chap wave to the couple, then notice me at the bar.

"Danny Boy! You made it."

I stand up and greet him with a manly hug.

"Well, I didn't seem to have a choice, did I?"

"Nope." He laughs. "Danny, this is Monty Milford." He motions to the man standing next to him. A white-haired chap in his late forties, at a guess. He's muscle toned, perfectly groomed, wearing some kind of sleek designer outfit in dark grey. I wouldn't be surprised if it was tailored. He shakes my hand with gusto.

"Pleased to meet you, Monty…"

"Don't say it." He smiles.

"Python? Ha. I wasn't going to."

"It's okay. Everyone does anyway." He laughs.

"You know Saffy." Roland waves her over. She's engaged in a discussion about pregnancy with the lady on the couch. "And these wonderful people are Keith and Lotty Myatt. Everyone, this is my brother, Danny."

The gent stands up again and walks over to me, hand outstretched.

"Pleased to meet you, Danny."

"Yes, and you, Keith. Err, Myatt, like the hotel?"

"Yes, exactly like the hotel."

"He owns the place," Roland interjects.

"Not quite, but the family does."

"Very nice. I stayed in a Myatt in Amsterdam, recently."

"Ah. Good choice. Excellent hot tubs in that one."

"It was indeed." I flash a smile and Keith winks back.

"Well, what are you drinking, Danny?"

"I just got water, thank you."

"I think we can do better than that. The bar is on the house for this special occasion. You partial to a Belgian ale?"

"Oh, well. Don't mind if I do. Thanks." I turn to my brother. "Roland, this is all very friendly and posh, but what exactly is the occasion?"

There's a pause of silence around the room. Roland exchanges a glance with Monty.

"This, mate, is my engagement party."

"What?"

"Monty and I are going to be married." He puts his arm around Monty. "These are all our best friends. Actually, where are Ben and Lucy?"

"Late, getting a sitter. They'll be here soon."

"Rollie!" I feel a tightening in my throat, my eyes moisten. "You sly bastard. Congratulations! You kept that quiet, didn't you? Bloody hell."

Three Belgian ale's later, and we're all in a circle around the couch where Lotty is firmly planted, due to her twin flames in her belly, she said. Not sure what that means, but she seems lovely. Another couple joined us. A hairy chap called Ben, salt of the earth type, and his wife, an American lady called Lucy. Everyone is friendly, happy, and a great laugh.

I found out that they are all somehow connected. Saffy and Lotty know each other from college. Ben is the hotel gardener and best friend of Keith. Lucy is Ben's wife he met online. Monty owns a small bed-and-breakfast across town and knows Keith and the family from years back. They hired Roland and Saffy to revamp the image of Myatt Hotels globally, about a year ago, which is how Roland met Monty in this very bar. Hence the summons here this afternoon.

I've been checked into a room, all expenses paid. Nice to have connections.

. . .

We move to the sumptuous dining room for an afternoon meal. Something between lunch and dinner. Delicious food is abundant and drinks are flowing. I'm feeling quite merry, and the atmosphere is wonderful. This isn't so much a party, as a relaxed dinner out with a group of friends. Roland tells me this is the gay version of a stag night and engagement party mixed together. New traditions are needed for new celebrations.

As we wander back to the bar, the natural resting place for everyone, I'm full, happy, excited and also a little jealous. Rollie is entering a new phase of his life with someone he cares about, while I linger and fester, turning more and more rusty as the weeks fly by. I need to do something about this. I resolve to organise a date with Faye as soon as I get back home.

Roland falls back as the throng goes into the bar. He tilts his head and waves me to come over, just as I'm going through the door.

"Really happy for you, dude. Seriously."

"Thanks, Danny. I appreciate that a lot. You've never once judged me, or made fun, or said anything at all about my lifestyle choices."

"Why would I? You do what you want, mate. I'll always be here for you."

"Cheers, bruv. About that, I have a favour to ask."

"Yeah?"

"We aren't going to have a traditional wedding, by any standard, but there're some things we've agreed we want. One of them is a best man." He smiles.

"Me?"

"Well, who else, you knob?"

I have to cough back a burst of emotion. "I.. I don't know what to say."

"Well, a fucking yes would be nice?" He laughs.

"Yes, of course, you muppet." I pull him over for a bear-hug because I'm too teary to speak, and I need a moment to compose myself. He slaps me on the back.

"You big soft shit."

"Shut it."

"There's one problem though."

I stand back. "What's that?"

"Mum and Dad."

"Oh, crap. Yeah."

"Worry about that later. Come on. We're getting blasted tonight."

———

Surprisingly, after an unknown quantity of Belgian ale, my drive back the next day wasn't hampered by a lingering hangover. I put it down to the vast, soft comfortable bed in the room, and the two litres of water I made myself drink that morning at breakfast. A good night was had by all. Lovely people. I'm genuinely excited for Roland.

I got to know my future brother-in-law a bit more. I couldn't hope for a nicer chap. He runs his own small bed-and-breakfast place almost entirely himself, and also occasionally works at the Myatt when they need help with waiting tables or cooking breakfasts in his off-seasons. He inherited the place from an uncle, twenty years previously, and that's been his life. Between him and Keith, I heard a swathe of anecdotes about terrible and ridiculous guests. By the end of the night, my cheeks ached from all the laughing.

I pondered, as I drove the miles of featureless motorway, how we will break the news to Mum and Dad? Do we just never tell them? Pretend it didn't happen? That isn't going to work, long term. I suppose we'll just have to go for it and let them decide how they feel.

.   .   .

I got home last night to chaos. Kids running amok like Lord of the Flies. Jessica packing bags, ready for her departure. Children begging her not to go. At first, it was joking, but then they were getting quite upset. In the end, I had to drag everyone out to the car and the clown-food emporium to calm down.

I understand their sadness. If I could think of a way for Jessica to stay and still go to University, then I'd do whatever it took, but that won't work. The best compromise I could come up with was that we'd all go in the car to take her to the dormitory. But I made them promise and swear on their iPads that there wouldn't be any waterworks at the other side.

I'm sceptical, but they all agreed.

When the kids finally went to bed, I took the opportunity to speak to Jessica. I thought perhaps she'd want to see her parents before she left, but she was quite adamant that she had no intention of going to their house. She hadn't even told them about her miscarriage.

It's entirely up to her, but I thought they'd want to know. I'm sure time will heal their wounds, but if it doesn't, and they let religion and stubbornness drive away their beautiful, intelligent daughter, they are bigger fools than I can imagine.

The first half-hour of the car ride was noisy with chat, singing, games, and endless questions for Jessica from the kids. They made her promise to text every day, even if she's busy. She agreed, foolishly, if you ask me. But I'm sure she genuinely loves the kids. They calmed down a tad, after a while. Each staring out of the window as we pass through strange towns and roads. Each plugged into their music.

I took a day off work and asked Alex to cover for me since I didn't plan this diversion.

We arrive at the building. I look over at Jessica in the passenger seat. She smiles, unplugs her headphones and picks up her bag.

"Well, here we are."

The children shuffle in the back, startled back into reality from their daydreams.

"I better go and register. Be right back, guys."

A few other students are milling around, going back and forth from the registration office, and what I presume is a dormitory building.

Oh, to be young and free again, embarking on a new chapter in their lives. Starting their path into debt, cynicism, broken hearts, broken marriages. Realising it wasn't worth the crippling debt to get their degrees, in some obscure subject they never end up working at. Slaving in a job they hate, but can't leave. Can't realise their dreams. Can't find someone to cuddle at night. Their only solace found in a never-ending stream of entertainment spewed at them from hundreds of thousands of rectangular screens.

Or maybe that's just me?

"I got my key." Jessica waves and jumps up and down. She makes a sound like 'Squeeeee', "I'm so nervous!"

"Come on, guys. Let's help Jessie up with all her stuff."

I open the door and two children bolt from the car like racehorses, around to the boot, scrambling to grab bags and boxes. If only they were like this after a Tesco grocery run.

The dorm is small but neat. There's a bed that will inevitably prove far too small to do any decent shagging in, but I suppose students don't care about comfort during sex. Any old back seat of a burnt-out car wreck is adequate. There's also a small desk, a water-stained mirror, a missing patch of carpet, and the sound of dozens of other people dragging in furniture and bags.

"It's great!"

I raise an eyebrow. I suppose I've grown old and used to more space and comfort.

"Fond memories will be made here. Mark my words."

Jessica smiles. I know she'll be fine, but I feel like this is my daughter leaving. It's hard not to be emotional. I blink back tears.

"Hey, you said no crying." She laughs, then buries her head in my chest one last time. The kids pile on for a group hug. We stay like that for a good two minutes before I break away.

"Come on, guys. We'll see Jessie soon, won't we?"

"Well, doh. I'll be back for Christmas."

"Yay!" The kids cheer and clap, then bounce back for one last hug I have to pull them away from.

The drive home is silent, all of us lost in our thoughts.

The house feels empty as we all disperse to our beanbag, couch, and office chair. Jessica has left the building.

Chapter Twenty-Seven

I probably should have checked my work email when I got back yesterday from dropping Jessica off. But instead, I vegged out in front of the mind-numbing stream of crap that YouTube throws up at you. The inescapable, bottomless pit of video, promising something a little interesting but rarely delivering. I learnt, amongst other things, about the making of a movie I've never seen, how shoes are manufactured, how to build a log cabin, what happens to illegal items after they are confiscated at the airport and three easy ways to clean my roof and driveway. Thrilling stuff. But I needed an escape from reality for a while.

What I needed to do was stop procrastinating and ask Faye if she'd like to go on another date with me. In the end, I did exactly that, but not before I had realised that I no longer had a babysitter. This made things more complicated since I don't want to trust the kids to anyone off the street. It would take a lot of investigation, background checking and interviews before I could make a decision and find someone suitable. It would be easier to find a real Au Pair.

If I had checked my work email, I might have done just that. Or at least kicked the process off.

I've been given a raise!

For the first time in I don't remember how many years, they have promoted me, with a meaningful salary increase. A message from D4 languished unread in my Inbox all day. I'm hoping he takes it as me being hard to get, rather than me being a rude twat.

The nature of the raise is a chunk more money, including a car allowance, ostensibly for me to travel around to my various team members, but since most of them are in mainland Europe, rather than the UK where I can easily drive to, it's just another perk. Plus, the new title of 'Regional Director'.

I don't know what that means, specifically, or how it differs from my current role, but I have a good notion that it's something to do with the chatbot situation. D4 wants me to own this and make it happen. I have to believe this is his way of making sure I don't bail to some other company doing similar things. Little does he know, I've been looking for something better for years, but there isn't much I can be bothered to go for. This job may not be thrilling or challenging, but I can get by with minimal effort, and a big reason I haven't felt like leaving was Alex.

Fair enough. I'm not entirely stupid. I respond that I've pondered the offer for all of thirty seconds, and accept.

This, and the imminent date with Faye this evening, call for celebration.

Since I don't have a babysitter already organised, I invited Faye to come to the house, and I'd cook her something. I asked if Josh would like to come, but she thought he'd be best with the neighbours. I had hoped that Josh would keep Ethan entertained playing games, and Rosie would likely vanish up to her room, leaving Faye and me mostly alone. Still, I didn't push it because anything is better than nothing.

It isn't Champagne, but it is fizzy wine with a poppy cork. I'm not precious about these things, and I know Faye isn't either. I bought two bottles, and some normal white wine. I'm risking a couple of drinks, hoping that my regular walking and cycling regime has done me some good, and Judas may yet see me through a few more years of sexual activity before he finally packs it all in and heads south. Permanently.

Chance would be a fine thing. Even though Faye and I are delightfully friendly lately, I have no idea if she plans on extending the relationship to the bedroom. These choices are always made by the female of the species in my experience.

I know, women like a strong man to demand sex of them, dragging them by their hair back to the cave, but I can't bring myself to be that man. I need a signal like Batman.

Sure, keep telling yourself that, Danny.

The rest of my shopping trolley tells a story of pasta, bolognese sauce, and fish fingers. The lady at the checkout nods at me in recognition.

"Did the pads work out, Dear?"

"Pads? Oh. Yes, sorry. Rosie was fine. Thank you, and the chocolate helped immensely." I smile.

"Good to hear. It can be a tough time if there's no mum around." She looks down at my ring finger.

"Err, yeah." I didn't realise I was checking out with Sherlock Holmes.

"Celebrating tonight?" She scans the bubbly.

"I am. Got a pay rise."

"Oh, well done you. Chance of that around here would be a fine thing."

"Sorry."

The rest of the transaction is conducted in silence until she announces the final price, which is inevitably well over what I estimated. Still, never mind.

Faye is punctual, and I open the door to a vision of elegant beauty. Her perfume as she kisses me is a spicy musk. Her hair is down, she's got her black leather jacket open, revealing an 'Echo and the Bunnymen' t-shirt and black jeans. I could have her for dinner right here on the doorstep and be plenty satisfied.

"Hey!"

"Can I come in?" She looks up at me.

"Sorry, yes." She giggles.

We go through to the kitchen, and she perches on a stool at the counter.

"Would you like a drink?"

"Sure, wine sounds nice."

I pour a glass for both of us then stir the spaghetti sauce-pot.

"Are the kids around?"

"They ate already and they've gone upstairs. Some peace, finally."

She smiles. "Better make the most of it then."

"Indeed. And I've got some news."

"Oh? Well, I've got some for you, too."

"Excellent. You go first then."

"No, no. Your house, you can go first." She sniggers.

"Fine. Well, I was going to save it for dinner, but what the hell. I got a promotion. More money, car allowance, and I don't even know what the upgraded job is."

"That's brilliant. Well done. I'm sure it was well deserved."

"Thanks. Shall I pop the cork yet?" I take out one of the bubbly bottles from the fridge.

"Oooh. Yes, excellent plan." I open the bottle carefully. No need to spill any.

"I have a feeling the promotion is because of the chatbot thing I got landed with in Holland. I haven't discussed it with the boss, or Alex, yet."

"Well, maybe a change is a good thing for you. Who knows what opportunities it will create?"

"True. I'm not averse to the chatbots. I just don't know much about the tech, yet. You should see the training manuals we got. I'm wading through them, slowly."

"I know the feeling."

"Well, anyway, I don't want to make this a business meeting. What's your news?"

"A toast first, to future opportunities." She raises her glass, we clink, then gulp down the wine. "Ah, that goes down easy."

"It does. Another?"

"Please." I refill our glasses. "Remember when we first met, in that café?"

"How could I forget?"

"I had a job interview that evening. You kindly fixed my phone so I could do the interview."

"I wondered what happened with that."

"I just heard yesterday. I got the job."

"Wow! Congratulations. That's wonderful. What is it?"

"It's almost the same as I do now, but for a bigger company. More money, better prospects."

"That's amazing, we both got upgraded. Double celebration then."

"There's one thing about it." I look over at her, suddenly awkward. "The job is in Albany."

"Albany? In New York State?"

"That's the one."

"Oh." A thud in my chest reverberates around my body. My guts sink to the floor. "You are going to America?"

"Yes, but it's only for three years, after that, I don't know. I could stay on or move back."

"Three years?"

Shit.

"I'm sorry, Danny, I know we're only just getting started. We can keep in touch, of course." She motions to her phone.

"No, no. If it's a good opportunity for you, you must take it." The selfish part of me wants to change her mind, ask her to stay, but I can't let her know I'm disappointed.

She's one of the few women I've met since Elise left that I thought could work out. But we aren't an item. I can't expect her to change her life for me.

"They've got an apartment for us, work permit, a place in a good school for Josh, a car… It is a good move."

"It sounds great. I'm happy for you." And there's always PornHub for me, I suppose.

"Thank you. I wasn't sure how you'd take it."

"I want what's best for you, and Josh. It's a shame it's so far away, but as you say, we can keep in touch." I stir the sauce again.

"That's good, because I like you, Danny. A lot." I look her in the eyes.

"I like you, too."

She stands up and walks around the counter to me at the cooker. She takes my arm and turns me around to face her, pulling me down for a long, hot, deliciously moist kiss. My underwear grows taught.

"That's for being understanding."

"Of course. I mean, what else?"

"Not everyone would be nice about it."

"I'm not everyone."

"No, that's why I like you." I smile and she kisses me again.

Over dinner, Faye tells me about the job and how she will uproot her entire life. She has to sell most of her furniture and stuff, including her car. Then some things are being shipped over in huge containers. Finally, she and Josh will fly out in eight weeks. That's all the time I have left with her.

Realistically, can I make a long-distance relationship work? Will I ever see her again, would she come back after the three-year job is over? I have no idea. I can't expect her to wait for me if she met someone local and more interesting. What if I meet someone here? Is it cheating to have sex while Faye is away? I have many thoughts, much confusion. No answers.

I should have known this wouldn't work out, that love was not my destiny. But that tiny glimmer of hope overtook me, reason and sensibility going out the window. Fantasy and desire taking over. Those are the dominant species in my brain.

I know one thing. The thought of going back to dreadful dating websites and apps fills me with a dire dread. I won't do it. The endless swiping, the two-second evaluation of dozens of hapless, bubbly outgoing women, all hoping for romantic walks on the beach. I'd sooner take a leaf from Jessica's book and stay single and celibate. At least that way there's no chance of heartbreak.

Maybe I should take up a new hobby, something the kids can enjoy. Instead of looking for women, perhaps women can come and find me for a change.

"If you need a hand with anything, give me a shout, okay?"

"Thank you, Danny, that's very kind."

"Least I can do. The kids can help too. I might buy some bits off you if anything is interesting?" Maybe a sack full of her knickers, for a start. Something to keep me going through the long, cold winters. A thought occurs to me. "How much do you want for the car? I'd love an electric vehicle."

"Oh, that would be great. I'll do you a deal. You better look after her though." She grins.

"I'll treat her good, don't you worry."

Ethan and Rosie show their faces briefly and grab a snack. Faye is easy with them, a great mother. I had hoped she'd one day, maybe, become a new mother for my babies. I guess not.

"I've been thinking of getting an Au Pair for them." I nod towards the door after they go back upstairs. "Jessica has only been gone a day and we already miss her."

"That's a good idea. Especially if you will be busier at work, now."

"That's a good point. This new title may mean I have to do some work all day."

She laughs. "Can't have that. Will there be much travel?"

"I have no idea. Perhaps, for training and stuff."

"To the US, maybe?" She smiles.

"Well, possibly. Our head office is in Texas."

"Flight layover?"

"Well, some kind of lay-over, maybe?" I grin.

"You never know." She bats her eyelashes.

Chapter Twenty-Eight

Once I'd talked to Alex, I found out she was also offered a promotion. But she declined it. I thought she was joking at first, one of her pranks, but she was dead serious. She didn't want to become the regional manager and take on the extra responsibilities that meant. I tried to tell her she was already doing the same job, and I did very little extra that she didn't. She didn't care. She preferred to stay as the team lead and nothing more. Fair enough, I suppose. I'm sure she has her reasons.

Since she's moved back to her parents' house and the break-up, I feel like she's been a bit distant. I'm not going to pressure her. I know she'll come to me if she needs anything. After a massive life change, you need some peace. The last thing I wanted after Elise left was people constantly asking if I was okay. I was trying to be. But like a quantum state, the act of observation changes the outcome.

I also had a long chat with D4 via video conference. He's a decent enough chap once you see past his Texan eccentricities. The promotion was apparently down to my outstanding work over the years. I don't know where that lie came from, but I'll take it. He did mention Faye's post on Facebook as evidence of my efforts. I must thank her.

D4 has big plans for the chatbot scheme; It feels like he's bet the whole darn company on this roulette wheel. Let's hope it comes in, or I'll be bringing the kids happy meals far more often after I finish cooking them at my new job with the clown.

He asked me how I'm doing with the training. I lied and said fabulous. That's what he wanted to hear. I hope that the computers more or less run themselves, and we only get involved if something goes tits up.

Today is a big day for the kids and me. With the help of an app on my phone, we are interviewing Au Pairs.

Narrowed down from a plethora of potentials to two girls who are visiting us at the house. I've spoken to both on the phone, and they seemed nice, as far as I could tell.

After discussing it with the kids, Faye, and deliberating over the pros and cons. In the end, I just went with 'fuck it' as the major decision-maker. Got to be worth a try? No one could replace Jessica, or indeed, their mother, but neither of them is around. I need someone to help. At least, it would make my life much easier, having gotten used to the help Jessica provided.

The app is like a mashup of a dating and shopping site. Dozens of hopeful girls listing all their credentials, attributes and achievements. Their photos mostly business-like headshots, but some girls can't resist the selfie duck-face even in a supposedly professional environment. I avoided those. I don't want drama. I also avoided the girls who I know I'd just want to coax into my bed. Sure, I could tease myself, try to live out my mid-life-crisis dream of shagging the Au Pair, but realistically, that will not happen, and even if it did, it's not a good idea.

My entire pay rise and a little extra will go to pay the successful candidate. But I think it will be worth it for my sanity and the kids' welfare. The summer holidays are almost over, and I feel guilty that we have done nothing together. Jessica took them to the playground and park sometimes, and the frequent burgers, but we haven't done anything as a family. I suppose I'm still shell-shocked from the disaster holiday at Forest Parcs. The children haven't complained at the lack of organised fun, but when they go back to school, and their friends ask what they did during the summer, and they say sod all, they may realise how apathetic and reactive my parenting style is.

The first candidate is Caterina from Spain. She's twenty-one, studied childcare, and wants to learn English. Our phone conversation revealed that her English isn't too bad already. She arrives on time, which is an attribute I value. She's petite, dirty-blonde, wearing a denim dress and sensible shoes. I don't know what I was expecting, maybe Mary Poppins? Caterina lacks the hat and umbrella. She has a nice smile and a fairly heavy accent that could take some getting used to. But maybe, while she's honing her English, we could all learn some Spanish? Which could be fun?

After some awkward pleasantries and introductions with the kids, we sit at the dining table with coffee and some notes I made for questions.

However, looking at my notes, they are all utterly irrelevant. I'm sure her childcare credentials are adequate, but only two people in this room have any real say about this. I look at Ethan and Rosie. They are quiet, polite and fidgeting. They don't like her.

Maybe they just need to loosen up and get to know her a bit. I'm still hopeful. I think she could work, and I don't even want to have sex with her. That says a lot.

"Tell us a bit about yourself, Caterina?"

"Please, you can call me Cat."

"Our cat puked in the laundry basket." Ethan states, matter-of-factly.

"I'm sure Cat doesn't want to know that, Ethan."

"I had to get a new school shirt."

"Never mind."

"Is YouTube different in Spain?" Rosie asks.

Caterina laughs. "No, is same."

"Does everyone sleep in the day and stay up late?" Ethan suddenly looks excited.

"You mean siesta? Only if it is too hot. I don't do it. But I like a long lunch."

"Guys, please. Let Cat speak."

"Is okay, no problem. Let me see. I am from Madrid, but I leave one years now. I work with one family since then, but they are, how you say? Strict."

"What do you mean? Strict with you?" I have visions of her being tied up and spanked for misbehaving. Stop it, Danny.

"No, no. With the children. Bedtime, routine, homework, TV time. My approach is more simple, not to force things, and they will come naturally. You know?"

"Ah, yes. That's how I think, too. Good. You want to leave the other family?"

"They are not terrible. I won't run away, but I don't stay much longer."

"Okay, good to know."

"Ethan, Rosie, do you like to show me how you play?"

"Games?" Ethan jumps up.

"Yes, sure." Caterina smiles and gets up to follow Ethan to the living room TV. Rosie remains seated. Looking unimpressed.

"Okay, Rosie?"

She shrugs. "Yeah."

"Sure?"

"Jessie helped me with my makeup."

I see what's wrong here. They are still loyal to Jessica. Maybe this was too soon?

"Well, I'm sure Cat could do that?"

"No, she can't."

"How do you know that?"

"She's got green eyeshadow on, which doesn't match her eyes, and her eyebrows are too faint and not shaped. Her lipstick is badly applied."

"Oh."

"Yeah. And she has a moustache." I have to admit, I noticed that. But I don't think that's reason enough to discard her application, unless she'd steal my razor and aftershave?

"Well, maybe you can help her, then?"

Rosie folds her arms. I guess not.

Caterina stays for a short while, looks around the house and garden, such as it is, and then departs on good terms.

"What did you think, Ethan?"

"She can't play games. She said they are boring."

"Not everyone can be interested in games. That's okay. I'm sure you'd find something in common with her, given time."

"She said she does jigsaw puzzles."

"Well, they can be… Rewarding?"

I may be fighting a lost cause here.

Małgorzata, thankfully known as Gosia, for pronunciation's sake, is our second candidate. She's twenty-five, also has an abundance of childcare qualifications, speaks fluent English, and is not currently employed. Thus available immediately. Her previous family no longer required her service, as the mother quit her job and decided to stay home. I've already seen her references, and on the surface, she seems great. Let's see what the kiddos think.

Once again, we gather around the table with drinks. Gosia is casual in jeans and a chunky sweater. Short brown hair and minimal makeup. I note that her tones are muted and natural. Hopefully, that is acceptable to Rosie.

"How long have you been in England, now, Gosia?"

"Five years. Seems like forever."

"Where are you from?"

"A city called Łódź. There is big manufacturing there, I worked in a factory before I came here."

"Do you have a big family?"

"Yes, five siblings, two brothers and three sisters. But they all stay in Poland."

"Do you see them often? Must be tough for you."

"We talk on Facebook, you know?"

The kids have been quiet thus far, but they seem to be listening, this time.

"Rosie, Ethan, do you have any questions for Gosia?"

"Do you play video games?" Ethan immediately asks.

"Can I tell you a secret, Ethan?" He nods excitedly. "I am addicted to Minecraft. Please, don't tell anyone." She stage-whispers.

"Yay! I love Minecraft. Do you want to see the secret underground bunker I made?"

"Cool. Yes, I would love to see." Ethan's face lights up. I think he's won over. I look over at Rosie.

"Do you have a boyfriend, Gosia?"

"Rosie, that's not a polite thing to ask."

She laughs. "It's okay. I don't mind. Not a boyfriend, but I talk to someone." She motions with her phone. Rosie seems satisfied.

We take the sixty-second tour of the house and garden. Gosia seems at home.

"Do you have any hobbies, Danny?"

I don't think she wants to hear 'chasing women'. "I've been trying to get out on the bike more, and I walk every day. I like to cook, sometimes."

"That's good. I do Geocaching. Do you know it?"

"No, what's that?"

"You download an app, and it shows trails and places where there is secret hidden treasure on a map. You have to go find it."

"That sounds fun."

"I've heard of it. Kirsty does it with her dad." Rosie perks up.

"Nice. I'll get the app. That might be fun for us to do something together, hey, kids?"

"Can I bring my skateboard?"

Ethan seems to be excited about something other than video games. I should call Sky News.

"Err, well, I don't know how much use it will be if the trail is in the woods, but sure."

"I'm going on a new hunt on Saturday if you want to come?"

"Can we, Daddy?"

"You know what, yes. Let's go Geocaching."

"Awesome. I will send you the details."

"Actually, why don't you just come with us?" I smile.

"I got the job?"

"Yes, Gosia, you got the job. Welcome to the family."

There's a cheer from everyone around the table. I think this is the right choice. At least she doesn't have any facial hair.

Gosia went off back to her current lodging to pack up her stuff, which is somewhat awkwardly with the family she is no longer employed with.

She arrives back with several suitcases and bags of food that she picked up from a shop in town I didn't know existed. A Polish food shop. She prepares dinner for us all from the bag of mysteries, wonderful dishes that none of us has ever tasted before. Makes a big difference from our usual pasta-based fare. I was concerned that the kids would complain, but they lapped it up with gusto. Especially the little Pierogi parcels.

I thought Gosia would need to go back for more of her things before she was ready to move in with us fully, but she says she's got everything already. She had a feeling she'd get the job and her bags were already packed.

Well, that's it then. We have an Au Pair.

Chapter Twenty-Nine

W hat is it about me that causes women in my life to leave? I suppose if I knew the answer to that, I'd be on every chat show and morning news channel, and running out of ink on my book signing tour of the world. The logic of why women do anything is far beyond me, and I suspect I'm not alone in this.

However, the reason is pretty clear in this case, and hindsight, being crystal clear, tells me I should have seen it coming. The signs were there. Perhaps I should have done something, or perhaps this was entirely out of my hands.

Regardless, here I am, trudging through Schiphol Airport once again. This time Alex isn't here to meet me off the plane.

She's leaving.

I make a mental list of all the dramatic female exits I've managed to live through and tell the tale of, as I walk the miles of corridor. It started with Emma, my first wife and love all those years ago. She drove a truck into my heart and then tore off with entrails gushing in her wake. I don't like to remember those thoughts. Then, just as I thought everything was calm and set in my life, Elise, the mother of my two children, my second wife. Her departure a deep stab wound into the scars of pain that took many years to heal. More recently, Jessica off to college, but I can't blame her for that, and Faye off to America before we even got anywhere.

Now Alex, my best friend, most valued colleague, and general tease has found new and better employment. I suppose it was inevitable. She is talented and smart, and her life was turned upside-down recently.

But still. Shit.

With Gosia installed only a week ago, I'm lucky that the kids are happy with her. I didn't like to ask Faye to help this time, as I'm sure she's busy, packing up and selling off her bits and pieces, as well as organising her imminent departure.

I flag down a taxi and direct the driver back to the luxurious grace of the Amsterdam Myatt hotel. A perk of being the regional director means no more per diem limited travel. For this combined recruitment and leaving piss-up trip, I'm entitled to some pampering.

Alex is arriving later, and because I simply couldn't face more interviews, our old friend from Paris is joining us tomorrow for his integration into the chatbot life. Victor Jacquard, the candidate who lost the previous job by the toss of a coin, gets another chance. It surprised me he was still available, and willing to come back to us, but he was even more interested when I explained the chatbot situation. He agreed to relocate temporarily to Amsterdam during the setup period and own the management and rollout. Perhaps this is for the best because even though I tried, admittedly, not that hard, I just couldn't get interested in the training documents. Alex never cared for this plan. Having Victor here to manage it for me is a godsend. D4 approved it all. I think this is what he intended for me to do, delegate the task to a minion. This will be a new chapter in work life.

Alex assured me we'd keep in touch, but I doubt that's true. When someone moves on, no matter what they think at first, it never ends up the same. Although, Jessica does keep in touch with the kids and me, even as she's started her first semester at university. I'm sure we will drift apart, slowly, unnoticeable at first, but one day we'll just realise it's been a month since we heard anything, and life goes on.

Maybe that's okay, and how things should be. Life evolves and changes; People come and go. Some stay for a long time. Others, like Faye, briefly light our lives like a flash of lightning and then rapidly dissipate into the ether. Part of me blames myself for hoping there could be something between us, part of me still hopes there could be, but the reality is staring me in the face. Faye will gradually fade away like everyone else.

I won't look for someone else, though. The accepted feeling seems to be that relationships come when you are least expecting them. Stop looking and something may just fall from the sky. At least, that's what the movies would have you believe.

I'm sceptical because that hasn't happened yet, however, since all my previous endeavours to find love resulted in bugger all, I reckon this approach has an equal chance of success.

I'm seamlessly transitioned from taxi passenger into hotel guest. My bags already in the room when I tap my phone on the door lock. I flop down on the bed for a moment of quiet pause, before sending a text to everyone that I have arrived safely.

Alex should be here soon, which gives me a little time to plan a fun evening for us. She said she didn't want a fuss, but I didn't come all this way just to wave goodbye.

I should have asked Alex for some suggestions. Aside from cycling and sex, I'm stumped as to what to do in Amsterdam for a colleague's leaving do. If Alex was a man, there'd be no question. Alcohol, smoke and hookers, or some lewd show at least. But this is different. I want to say thank you to her for all the years of pleasure and hard work she has given me. A meal seems irrelevant, no matter how good the restaurant. A night of drinking is inevitable, but hardly anything special. I should buy her a present, really, but what?

I remember seeing a shiny looking gift shop in the hotel foyer. Typically, this is something I wouldn't give a second glance at, as those places usually contain overpriced crap I have no need of. But in this situation, overpriced crap is exactly what I do need.

I wander down for a gander.

The moment I enter the room, I'm accosted by the immaculate assistant. She's got the resting-bitch-face thing going on but transforms to smiles instantly as she approaches me.

"Goedemiddag meneer."

"Err, sorry. Do you speak English?" I feel like a fool having to ask, but I'm sure she is used to it.

"Yes, of course. Good afternoon, Sir. Can I help you?"

"I'm looking for a gift for a colleague."

"Excellent, do you have something in mind?"

"Not really. She's a dear friend, leaving the company."

"Ah, a lady. Let's see." She pretends to think for a moment, then moves over to an expensive-looking and sparkly glass cabinet. "Anything here that you fancy?" She looks up at me, and I'm sure I noticed a flirty glance. She's ridiculously gorgeous but so far out of my league and style, I wouldn't even try. The cabinet is full of crystals and jewellery, with no price tags. I assume everything is just horrifically expensive, and they dare not advertise the cost.

"Well, my friend is about your age, very smart and stylish. Do you recommend anything?"

She smiles. I imagine her sales commission will get a fine boost from my credit card. "How about this?" She picks up a clear-blue crystal set of jewellery. A necklace, earrings and brooch, all styled to look like cracked ice. It's beautiful, but probably costs an arm, a leg and a couple of balls, too.

If I was a smooth, James Bond type bloke, I'd ask her to try it on for me, to see how it looks, but I'm not.

Instead, I pick it up and awkwardly look at the details. "It's lovely. I think Alex will like it. Dare I ask how much?"

"This set is five hundred Euro."

"Fu… Err, right. Maybe I'll keep looking."

"I can charge it to your room if you like? You are staying in the hotel?"

"Yes, I am. Oh, that could work." I wonder if I can get away with charging the expense to the company on the room bill. Would D4 shit his pants when he sees it going through, or would he not even bat an eyelid? My guess is he wouldn't notice since the room cost is almost that much per night. Time to make an executive decision here, as regional director.

"Go for it. I'll take it."

"An excellent choice, Sir. Shall I gift wrap it?"

"Alstublieft." She smiles again. I hope this expense doesn't end up costing me my job.

After a long and glorious shower to freshen up, I go back to exploring the nightlife possibilities and somewhere suitable to take Alex. There's too much choice. I'm lost in a sea of complication. I guess I'll just ask her where she'd like to go. Perhaps she has a favourite restaurant or bar she used to go to? Then again, that could stir up memories she'd rather not have. I know I'm haunted by thoughts I should have long since buried, anytime I go to the Kings Head in my town.

I'm saved from too much self-indulgent pondering by a knock on the door.

"Alex!"

"Hey, Danny."

"You look wonderful." And she does. She's wearing a clingy blue dress under a long jacket, and there's something different about her hair. I notice a porter standing awkwardly behind her with luggage. I motion them in.

"Thank you." She hands the porter some currency, and he slips away. "Well, do I get a hug, or are you mad with me?"

"Of course you do." We embrace and I squeeze her tightly. She smells like a woman should. A heady, intoxicating scent. "I'm not upset with you at all?"

"Really?"

"I'm happy for you, Alex. Yes, really. Don't worry about me. I'll be okay."

"Good, because I felt bad about it. You know?"

"Hey, it's not like you are dumping me. It's the job, isn't it?"

She raises an eyebrow, but I'm not going to be fooled by her teasing this time. She sniggers. "Of course not you."

I grab us both a beer from the minibar and we move to the sumptuous couch.

"You going to tell me about the new job, then?"

"My Dad, you know he worked at Philips for basically his whole life?"

"Yes, I think you told me."

"When I moved back home, he kept telling me about possible jobs coming up all the time. I ignored him at first because I didn't want to leave you." I look her in the eye, a stab of emotion throbs in my heart. "But you know, I thought about it and it made some sense. It's in the medical research division. Global marketing for the mammography scanner range of devices."

"Oh, wow."

"They want me to learn Hebrew and spend some time in Israel."

"That's amazing, sounds right up your street, well, if your street is in Jerusalem, I suppose." As the Dad-joke comes out of my mouth, it brings to mind my other fleeing woman. I feel a frown form on my face.

"What's wrong?"

"I didn't tell you yet, did I?"

"Tell me what?"

"Faye got a new job, too." Alex leans forward, curious. "Yeah, but it's in America."

"Oh, no…"

"Indeed. I mean, she says we'll keep in touch and it's only for three years, but…"

"I'm sorry, Danny. I know you liked her."

"I did. I do. I haven't given up all hope, yet. It's okay, I have the kids to keep me company. I know they won't leave me, at least for a while longer." Alex scrunches up her face in sympathy.

"No, it's good for her. A great opportunity. I can't expect her to put her life on hold because she met me. I mean, we aren't officially an item or anything. It's just been a few dates and the odd snog."

"Danny… Come here." Alex pulls me over to her and wraps her arms around me. "You are such a nice guy."

"Ha. Yeah, that's what all the girls say. Then they shag someone else."

She slaps me on the arm, but then tips her head over and kisses me on the cheek.

"Look, enough of the misery. Everything is fine. You have a great new job. I'm super happy for you. It sounds amazing and you'll change the world."

"Thank you, Danny. It means a lot."

I stand up. "Well, I suppose this is as good a time as any."

"For what?"

"If you are going to Israel, I expect it can get hot there, can't it?"

"Not bad, I don't think. Kind of like here."

"Well, it's too hot here. You'll need something to keep you cool."

"What are you talking about?"

I get the parcel from the minibar ice-freezer and hand it to her.

"What is it?"

"Open it and see."

She looks up at me, then down at the little box and tears open the wrapping. As she opens the box and takes out the now ice cold, cracked ice style crystal necklace, she gasps, her hand over her mouth. "Danny!"

"You don't like it?"

"No, I love it, it's beautiful. Oh, my god, where did you get that? It must have cost a fortune."

"It's a leaving gift from the company. I just appropriated it on their behalf. You deserve much more."

"Thank you, thank you. I will put it on now, but it's freezing cold."

"It's meant to be ice or something. So I put it in the freezer."

She laughs. "You crazy!" She walks over to the mirror and adorns herself with the jewellery. It suits her in the clingy blue dress. "What do you think?" She smiles and holds her hands up, tilting her head.

"Absolutely gorgeous. Oh, and the crystals look good, too."

"Oh, Shush." She blushes a little and my heart melts.

"You hungry?"

"Yes, a little, now you say it."

"All right then. Well, this is your special night. Where would you like to go for dinner in this fine city?"

"Nowhere. This is fine right here."

"Really? The sky is the limit. No per diem anymore for me. We can go crazy."

She looks around the room, then back at me, an angelic smile on her perfect face. "No, Danny. Why would I want to go out when I have everything I need right here?"

Chapter Thirty

Victor was installed successfully into the chatbot factory. I tried to set him up a tad more gracefully than D4 did to me. The chap was in his element. When Janwillem gave him the tour and hours of the tedious demo, he seemed to enjoy it. Strange fellow. But excellent for me. I left him enthralled and deep in the training documents I couldn't make any sense of. This is most definitely the right choice. D4 is happy; I'm happy. Well, as happy as a chronically single man can be when teased by beautiful women, who always seem a hairsbreadth away from sex, but never quite reaching the bedroom.

I tried. I really did.

What's the word for that feeling of an overwhelming desire and lust to jump on the bones of a beautiful woman, only to be held back by niggling self-doubt, fear of loss, the terror of rejection, and all-encompassing anxiety of making a total arse of oneself, in front of someone you love?

Oh, yes. That's it. Fucking idiot.

I could have made it happen if I just pushed a tiny bit further. But reality kept slipping back through the wine fug in my brain. Alex lives hundreds of miles away in a different country, she's got a fabulous new job, she's going to Israel of all places. What could I possibly offer her that would make her come with me to boring suburbia?

Nothing.

A one-night-stand was not what I wanted.

Sure, it would have been nice, a temporary relief. But the regrets would be too much to bear. I love that woman enough already. To be taunted with memories of that one night. The sweat and desperation of addiction clamming at my skin for more of the same. No. That Tennyson bollocks about 'Tis better to have loved and lost than never to have loved at all' is all very well, but I don't think he took into account the decades of misery that inevitably follow. I've already loved and lost enough. What I crave now is love that stays. Alex is not that love.

Faye is not that love either. As evidenced by her son, here now at my house, playing video games with Ethan.

She rang me last night to ask if I'd watch him for a day, while she got on with some hardcore packing up. Her normal babysitters, the neighbours, away for a weekend. Josh asked specifically if he could come here and play with Ethan.

That's a good sign. She wouldn't leave Josh with just anyone. Still, the cause is hard to overcome. She's leaving. Yet a niggling thread of hope still tangles at my thoughts. I'm stuck in her web of uncertainty and maybe's.

There are only two ways out of a web. Either I buzz off completely, and never come back, or I let her consume me until my withered husk blows away one day in the wind.

Josh is a good lad. He and Ethan seem to get along very well, at least while playing games together. It's a shame they won't get to be long-term friends.

Rosie retreated to her room, and Gosia is helping the boys with their game strategy. I'm getting the cosy family feelings again, but I can't shake the reason and logic my brain presents me with. Don't get used to it, Danny. It won't last and it isn't worth the emotional stress.

Judas doesn't care about that. He wants me to ask Faye to stay for dinner when she picks Josh up later. I mean, it makes sense. If she's packing up her life, I doubt she'd have had much time to cook anything, plus she's probably tired. I'm sure she'll welcome a cooked meal and no washing up.

My phone rings. Which is always an ominous sign. Elise's face appears on the screen.

Shit.

"Hello."

"Hey, Danny, how are you?"

"Err, fine, thanks. You?" No one wants to hear the truth when they ask how you are. I learnt that the hard way. A default answer is always preferable.

"Just wondered if you'd meet me for a drink? Are you busy?"

What the…? "A drink? You mean, in a pub? With you?"

"Yeah, Kings Head, if you like."

"Why?" This is highly suspicious.

"Well, I wanted to have a chat. It isn't something I can say over the phone."

"Err, well. Okay, I guess?"

"Meet me there in half an hour?"

"Yeah, sure. I can't stay long though." This must be a trap? What is she cooking up?

"Thanks, Danny. Appreciate it."

On the walk to the pub, having made sure Josh is happy in the capable hands of Gosia, I ponder the sanity of this encounter.

Am I voluntarily walking into the fiery pits of hell? How is she going to torture me this time? Does she need something from me? More money? Is this some kind of scam to get the kids away from me? Not happening. Why not just come to the house and talk to me?

I take my customary bar stool at the Kings Head and order an orange juice, but my nerves demand something else. I get it topped up with a shot of Vodka. Never a good plan, but some Russian courage is needed here.

"Hey, Danny."

I spin around on my stool. Elise, a vision of elegance and beauty in front of me. She never lost her looks when her love waned.

"Hi, Elise, you are looking well."

"Thanks." She takes a seat next to me. I wonder if she remembers this is exactly where we sat all those years ago when we first found out she was pregnant with Rosie? "And thanks for coming, Danny. I didn't know if you would."

I nod. "Drink?"

"Please. Half a Guinness." I call over the barman and order her chilled dark stout to go with her cold black heart.

"Cheers."

"What's this about?" I've learnt that it's best to cut to the chase, with Elise. Beating about the bush is what got me in trouble in the first place.

Elise stands up and motions to a comfortable seat at the back of the pub. "Can we sit over there?"

"Sure, if you like."

Once we are tucked away in the quiet corner, Elise takes a big gulp of her drink and then sits back.

"I guess there's no easy way to say this, so I'll just say it." I raise an eyebrow. "Brian is dying."

For a split second, I have to think who Brian is, but then it hits me. He's her current partner. The man who stole her away from me.

"Dying?"

"He's been sick for a while. Stubborn fool, wouldn't see anyone. But it was recently diagnosed. He's got terminal brain cancer."

What do you say to that? "Fuck. I'm sorry to hear that."

"They've given him twelve to eighteen months, but they say it could be anytime." Elise delivers this news clinically calm. I know she's not calm though. I can see clearly through her poker face, even after all these years.

"Brutal… I'm sorry, Elise. This must be tough."

"Well, you know. Life is tough, then you die." Funny how Rosie has her mothers' matter-of-fact way.

"Indeed." She takes another gulp of her drink. "Elise, look, I'm sorry this is happening and everything, but why are you telling me?"

She looks over at me, then looks away. "Brian asked me to become his widow."

"To marry him?"

"Yeah."

"Oh. Right."

She looks back over at me. "What do you think?"

"What? What do I think about what?"

"The whole thing."

I'm confused. "Elise, I'm not sure what to say here?"

"Danny!" She raises her voice, then seems to remember where she is and quietens down, "I'm asking for your help."

"Me?"

"I don't know who else to ask…"

"Oh." My mind flits back to how we were, long ago, when it was love I saw in her eyes, not hatred or scorn. She was a timid girl when we first met, I remember it was a slow and delicate process to get her to take notice of me, like taming a wild cat. Leave a morsel out and step back, see if she comes to grab it. Then slowly getting to know each other better, we finally became an item. After we married, over the years she gradually changed. A nervous, shy girl became a strong, independent woman. Then she ran away.

She never had many friends, never liked to talk about feelings with her family. I suppose she's right; she doesn't have anyone else who knows her as I do. Even so, this is weird as shit.

She's the young, nervous Elise, for a brief moment. "I suppose you have to ask yourself a couple of questions."

She looks over at me. Her eyes are moist; She seems desperate. "I have. I mean, I've thought about this a lot, but I'm running out of time."

"Well, then you already know what you want to do. Don't you?"

"Yes, I do. But I just need some moral support, I suppose."

"Do you love him?" The words stick in my throat as I say them.

She puts her hand on mine. "Yes, Danny."

"If he wasn't going to die, would you have considered marrying him?"

"Well, not really, there didn't seem to be a need. You know?"

"But now?"

"I suppose it's symbolic, or something."

"Marriage is always symbolic. I mean, what else could it be? Nothing changes, does it, if you are already living with someone. Some jewellery and a day of drinking, and then it's all forgotten." I'm reminded of my best man duties coming up soon. I should probably do some preparation for that.

"Hey, guess what?"

She looks up. "What?"

"Roland is getting married soon. I'm the best man."

"Roland? Your brother?"

"Indeed."

"But, isn't he gay?"

"He's marrying a man."

"Oh, wow. What do your parents think about that?"

"Err, well, I don't think they know, yet."

"Bloody hell."

"Yeah." I smile. "Elise, look. The man is dying, and he wants to marry you. If you love him, you know what you need to do."

She looks at me, on the verge of tears. Jesus. Here we go again. I open my arms and beckon her over for a hug. She rests her head on my shoulder and sniffs back the emotion.

"Thanks, Danny. Yes, I do."

She stays in my arms for a long time, then moves back and takes another drink.

"Rollie, eh? Who'd have thought?"

"I know, it was a shock. He never said a word. I was summoned to a secret engagement party down near London."

"Who's the lucky groom?"

"Chap called Monty. He's nice. Not what I expected at all."

"What did you expect? Village People?"

"More like Rocky Horror." We laugh. "No, I didn't know what to think. But I'm happy for them. It's a bold step."

"Yeah, I suppose."

"Have you thought about what you'll do… You know, after?"

"I try not to, but these things niggle at you, don't they? I mean, there's no point trying to deny facts. I think I might travel, for a while."

"That's always good."

"Might take Rosie and Ethan for a break, at some stage. I mean, if you don't mind?"

"I'm sure we can work something out."

She nods. "It brings it all into focus, doesn't it? Death. I mean, make the most of the time you have. Death comes for us all, inevitably."

"Can't argue with that."

"How are the children? I'm sorry I haven't seen them for a while. Things have been a bit… Intense."

"Understandable. They are good, thanks. We have a new Au Pair. Gosia. Polish lady. They seem to like her. She's making dinner. I should probably get back." I need to get home in time to ask Faye to stay.

"A Polish Au Pair? Look at you."

"Got a pay rise recently, but it doesn't cover her wages. Still. It helps to have someone around."

Elise looks down at her hands. I stand up to go.

"Danny. Thanks, for this chat, it helped…. And, well, thanks for looking after the kids. I'm glad they have you."

"Least I can do. They are my babies, after all."

Chapter Thirty-One

I thought about asking Faye to come to the wedding as my 'plus one' but it was far too complicated.

She's busy with her packing. What would the sleeping arrangements be? What would she do with Josh? Would he be comfortable with all the strangers? What would I tell Roland and our parents about the situation? They'd all assume we were an item, and, much as I'd like that to be true, I just don't know. Even asking her would cause confusion and stress. I left her alone.

I do feel bad, not asking. Too late, now. Story of my life.

Instead, I'm accompanied by Gosia and the kids, and on the drive down to the hotel, they are all asleep. Quite the normal family scene for us.

Roland has organised two rooms in the hotel for us. Kids share with Gosia, who seems very excited about the whole thing. Any excuse to go shopping for new clothes.

And I'm in a room on my own, unless I can pick up a spare bridesmaid and coax her back. Oh, wait. No bridesmaids. No bride.

· · ·

The, admittedly, minimal research I've done regarding best man's duties at gay weddings has garnered me nothing of use. Roland, as vague as ever, wasn't much better. He said, "Just enjoy yourself and go with the flow, bro." And various versions of "Stop worrying." All I know is I'm holding the rings and there's no need for a speech. Thank heaven for that, because I was quite freaked out about the possibility.

Another thing I was a tad concerned about was the reaction of our parents. However, much to my shock, they are happy and will be attending. As with all things, the details of how this miracle came to be are unknown, but I expect all will become evident when we arrive.

I didn't know what to wear, and Roland was of no help. I ended up in the suit I wore for my marriage to Elise, all those years ago. I'm surprised it still fits me. Sure, I had to change the trousers and shirt for new versions; the jacket is a little tight, but the shoes fit. Basically the same suit?

I park at the elegant Myatt hotel. Kids awaken, impatiently pulling at door handles. Gosia lets them out and they bolt onto the immaculate lawn.

"Guys! Come back. You probably aren't allowed on the grass."

"Hi, Danny." I turn around and find Ben, the hairy chap from the engagement event, beaming a smile. "Don't worry about the grass. It's meant to be played on."

"Ben, good to see you. Thanks. The kids are hyper."

"Good to get some air then. Come on in, we'll get you sorted."

Gosia goes off to round up the children, who are by now half a mile away into the garden, and I'm shuffled into the hotel. I'm checked in, given two room keys, and a free drink of something bubbly.

Ben leaves me at the bar.

There's no sign of Roland or Monty yet, or my parents for that matter. Looks like I'm the first to arrive.

Ethan comes flying in, quickly chased by Rosie and then Gosia. They flop down onto the antique leather couch. I cringe at the damage they will inevitably do to this regal old building. Probably stood for hundreds of years, through war and revolt, but finally razed to the ground by my kids on a single weekend.

"This place is amazing." Gosia comes over to me.

"It is nice, isn't it? Roland knows the owner."

"Very posh."

Saffy, as gorgeous as ever, clad in a tight little red dress, struts into the bar holding a glass in one hand and the hand of another girl in the other. She sees me, waves and comes over.

"Danny!" I stand up and engage in some excited hugging and triple kissing, no complaints here. "This is Leala." She introduces me to her friend. Leala has long electric-blue hair, pierced everything, and wears a lot of black fishnet, with huge black boots. Stick thin, total goth chick. She's the sort of girl I'd be scared stiff to talk to when I was a young lad, but I'd desperately want to. Come to think of it, she still is. She smiles and shakes hands, then sits down at the bar with her drink. I have a feeling she's only interested in fannies, too.

I introduce Saffy to Gosia and they start talking about clothes shopping almost immediately. I roll my eyes and get myself a beer. The kids are getting fidgety. They heard there was a swimming pool, and it's all they can focus on. Uncle Roland's wedding? Meh. But a free pool and they are like moths to a flame. I told them we'd try to get a dip at some point. I'm sure it's the only dip I'll get this weekend, or for a long time.

A gaggle of folks stroll into the bar. It's Keith Myatt and his wife Lotty, who is even riper and more pregnant than last time, she looks like she could burst at any minute. She sits down on the leather couch next to the kids. Then Ben and Lucy with their baby in a buggy. They come over to us and we do the shake and hug ritual.

"Does anyone know where Roland and Monty are?" Keith asks, looking around the group and settling on me. Everyone else shrugged.

"No idea, he's told me very little. But don't worry, this is how he likes it. I'm sure he's got a plan."

"Fair enough. Time for a beer, then?"

"Sounds good to me."

Mum and Dad appear in the bar doorway, pausing for a moment until the kids spot them, jump up and run over to greet them. I follow.

"Hi, Danny. Wow, isn't this place posh?"

"We couldn't afford a fancy do like this when we got married. Registry office and fish and chips after, wasn't it Sally?" Dad is in his favourite old suit. Starched collars and shoes so polished, you can actually see your face in them.

"That's right, and my old Mum tutting because we didn't have it in a church the whole time."

I've heard this story ten thousand times and again emphasised at both my weddings. It looks like Mum has been shopping for new clothes. A fancy hat and outfit. She looks uncomfortable.

"Hi Dad, Mum. Glad you could make it."

"'Course, this is bound to be an unconventional one, isn't it? What with Roland and his ways."

"I wasn't sure you'd come, to be honest."

"Of course we'd come, Danny," Dad exclaims. "Your little brother's wedding? We wouldn't miss it."

"Well, that's good. I just didn't know how you'd feel about it." They seem to have changed their tune quite drastically.

Mum turns to me. "Roland and Monty came to visit us a little while ago. Lovely chap, isn't he?"

"Yes, he is."

"Ex-military man." Dad grins.

"Really? I didn't know that." He nods, knowingly, and the matter is closed.

We go over to the crowd at the bar, and I introduce everyone to Mum and Dad. Keith gets them a drink. Dad and Keith discuss the qualities of Belgian ale, and Mum dotes on Ethan and Rosie, giving them a bag of sweets when she thought I wasn't looking.

Saffy sits down next to me.

"Danny, come outside with me for a second?" She winks and smiles.

"Err, okay…" This seems a bit cloak and dagger, but I'd follow her anywhere if I'm honest.

She leads me out to the back of the hotel and gardens. A few dozen chairs are being set up inside of a big open marquee tent on the grass. There are huge speakers and a little stage at the back.

"An outdoor ceremony? Lovely day for it."

"Yeah, lucky it isn't raining or windy."

"Do you know when he's arriving?"

"Roughly, but no one else does." She laughs. "Here, you'll need these." She takes two little boxes out of her bag and hands them over. The rings I presume. "Oh, and you'll definitely need these." She gives me a set of little earplug things. Then another bag full of them. "Give these to your family."

"Err? What for?"

"You'll know when to put them in." She laughs, then pats me on the arm. "Trust me. Everyone else has them already."

"Right. Okay."

She looks up and all-around at the sky, then back down at the marquee. "Not ready yet. Let's go back in for a bit."

We rejoin the throng and find my Dad holding court, regaling everyone with tales of submarine sewage processing. Not sure that's appropriate, but people seem engaged. I pass around the earplugs to the family. When they look at me quizzically, all I can do is shrug.

A few more people arrive whom I don't know. I presume they are Monty's guests. Saffy hands them earplugs and receives a lot of raised eyebrows.

More drinks flow, and the crowd seems happy and excited, dispersing off into groups.

Ethan pipes up. "What's that noise, Dad?"

"What do you mean?"

"That growling noise." I listen, and as the chat stops all around the room, the low throb of an engine becomes evident.

"Err, I don't know."

"We should go outside, ladies and gents." Saffy taps her glass with a pen and calls out to the crowd. She leads the way, and everyone stands up and follows.

The throb of the engine increases in volume as we go out into the garden and the source of the sound becomes visible. A gigantic army tank, coming into the car park, with Monty atop, dressed in camo gear and a helmet, poking out of the hatch. He's pointing up at the sky to a small plane, circling the grounds.

"There he is. Take aim!"

The turret of the tank gun swivels up and around, following the plane in the sky. Saffy puts her earplugs in, and motions to the gathered throng to do the same.

The plane circles around, swooping up and down. It looks like an old military thing, twin propellers at the front, painted in dark green.

"That's an old Bristol Beaufort." Dad excitedly announces. "Don't see them every day."

"He's going to shoot it down!" Ethan points at the tank turret, and it certainly does seem that way.

Monty looks over at Saffy and she gives a thumbs up.

"FIRE!"

The tank fires a blast of the gun, and even with the earplugs in the sound is deafening. He missed. The plane circles around again and climbs up higher. I look down at the kids to make sure they are okay. They are shocked, but absolutely loving it, jumping up and down in glee.

"FIRE!"

The turret swings around and takes another shot. My ears ring with the noise. This time the plane engine stalls and a stream of black smoke pours from the tail. The crowd gasps.

"Got him!" Monty roars and then jumps out of the tank and runs over to the marquee.

We look back up at the plane, the engine stuttering now. The smoke changes colour to red. Someone jumps out, and after a second a parachute opens. The plane flies away into the distance, leaving a trail of dissipating smoke in its wake. The crowd cheers as the parachutist descends, steering into the hotel grounds. As he gets closer, I can see it's Roland, dressed in a suit underneath the parachute straps. He waves and everyone cheers again. I didn't notice, but a photographer has joined the crowd, snapping away at Roland as he falls quickly into the garden.

He lands in the middle of the lawn, breaking into a run as he touches down, then releases a clip and his 'chute billows off and flops down. As he runs over towards the marquee, he takes something from his jacket, a small white sheet. He waves it like a flag.

Saffy leads the way and beckons everyone to follow over to the chairs in the tent. She grabs my hand and we head up to the stage, where Monty and Roland are now standing.

Roland picks up a microphone and holds up his flag, waving it high.

"I surrender, I surrender!"

"Got ya!" Monty yells into his mic and then they embrace to a massive cheer from the crowd.

Roland always does like to make an entrance!

.   .   .

279

A lady comes from the back of the tent with a clipboard. Presumably, she's the registrar. She picks up another microphone and comes to the front of the stage. Saffy and I are directed at a couple of chairs to the side. Roland and Monty stand with the registrar.

"Good afternoon ladies and gentleman, and welcome to the Myatt for the marriage of Monty and Roland." Another cheer erupts from the crowd.

The opening chords from Europe's 'The Final Countdown' blasts out suddenly. Roland plays air guitar to raucous cheers from everyone. Monty, in his camouflage outfit, struts up and down the stage lip-syncing to the lyrics. This is amazing, ridiculous, and they are loving it. Thinking about it, this is exactly what I should have expected from Roland's wedding. He's never been one for tradition and convention. A few people in the audience get up and dance to the song.

The registrar continues once the music fades. She's finding it hard to be serious, you can tell.

"Marriage joins two people in the circle of its love. It is a commitment to life, the best that two people can find and bring out in each other. It offers opportunities for learning and growth that no other can equal. It is both a physical and emotional joining that is promised for a lifetime."

In the front seats, I can see Mum reach for a handkerchief and wipe away tears from her eyes. Dad stifles back a choke, too.

Monty and Roland come to the front of the stage and stand facing each other. The registrar continues.

"Roland and Monty, you have invited your guests here today to receive their encouragement and support and to celebrate with you at this special time. I ask you now."

She turns to Roland.

"Roland, do you take Monty to be your lawful wedded

husband, to be loving, faithful and loyal to him for the rest of your life together?"

Roland pauses for a moment, looks out at the crowd, then up to the heavens.

"Yeah, what the hell. Go on then. I do." There's a laugh from the audience. I'm sure I saw the registrar roll her eyes. She turns to Monty.

"Monty, do you take Roland to be your lawful wedded husband, to be loving, faithful and loyal to him for the rest of your life together?"

"I do."

Saffy nudges me, I turn to face her. "The rings." She whispers.

"Oh. Right."

I get up and walk over to the couple, handing them the boxes. They are labelled so I know whose is whose, thankfully. They nod in thanks and the photographer rattles off a dozen photos of us.

They chime in unison, "I give you this ring as a symbol of our love. All that I am I give to you, all that I have I share with you. I promise to love you, to be faithful and loyal, in good times and bad, may this ring remind you always of the words we have spoken today."

They look up at each other with a huge grin.

The registrar continues. "Today is a new beginning. May you have many happy years together, and in those years may all your hopes and dreams be fulfilled. It now gives me great pleasure to tell you both that you are now legally Husband and Husband. Congratulations."

The audience cheers again, and from the car park, the tank fires another round. The boom nearly blowing the marquee into the atmosphere. I assume the gun is firing blanks, but you never know. It's damn loud, either way.

I turn to the couple and hold out my hand to shake, but they both grab me in an embrace. Saffy comes over to join us, and several people from the audience run up onto the stage until we are one huge circle of group hugging. Rosie and Ethan clasp around my legs. I wish I had invited Faye, now. The emotion overpowers me and I feel a choke of tears at my throat.

"Congratulations, mate." As we finally disperse and head back inside the hotel for drinks and the meal, I catch up with Roland.

"Cheers, bruv. You enjoy the show?"

"Rollie, I can safely say that was the best fucking wedding ceremony I've ever witnessed. Amazing."

"Nice one. Wanted to make a bang, you know."

"Certainly did that. Where did you get a tank and a bomber plane?"

"Monty has contacts." He taps his nose. "You ever jumped out of a plane? It's exhilarating."

"No. Fuck that. Faye has, though."

"Who's Faye?"

"This woman I'm sort of seeing, but… Well, she's going to live in America, so, ugh. I don't know."

"Mate, what did I tell you? Grab life by the balls. You like her?"

"Yeah, she's amazing. Gorgeous, smart, kind."

"Snap her up, you muppet. Why isn't she here with you?"

"She's busy, and I was worried about the sleeping arrangements, plus her kid… What am I meant to do? She's got this new job; she's packing up her life as we speak."

Roland shakes his head. "You'll find a way if it's meant to be. Live for now, don't think about what happens tomorrow."

"I wish I had your confidence."

He slaps me on the back. "Don't worry about it. It'll work out, trust me. Anyway, enjoy the rest of the day, that's all your duties done."

"Really? I thought best men had a load of stuff to organise."

"Monty is the real best man here, mate. Nah, none of that, we want everyone to relax and have a laugh."

"Fair enough."

The restaurant is closed off apart from our wedding party, which is only a couple of dozen. The atmosphere is relaxed and cosy. I'm on a table with the kids, Gosia, Mum, and Dad. The children are bursting with excitement still. Ethan wants to know if he can ride in the tank. Dad seems to know exactly how many rivets and bolts are used in its manufacture and isn't shy about telling everyone the excruciating details.

I feel like a complete twat, why didn't I ask Faye to come? It would have been an excellent chance for us to get more intimate. Roland is right, so what if she's leaving soon? I should enjoy the time there is left. I send Faye a photo of the gathered throng at our table with a simple message. 'Wish you were here'.

Chapter Thirty-Two

I don't know what it is about those Myatt Hotels, but it seems like whenever I stay in one; I end up in a hot tub with gorgeous women.

Now that I know him, I have a sneaky feeling that is the intended plan by the owner.

This time, it was Saffy and Leala, along with Gosia, Monty and Roland, and we wore swimming cozzies, well, most of us. Roland said you just can't tame the beast and Saffy. Well… After an unknown quantity of alcohol, and once the kids had finally settled down enough to be put to bed, someone mentioned Jacuzzi, and the rest is history, as they say.

The evening was going well, with Keith Myatt doing the DJ duties, playing an assortment of hits from the nineties. That was until his wife's waters broke at the buffet table. Someone said it was the tank gun blasts that triggered it, but she was bursting at the seams, anyway. They rushed off to the hospital. We found out the next day that her twin girls were born during the night, named Kay and Kenna. Mother and babies doing great.

I was yanked up on the dance floor by Saffy during one of the slow songs. She was drunk and clumsy, but since I can't dance to save my life, that's a good thing. She didn't notice I froze up and then pranced around like I was having a seizure. She grabbed me and pulled me close and didn't seem to mind that my boner was pressing up against her. Gorgeous women love to tease me. After two songs, Leala replaced me, and I watched them dance together, lustfully. I found out later in the hot tub they have matching tattoos in places where few men have seen.

Inexplicably, Mum gave Rosie a beer. She asked to taste it and Mum went and got her one at the bar. Shandy, she told me later, but still. I was a bit taken aback. Mum said she may as well taste it there in a safe environment, rather than in some boy's bedroom, or down by the river one day. I have to agree, that's a better plan. Rosie turned her nose up at first, but she did drink the whole glass.

As we left the next day, Mum and Dad were all over Roland and Monty. Mum said it was the best wedding she'd ever been to. I don't know exactly what it was that changed their minds about Roland, but I'm glad they are all happy and friends now.

All in all, we had a wonderful weekend.

I spent most of Sunday texting with Faye. I sent her the photos of the tank and Roland with his parachute. Explaining it all to her made me sad again that I didn't invite her with me. I'm such a fool.

Well, no longer. I'm taking her on a date today. It may be our last, or it may not, but it doesn't matter. I'm going to carpe the shit out of this diem.

It took a bit of organising, especially as I didn't want to tell Faye exactly what I was planning, but she agreed that Josh would come to our house, spending the day with Ethan, under the watchful eye of Gosia, while we head off for an adventure. It starts early, with a short trip to Oxford, then goes rapidly up about two or three thousand feet, after that, the elements decide where we go.

"Where are we going?"

"You'll see."

Faye twists her mouth in a devastatingly cute way. "Lucky I trust you, isn't it?"

I look over at her, in the passenger seat of her little electric car. I wanted to take it for a test drive, as I'm fairly certain I want to buy it off her when she leaves; because I want an efficient vehicle to take the kids to school in, not so I can sniff the driver's seat...

"Yes, it is." I smile and put my foot down. We accelerate silently. Love it.

We arrive at the car park for the ice rink, which is not where we're going, but this is where the adventure starts.

"Skating?" Faye looks at me and laughs.

"You'd be forgiven for thinking that, but, no."

"You are being very mysterious, Danny." She smiles.

"Really? Do you like it?"

"I don't know yet. We'll have to see."

"Ha. Come on then."

We walk straight past the ice rink doors, and around to the back where there's a small park area. I can't hide the surprise any longer since there's a huge, bright red, deflated hot-air balloon laid out across the majority of the green.

"A balloon ride?"

"Yup."

"Danny! That's awesome."

"Glad you think so. I had many doubts if this was a good idea, but I decided to 'just fucking do it', as my brother would say."

"Tell him thanks, then. I've always wanted to go up in a

balloon."

"Really? I thought it was just a load of hot air."

She slaps her forehead. "Oh, my god, Danny. Shut up, Dad!" Faye smirks and then smacks my arse, before running off towards the balloon. I chase after her. She won't get very high without me. I've got the tickets.

"If you were a bird, do you think you'd maliciously shit on people?" I know the basket sides are plenty high, but Faye hangs over the side, taking photos with her phone. I insisted I needed to wrap my arms around her to make sure she didn't fall out. She didn't seem to object much.

"No question about it. I'd deliberately find berries that made me shit purple, then I'd go crazy. I'd paint the town purple." She chuckles.

"It would be wonderful payback, wouldn't it? For all the people who have shat on us from a great height in this life."

"Shame it would be frowned upon to practice now."

We are in the basket with half a dozen other ballooners, plus the pilot. Between gas burns, the balloon drifts silently. It's wonderful and crisply cool. The pilot looks over at us. I flash a smile back. He pulls the burner lever and I take the opportunity to whisper in Faye's ear.

"We could probably spit on someone, though." She laughs, but nods.

We pass high over a golf course, which is absolute prime target practice. I point at the golf club and a group of people standing outside, waving up at us. Faye gives me a thumbs-up sign. We prepare to hock a massive loogie.

"Next burn?"

She nods. We're giggling like kids on a school bus, immature and stupid, but, how often do you get to spit on a golfer from two thousand feet up? You can't let an opportunity like that pass by. The other passengers seem to be busy with their own observations. But the pilot keeps giving us an evil eye.

We pass as close to the golf club as is likely. It's now or never. I look up at the inside of the balloon, it is just a thin bag of hot air holding us up in the sky. A bit insane when you think about it. Physics is wonderful.

The pilot pulls the burner lever and lets rip. I look at Faye and she nods. We hock, aim and FIRE!

For a second it seems like the pair of loogies will land true on target, as we're almost directly over the group of golfers now. I strain to watch as a gust of wind carries the spitballs far off course, vanishing into the distance.

"Bugger."

"I guess if we were birds, we'd have had more aiming practice." Faye turns to face me and offers a hug as consolation.

"Yeah, oh well, there's always the next life."

She peeks around to see if anyone is looking at us, then pulls me down for a long, passionate kiss. "Thanks, Danny. This was really sweet of you."

"My pleasure, Faye." And it is, too.

The flight is only around one hour, but that's probably enough, as it does get a bit chilly up there. I didn't mind though, because Faye had to snuggle up to me for warmth. We took some great photos as we passed over a castle and grounds, then descended into an open field, and had the fun task of helping to fold up the vast balloon into a little box, before being taken back by the follower van to the car park.

I have a whole day planned out for us, I told Faye she probably needed a break from the stress of packing up her life, so today she doesn't have to worry about anything. Josh is taken care of, and I'll take care of all her needs. You never know, those needs might even extend to the bedroom.

. . .

Lunch is a picnic in a park by the Thames. The food has been in a cool-box in the back of the car, but it's all carefully planned food that would survive. No soggy sarnies for us.

I transfer the contents into a wicker picnic basket, including a selection of beers, with some non-alcoholic, since I still have to drive home later.

There's a short walk through the woods to a bench by the riverside, in a quiet area. Hopefully, there won't be many people around, but you can't seem to avoid the dog shit that is always a default, despite the poop scoop shit-post-boxes everywhere.

"You needn't have gone to all this trouble, Danny."

"I did need, Faye. I wanted you to have a lovely day before you go."

She squeezes my hand tight as we walk and pulls me close.

"Thank you. It's nice of you. I do appreciate it."

"It's as much for my benefit as yours. I enjoy spending time with you."

She looks up at me. "Me too. With you, I mean." There's a hint of sadness in her smile this time. Now I feel guilty.

We get to the riverside path next to a bridge that has been entirely sprayed with graffiti underneath. Apparently 'Baz has a twelve-inch cock' and 'Mel wants to suck it'. Good for them. I wish them a happy life together. Sounds like they have something to build a great relationship on. Who says romance is dead?

We turn the opposite way and carry on down the path for a while until we get to a little clearing in the woods with a bench. That too is completely covered in scrawls and carvings, but I thought ahead and brought a blanket to throw down.

"This is lovely." Faye smiles, then sits down on the blanket. "My work said I could come back. You know, after the three years is up, if I wanted."

"Yeah?"

"They even offered me some consultancy while I'm in America. But I don't know if I'll have time."

"That's good, though. Means you have choices?"

"Yup. It's a bit scary, this whole moving country thing, now I'm actually doing it."

"I don't doubt it. You are brave. But I have every faith in you. You'll make a big dent in the Americas."

"You mean from my fat arse?" She sniggers.

"Your arse is anything but fat. Quite delicately peachy, in fact."

"Thank you, Danny. I didn't know you had noticed." She flashes a coy smile.

"I can't think of anything else."

She laughs. "Maybe we can do something about that, then?"

"Oh?"

She moves the picnic basket to the side and stands up, then sits down on my lap, her legs straddling me. She grabs my hands and pulls them around her, placing them firmly on her squeezable behind. She pulls me towards her and plants a kiss on my lips, deep, hot, moist. I pull her closer by her bum and let her explore my mouth with her lips and tongue. After a heavenly minute, she moves to my neck, nibbling softly, then licking and gently biting. My pants stretch as Judas wakes up from his slumber. Faye returns to my lips but gropes at Judas through my tight jeans, which only makes him fight to escape more. I feel a clawing at my button, then the zip of my fly and pressure released as my boxers are exposed to the air and Faye's grasp, all the while snogging my face off. I move one hand up inside her jacket and shirt, then clasp at her boobs like a baby trying to get fed. She's wearing a sports bra though, it's impossible to get any skin. I move back to her delightful rear and slip a hand into her leggings and squeeze. She squeals as I do and puts her hand inside my underwear, running a finger up and down the length of Judas. I gasp, her hands are cold but most welcome.

"Excuse me, Madam, Sir." We are startled into reality by a stern voice. We turn and see two policemen standing next to us; one of them is smirking behind his walkie-talkie.

"I'd take that inside somewhere, if I was you, folks."

"Err, yeah, sorry we just…" My face flushes bright red, Faye leans in to cover my rapidly deflating boner.

"This is a residential area, you know." He points at the riverbank opposite. I have to admit, I didn't know the odd rats' nest and litter dump was classed as a housing zone now, but I'll take his word for it.

"Right, sorry." Faye tries to suppress a giggle.

"We just came for a picnic, and, you know."

"I do indeed. Just take it easy, okay?"

"Yes, officer. Sorry, again."

"And make sure you take your litter home, please."

"Absolutely."

The cops walk away, but I remain frozen until they disappear around a bend. Faye sits up. "Never one around when you need one is there?"

"Bloody hell…"

"Don't worry, there's always later." Faye kisses me on the cheek and stands up, allowing me to adjust my clothing and zip up.

"Scotch egg?"

"Pardon?"

"From the picnic basket. Would you like one?"

"Oh, yes. I'd quite forgotten why we came."

"I didn't come, yet." I snigger.

"Danny!" She laughs. "I told you, there's always later." I think my luck could be in, here?

. . .

ADAM ECCLES

After our picnic, I had planned a movie at a nearby cinema. Since I had no idea what any of the movies were about, in the end, I plumped for something that was meant to be vaguely funny and romantic. Can't hurt to reinforce the subliminal thoughts and keep the mood alive. We made sure to leave the riverside as we found it; utterly filthy and drizzled with dog shit. But not our litter, therefore all is well in the eyes of the law.

"Where shall we sit?" The theatre is almost empty; We have our choice of the layout.

Faye points to the back seats. "Isn't right at the back traditional?"

"Traditional? Oh, you mean… Oh." A smile erupts on my face.

We take our horrifically expensive popcorn to the back, right in the middle. We've smuggled in cans of beer in Faye's bag.

We're really doing the teenage couple thing today, what a terrible scandal.

"I haven't been to the pictures in forever. Maybe ten years."

"Really? I bring Josh every so often. He wanted to see the Marvel movies on the big screen."

"I should probably bring the kids, but there's always something else to do, you know?"

"I do know. Life is hectic, but sometimes you just have to do it."

"I know. I try, but… They usually fight over what to watch at home, let alone choosing a movie."

"It's hard, being a single parent, isn't it?"

"It is. We deserve medals or something."

"Or at least a little treat, like today, now and then. I'm having a wonderful day, thank you again, Danny."

"Aside from almost getting arrested for indecent exposure, I agree, a wonderful day."

"Hey, that's how you know it was good. Who hasn't been

caught necking in the park?" She chuckles and grabs my knee, squeezing gently.

"Shh!" A grumpy old codger six rows ahead of us turns around and scalds.

"The adverts haven't even started yet."

"Some of us are trying to get some peace and quiet. Will you please shut up?"

He turns back around and Faye throws a popcorn down towards him. I have to cover my mouth to stifle a laugh. Thankfully, it falls short.

"Damn."

I whisper. "We keep missing things, just by a hair, today."

"Must try harder." Faye snuggles down low in her seat as the lights dim for the hour of pre-film adverts. "Well, Danny. You gonna kiss me, or what?"

"Don't have to ask me twice." I slip down to her level and she covers us up with her jacket. Privacy at last.

Chapter Thirty-Three

After the movie, that neither of us saw a single minute of, we went back home for a checkup on the kids. Faye was a tad concerned about Josh, but her worries were unfounded. He was fine at that point. So, to work up an appetite for dinner, which I had planned back at the Italian I favour, we went for a walk along my daily cardio-stroll route. Gosia and the kids came along, which wasn't exactly what I had in mind, but it worked out well. They ran around us in circles, and Gosia was planting one of her Geocaching capsules. The children had a blast helping her find a secret location. Faye and I took up the rear of the party, slowly ambling all the way, and she told me some more about her job and plans in America. They have secured Josh a place in a school that focuses on autistic children, which Faye is excited about, but she's also nervous about how he'll settle into a group from such a different background. It will be a challenge, for sure.

Some of her possessions are sailing off on a boat soon in huge shipping containers, ahead of her and Josh. Then they fly out themselves the day before Halloween. They've been allocated an apartment in a decent part of the city and a car rental until she can organise a lease herself. She said she'll miss her electric vehicle, but I promised to take good care of it for her.

She's looking forward to the Halloween costumes and candy that the Americans love so much. I never really bother with the holiday myself, just a pain in the arse with people ringing the doorbell all night. I usually turn the lights off and make the kids hide upstairs. I know, I'm a grumpy old sod, but the kids don't seem to care. They think it's fun to hide.

Elise used to take them out trick or treating, a long time ago now, but I've never really got into it. Maybe this year we'll do something. It might take my mind off things.

Anyway, when we got back to the house, Faye took a shower and changed into an evening dress, which was quite the vision in tight black, with a smear of bright red lipstick.

I let her get changed in my bedroom, which is the first time a naked woman has been in there for a long while. Shame I was too gentlemanly to sneak a peek.

She sprayed on some perfume that made me want to cancel dinner and just eat her there and then. But she deftly batted me off. I think she enjoys teasing me.

I showered after. I needed a cool one to calm me down. She had promised me 'later', after all. I just needed to wait a little longer. The prize was most certainly worth it. I'd had my starters already, now I wanted the main course.

Dinner at the Italian was delicious, as usual, and, having decided to walk into town, we both got a little tipsy on Chianti. There were many candlelit moments of hand-holding and eye staring, and reflection on a lovely day, and, I dared to mention that I'd very much miss her when she's gone. She said she'd miss me, too. That it was a shame we hadn't met much earlier; Perhaps things would be different? It certainly is a shame, but as my Dad always says, there's no point in dwelling on what if. If your Aunt had bollocks, she'd be your Uncle.

As we exited back into the cool evening air, we realised we may be a little drunk to walk all the way home, and much too full and lazy. Instead, we called a taxi, or whatever the modern equivalent of a taxi is these days.

As I unlocked the front door, the merriment and lust that was lingering between us dropped to the floor. The mood changed rapidly, and Faye let go of my hand.

Screaming children from inside the house will do that.

We could hear it was Josh that was crying as we went into the hallway. Faye sprang into sobriety immediately and rushed into the living room. Gosia was trying to calm him, and Rosie and Ethan could only look on in a mix of horror and awe.

They'd had a great day together, mostly playing games, and in the evening as Faye and I dined out, they watched a movie. But it was when Gosia suggested it was bedtime and everyone go get ready, and that Josh could sleep on the couch, or in her bed and she'd take the couch if he wanted, that all hell broke loose.

Bedtime is at nine-thirty, he said. Not ten, and definitely not ten-thirty. Bedtime is in his room at home with Mum, not in someone's house with strangers. He was adamant about this. No amount of discussion would change his mind. It got a bit heated, apparently, and he became rather upset, which made it all worse. Faye hugged him and motioned for us to leave the room. She got him settled after a while, then came into the kitchen where I sat, already knowing what she'd say.

The kids had gone up to bed, and Gosia had followed shortly after, once she'd explained what happened, leaving me to mulch in my disappointment, and then my guilt at my only concern being getting the shag I was promised. Of course Faye had to look after her son. I'd do the same, without question. She asked me to order another taxi and take them home. I had already booked it.

She apologised, over and over, but I told her not to worry. There'd be another day; it would be fine.

But with their departure to the other side of the world ever more imminent, I don't think there will be another day. At least not for three years, give or take.

Faye dropped by this morning to pick up her car. All was fine once Josh got home to his bed. She apologised again and kissed me many times, but she had to go and finish up some work things, and she couldn't stay. I managed to get another tentative date promise before she left. She said, of course, she wouldn't just fly away, we'd say goodbye, one way or another.

So close, but no cigar.

"Danny!" Gosia appears at my office door, she has her phone in her hand and tears in her eyes. Oh lord, what now?

"Hey, are you okay?"

"No. My Babcia died this morning." Tears flood from her eyes. I stand up and offer my arms for a hug. She comes forward and falls onto my chest.

"Your what?"

"My grandmother." A muffled voice comes from my shirt.

"Oh, I'm sorry." I pat her back, soothingly. "Was she sick or something?"

"No, I don't think so. Eighty-seven next month but she was strong as a bull."

"What happened?"

Gosia pulls away and sits down in my chair. "She didn't wake up this morning. I guess her heart or something? They don't know for sure yet."

"Well, you know, I hope I go in my sleep. Probably the best way." Gosia nods. "Were you very close?"

"Yes. Well, when I was young. I didn't see her much since I lived in England."

"I'm sorry, again. This must be tough."

"Funeral is in three days. I was just talking to my mother."

"You should go."

"I was going to ask, you don't mind?"

"Gosia, of course not. You must go. Do you want some help with travel arrangements?"

"You are such a nice boss. Thank you, Danny."

"Don't mention it. Go pack your bags. I'll find you a flight as soon as possible."

After some cursing at the various cheap flight websites, that mainly just infuriate rather than help, it turns out that it's hard to find a good flight deal with such short notice. The only seat on a direct flight we could find was three times what Gosia expected to pay, but rather than piss around and lose the opportunity, I booked it on my credit card. She's a good lass. I help where I can. She leaves in the morning, ridiculously early.

"I was thinking, Danny, I might stay in Poland for a while after, with my family, you know?"

"How long do you think?" I booked her a one-way ticket. She said she'd worry about the return flight later.

"Well, maybe a long time. Like, forever."

"Oh. Right."

"Sorry, I know this is unexpected."

"No, don't worry. I understand. Tell you what, just see what you think and let me know when you get your head together. Okay?"

"Okay."

I guess that's over. Another woman leaving me. I should just expect this now. They don't last long. Gosia has been a real help, but thinking about it, I don't think I'll hire a replacement. We'll muddle through as we did before Gosia and Jessica.

I somehow kept the children alive and entertained. I don't want us all to go through another cycle of acceptance and loss.

With them back at school now, we're getting into our normal routine. School runs, work, eat, YouTube, sleep, repeat. I guess this is my life now for the foreseeable. I may as well try to get used to it.

I have noticed something about the kids lately. A visible change. Their rooms are tidy, they do their homework before dinner most nights, and not in the morning, as we're trying to scramble to get everyone out of the house on time. I even saw them playing a board game with Gosia a few times. They seemed to enjoy it, and there were no iPads anywhere near.

I think the female influences they've had recently have done them good. If only I could find someone who would stay, long term.

Gosia made us a spread of Polish food for dinner. She said it was in honour of her Babcia, and her leaving gift to us. A veritable feast. I'm stuffed, but in a good way. The kids lapped it up. I must try to get the recipes, but I doubt I'd be able to do these dishes justice.

The kids were sad at the news of Gosia leaving, but they seemed to accept it with little fuss. I expect they are getting used to the high turnover of staff. I'm sure these experiences are setting them up in life to be resigned to disappointment as the default state. Whilst that's sad, it is pragmatic.

Never mind. We'll figure it out, and Jessica still wants to come to visit over the Christmas holidays, which aren't that far away.

Chapter Thirty-Four

I feel like it's a tad unnecessary, but D4 insisted.

I am headed back to Amsterdam once more for the debut of the much-celebrated Chatbots. Victor has them primed, ready, tested and keen to be released on an unsuspecting public. The machines are coming. Humans lookout. You are obsolete.

I hope they function correctly because my directorship is on the line here. "Make it work, Danny," D4 said. And I have to admit, I've been somewhat hands off throughout the setup, trusting it all in the capable hands of Victor. Have I bet my life on a crappy hand of cards? Or have I bluffed my way to a win? I'll find out soon. Not that I'm worried or anything.

With Gosia gone and her grandmother buried, my suspicions were correct. She decided not to come back, at least not in the foreseeable future. Maybe one day, she said. But my kids could have left for college by then. I guess our brief relationship is over.

This explains why we're in the car, headed to my parents' place and the kids are asleep in the back.

. . .

Elise got married yesterday. I found myself strangely not caring. There was a time when the thought would give me cold chills and jealousy pangs, but now I'm sure I've moved well along. Ambivalence was all I felt. It's a temporary situation at best, but I think she made the right choice.

Unsurprisingly, I was not invited to the event, but she sent me a text after. The celebration was likely quite muted, conducted at the registry office in town. Speed was of the essence. Things took a turn for the worse recently, she said.

I was in two minds if I should even tell the children about it, but Elise wanted them to know. She took them for a fast food treat and broke the news in the clown's presence. The cynical part of me thinks that's highly appropriate, but the mature part, stunted in growth as it is, realises that would be mean. The man stole my wife away, but maybe she'd already gone when he met her, maybe he just pushed her over the cliff edge, but I drove her up the mountain in the first place. I don't wish him dead because of it.

When Ethan asked me later if Brian was sort of their daddy now? The answer was a definite 'No.' and they said no more on the subject. Rosie, in an uncharacteristic move, probably sensing the tension, came and sat next to me on the couch and snuggled up as we watched TV that evening. I appreciate the thought.

I look up in the rearview mirror at them, asleep and yet still plugged into iPads. They aren't bad kids, all told. They've had their moments, but I couldn't be without them.

We pull up at Mum and Dad's house, and as I turn off the engine, they awaken. I enjoy the moment of peace as they stretch and yawn, but then, as they realise where we are, the chatter and excitement begins. I get out and stretch my joints, leaving them to jiggle at door handles and yelp to be released. I take my time, teasing them for a few seconds.

.   .   .

"You must be very important, Danny, to be travelling for work all the time?" Mum might have exaggerated my value a little, but I don't mind the boost in ego.

"Something like that…"

"Someone has to lead the rabble, eh, Danny?"

"Too right, Dad."

"Ethan, you've grown again." Mum fusses over the lad. He smiles, but a little sheepishly. He is getting tall for his age, but I don't like to call it out. No need to give him any reason to be self-conscious. Life is complicated enough.

"I've got something for you kids later." Dad winks and Ethan beams a smile. Rosie is busy trying to hack into the neighbours' WiFi.

After Sunday dinner, which was traditional fare as Mum likes to make, Dad takes us up to the box room.

"Remember the train-set I made you boys, Danny, when you were a lad?"

"Of course. How could I forget? Is it still around?"

"Up in the attic, somewhere, yes." He chuckles. "Well, kids, here's version two."

Dad flicks on a switch and the room lights up with hundreds of tiny bulbs suspended around a model railway on a table.

"Wow!" Ethan's eyes widen, Rosie beams a smile, too. The diorama is intricate and detailed. A small electric train moves around the track, going into a tunnel that's part of a mountainside.

"It's amazing, Dad. Beautiful."

"Glad you think so. It's for the kiddos to take home."

"Oh. I'm not sure it will fit in the car."

"Don't worry; it all comes apart. Remember all those beer cans?" I nod. "I made most of this from smelted aluminium."

"You made this? It's awesome!" Ethan looks up at his grandpa in wonder.

"Grandpa is very resourceful." I turn to Dad. "You melted down old beer cans and made a train set?"

"Well, the shell of the trains, the underpinnings of the landscape, all the little houses and people. Yes." Dad looks very proud.

"He's been working on it for ages." Mum comes into the room. "To the detriment of my lawn, I might add. That smelter always singes the grass."

"Just like a big barbecue." Dad laughs.

Ethan is enthralled, playing with the controls. Rosie takes a close-up photo of the station with her iPad.

"This is wonderful, Dad. Thank you so much. Say thank you, kids."

"Thanks, Grandpa. I can't wait to show Josh." Ethan flings himself at Dad for a hug. At least they won't be bored while I'm away for a few days.

———

Dad dropped me at the airport again. I think he enjoys getting up before the dawn, in some kind of sick, demented way. He regaled me with in-depth details, on the journey down, of how he made each of the trains using his metallurgy skills. I think he's something of an alchemist as well as an engineer. He brings a sense of magic and wonder to simple lumps of metal.

I make my way to the, now familiar, Myatt hotel to dump my bags before heading straight over to the data centre where Victor and Janwillem await my arrival. No ceremony, we're launching straight into a phased release. English-speaking countries first.

Leave them to soak for a day, then switching on the rest of Europe tomorrow.

Fingers and toes crossed.

I went back and forth about telling Alex I was in the country. On one hand, I'd love to see her, on the other, she's probably busy and I don't want to disturb her. Guess which devil on my shoulder won that debate? Alex said she'll pop up later after she finishes her work. We've got some catching up to do. A lot has happened since I saw her last.

I wasn't sure if she'd still be here, but she hasn't gone to Israel just yet.

At the data centre, I'm greeted with a pair of blue-cloth-shoe-bags and shuffled through into the hall full of those churning monoliths, spewing out a constant stream of binary electrons, creating an invisible world we all know intimately. Delivering movies, videos, photos, books, social media and all our files we create and store for massive corporations to suck up and analyse, to figure out what crap they can sell us. The cycle continues. We feed the machines and they feed us.

Victor and Janwillem are waiting in the little office. After some vigorous handshaking and much-needed coffee, Victor, in his oversized suit, opens up a window on his laptop.

"Ready?"

"I feel like we should get a photo or something to mark this significant event?"

"Ah, Oui. If you like."

I stand up and snap a shot on my phone of Victor and Janwillem next to the laptop. It lacks pomp and formality, but the moment is captured, nonetheless. I send it to D4.

"Okay… Make it so." I've always wanted to say that.

Victor types a command and presses enter. Nothing happens.

"They are live."

"Bit of a damp squib. I thought there would be something audible at least."

"Ah, I had my volume muted. Shall I start again?"

"No, no. That's fine, Victor. Sorry, don't mind me. Well, now what?"

"We wait for some people to log on and talk to the bots. Then analyse the first conversations."

"Time for lunch, then?"

I had my suspicions before, but now I feel they are definitely confirmed. Janwillem is a robot. He declines my offer to go for lunch. Said he wanted to stay and monitor the systems. Fair enough. Victor and I head to the canteen.

"Are you confident the bots will work out, Victor?"

"Oui. No problem." He smiles, he seems assured. "We have run many tests. It works well." His face falls. "… Unless, oh merde."

"What?" Oh, holy shit balls. He's forgotten something. It will go pear-shaped and explode. D4 will have my balls for bookends and Victor's arse in a burger bun.

"Just kidding. Everything is fine."

"You had me there for a second."

He laughs. The little twat. I'll get him back for that.

"How are you doing, Victor? Generally, I mean."

"Very good, thank you, Danny. I am glad you took a chance on me."

"Dude, you've been a godsend. With Alex leaving and my ineptitude with this, I'd be screwed without your help."

"My pleasure. It has been fun learning the city."

"Do you get home much, at the weekends, maybe?"

"I stay here until now, but maybe soon I visit."

"You should. Do you have someone special to go to?"

"Just parents, no girl right now." He grins.

I know that feeling. "Your day will come."

"Too busy with work."

"Well, now the bots are up and running you can relax. We won't need you anymore."

"Ah, pardon? I thought this was a permanent role?"

"Hey? Who told you that? No, mate."

His face falls again. "Oh, this is not good." I raise an eyebrow. "I was hoping to save up for my business."

"Got you back." He looks up. "Just kidding, Victor. Now we're even."

"You are funny man." He grins nervously.

"Come on, let's go see how the bots are doing."

The website has been directing calls to the chatbots, instead of phones, for an hour now, and they've already taken two hundred and thirty requests. Of those, they redirected about ten percent back to humans, because they didn't understand the questions. The rest they handled entirely. We look through a sample of the conversations they've had. Some ended with the user just disconnecting as they discovered they were talking to a machine, but others had an entire conversation and resolved the users' problem, they even thanked the bots. We focus on the conversations where they were redirected to humans to see what went wrong. Of those twenty or so, some people couldn't seem to spell accurately enough for the machine to understand, some didn't want to type out their problem in-depth, requesting a call instead, others just had a strange way of asking their question. A human needed to interpret their thoughts. For example, the bot didn't know what to make of this one:

'My daughter bought me this smart telephone thingy, but I don't understand anything about it. Can you help?'

One chap had been infected with some kind of porn virus and wanted to talk to a man only. The chatbots all have female names; it makes them seem more approachable. Another person had dropped his phone in a cup of coffee, but because he called it Java, the bot wildly misunderstood.

Teething problems, but the majority of the conversations went well. I think we have a winner here.

I sent D4 an update on the status. Attaching the first hour reports. Got to keep the big man happy.

"Victor, this is excellent work. Well done, mate."

"Merci, Danny. My pleasure. Still, we need to monitor it for some time."

My phone buzzes in my pocket. A text from Alex. She's got off early, and she's coming to Amsterdam now.

"Ah, something has come up. I have to split, but will you join me for dinner later at the hotel?" I look over at Janwillem who is deeply engrossed in his screen. He shakes his head.

Victor smiles but also shakes. "Perhaps tomorrow evening, if you are still here? I want to watch the bots this evening."

"Seriously?"

"To be safe, I will stay."

"Wow, that's above and beyond, Victor. I certainly appreciate your dedication. Make sure you remember to eat, though." I look back over at Janwillem; He doesn't flinch.

Victor nods.

"I'll see you tomorrow then."

I'm glad of the excuse to leave. The constant drone of the machines in that place always gives me a headache.

"We meet again." Alex arrives at my hotel room just as I step out of the shower.

"You didn't think I would let you get away that easily, did you?" She flashes her heart-melting smile. She's in a smart business suit, heels, hair tied up. She looks the part. Still gorgeous, but differently to Faye.

"You don't mind if I change? I see you are already comfortable." She laughs. I'm wearing nothing but the hotel bathrobe, which I may consider pilfering. I'm sure Keith Myatt won't mind. Mine has seen better days, though it has stretched out a little of late.

"Of course not, go ahead." I flop down on the couch. "Throw me a beer while you pass the bar, Alex?"

"Ha. What did your last slave die of?"

"Of not getting me a beer quick enough." She flips me a finger but laughs. "My Au Pair has gone. Did I tell you?"

"Oh? No, you didn't." She yells from the bedroom.

"We have a lot of catching up to do."

Alex comes out, wearing the other fluffy white bathrobe. She laughs as I look up at her. "Well, you look cosy, so, when in Rome…"

Chapter Thirty-Five

Victor is now a proud father, to thousands of autonomous chatbots. He gave them life, now they do his bidding and patrol the corners of the internet, looking for lost souls who need help. We deployed our bot-farm all over Europe, and now they field thousands of help requests per day in multiple languages. So far, they haven't attacked our humans, and we all still have a job. For the time being at least. We just help more people overall.

D4 is thrilled at the results, although we still keep a close eye on things, probably for the foreseeable. We don't want the bots going rogue and telling people where to shove their iPhones.

It's surprising how many people don't even realise they are talking to a machine, saying 'thanks' at the end of their conversations. It's funny, but I suppose we should get used to this revolution.

I, for one, welcome our new AI chatbot overlords.

Alex has gone to Israel. There's a big thirst for medical imaging systems there. She's on her first of many visits. Some will last months. She's excited to learn another language and get to know the culture.

I can't help but wonder if I will ever see her again.

Sure, we'll talk online, but will I ever get to spend a crazy evening getting drunk and silly in a hotel with her again? Probably not. Those glory days are over. She's moved along in her life. I suppose I should, too.

Where to though? I've been pondering the possibility of moving to the US, but I doubt my skill set is much use out there. I excel in doing bugger all.

Even if I somehow convinced D4 I needed a transfer, he's in Texas, and that's a world away from where Faye will be in Albany, New York state. Not much use.

Plus, the kids. Could I drag them away from their school and friends? It would devastate Rosie at this tender age. Although it makes for a nice daydream, I can't see it happening.

I'm stuck here, Faye is leaving for at least three years, and who knows if she'd ever come back after that. A lot can happen in three years.

A lot can happen in one day. Maybe today is the day?

With Gosia gone, I moved furniture around in the spare room to make space for the wonderful train-set that Dad made. He helped me disassemble it for the car ride home and showed me how to put it all back together again.

In truth, Ethan did a lot of the re-assembly. He's starting to show a real interest in mechanical things. Must be Dad's influence rubbing off, because I can break a can-opener just by looking at it.

I'm in awe of the detail Dad put into the landscape and trains. Cast and moulded from old discarded beer cans. I told him he could make good money selling things like this online, but he wanted none of it. He does it for the joy, not for money.

Said he's too old to start a business, and he doesn't want to deal with punters, tax, shipping and complaints. Can't say I blame him. I have enough business crap to deal with at work and we don't have physical products.

Ethan can't wait to show it to Josh. He's been sending him photos already.

They talk online all the time, and he's not one bit worried that Josh is going away soon. They'll still be able to talk, he says, albeit with a five-hour time-zone delay.

I suppose I should take a leaf from his book and be thankful for the wonders of the Internet. I'll still be able to talk to Faye every day if I want to, and it won't cost a penny. If this was twenty years prior, my phone bill would be astronomical, but now a high-quality video call is just something we all expect for free. Amazing progress.

Not quite the same, though. I know I will miss the warmth and smell of Faye's skin. Ah well, there's always my pocket-pussy, and Internet-enabled sex toys, I suppose.

"They're here," Ethan yells from upstairs. He's been peeking out of the window.

I go to the front door and watch Faye park my new motor in the driveway. She's leaving it here this time. I must flog my old crap-heap at some point; might get enough for a clown-food takeaway.

I'm joined by children at the doorway. Ethan bubbling to show Josh the trains, and Rosie proud of the food she's made for our lunch. This is it. Our last day together. Better make it a good one.

"Hello."

"Hiya. Sorry, I didn't change. We've been painting and cleaning for the rental inspection, and we're living out of suitcases for now."

Faye is in old blue dungarees and a white t-shirt underneath, with daubs of magnolia paint on her hands and face. Her hair is tied up. No makeup. She looks delicious. Women make such a fuss about their appearance, but all we men want is natural beauty, unadulterated with face paint and fancy clothes. Elise used to moan at me that I never complimented her on her nail polish. I never looked at her fingers, why would I? If she'd worn a bin-bag with holes poked for arms and legs, I'd still think she was gorgeous.

"You look great. Come in."

"Josh, come see the train-set." Ethan beckons Josh in. He looks up at Faye for approval and then runs in after Ethan, up the stairs.

I steal a kiss as Faye passes me by. She smiles and lingers for a longer snog. I sneak a bum squeeze in. Love a nice pert buttock grab.

Rosie rolls her eyes, tuts, then escapes into the kitchen. I'm sure she thinks adults shouldn't be kissing, especially ancient old adults like me.

"Rosie has made her world-famous lasagne. She's very proud, aren't you Rosie?"

"Dad. It's just lunch." She blushes a little.

"You've done a great job, sweetheart."

"It smells delicious, Rosie. I'm starving. Can't wait." Faye smiles and flops down at the table.

"Drink?"

"I shouldn't really, loads more work to do later." She sighs. "Oh, go on then, you've talked me into it. Just a small glass, though."

I grin and pour her a white wine. "What's left to do?"

"There are still two rooms and the halls to paint. The bathroom to scrub, kitchen to blitz." She throws up her hands. "Otherwise I'll never get my security deposit back. You know how miserable landlords are."

"Why don't we come and help, after we eat and relax for a bit?"

"Oh, no I can't ask you to do that."

"You didn't ask. I offered, and I insist. Shut up and drink your wine. We're going to paint your house."

Faye laughs. "Well, if you put it like that. Thank you."

"Be a laugh, won't it, Rosie?" She looks sceptical, but nods. I think she can sense that I want to eke out every last minute I can with Faye. If that means cleaning a kitchen and getting covered in paint, then so be it.

"Ethan is a dab hand with a mop. We'll have you all cleaned up in no time."

"What would I do without you guys, huh?"

"Indeed."

Lunch is delicious, of course. Rosie is becoming quite the domestic goddess. She's picked up some tips from Jessica and Gosia recently. The kitchen is clean and food is served. Garlic bread, salad with dressing, the super-tasty lasagne, and freshly grated parmesan. Food of kings. Everyone tucks in with gusto. Faye, petite, somehow manages second helpings. I admire a woman who isn't afraid to eat.

I also coaxed another glass or two of wine into her.

I'll be driving us to her house later. She doesn't own a vehicle anymore. I transferred a chunk of money into her bank account earlier. I shall treasure that little electric car.

Josh excitedly tells Faye all about the train-set, with Ethan backing him up.

Who'd have thought they could be this happy about some little trains going around and around? It's more than that, though. Grandpa made it for the kids; No one else has one of these. That gives it massive kudos. They drag Faye up to see it after we eat.

313

Ethan draws the curtain and turns the main room-light off, then flicks on the tiny model lights. Hundreds of them suspended all around the track, vanishing into the tunnel and coming out the other side, up into the little hillside. Faye gasps in awe and I look over at her, a sparkle in her eyes from the lights. A moody amber glow lights her up, and I could bathe in her delicate beauty forever.

"Wow. You're right guys, it is amazing."

"It really is." I reach behind and put my arm around her, pulling her close to me. She doesn't object.

If it were me, I'd take the risk and skip painting the walls. As we look around Faye's house, all I see is normal wear and tear, but she's paranoid and wants to leave the place spick and span. Do as you would be done by, and all that.

There are two buckets of paint, and we stopped for extra brushes, cleaning materials and plenty of sugary drinks to keep us going. Faye may be a little tiny bit merry from the wine, but I'm not complaining.

Rosie is plugged into headphones, painting the hallway, as high as she can reach, then I'll go around with a step-ladder and finish off. Faye is cleaning the bathroom, and the boys seem to have found a way to get out of doing hard graft, by walking up and down with a mop and bucket downstairs in the kitchen. I'm painting around the small bedroom while I wait for Rosie to be finished.

The house is nearly empty. They have either sold or packed up almost everything. I suppose there's no denying it now, with the evidence staring me in the face. This is the last time I'll see her.

"Come on, slowpoke." Faye sticks her head into the room I'm painting.

"I'm trying to be careful and not get paint everywhere." I

314

grabbed a pair of overalls at the DIY shop on the way. They don't fit particularly well, but they do the job, even if they do rub the old family jewels a bit.

"You are covered in paint, Danny." She looks me up and down and laughs.

"Well, yes, but I'm trying not to get it on the floor."

"Give me the brush, let me show you." She grabs the brush from my hand and dips it into the bucket of paint.

"Here, long even strokes, up and down, up and down." She beckons me over. "Do it with me, up and down, up and down." I hold her hand and she guides the brush. "That's it, see?"

She turns to face me, then snaps the brush out of my hand and slaps it, full force, onto my chest, painting a line down to my groin. "Up and down."

"You little…" She bursts out laughing, doubling over. I grab the brush back out of her hand, and, as she stands back up, in one deft move, I dip the brush back in the pot and then slap it full on her breasts, one dab on each.

"Got ya." Faye squeals and tries to wipe paint from her dungarees.

"Come back here, you." She lurches after me with hands covered in paint. I back into the door, but it slams shut, and I have nowhere to escape to. Faye's paint-hands reaching for my face.

I instinctively put my arms up to block her, but she planned this and changes course for my tummy.

Before I can flinch, she's got her hands around my waist, splatting the paint all over my arse cheeks, and pressing her paint-covered breast against me. Grinding up and down.

I still have a loaded brush. I run it down the length of her back, stopping at her bum and slapping it against her cheeks.

"Oh, I like that." She giggles.

I raise an eyebrow. "You know… I'm not wearing anything under this overall."

"You dirty boy."

She pulls me down and kisses me, violently, grabbing at the zip on my front and yanking it down.

"You liar! You've got underpants on."

"Well, these overalls chafe something rotten."

"Here, let me help." She fumbles, trying to find how to pull the overalls off me, but as they are way too small, the arms are stuck fast and they won't come off without a struggle. The boner in my pants isn't helping, as now I'm fighting to be released on two fronts.

Faye gives up trying to disrobe me, and instead puts her arms inside my top, making sure to rub the remnants of paint all over my back. I will be scrubbing for days to get clean, but as this is the dirtiest I've been in a long time, I'm not complaining.

She kisses me, hot and wet, then glances around at the small bed, covered in a painters tarpaulin, and steps back, dragging me with her. Then twists me around, pushing me down and jumping on top of me. I might get lucky, here.

I reach up and try to undo the straps on her dungarees, but I have no idea how they work. If only I had listened when my dad was talking about mechanical engineering.

She slaps my hand away and unclips the buttons, letting the front hang down. My hands immediately stray to her shirt and pull it up, revealing a fraying old bra. Do I care that it's old and threadbare? No, I don't. I'm one step closer to heaven, and the condition of the stairway isn't important.

Faye takes my hands, stretching my arms above my head, leaning down over me and biting at my neck, running her tongue up and down. I let out a moan of pleasure; she stifles me with a long, drenching kiss.

"Dad, I've finished the hall walls." The door bursts open with Rosie, pulling headphones out of her ears. She sees us on the bed and stops dead in her tracks. Mouth falling open, she slowly backs out and closes the door.

"Oh. Shit. Kids."

Faye bursts out laughing. "Foiled again." She gets up and buckles up her straps. Bugger.

I clear my throat. "Thanks, Rosie. I'll come to check the walls in a second. We were just, erm, checking something." Faye stifles a giggle. I stand and zip up.

I step to the door and reach for the handle. "Danny," Faye grabs my hand. I turn to face her. "I'm really sorry we didn't get to, you know, do stuff." She offers a sympathy smile.

"Me too." I squeeze her hand. "Maybe I can come to visit you soon, in Albany?"

Her eyes light up. "Yeah? That would be nice."

I nod and go see what the kids are up to.

Walls painted, kitchen and bathroom scrubbed, and an impromptu takeaway eaten and cleaned away. Faye is all set to hand the keys back to the landlord and go off on her new adventure. I round the kids up for us to go home.

At the door, I have an idea. "Can I give you a lift to the airport?"

"No, thank you, Danny, but we've already booked a taxi."

"I don't mind. You could cancel it?"

"It's okay. Honestly, I hate airport goodbyes."

"Oh, yeah. Good point." I look down at my hands. I'm picking at the paint, now dry on my nails. "Well, I suppose this is it then."

She nods, twisting her face to hold back a tear.

"Bye, Ethan, Rosie. Hopefully see you soon, yeah?"

They nod. "Bye, Josh. I'll send you a video of the train coming out of the tunnel."

"Awesome!"

Ethan and Josh shake hands. Rosie waves then goes to stand

next to the car. I blip open the lock and she gets in. Ethan follows and Josh goes into the house.

I linger on the doorstep. Faye starts to shut the door. "See ya then, Danny. Thanks for the help."

"Wait!" She opens the door again, laughing.

"Just kidding!" She pulls me back for a long, slow and passionate kiss. The kids are probably watching from the car, but I don't care. I want to savour this moment, it will need to keep me going for months until I can organise a trip to America. I've already checked the price of a flight, and now I don't have to pay an Au Pair, I could make this happen in a few months.

"Thank you, Danny, for all the sweet things you've done for me." Faye finally releases me from her kiss and blinks back tears.

"It was my pleasure, Faye."

"And you will come and visit soon, won't you?"

"You can bank on it." She smiles, but now her eyes are wet. She wipes away a tear and sniffs.

"Well, bye then. I'm going to miss you, Danny Watts."

My chest tightens, my eyes moisten, my heart melts. "I'm going to miss the absolute crap out of you, Faye Lovering."

She pulls me back for one last kiss and then whispers gently in my ear. "I love you."

My knees buckle, a thud of adrenaline courses through my veins. I stand up straight and look down at the beautiful creature in front of me.

"I love you, too."

Chapter Thirty-Six

This is my third shower since the paint fight. Well, not so much a fight as a paint snog. It's surprisingly difficult to get off, especially when it's all over my back and chest. I've scrubbed until I'm raw, and there are still remnants mottling me. How on earth did it get in my ear?

Faye has gone.

I'm waiting for her to text me she's landed okay. Trying not to think about it. Instead, I will focus on the good things, like those three words Faye whispered to me, three words I never thought I'd hear, or believe ever again, but now I will never forget. "I love you." Such little words, but they stir up so much emotion. Rosie asked me in the car home if Faye was my girlfriend now. I surprised myself and said "Yes." Rosie thought about that for a moment, then said: "But, she's going away?"

Yeah. I know.

I'm planning to save up my pennies and organise a holiday to the States to visit her as soon as possible. The kids will enjoy it, too. There must be something fun for them to do in Albany?

Meanwhile, I'll occupy myself with work, kids, school runs,

grocery shopping, and sleep. The normal old routine we all know and hate. It passes the time, at least.

I linger long in the shower, putting those memories of our fun times together to good use, while they are still fresh.

Oh, Faye. Why couldn't we have met years ago? Why did you have to leave now, just as things got interesting? Sod's bloody law, I suppose.

The faint sound of the doorbell from downstairs breaks me from my concentration. Bugger. But Judas wasn't playing ball, anyway. I wonder if Faye knows what 'sexting' is? Can I stoop that low and ask her for some photographic material? That's what all the kids are doing these days, isn't it?

The bell rings again. It's early for trick-or-treaters already at noon?

"Rosie. Can you get the door?"

Knocks on the door now. "ROSIE?"

The silent sound of tumbleweeds comes from Rosie's room, I expect she's plugged into some inane crap on YouTube. I should have found them something more interesting to do over the half-term, but I've been busy with work and life. I thought maybe we'd go out trick-or-treating this evening, but they turned their noses up. Said they were too old now. I guess I missed those opportunities. They grow up so quickly.

No point calling for Ethan, as he is permanently glued to his games or train-set.

I step out of the shower, grab the wonderfully soft Myatt bathrobe that I stole, and stomp downstairs. If this is a Jehovah or a window-cleaner, they will feel my fluffy white wrath.

The bell rings again as I get to the door.

"All right, all right. Keep your hair on." No patience, some people.

I open the door. "Oh. Hi, Elise." She's not so much treat, mainly trick. She looks rough, tired, puffy red eyes.

"Danny. I nearly didn't knock. I thought you might have company." She motions to the second car in the driveway.

"No, no. I just bought it. It's electric."

"Can I come in?"

"Of course." This can't be good.

She goes directly through to the kitchen. "Are you okay?"

Her lip trembles. "No." She bursts into tears and rushes towards me, throwing her arms around me. I'm still damp from the shower, but she doesn't seem to care.

"What happened?"

"Brian. He's dead." She coughs out the words through the storm of tears.

Oh, fuck.

"God. I'm so sorry." I pat her back, awkwardly. Waiting for the emotion to calm down.

I made us a nice cup of tea when Elise regained her composure. Because, as we all know, tea is the ultimate cure for everything and anything.

"When did it happen?"

"This morning. He said he had a headache last night. I told him to go to the hospital and get it checked, but he waved me away. Said it was nothing that a good sleep wouldn't take care of. I woke up this morning, and he was gone." She pauses. "Well, it did take care of it, didn't it? Once and for all."

"Jesus, that's terrible. You poor thing." It wasn't that long ago Gosia told me her grandmother went in her sleep. But to wake up next to a corpse? Shit. "I know it's a cliché, but I guess I'd prefer to go in my sleep if I had to go."

Elise nods. "I knew it was coming, but did it have to be this fucking soon?"

What can I say to that? "It isn't fair, is it?"

"Life isn't fair." Elise uses her pragmatic tone.

"Indeed. Has he been taken away? He's not still in the bed, is he?"

"No, Danny! They took him already. I didn't know where else to go, so I came here. Didn't want to be in the house alone. Where are the kids?"

"In their rooms. You should see the train-set that Dad made for them." She looks up, confused. "Yeah. Maybe another time. I'll fetch them down."

Elise goes into the downstairs toilet to wash her face while I go upstairs and drag the kids out. They are annoyed at first, but when I explain their mother is here, with some sad news, they plod down to see her.

I take the opportunity to get dressed and pause for a moment to breathe. Too much emotion lately, I'm drained from it all.

Dying on Halloween; Does that make it the best or worst time to enter the spirit realm? I have no idea how these things work.

There was a time when I'd have happily wished Brian dead. Soon after Elise left me to be with him, I'd have run the fucker down in my BMW if I could have, but now, it doesn't seem appropriate to think that way. Things have changed, we've all moved on. It didn't go well for Brian, in the end.

Aside from tea and hugs, I don't know what else to do. I suppose just listen and be here if she needs me. I didn't go to the wedding, but I probably should go to the funeral.

I head back downstairs.

The children are clasped around Elise in the kitchen. They aren't crying, but they are by no means happy. They didn't know Brian, thankfully, but I'm sure they can tell their mother is upset. Rosie is the spit of Elise, standing next to her. Funny how you think of these silly things in times of stress.

The kids disperse as I approach and vanish back upstairs in silence. Perhaps I'll take them out for some McDs later, cheer them up a bit.

"I better go, Danny. I have to go fill in forms or something at the morgue."

"Right, do you want me to come with you?" Please say no. Please say no.

"No, I'll be okay. I don't want the kids in that place." Thank fuck for that.

"Ah, yeah. Well, you know. Call if you need anything." I offer a sympathetic smile.

"Thanks, Danny." She kisses me on the cheek. "I always could rely on you."

"Of course. I'm a rock, me."

After dining with the clown, we stop at Tesco on the way home. The vast piles of Halloween sweets dominate even the barrels of pumpkins and cheap witch costumes, broomsticks and spray cobwebs. Still, I'm sure this is nothing compared to what Faye will find in America. They sure love to dress up and decorate, over there.

I grab a few of everything and drop them in our trolley. The kids seem to have perked up a bit and they are looking forward to handing out sweets at the door, and no doubt, taking the bulk for themselves. We usually hide, but this time they thought it would be fun to see what people are wearing. Ethan said Jack might come by our house.

It has crossed my mind that Rosie might want to go to parties around holiday occasions, like this soon. Which is a tad worrying. The costumes for teenage girls tend to all be prefixed with the word 'sexy'. Sexy witch, sexy vampire, sexy scary-clown, sexy pumpkin... I'm thankful that I still have a little time before these things become a problem. Hopefully, anyway.

. . .

The kids said they wanted to get pumpkins, but oddly enough, I seem to be the only one carving. They recoiled in horror when I showed them they'd have to put their arms into the pumpkin to scrape out the guts. "Disgusting!" Oh well, I'm saving the seeds for the squirrels. It's quite relaxing.

My Jack-o'-lantern face looks a tad drunk, but he'll do. I stick him outside on the wall, with a candle inside, and await the onslaught of demanding kids, wielding candy buckets and burning bags of dog-shit, if last year's doorstep the morning after is anything to go by.

I nip up to the office to check on work emails. I've sort of neglected my duties today, with all the drama. But it doesn't seem to matter. It's true, the higher up you go, the less work you need to do.

Victor has the chatbots running silky smooth, and he's planning to head back home to Paris soon. He thinks he can run everything remotely now. He's a good chap, and I'm thinking about making him the team lead. No one could ever replace Alex in my heart, but Victor has the brains and guts to make a decent go of it. I pop an email to D4, suggesting the promotion. He replies within a minute; 'Good plan, dude. He's a keeper.'

I'll give the lad a call tomorrow and see what he thinks.

Faye's a keeper, too, but I didn't do a very good job of hanging onto her. Hardly my fault she's going, is it? But maybe if I'd been more charming or something, she'd have changed her mind and stayed. Not much point in torturing myself like this, but my stupid brain won't leave me alone.

She should have landed by now. Weird, she hasn't sent me a message, but I expect she's busy getting settled. Maybe Josh was upset on the plane and she's got her hands full. I don't like to bug people when I know they could be busy. It's okay. She'll get in touch soon. Don't obsess.

. . .

In a moment of insanity, I picked up a 'Spooky Doorbell' for our Halloween night entertainment. It rings, and now I realise that the evil laugh sound it makes will quickly become extremely annoying. It's headed for the bin.

The kids suddenly appear with plastic cauldrons full of sweets and chocolate, then bound to the door.

"Trick or treat?"

A group of young girls is at the door, dressed in what looks like an emulation of the Spice Girls iconic outfits. Odd, as I'm sure they are far too young to even know who the Spice Girls were. I imagine their mothers harbour some latent passions. Wasn't only one of them meant to be scary? The nature of Halloween has changed somewhat since I was a lad.

"Zig-a-zig-ahh." They chime in unison and perform an obviously rehearsed two-second dance move, as their accompanying adults video the entire event on their respective phones. Good grief.

The kids present their buckets of sugar and the girls grab a selection and move along. Same as every woman I've ever known.

The next doorbell brings a group of kids from along the street, one has a sheet on his head with eyeholes cut out, another some black makeup, the third a cardboard witch hat. That's more like it. Good old British apathy and last-minute choices. We hand over sweets and they bugger off.

After the seventeenth doorbell, I stopped getting up and let the kids handle it alone. Even they are getting bored now. We've seen a plethora of completely inappropriate sexy nurses and catgirls, and a smattering of various superheroes I don't recognise, and the odd few vampires and witches. I'm calling it a night. I take down the evil doorbell and blow out the pumpkin candle. Humbug.

. . .

I'm disturbed from watching inane junk on the TV when the normal doorbell rings. Bloody hell. I was going to ignore it, but it rings again.

"GO AWAY! We don't have any sweets left."

They ring again and bang on the door. Fuck's sake. I get up and switch the porch light back on, opening the door.

"What the…" The sexiest of all sexy witches stands on my doorstep, with Josh behind her. "Faye?"

"Trick or treat?" Faye laughs. "Can we come in?"

"Omens."

"What?" I pour Faye a large glass of wine and get Josh a hot chocolate. They sit down at the kitchen table and the children buzz around with excitement. "Why aren't you in America? I mean, not that I'm complaining."

"A series of omens, Danny. Sometimes you have to listen to what the universe is telling you and change accordingly."

"Right, okay. What happened?"

"Oh, where to start…" She lets out a sigh. "We got to the airport fine, got checked in, but then our flight was delayed an hour. No big deal, we got some food and just relaxed. But then it was delayed again, and again, then finally it was cancelled. But they kept saying there'd be a replacement plane soon, and just to hold on." Faye looks tired and stressed, I top up her wine. "Eventually they organised a grotty airport hotel and asked us to be back at five in the morning for a new plane." Josh makes a face at the mention of the hotel.

"God. That's awful. Sorry."

"Yeah, well. That's not all. During the night, I got a message from the importer. All my furniture and stuff has been held up in customs, and could be stuck there for months while they thoroughly investigate it."

"What?"

"The only thing I can think of is, they mistook my sage smudge stick for weed. There's nothing dodgy in there unless someone used my boxes to smuggle drugs or something?"

"Shit! You mean, everything you own is stuck in a customs warehouse?"

"Yep. Apart from the suitcases we finally got back from the airline." She nods to the bags in the hallway.

"Bloody hell."

"Then there's the apartment that work had organised for us. It got broken into yesterday and ransacked. They sent some photos. All the stuff they had furnished it with is gone, and the door bust in." She shows me her phone and the photos of the empty apartment. Someone has sprayed a large penis shape on the wall in red spray-paint. Lovely.

"They said they'd organise a hotel instead, while they clean it up and fix it, but honestly, I'm not sure I want to live there now."

"I can understand that."

"And what put the icing on the cake, was that when we got back to the airport this morning, at five in the bloody morning, the flight was yet again delayed all day, and then overbooked. They asked for volunteers to be bumped off. So, here we are. I've changed my mind about going."

"That sounds horrible, Faye. I'm sorry."

"We have nowhere to live now. I was wondering if we can stay with you for a while? I'll have to see if I can get my old job back."

"Of course you can! Stay as long as you like, stay forever." I may sound a little too keen, but I don't care.

She laughs. "Thank you, Danny."

"My absolute pleasure."

.   .   .

327

We rapidly converted the spare room back to a bedroom, shuffling the train-set over and making up the bed. Josh was exhausted. He's had a couple of very bad days at the airport. Faye had her hands full coping with him, trying to keep the stress at bay. I feel sorry for them. They had all these plans and hopes for a new life, all dashed away with a series of unfortunate events. But I also feel wonderful. Faye came back, and she's here, in my house, children all asleep in bed, we're on the couch cuddled up with a glass of wine.

"There was one other reason I didn't go, in the end." Faye looks up at me, those big gorgeous eyes melting my heart once again.

"Oh?"

"Well, you know, there's this small matter of something we didn't get to do…" She grins and licks her lips.

"Oh!"

I think my luck could finally be in, here?

I wake to the harsh morning light, blinding me for a moment before I blink away the crust of night. I turn over, and I must still be dreaming. Faye, lying in my bed, the glisten of sweat on her lips from our heated passions, her hair flowing over my pillows.

"Am I dreaming?" I reach over and touch her arm. She stirs and creaks open an eye.

"Mmm. Morning, Danny."

"You are really here?"

"Yes, as far as I know." She opens both eyes and smiles, then shuffles over for a kiss and snuggle.

Even if I'm not dreaming, this is most certainly a dream come true.

Do me a favour?

I genuinely hope you enjoyed this story and I'd love to hear about it. So would other readers. I would be eternally grateful if you would leave a review on Amazon for me.

I don't have a big-name publisher or agent, or any marketing help. I rely on the kind words of readers to spread the word and help others find my books.

In a world of constant rating requests from everything you buy, I know it's a pain, but it does make a huge difference and it encourages me to keep writing.

Thanks!
Adam.

www.AdamEcclesBooks.com

Also by Adam Eccles

In order of publication:

Time, For a Change

The Twin Flame Game

Who Needs Love, Anyway?

Need a Little Time

The Soul Bank

facebook.com/AdamEcclesWrites
twitter.com/AdamEcclesBooks

Audiobook

Need a Little Time, unabridged audiobook.
Narrated by Mark Rice-Oxley